Blind Bake

Maddie Baker Mystery #1

Denise Grover Swank

Copyright © 2022 by Denise Grover Swank

Cover: Momir Borocki

All rights reserved.

No part of this book may be reproduced in any form or by any electronic or mechanical means, including information storage and retrieval systems, without written permission from the author, except for the use of brief quotations in a book review.

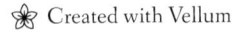

❀ Created with Vellum

Mystery Books by Denise Grover Swank

Maddie Baker Mystery
Blind Bake
Bake Off

Carly Moore
A Cry in the Dark
Her Scream in the Silence
One Foot in the Grave
Buried in Secrets
The Lies She Told
Shades of Truth
Keeper of Secrets

Rose Gardner Mystery and Investigations
Magnolia Steele Mystery
Darling Investigations

Chapter One

Maddie

I tapped my finger nervously on my steering wheel. Where was this guy? I knew I shouldn't have accepted an Uber request out at the industrial park after six p.m. on a Monday night, but desperate times meant taking risks.

I picked up my phone and sent a message to the guy who'd made the request. *I've been here five minutes. If you're not out here within the next sixty seconds, I'm leaving.*

I'll be good and pissed if I made the trip seven miles outside of the city limits on a cold November night for nothing, but a part of me rather hoped this guy would tell me to get lost. I'd seen enough horror movies to know when something was a bad idea. And this reeked of it.

A door flew open in the metal warehouse I was parked next to, and a short stub of a man hurried out, shuffling down a few concrete steps and then rushing over to my car and flinging open the back door.

The first thing that hit me was the smell, and I fought the urge to gag. The older man who'd just climbed into the back seat reeked of three-day-old egg salad and BO. I wasn't sure the can of Febreze in my trunk would get that stench out of the vinyl seats.

Why hadn't I just left?

Forcing a smile, I glanced over my shoulder at the balding man and hesitantly asked, "Marty the Man?" Which, now that I thought about it, seemed like a pretty sketchy nickname. "Going to 1435 West Walnut Street?"

"Yeah," he grunted, looking out his side window at the warehouse. "Go already."

So I did.

I could hear my friend Mallory's voice in my head. *If I've told you once, I've told you a million times, Maddie, do* not *pick people up from shady places, especially after five. Why would someone at an industrial park need an Uber? This man is trouble with a capital T.*

But desperate times often called for risks with a megaphone, and truth be told, there weren't many calls for Uber rides in Cockamamie, Tennessee, with a population of only twenty thousand. A fact that failed to impress the Middle Tennessee Teachers' Credit Union the last time they called about my late car payment.

So here I was with a rank older man who looked nervous as hell sitting in the back seat of my Ford Focus, which I was still fourteen payments away from paying off.

"Can't this thing go any faster?" he asked, looking out the back window for the fifth or sixth time.

"Making a fast getaway?" I half teased as I pressed harder on the gas pedal. The industrial park had a twenty-five-mile-per-hour speed limit, but hardly anyone was around this late, so I pushed it up to thirty-five. Still, it was hard to believe this old fart was making any kind of getaway that didn't involve finding the nearest shower. Or maybe that was just wishful thinking.

"Ha," he said weakly. He seemed to settle back in his seat, setting a brown paper lunch bag on his lap.

"You might want to toss out that sandwich," I said, looking at him in my rearview mirror. It was none of my business, but I couldn't see how he could carry that around if he actually knew how badly it smelled. My Aunt Deidre had lost her sense of smell a few years ago. Maybe his was gone too. "It smells like it went bad a couple of days ago."

His gray eyes, which were partially obscured by his drooping eyelids, met mine in the mirror. Confusion registered on his face for a few seconds, and then he shot me a glare as he tightened his grip on the bag. "I ain't payin' you to tell me what to do. I'm payin' you to drive. So how about you mind your own fuckin' business?"

I gasped in shock and tried to tell myself that maybe he was lashing out because he was embarrassed. I mean, some people didn't take well to humiliating suggestions, no matter how well intentioned. I pressed my lips together and pulled to a stop sign at Highway 75, the two-lane highway leading back into Cockamamie. Thank God I had power windows. I used the buttons to crack all four windows in the car before pulling out.

As I took a left turn, I noticed he was looking out the back window again. Did he think someone might be following us? I'd been sort of joking when I'd asked if he was on the run, but what if he really *was* making a getaway?

A man who looks like he's in his seventies? Carrying a smelly lunch bag?

No, this was what my mother used to call my wild imagination.

Still, when you put two and two together and came up with four, it didn't hurt to pay attention.

He leaned forward and gripped the headrest on the front passenger seat. "We need to make an extra stop."

"Okay," I said, "but that'll cost you extra."

"That's thievery," he grumbled.

I squared my shoulders. "Hey, time is money, and extra mileage means more gas. I'm not doing this for funsies."

"You need to get yourself a husband," he said, gesturing to my ringless hand on the steering wheel. "A woman your age shouldn't be driving strange men around in the dark for money. People are gonna think you're a hooker."

"*A woman my age?*" I asked in a huff, glaring at him in the mirror. If I weren't so fired up over the insult, I might also have pointed out that he'd gestured to my *right* hand. "How old do you think I *am*?"

"Over thirty," he said. "A spinster."

What era had this guy teleported from? Was he a time-traveling agent on the run?

"No one has unironically used the word spinster for about a century now," I said. There was no point arguing with him about the "over thirty" comment. My recent thirty-fourth birthday found me guilty as charged.

"You're still unmarried," he said, clutching his bag to his chest. "It ain't right."

This guy was starting to piss me off. "Some of us don't have a say in the matter," I snapped. "If I had my way, I'd already be married, but *Steve* had other ideas."

Great. Not only was I thinking about my asshole ex-boyfriend, but I was sharing my shame with this cranky, smelly old fart.

This car ride just kept getting worse.

"Women are meant to be meek and mild," he retorted.

"You got in the wrong car if that's what you're looking for," I muttered, catching a glimpse of him in the mirror. He was glancing out the back window again. "Why do you keep looking behind us?"

"I told you—none of your fucking business," he snarled as he turned back around. "Just drive."

I really wanted to stop the car and drop-kick this guy to the curb, but I needed the money, and although I seriously doubted he was a good tipper, or any kind of tipper, I had to start being nicer. I was oh-so-close to having enough to make my car payment *and* make the minimum payment on my credit card balance. Every dollar counted at this point.

Blind Bake

"So do you want to make that extra stop?" I asked.

"Not if you're gonna rob me blind."

Depending on how far off the route he wanted to go, I suspected his stop would have added a dollar or two at most. But I didn't love the idea of spending more time with this guy than necessary, so I kept that to myself.

We drove in silence for several minutes, and I darted glances at the map on my phone, realizing his destination was in the Bottoms, a.k.a. the old and mostly abandoned part of downtown Cockamamie, not the newer section. If I'd realized that, I never would have accepted the job. The sun had just set, and his destination wasn't exactly in the nicest part of town. The sooner I dropped him off and got home to Aunt Deidre, the better.

Thankfully, we soon pulled up to the dark doorway of 1435 West Walnut, which looked to be an abandoned building sandwiched between several other abandoned buildings. Other than a run-down convenience store on the corner of the opposite side of the street, there was a whole lot of nothing around us.

"Drive around the block," Marty the Man said, flicking his hand next to my head.

His hand smelled like rotten eggs, and I tried not to gag. "This is the address."

"Go around the block anyway," he said more insistently.

"Just know that the app's gonna charge you extra." Especially if he kept flailing his stinky hand in my face.

"Fine." He waved his hand next to me again.

I wanted to kick him out anyway, but if I were him, I wouldn't want to go in there either, so I tried to breathe through my mouth and drove around the block.

Old downtown Cockamamie had been pretty much deserted after Briny River flooded about twenty years back. For whatever reason, the town's forefathers had chosen the low area by the river to build their community, and subsequently, the downtown area regularly found itself covered in six feet of water. I'd been in middle school at the time of that last major flood twenty years ago, and I remembered Uncle Albert, Aunt Deidre, and my mother helping build sandbag walls to save downtown. It hadn't worked. While it hadn't been the first time the area flooded, it had served as the last straw for many, as it was sure not to be the last. So the city council had offered businesses incentives to move about six blocks to the east of the river bottom, an area at least twenty feet higher in elevation. A few businesses refused to make the transition, and some of them had managed to stay open, but given the less-than-ideal location, whatever business they operated now was likely shady. Which meant I needed to drop off my passenger and get the heck out of here.

Once I drove up to the curb the second time, I put the car in park, told the app the ride was done, then turned back to give my passenger a big smile. "You have a good night, Mr. Man."

He glanced at his phone and scoffed. "That seems unlikely after you charged me an extra dollar to go around the block."

I didn't tell him that if I'd had my way, the app would have charged him five.

He opened the back door and looked down both ends of the sidewalk, seeming to hesitate. As he leaned out, he leaned out, he accidentally dropped his bag onto the floor of the back seat.

"Shit," he grumbled. "Can you turn on the light?"

"It's already on." But I'd be the first to admit it wasn't very bright.

Cursing under his breath again, he sat up with his bag clasped to his chest and got out, slamming the car door harder than necessary. He scurried across the sidewalk and stopped at the front door. It may have been a full glass door at one point, but now it was boarded up with graffiti-covered plywood. Uncertainty etched his face, and he looked around the block again before finally knocking.

I started to pull away from the curb when my phone dinged

with a message that Mr. Smelly Pants had not only given me zero tip but had also given me a one-star review.

Bitchy feminist who robbed me blind.

"Mother Forker!"

I slammed on the brakes, threw the car in park, then climbed out.

"Are you fricking kidding me?" I shouted over the roof of the car.

He was about twenty feet away, still on the stoop of the address he'd given me, staring at me with a look of *oh shit*.

"A one-star review and no tip after I had to endure *that smell* and your *paranoia*?" I shouted, striding around the back of the car toward him, holding up my phone screen as though he could read it from that distance. In the back of my head, I knew this was the worst decision I'd made in a year, possibly several years, yet I couldn't seem to stop myself.

"Do you have any idea how hard my life is right now?" I shouted. "Two months ago, I lived a quiet, happy life and then boom! My whole world imploded! Do you think I *like* driving crabby old men with rotten-smelling brown bags around in my car? Do you have any *idea* how long it's going to take me to get that smell out of my upholstery?" I flung my hands out at my sides. "Because *I* sure don't!"

"I'm going to report you!" Marty the Man hissed. "Leave me the fuck alone!"

"Go ahead and report me!" I shouted, pointing my phone at him. "*But you'll regret it!*"

It was then I noticed a man standing next to his car at the gas pumps at the convenience store across the street. He gave me a wary look as he got into his car.

Great. Now I'd officially turned into a public spectacle. How much lower could I fall?

No, don't show me! I mentally shouted to the universe. The last thing I needed was a game of chicken with the cosmos.

The door behind Mr. Smelly Pants opened slightly, the person behind it out of sight, and he slipped into the darkness beyond the threshold.

I usually kept all of my angst and anger bottled inside and let it stew, but all those Brené Brown podcasts I'd been listening to, to help me take control of my life, must have sunk in, as I'd really let him have it. Too bad it hadn't felt as cathartic as I'd hoped.

No, now I just felt like a first-class bitch.

I sure as hell wasn't going inside and apologizing, though, so I headed back to my car.

"They make that deodorizer stuff in a can now," a man said from the shadow of the building next door. He was sitting on the sidewalk with his legs extended in front of him, a large black trash bag next to him. "And if that don't work, try baking soda."

He'd startled me, but then I realized it was Mr. Ernie, a homeless man I'd seen around town several times since moving back two months ago.

From what I'd seen, most people ignored him, but I decided to make up for my bad karma and headed over to talk to him. "Thank you, Mr. Ernie. I'll try that. Are you hungry? Can I take you somewhere in my stinky car and get you something to eat? Or maybe see if they have a bed at the Methodist Church shelter?"

He held up a to-go cup of coffee. "I done got me some food a short bit ago. And I don't much like staying at Methodist's shelter. They always steal my stuff."

"Who steals your stuff?" I asked in concern.

"Some of the shifty people there." He leaned forward and lowered his voice. "There are some not-so-nice people in this town, Miss...?" He looked up at me expectantly.

"Maddie," I said. "Maddie Baker."

He squinted up at me. "Miss Andrea's girl?"

My eyes widened in surprise. "Yeah. Did you know my mother?"

He offered me a warm smile. "That's a story for another day." He cast a glance at the door Mr. Smelly Pants had gone through. "You best get on out of here. There's seedy things happening in these parts. Especially after sundown."

"Then why don't you let me take you somewhere else?" I asked, reaching my hand out to him.

He chuckled. "Don't you go worryin' about me, Maddie. I'm exactly where I'm supposed to be. Go on now. Git."

I started to head back to my car, but then I turned around, tugging a business card out of my jeans pocket. Squatting in front of him, I handed him the card and looked into his eyes. "If you ever need a ride or food or *anything*," I said, "you call me. Okay, Mr. Ernie?"

He took the card and looked it over, then glanced up at me, giving me a wobbly smile. "Thank you, Maddie. You're a sweet one, just like your mother. You have a good night."

The reminder of my mother stung, but I smiled and said, "You too."

Chapter Two

Maddie

The windows in every room of my Aunt Deidre's nearly one-hundred-thirty-year-old Victorian blazed with light, which meant I'd have to go inside and turn them all off. My aunt was living on a fixed income now, and the gas bill was high enough to make me consider renting to boarders.

I parked my car in the driveway of the Cabbage Rose House, then got a can of Febreze out of the trunk and used half the can on the whole interior. I considered leaving the doors open to air it out, but it seemed like a bad idea. I wasn't afraid of getting robbed—there was nothing of value inside the stupid thing—but it might rain, and the last thing I needed was for the interior to get soaked. So I shut the doors and prayed the Febreze actually worked. At least I wasn't planning on making any Uber runs tomorrow.

"Aunt Deidre? Margarete?" I called out as I entered the front door. "I'm home!"

Margarete Jennings, my aunt's sixty-something next-door neighbor, popped out of the kitchen doorway at the end of the hall next to the staircase. "In here. We just finished cooking dinner."

Guilt hit me hard. I could always count on Margarete to help in a pinch—in this instance to cover the gap in time between the home health nurse leaving and me getting home. But sometimes she started dinner or a load of laundry, and while I appreciated her help, I hated that she felt obligated to do it. That was why *I* was here now. To take over Uncle Albert's responsibilities.

"Margarete," I protested as I walked across the hall's creaky wooden floor to the kitchen, "you didn't need to cook. I'm just thankful you could stay with Aunt Deidre until I could get home."

"Oh honey, I'm not cooking. Deidre is."

Shock roiled through me, drowned out by a rush of happiness.

Margarete motioned to me with a huge grin. "Come see."

Sure enough, my sixty-eight-year-old aunt was standing in front of the stove, stirring something in a large skillet. Her eyes were bright and clear, and she looked happy.

"Oh, Maddie! You're home! Dinner's almost ready."

So Aunt Deidre was having a *good* day. Finally something was going right.

"It smells delicious," I said. "What are we having?"

"I wanted to fry a chicken, but we didn't have one, and Margarete said she couldn't take me to the store." A glower filled her eyes. "And, as you know, that home health nurse refuses to take me *anywhere*."

"It's not Linda's job to take you anywhere," I said.

"No, it's her job to babysit me like I'm a toddler," Aunt Deidre moped.

I decided to ignore the complaint and focus on the main issue. "How about you and I go grocery shopping together tomorrow afternoon? I get off from my shift at Déjà Brew at three. I can come home and pick you up, and we'll get everything we need to make the chicken."

My aunt eyed me with a dark look. "What about Linda?"

"We'll send Linda home early for the day," I said. "I bet she'll like that."

"Be sure to go to the Piggly Wiggly," Margarete said, clasping her hands at her chest. "Stan McIntire owns it, but his son took over as manager. I know for a fact that Peter was excited to hear you were back in town."

Disgust stole my appetite. "Peter McIntire?" Peter had been an all-season jock—on the football, baseball, *and* basketball teams all four years of school, plus middle school—which had only seemed to fuel his arrogance. "He was excited to hear about *me*?"

While I hadn't been *un*popular in high school, I sure hadn't run in the same crowd as Peter and his off-and-on girlfriend Becca. Not that I'd wanted anything to do with Peter and his superficial friends. Shoot, I'd barely kept in touch with my own friends, my best friend since high school included.

I opened the cabinet to get three plates. "Isn't he married?" And not to Becca, if I remembered correctly.

"Divorced," Margarete said with a touch of smugness. "I knew he never shoulda married that trollop."

"Margarete," I softly admonished. "We shouldn't call women trollops."

A hard look filled her eyes. "I firmly believe in callin' a spade a spade. And she slept with plenty of men to earn it."

I cringed. "Miss Margarete, it's wrong to shame a woman for her sexual history and call her names, especially since men's sexual exploits are usually glorified as a sign of prowess and conquest. Women are just as entitled to explore their sexuality as men."

In this town, misogyny had been bred deep into the women my aunt's generation, and I was determined to squash it out of them.

Margarete's mouth pinched and her brows flew sky-high. "Not if she was *married* while exploring her sexuality, dear."

"Oh," I said, properly chastised. "Well, then trollop it is."

Margarete waved her hand when she saw I was carrying a plate for her to the table. "Oh, no dinner for me. I have plans."

"What on earth could you be doing?" Aunt Deidre asked.

"Pincher doesn't like to go out on weeknights. He's quite stodgy about it."

Margarete stiffened slightly, then flashed a smile. "Pincher's been gone for six years, God rest his soul, but you're right, he wasn't one to go out."

Confusion floated over my aunt's face. "But he was here just yesterday. He and Albert were playing a game of checkers." She looked around. "Albert? Come down here and tell Margarete she's crazy."

Margarete suddenly looked tired, not that I blamed her. Her husband Pincher had been a good man and the love of her life, much like my uncle Albert had been to Aunt Deidre.

"Aunt Deidre," I said, "why don't you finish setting the table, and I'll walk Margarete to the door."

"Where is Albert?" she asked with a frown. "It's not like him to be late."

"He had a meeting at church, dear," Margarete said. "He'll eat there."

Aunt Deidre's face fell. "Oh."

I headed to the hallway and walked to the front door, Margarete following.

"Will you be needing me tomorrow, dear?" she asked.

"No. I get off at three from the coffee shop."

"You need some time to yourself, Maddie," she said. "I love Deidre to absolute pieces, but she can be exhausting. Even Albert took time for himself."

That was news to me. "What did he do?"

"He spent plenty of time at church, and sometimes he'd just be gone—I have no idea what he was doin'. Probably helpin' out unfortunate souls, just like your mother used to do. But we're talking about *you*. Just let me know when you decide to take some time for yourself, and I'll be over to help. Only not tonight. I have plans."

"What are you up to tonight?" I asked, because Aunt Deidre

was right, Pincher hadn't gone out much in the evenings, and it had rubbed off on Margarete. But mostly I asked because I could tell she was dying to share.

She puffed out her chest, not an easy thing to do since she couldn't weigh more than one hundred twenty pounds sopping wet. "I'm the newest member of the church building committee, and we have a meeting tonight. We're discussing the church hall renovations."

I blinked in surprise. "That was Uncle Albert's position, wasn't it?"

Margarete gave me an apologetic smile. "I'm sorry, Maddie."

"Why on earth would you be sorry?" I asked, then gave her a hug. "Congratulations. That's a huge honor." I bit back the urge to tell her she had every right to be on the committee, that they'd been stupid not to bring her on in the first place. She and Pincher had run a construction company, for goodness' sake. Their oldest son Brick ran it now, but Margarete still had plenty of construction sense. Probably more than Cole Simpson, the restauranteur who chaired the building committee.

"It's just that Deidre hates that life is moving on without her beloved Albert. If she found out, it would kill her." She made a face. "Well, when she remembers."

"You deserve this position, and they can't leave it open. Life doesn't stand still, Margarete. I learned that lesson long ago."

She searched my eyes, then reached up and cupped my cheek. A soft smile shone in her eyes. "I know you did, child. And I'm sorry for that too."

I frowned, hating that I was thinking about my mother *again*. Time to change the subject. "Margarete, you have been *such* a lifesaver. I don't know what I'd do without you."

"There, there," she said, patting my arm. "That's what friends and neighbors are for. And I hate seein' you working yourself into a frazzle trying to earn money. Did you check again with the school library?"

I fought a grimace. She'd asked me this question every few days since I'd moved back. "They know I'm looking, and they know my experience, so no need to pester them. Librarian jobs are kind of hard to come by. Especially in a town this size."

She pursed her lips in disapproval. "You *know* your aunt has some money—"

"No."

"She would hate to know how much you work."

"She knows I work."

She shook her head. "While she knows on some level, she doesn't necessarily remember. Or put two and two together." Margarete reached for my hand and squeezed. "Madelyn. Seriously. You're doin' a good thing here, givin' up your life to come back to Cockamamie to take care of your aunt. You *know* she'd want you to use her money. You *have* to know that you're the beneficiary of it all when she dies. For heaven's sake, your uncle gave you power of attorney for her and the estate."

"Maybe so, but it's not my money yet, and I *do* use her money," I said, steeling my back. "I use it for utilities and bills and food, and it'll pay the taxes on this place. But I need to be frugal. Despite secondary insurance and Medicare, Aunt Deidre's medications cost a fortune. She's only sixty-eight and has many years left. The money's going to have to stretch."

"Honey," she said, squeezing my hand so hard her ring dug into my flesh. "She might live two more decades, but she won't be spending them all here at this house. We both know that at some point she'll have to move to a long-term care facility. You only delayed the inevitable by moving back to care for her."

"It would kill her to move into a place like that before her mind is completely gone," I said, my eyes stinging. "There was no way I could let that happen. Especially since she and Uncle Albert took me in after Mom..."

Releasing my hand, Margarete pulled me into a tight hug. "Maddie. Your aunt and uncle took you in because they loved you. They never expected anything in return."

"And I'm here because I love Aunt Deidre," I said with a sniff. "Same thing."

Margarete pulled back and cupped my cheek again. "I see so much of your mother in you."

Before I could register my surprise, she kissed my cheek, opened the front door, and left.

Up until today, no one had mentioned my mother around me in years. Steve had never brought her up, and neither had I. So far, Aunt Deidre hadn't brought her up either, other than a few comments in passing. But my aunt's mind was slipping, and I knew the day would come when she'd talk about her and the horrible thing that had happened to her. I needed to prepare myself.

* * *

Dinner was uneventful. Aunt Deidre complained again about her home health nurse, but when I suggested that I call the agency and request a new nurse, she stopped me.

"Better the devil you know than the devil you don't."

"Surely she's not that bad, Aunt Deidre."

She made a face, her chin trembling. "Maybe not. But she's not Albert."

She remembered he was gone. That was the hardest part of taking care of her—when she asked for him, forgetting that he'd died. It was like she had to go through losing her husband of forty-nine years all over again. He'd died two months ago, his heart attack unexpected and devastating to everyone who knew him. Me included. "*No one* is Uncle Albert."

"That is most certainly true." she gave me a watery smile, then pushed her plate away. "I think I've lost my appetite."

"Just eat a little bit more," I encouraged, reaching over and nudging the plate back. She'd lost so much weight over the last couple of months, she was practically skin and bones. "If you want me to take you to the Women's Club meeting on Wednesday, then you need to build up your immunity."

"That's what vitamins are for," she grumped, but she picked up her fork and took a few more bites before declaring she was done.

She helped me clean up the kitchen but kept quiet, giving me plenty of time to think about Marty the Man and all it led to, including my surprising exchange with Ernie.

"Aunt Deidre," I said as I washed the skillet in the hot sudsy water. "Do you know anything about the homeless man I keep seeing around downtown?"

There was a chance she might know who I was talking about. Her memory worked in weird ways. Sometimes she remembered things that seemed inconsequential and forgot the important stuff. Thankfully Ernie was so far removed from her normal life there was little chance of upsetting her if she didn't remember him.

"Which one?" she asked. "There seem to be more and more homeless people lately."

I had to agree with that statement. I didn't remember seeing any of them when I was a kid. Then again, do children look for that kind of thing?

"Mr. Ernie," I said. "He's older, maybe in his seventies. He's skinny and has gray hair and a scruffy beard."

"Ah..." Her eyes got the faraway look she got sometimes, when she got lost in herself, but this time she must have been absorbed by her memories because she said, "Ernie Foust. He was the high school janitor. He worked there when you were a student."

"I told him my name, and he knew I was Mom's daughter.

When I asked if he knew her, he said he did, but it was a story for another day."

"He must have known her from school," my aunt said with a soft smile. "Everybody loved Andrea."

It was true. Everyone loved my mother. Her students. Their parents. Her coworkers. Andrea Baker was practically a saint in Cockamamie, especially after her tragic death. Her funeral had drawn so many people, they'd had to have it in the high school auditorium. An audio feed of the service had been piped out to the three hundred people in the school parking lot.

"It's just that it seemed like there was more to it," I said, then shook my head. I was imagining things. Everyone had a story about my mother.

"Are we really going to the grocery store tomorrow?" Aunt Deidre asked excitedly as she dried the pan.

I'd done all the grocery shopping on my own since I'd moved in, and now I felt guilty. She was used to going out on errands every week with Uncle Albert. And Aunt Deidre did have her good days. Problem was sometimes a good day could quickly turn into a bad day without notice. I couldn't imagine taking her out during one of those confused times.

Still, I couldn't keep her holed up forever. She needed to get out of the house for her own well-being.

"Definitely. In fact, after we finish here, we should make a menu for the rest of the week. Fried chicken sounds delicious, but we need to make some of your mashed potatoes to go with it. What do you put in your potatoes to make them taste so good?"

She narrowed her eyes. "You've been helpin' me make those mashed potatoes since you were a toddler. You know darn good and well it's sour cream."

She was right. I knew, but I'd met with her doctor a week after Uncle Albert's death, and Dr. Snyder had told me the best thing I could do for my aunt was to exercise her brain. Any way I could get her to use both her long-term and short-term memory, the better.

"We need to add it to the list," I said. "And when we're done with that, let's play the memory game before we watch a few episodes of *Grace and Frankie*." I'd replaced my aunt and uncle's dinosaur of a TV in the living room, which had required an antenna, with my 45-inch smart TV. I'd also promptly gotten Wi-Fi for the house and introduced Aunt Deidre to Netflix. Now she had a plethora of shows to watch.

Aunt Deidre rolled her eyes. "I already played that stupid matching game with Linda after my nap."

"Indulge me and play it again. I bet I can beat you."

"You're incorrigible."

I gave her a cheesy smile. "And that's just how you like me."

Her eyes welled with tenderness. "Yes, Maddie. It is."

Chapter Three

Noah

"Hey, new guy. Feelin' like a hotshot now?" asked Officer Eddie Dunst, the uniformed cop manning the log sheet, as I walked up to the crime scene.

"I'm not sure what you're talking about," I said dryly as I signed my name, then scanned the list to see who'd arrived before me. I'd gotten lucky. The only people who'd shown so far were a couple of patrol cops, one of whom I actually respected, and the EMTs. I'd even beaten the sergeant and coroner.

"You know," Eddie explained, "because you had to get up so early."

"It's part of the job," I droned as I pulled booties out of my jacket pocket, then squatted to put them on my feet. But my gut was churning, and the back of my neck was clammy.

"You always carry booties around in your pocket?" Eddie asked with a laugh.

"I do when I'm going to a murder scene."

Eddie stopped chuckling and gave me a look so dark I wondered if this was about to become the scene of a double homicide.

Okay, so I hadn't made many friends since I'd joined the

Cockamamie police force three months ago, but I wasn't here to make friends. From the chief's perspective, I was here to improve their crime clearance rate. Bozos like Eddie Dunst were a big part of why the force only closed twenty-two percent of the crimes in this godforsaken town. This was the first murder since I'd come to town, and of course it happened when the only other detective was on vacation.

This would be a true test of whether I was still up to being a detective.

"What time did the anonymous call come in?" I asked. Although I already knew, the professional thing to do was to get confirmation.

Play it by the book, Noah. You've got this.

"Right before three a.m.," Eddie said. "The call was placed from a pay phone across the street, outside the convenience store. The male caller said there was a murder in the abandoned butcher shop, so I answered the call to investigate. I arrived at 3:08, checked out the shop, and confirmed there had been a murder. So I called the shift sergeant."

Who had then notified me.

"Sarge called Officer Forrester in early to help lock down the crime scene and babysit the body. He's inside."

I turned to take in the abandoned block around us.

Focus on this murder, I reminded myself. *This isn't Memphis.*

The convenience store was the only place operating in the immediate area. Crime scene tape was strung up about six feet around the outside of the building. "Since the Stop and Go is the only thing open, extend the crime scene to include the rest of the block."

"The whole street?" Eddie asked in disbelief. "It's just an old guy that got offed in a bad part of town."

"Exactly," I said dryly as I pulled on my black nitrile gloves. "An area riddled with drug deals and assaults. There might be evidence in the street, but we'll never know until we look." I wasn't missing anything this time.

"You want us to look in the gutter for evidence?" he asked, shocked.

"Yes, Officer," I said bluntly. "We'll even look up your ass if we have to."

Without giving him time to respond, I opened the door and went in.

Okay, so I probably went too far with that last quip, but goddammit, I'd only had one cup of coffee after being woken up at four in the morning, and my nerves were shot. I had a right to be cranky.

The front room was full of empty refrigerated display cases. The electricity to the place probably hadn't been turned on in years, but there was a battery-operated lantern on the counter, most likely placed by another officer. A dark stain lined the walls, about five feet above the floor, and I realized it was probably a water line from the big flood twenty years ago. There were about six other similar marks on the wall, which made me thankful the place wasn't covered in black mold.

Small favors.

I walked past the empty refrigerated cases, shining my light on the floor to see if anything jumped out at me—both figuratively and literally. But there was nothing. I continued to the back and found myself in some kind of prep room with stainless steel tables pushed up against the wall to my left and a large stainless steel sink with a pull-down, heavy-duty faucet/sprayer. Everything was grimy and rusted, looking like it was a tetanus case in the making.

Centered in the wall opposite the door was a large doorway with a barrier made of hanging six-inch-wide vinyl strips. Once upon a time they'd probably been clear, but now they were opaque and dingy. This must be the entrance to the refrigerated meat locker. A muted glow radiated out from the other side of the vinyl.

"Lance?" I called out the name of the cop from the log sheet, the cop I liked, as I panned my light over the prep room.

"Yeah," a male voice answered from behind the vinyl. "The vic's in here."

I carefully pushed through the vinyl sheets to see Officer Lance Forrester and two EMTs standing to the side. The victim was lying on the concrete floor next to the back wall.

Thank God it wasn't a kid.

I could handle this.

I didn't have to ask if they were sure he was dead. The old man was on his side, staring up at me with glazed-over eyes and a slice from one side of his neck to the other. The blood from the gaping wound had dripped onto the floor and had conveniently—from a cleaning standpoint, not an evidence standpoint—run into one of the drains built into the room. The space smelled of copper and mildew.

"It's a meat locker," Lance said. "I guess we're lucky they didn't hang him on one of those hooks before they killed him."

I glanced up, and sure enough, there were still a few S-shaped hooks hanging on a metal pipe.

"It looks like this place has flooded a time or two since it was abandoned."

"Good eye," Lance said appreciatively. "This whole block has been flooded more times than I can count."

"That's why they pay me the big bucks," I muttered as I surveyed the room. It was a large space—about twenty feet wide by thirty feet deep. Our flashlights were barely lighting the room. "We'll need to bring in outside lighting and a generator if there's no safe electrical source we can tap into for the coroner and the crime scene crew."

"Already on it," Lance said. "I got someone from the department bringing a generator and lights. The coroner's on his way, and so's the county crime lab."

"County may collect the evidence, but this is still my case," I said in a dark tone.

"I already made sure they knew that," Lance said. Then his body relaxed slightly. "With all due respect, Detective, I know why you're here. We all know why you're here. We don't even bring a quarter of our cases to court and conviction. And yeah, I know the county's a big part of that, but there've been plenty of mistakes on our side too. Most of us want that to change. The chief's made sure we know to tell the sheriff's department we're keeping control of all cases within Cockamamie city limits." He held my gaze. "I've got your back, Langley."

While Lance and I had only interacted a few times since I'd joined the force, he was one of the few who hadn't needled me about my reasons for leaving a crime-ridden city for a smaller, more sedate one. Most assumed I'd left because I wanted a quieter life, but something in Lance's eyes had suggested he knew the truth... and also that he'd keep it to himself. That had earned my respect too. So many people ran their mouths just to hear themselves talk, and Lance was one of the few who soaked in more than he doled out.

I reached out my hand and he grasped it, each of us giving a firm squeeze and a shake before releasing.

"Thanks, Officer Forrester. I appreciate that. Which is why I'm going to request that you help me with this investigation."

"Sir?" he asked in surprise.

"This is my first major crime since I arrived in Cockamamie, and Max is on vacation. I need someone I can trust to help me keep an eye on everything. We're going to watch every piece of evidence the Wayfare County crime lab collects and make sure every *i* is dotted and every *t* crossed on the chain of evidence logs. You're also going to help me conduct interviews. You good with that?"

"I am, sir," he said, then swallowed, his Adam's apple bobbing.

"I'll let the chief know, but first, let's get a good look at the crime scene before it starts getting trampled by a whole bunch of people."

We both spun in a circle to survey the room.

"A messy murder like this would produce a lot of blood," I said, "which means it would have been hard for the perp not to get blood on them. But the only blood I'm seeing is the stream that went down the drain."

"No bloody footprints," Lance said.

"Any chance they were trampled or smudged?" I asked.

"No, sir. I arrived soon after Officer Dunst, who found the body and then waited outside and called it in. I made sure everyone wore foot coverings."

"Even the EMTs?" I asked, noticing they were wearing them now.

"Yes. The sarge called them too, of course, but they were out on another call. I got here before they did," Lance said. "Eddie stayed outside, and I knew the vic was dead the minute I saw him, so I greeted the techs at the door."

It seemed like waste to have them there, but per Tennessee state law, EMTs weren't qualified to pronounce a death. A coroner had to do it, but they still had to be called. In a situation like this when the victim was obviously dead, they left the body in place to preserve the crime scene, then waited until someone with more authority released them.

"I looked around the room, Detective," Lance said. "We didn't destroy any footprints."

He could have been covering his ass, but I suspected he was being truthful. Which meant he had a good head on his shoulders. I may have just found my partner. Now the question was how the killer had murdered a man in a messy way without tracking blood all over the place.

"Any evidence of a cleanup?" I asked, squatting and shining my flashlight across the floor to look for telltale signs.

"None that I could see and no scent of any cleaning fluids, but I guess the crime lab will be better equipped to gauge all of that. But…" He hesitated.

"Yeah?"

"The buildings on this block are known drug dens, but this entire place is clean. None of the usual debris you'd find."

I narrowed my eyes. "You think someone cleaned it up."

"Yeah, but the question is who. And when."

I nodded and stood. "We'll talk to the property owner and see what they have to say." I motioned to the body. "Got an ID on him yet?"

"I could see the lump of his wallet in his back pocket, and he's wearing an expensive-looking watch, so it's not likely that robbery was a motive. But I don't need his ID to know his name is Martin Schroeder. He's a retired schoolteacher in his seventies."

"You a mind reader?" I asked in surprise. "That could come in handy for solving crimes."

Lance grinned. "Had him in high school for chemistry and physics. Shit teacher, but he was born and raised here in Cockamamie. He probably figured he'd die here."

"Guess he got that part right," I said, bending over to get a good look at the wound. "Clean slice. Looks like the perp cut pretty deep. Any sign of the murder weapon lying around?"

"Like I said, sir. I checked the floor, and as you can see, there's nothing in here. No one accidentally kicked anything either. At least not after I got here."

"We'll wait to see what the coroner says is the likely murder weapon, but for now, I'm guessing something extremely sharp with no serrated edge. The incision is too clean. Possibly a tool used by butchers? I didn't see any knives out in the other two rooms."

"I didn't see any either, Detective, but then again, I haven't left the body since we found him."

I raised my brow. "Why not?"

"Just being careful, sir."

I gave him a sideways grin. "Let's get one thing straight, Lance. You need to drop the sirs and the detectives. It's Noah. Got it?"

He grinned back. "Got it."

"Good, because I have a feeling you're a goddamned godsend, Lance," I said, rubbing the back of my neck.

"Don't know about that, sir—Noah," Lance said. "But I do know two things."

I propped my hands on my hips. "Okay. I'll bite. What would those be?"

"One," he said, "once news about the way he was murdered gets out, the town's gonna lose its damn mind."

It wasn't hard to believe that. Murders were frightening to a community, but gruesome murders could produce hysteria. Especially in a small town like this one. "And two?"

"You're gonna have a hell of a time finding out who did this."

"Why?" I asked, scanning the room. "You know something about this murder I don't?"

"Not about the murder, no," he smirked. "But just about every person in this town knows Martin Schroeder, and more than half of them likely wanted him dead."

Well, shit.

Chapter Four

Maddie

I had a hard time getting out of bed when my alarm went off, and not for the first time I shed a few tears about losing my old life. I missed the kids at the middle school where I'd worked as a librarian since finishing grad school. I missed the teachers and everyone else. I especially missed my best friend Mallory and our weekly girls' night in to drink wine and watch trashy reality TV. I even missed my apartment, right down to the dripping bathroom faucet. Oddly, I didn't miss Steve.

Shouldn't I miss the guy I'd wanted to marry?

I'd wasted five years of my life on that asshole, and he'd squandered my meager life savings to buy a hellhole house he'd insisted he was going to flip. No doubt I could kiss all fifteen thousand dollars of my life savings goodbye. I'd likely see cows eating at a steak house before he'll ever pay me back.

Well, maybe that was why I didn't miss him.

Wallowing wasn't helping anything, though, so I rolled out of bed. A hot shower and steaming cup of coffee helped perk me up before I checked on my aunt.

Aunt Deidre was already up and dressed by the time Linda arrived. I kissed my aunt on the cheek and told Linda that I'd be home by three thirty to take Aunt Deidre to the grocery store, at which time she could take off early for the day.

"Thanks, Maddie," she said, looking relieved, and I wondered how much grief my aunt had been giving her. I suspected it was a lot. If I had more money, I'd give her a bonus. I wondered if she'd take ground coffee from Déjà Brew and maybe some leftover pastries instead. I know *I'd* jump on that offer.

The coffee shop was already bustling when I got there at about 8:10, but with its downtown location, the majority of the shop's customers were people who stopped by on their way to work, which meant most of them arrived between seven thirty—when we opened—and nine. Honestly, my boss, Petra, should have never hired me. She needed someone to get there by seven thirty, and the soonest I could get there was a bit after eight. But she had a heart of gold and my mother had been her English teacher in high school, so she'd hired me anyway.

I grabbed an apron and got to work right away, surprised to see we were even busier than usual.

"Oh, man," I said. "What's going on? Did the coffee grinder break down again?"

"No," my coworker Chrissy said, turning her back on the customers to talk to me. Chrissy had started working at Déjà Brew a couple of years ago, after dropping out of college. She had an edgy look, with short dark hair and multiple piercings in her ears and nose, and a nearly encyclopedic knowledge of coffee.

She gave me a pointed look. "There was a murder."

A jolt of fear shot through me, and my blood pooled in my feet, leaving me light-headed and shaky.

There hadn't been a murder in Cockamamie in years. So it was little wonder that my mind shot back to that cold, rainy April night nearly twenty years ago, when the police officer had shown up at my door to tell me my mother was dead.

No. I wasn't letting my mind go there.

This murder had nothing to do with my mother.

Taking a deep breath, I asked, "Who was murdered?"

"No one knows anything, which is why we're so busy."

"Why would that make us busy?"

She lowered her voice and leaned into me. "They're not here for just the coffee. They're here to gossip. The scuttlebutt is that the police aren't saying who was murdered yet, but it happened somewhere downtown. I guess people are gawking at the crime scene."

I'd thought I'd left major crime behind in Nashville, but then again, murderers likely didn't care about zip codes. I had to admit it made me nervous. Aunt Deidre wasn't a fan of locking doors, and I often found them unlocked after I'd locked them. "The new downtown or the Bottoms?"

"Don't know."

Cockamamie had its quirks, but other than my mother's murder, it had always been a fairly safe town, hence my aunt's habit of never locking doors. And it had been determined that my mother's killing was a personal matter given the nature of her death. No wonder this news had thrown the town's residents into a tizzy.

Over the next few hours, the murder was all people could talk about. We eventually found out it had happened down in the Bottoms, but everything else seemed to be speculation. The older women were sure there was a rapist/murderer on the loose. A couple of younger women who were avid true crime podcast listeners suggested almost hopefully that it was the first murder by a serial killer (or at least the first known murder). The men weren't as loose with their speculation, but most of them theorized it was either a rape/murder or a drug deal gone wrong.

When we had a lull in customers, I ran out to the dining area to wipe down several tables. Of course, several customers at the table next to me were discussing the murder.

One of them, a man whose hair looked like a bird's nest after a storm said, "It's drugs. No question about it. You know what they get up to in that section of the Bottoms."

An elderly woman sitting near him gasped in horror. "We don't have drugs in Cockamamie."

"Sure we don't," the man said. "You keep living in denial."

The woman released a huff. "I've lost my appetite," she said, although she didn't appear to have any food, and got out of her seat and left. I wiped down her table. Then, against my better judgment, I asked the man, "Does Cockamamie have a drug problem?"

He laughed a little. "Doesn't everywhere?"

I'd grant him that, but the way he said it made it sound like it was an actual problem here, not just a nuisance.

When I went back around the counter, I asked Chrissy if that man was right when he said Cockamamie had a drug problem.

The look in her eyes suggested I was being naïve. "Well, every town does, don't they?"

"But has it gotten worse here? Like more than usual?"

"What makes you think I'd know?" she said. Something about the way she said it suggested she knew more than she was sharing.

But we got busy again, and soon it was noon, and it shifted to a lunch crowd. We didn't have a huge lunch selection, but we had a few sandwiches and some protein boxes in the refrigerated display case. Around one, the buzz about the murder had died down, but I heard a woman in line tell her friend, "You have to admit the Bottoms are creepier than usual lately. Especially West Walnut Street."

"Wait," I said, narrowing my eyes. "Did I just hear you say the murder was on West Walnut Street?" That was where I'd dropped off my passenger the night before.

"Yeah," the woman said. "At the old butcher shop."

I shook my head. "I don't know where that is. I've only been back in town a couple of months."

"Oh! *You're* Maddie Baker. I heard you were back but never put it together. It's such a shame what happened to your mom."

I stuffed down my unease at the mention of my mother. "Ancient history. What else do you know about the murder at the old butcher shop?"

Her eyes lit up. "Not much. All I've heard is that someone was killed in the meat locker. Strung up and bled."

My stomach soured, and I felt light-headed. "Say what?"

"Yeah, hung right up and bled out like a butchered cow or pig. Heard his blood ran down the drain and now there ain't any left for DNA analysis."

That didn't make any sense. Why would they need to do DNA analysis on the victim's blood? A tox screen, sure, but DNA? (Okay, I listened to a true crime podcast or two myself.) But one other thing I'd gotten from her information was that the victim was a man. Of course, I wasn't sure I could believe anything she was telling me, but if a man had been murdered on West Walnut hours after I'd dropped that creepy guy off in the same general location…

I was being ridiculous. Right? What were the chances?

But I couldn't get the thought out of my head. For the next hour, I kept running it over and over, until I finally mentioned it to Petra. I found her in her office, sitting at her desk and totaling up the receipts from the second register. She was a large woman—tall and wide—and she kept her dishwater-blond hair cropped close to her head, saying she didn't want to spend her life fussing with her hair. But her most memorable feature was her infectious smile. She smiled so much, sometimes I wondered if her cheeks hurt.

"Say, Petra, you know that murder everyone is talking about?"

"How could I miss it?" she asked, glancing up at me. "It's all everyone can talk about today."

"I think maybe…" I couldn't really say it out loud, could I? "Never mind."

She stopped punching numbers into her adding machine and

took off her reading glasses to get a better look at me. "You feelin' okay, Mads?"

"Yeah, I'm just a little tired."

"You haven't had your lunch break yet, have you?" she asked with a frown.

"No, but it's okay. We were too busy."

"Maybe you've got low blood sugar." Petra was a worrier and a fusser, and honestly, she was probably too empathetic for her own good. Which was why she'd hired me even though I wasn't exactly what she needed.

"Good karma," she'd said when she'd hired me. "What goes around comes around."

But now she was studying my face with an intensity that was unnerving. "You look pale. Go grab a sandwich and take off early." She held up her hand. "And don't you go worryin' about your hours. I know you need 'em. You can just call it your lunch."

I glanced up at the clock on the wall. It read 2:24, which meant I'd have enough time to stop by where I'd dropped off Mr. Smelly Pants to check whether it was the center of a crime scene.

"Thanks, Petra. If you're sure…"

"Of course I'm sure, so go on," she said with a wave and a smile. "And be sure to take your aunt one of those lemon bars she loves so much."

She was a great boss. I'd had enough bad ones while working service jobs in college and grad school to recognize a really good one when she was shoving pastries and sandwiches at me.

I grabbed the lemon bar for Aunt Deidre and a cinnamon roll to bring to Linda, then headed out to my car. For several seconds I held the steering wheel, staring at the building. Part of me was scared to drive by the location where I'd dropped off my Uber passenger last night. I was almost certainly wrong about the connection, but…

What if I was right?

Chapter Five

Maddie

A cold chill spread through my blood when I got to the Bottoms and saw West Walnut Street was blocked off.

Did I really want to know whether I was the last person to have seen my Uber passenger alive? Well, other than the person who'd killed him, of course. No. No, I did not. I wanted to drive on past, pick up Aunt Deidre and head to the grocery store, but that was the chickenshit way out. I couldn't hide from this. Besides, it might not have been him at all? What if poor, homeless Ernie had gotten caught in the middle of something? Shouldn't I at least tell the police what I knew?

This was ridiculous. I was jumping to all kinds of conclusions. The victim could be someone completely different. There was one sure way to find out.

I parked in a lot a block over and got out of the car, wishing I'd worn a heavier coat. It was early November, and while some days were in the sixties here in southern Tennessee, today was cloudy and in the low forties. I wrapped my thick cardigan around me and headed into the crowd that had gathered at the corner of West Walnut. A news crew was huddled on the sidewalk, their van parked on the other side of the street, although they didn't seem to be broadcasting anything. Like everyone else, they seemed to be waiting for something to happen.

I walked up to the edge of the crowd and stood next to a teenage boy who looked like he should be in his high school calculus class and not standing on the sidewalk next to crime scene tape. "Is this where the murder happened?"

"Nah." He snuck a look at me, then puffed out his chest and stood up straighter as though he was trying to make himself look older. "It's further on down. For some reason they've got the whole street blocked off."

"I heard it happened down at the abandoned butcher shop?"

"Yep," he said, pointing to the middle of the block. "We keep seeing police coming in and out of the building, but they ain't sayin' anything. They ain't even admitting there was a murder. But my friend Edgar's uncle is friends with a guy whose stepson is dating a woman whose father is in the police department. *He* said there was a murder in there."

Uh-huh, *that* sounded totally unreliable, but it explained why there were so many rumors flying around town. Everyone probably knew someone who knew someone. I looked down the block, and my stomach sank to my feet at the sight of a police officer standing outside of the building where I'd dropped off Marty the Man.

"Is the butcher shop the door that police officer is standing next to?" I asked with great trepidation.

"That's the one."

Panic spiraled through me, but I tamped it down.

"Did your uncle's stepson's husband…" I shook my head. "Did your source know who was murdered?" I asked as I craned my neck to get a better look.

"Some old dude."

That would fit either Ernie or Marty the Man. Which meant one of them definitely could be dead.

I had to tell someone in the police department what I knew. It didn't seem like much, but it might lead to something. I needed to find a police officer to talk to.

All the officers I could see were hanging out around the butcher shop door, about forty feet away. I needed to get closer. Going under the barricade didn't seem like a good idea, but the sidewalk on the other side of the road wasn't blocked off. I pushed my way through the crowd and headed toward the corner on the opposite side of the street, figuring I'd have a better chance of getting an officer's attention if I were directly across from the butcher shop. I'd talk to someone, and then I'd get the hell out of here. Especially since people would definitely be watching me, curious about what I was up to.

People really valued their positions next to the crime scene tape at the end of the street, because they shot me dark glares as I walked past them, as though they thought I was trying to weasel my way in front of them to get a better view of a door. Surely there were better things for them to do.

I'd nearly made it to the curb on the other side of the street when a woman in the crowd shouted, "Oh my God! Are they bringing out a body?"

I turned to look at the guarded door just as I heard the same voice say, "Never mind. It's only a couple of donut boxes."

A police officer had emerged from the door, carrying a dark bag marked "evidence." The screamer either needed glasses or she was hallucinating.

Unfortunately, I'd continued walking as I took in the scene, and I tripped on the curb, which was apparently closer than I'd remembered. My arms pinwheeled as I began to fall flat on my face, but then a pair of strong arms grabbed me and set me upright...but not before my flailing hand connected with his head.

"Oh my God. I'm so sorry!" I cried out. The look in his blue-gray eyes made my *thank-you* freeze on the tip of my tongue. I'd expected concern or friendliness, but I saw only anger. And also a bright red splotch on the side of his face next to his eye.

Oops.

"What the hell do you think you're *doing*?" he shouted.

His hostility caught me off guard, and I stumbled over my words. "I...well...uh..."

"Would you like me to have you arrested for interfering with an investigation?" he snapped. "Not to mention assault?"

"What?" I asked, incredulous. I pulled myself free of his grasp and took a step backward.

He jabbed his finger at the loosely hung tape that had been attached to the stop sign and which was currently flapping in a small breeze. "The crime scene tape is there for a reason."

This guy was starting to piss me off. He wasn't wearing a patrol uniform, but I knew right away he was a cop. He had the arrogance of one, something I knew from past experience. But he wasn't just a cop. His rumpled dark gray suit, blue shirt, and navy tie marked him as a detective, which meant he was an even bigger asshole. The badge hanging from a lanyard around his neck only confirmed my suspicion.

He was tall and youngish, probably in his thirties, definitely younger than the detective I'd dealt with during my mother's murder investigation. Too young to have been on the force back then. He also looked slightly too polished for Cockamamie, suggesting he hadn't been born and raised here. With brooding eyes and windblown brown hair streaked with blond, he was a handsome man. Too bad his looks were wasted on a shit personality.

"Look," I said, my irritation rising. "I wasn't going under your stupid crime scene tape. I was trying to walk *around it* to the sidewalk over here. Then I tripped."

"And assaulted me."

"I was falling," I snapped. "You're the one who chose to help me."

His mouth opened as if to retort, but then he closed it and looked me over, pulling a face that suggested he was sorry he'd done his job of serving and *protecting*. Or maybe I was imagining it because of the way his right cheek was beginning to swell.

He took a breath, the rest of his face turning red. "Stay away from my goddamned crime scene."

Then he ducked under the tape and strode down the middle of the street toward the murder scene.

I almost called after him to report that I might have information about the victim, but I clamped my mouth shut. I wasn't telling Detective Asshat anything. If he thought he was so great, then he could probably find the murderer with one eye swollen shut. So let him. I'd wanted to do my part as a good citizen, and now I was running late to take my aunt shopping. I'd promised her we'd go, and if she remembered, my promise would be important to her.

I spun on my heels, good and pissed, but I still felt a tiny pinprick of guilt. First of all, I hadn't meant to hit the guy. It had been a complete accident. More importantly, I owed it to whoever was dead in that building to tell the police what I knew.

Then again, whatever I had to tell them wasn't going to bring the murder victim back, and unless Ernie had killed someone or been killed, I didn't know much they didn't already know. A trip to the grocery store wasn't going to make much of a difference in the end. I'd take Aunt Deidre shopping, then call the nonemergency number and ask to talk to someone with an actual soul.

Chapter Six

Noah

"Goddamn gawkers," I fumed as I walked back over to the butcher shop. Officer Dunst was gone for the day, thank God, and he'd been replaced by a rookie. Neil Erickson, a kid so green he looked like he'd hatched out of a cabbage patch last week. But I could work with green. Especially someone like Erickson, who was eager to learn.

"What happened to your face?" Erickson asked, his eyes wide with shock.

I reached my hand up to my right cheek and winced. "Had a run-in with an exuberant bystander."

"That big burly guy over there?" Erickson asked, pointing to a guy standing in the convenience store parking lot. He looked like a body builder who had a steady diet of lean chicken breasts and steroids.

I could have given a noncommittal answer, but something in me insisted on honesty. "No." I motioned to the crowd. "Her."

"Which her? There have to be about two dozen hers."

I glanced over but didn't see her, which was probably a good thing. I was pissed at her for trying to get a closer look at the crime scene but also pissed at myself for jumping down her throat like that. She was right. No one had forced me to keep her from falling. It wasn't her fault she had a great pinwheeling left hook.

I couldn't help wondering if part of the reason I was still dwelling on it was because she was so cute. Dark, wavy curls had spilled out underneath her knit cap, tumbling just past her shoulders. And her bright green eyes had been full of horror over smacking me…until I reacted poorly and they'd turned to pools of anger. I couldn't say I blamed her. I wasn't exactly Mr. Charming. I'd been on edge about handling this case and my nerves had only just begun to settle. Now they were flaring again.

I couldn't let a clumsy gawker get to me. This was a run-of-the-mill murder. Piece of cake.

"She's gone. I must have scared her off. Is the evidence team still in there?"

"They finished about an hour ago. Oh, but they found a shell casing in the street. Bagged and tagged it."

I doubted it was tied to this case, especially since the murder weapon definitely hadn't been a gun, but I knew from experience that it was better to have more than we needed than not enough. It was too early in the investigation to rule anything out. I opened the door to go inside.

"You know, this place is scheduled to be torn down next week," Erickson said.

I kept my hand on the door handle and gave him my full attention. "What?"

"The same guy owns most of the buildings on this block, and he's tired of dealing with all the vagrants and drug dens. He's tearing it all down."

Couldn't say I blamed him. "And how were they going to bring it down?"

"Backhoe, I think, but I'm not sure. Maybe explosives on the building next door." He nodded to the three-story building next to the butcher shop.

"Mmm." If the murderer hoped to get rid of the victim's body in the demolition, it wasn't a very good plan. Especially since they hadn't left his body in the building next door, and if the body hadn't been called in, it almost certainly would have been found by the wrecking crew when the building was torn up. Or even before that point, as the explosives team probably would have gone from room to room to check for vagrants before blowing the building sky-high. Maybe the killer wasn't that bright, but I was willing to give them the benefit of the doubt. They'd been careful here. Last time I'd checked in, the crime lab hadn't found much evidence. Maybe it hadn't mattered to the killer whether the body was found, or they'd hoped it wouldn't be discovered until it—and the murder scene— was displaced by the backhoe.

Lance was still in the cooler even though the body had finally been picked up by the coroner a couple of hours ago. When the evidence team had arrived, I'd gotten the impression they wanted to rush through their collection, but I'd put the fear of God in them, insisting they be slow and methodical. In retaliation, they'd moved at a snail's pace.

I'd just returned from following the coroner's team to the morgue, where I'd met the county coroner for the first time, and I'd been pleased when he and his team had concluded their intake process.

"Well, you were right," I said. "The victim's Martin Fitzgerald Schroeder. His license lists his address as 2389 Hillsdale Avenue in Cockamamie. He had a debit card from the Cockamamie Savings and Loan, a Chase credit card, his insurance and Medicare cards, and a slip of paper with #293 scrawled on it in black ink."

"Find out anything from the coroner?" Lance asked.

"The cut on his neck was a downward slice, consistent with

someone slashing him from behind. Dr. Mueller couldn't give us an idea of what was used to make the cut, but he agreed it was something with a clean edge. They emptied his pockets and found a few interesting things."

His brow lifted in anticipation.

"Besides his wallet, there was a key ring with four keys, a tube of lip balm, a condom, and fifty-three cents in change. No cell phone." I gave him a second for one of those items to sink in.

Lance's eyes flew wide. "Jesus. A condom? What the hell was he gonna do with that?"

I grinned. "Well, Lance, when a man is turned on by a woman—or a man—and he wants to insert his—"

He held up his hand and waved. "Okay! Okay! I got it! But it's not a pleasant mental image when I'm associating it with Schroeder." He glanced up with a hopeful look in his eyes. "Maybe he carried it around for wishful thinking."

"I don't think so," I said. "The condom looked pretty new. Not like he'd been carrying it around for a while. He was widowed. Could he have had a girlfriend?"

He shuddered. "I'm struggling to see how he could have gotten a girlfriend. Not only had he let himself go, but he was *not* a nice man."

"It takes all kinds. I've seen plenty of relationships that didn't seem to make sense." Like my parents.

I added that to my list of things to look into—Schroeder's sexual history, not my parents' marriage. I'd given up trying to figure that out ages ago.

"He said the time of death was likely between six and nine p.m. last night. The autopsy's scheduled for eight tomorrow morning." I chuckled. "Dr. Mueller told me he takes his coffee strong and black."

Lance grinned. "I've heard he's a character."

That was an understatement. "After I left there, I stopped by to see his son, forty-two-year-old Darren Schroeder, who had been listed as next of kin. I didn't have any trouble tracking him down."

I shifted my stance, unwittingly giving him a good view of the right side of my face. He did a double take when he saw my eye. "Jesus, did his son punch you?"

"No," I muttered absently reaching up to touch it. There was a small welt, but I'd suffered worse. Much worse. The scar on my chest ached at the reminder. "Had a run-in with a bystander on the sidewalk."

"Get into a scuffle?"

"Something like that." I didn't want to admit to anyone else that I'd been accidentally clocked by a woman on the street.

"You arrest him?" he asked, looking pissed.

"Nah, it wasn't intentional." I quickly changed the subject. "Schroeder's son was eating a late lunch when I showed up at his front door. Said he hadn't talked to his father in weeks because the two didn't get along. Claims he has no idea why his dad would be in an abandoned butcher shop."

"Huh," Lance said. "He say anything helpful?"

"His son was the one who told me he was widowed," I said. "Says he didn't think his father had a girlfriend, but he didn't know much about his life. He confirmed that lots of people hated the guy, from his neighbors to his former students, to the teachers he worked with and more. Hell, even *he* hated his father, but he claims to have an alibi, so I suspect he's not our murderer."

A grin cracked his pinched mouth. "Told ya."

"We'll figure it out. His reputation as the most-hated man in Cockamamie might make it difficult to pin down who murdered him, but we'll solve it."

I was closing this case, dammit. This was the whole reason I'd been hired.

. . .

"His hands weren't bound." I said, "And no visible ligature marks on his wrist, but the autopsy's tomorrow morning, so we'll know more then."

"Could have been more than one person. Someone holding a gun on him while the other slit his throat."

"The possibilities are endless," I said. "We need more evidence to help steer us in the right direction."

"What do you think about the slip of paper?" he asked.

I pulled up an image of the slip.

"So it's a torn-off piece of paper with a pound sign and the number 293. Who knows what it's for."

"Hopefully, we'll find out more at his house. I'm waiting on the search warrant to be signed. Apparently, the judge is playing nine holes of golf and said not to disturb him unless it was life or death. His clerk claims this doesn't fit the bill."

Lance shook his head. "Let me guess, the Honorable Stanley T. Neilson."

"That would be the one."

"He's as lazy as they come, but the good citizens of this county just keep voting him back in. I suspect it has something to do with his barbecue food truck that he parks at the fairgrounds in the summer."

"He has a barbecue food truck?" I asked in disbelief.

He shrugged. "His dry-rub ribs are no joke."

Great.

"I talked to the owner of the building," Lance said. "He was driving by and saw the commotion and stopped to investigate."

"He have anything helpful?" I asked.

"He confirmed the building's set to be torn down next week. He said he'd had the place cleared out multiple times, but the drug addicts kept coming back. The last time he was here was last Thursday, talking to the demo crew. There were loads of trash everywhere."

I perked up. "So someone cleaned it out between last Thursday and this morning. Four days." I took stock of the room. "Has the demo crew been in since? Would they have cleaned it up?"

"Doesn't seem likely," Lance said. "But I'll check. The owner left the name of the company."

"Did we get the surveillance video from the convenience store across the street?" I asked.

"The owner of the store said he'd be more than happy to cooperate but claims that camera has been broken for a few weeks."

"How convenient," I grumbled.

"I thought so too. No one knows who called in the tip from the pay phone at the Stop and Go, but the 911 operator says it sounded like a male voice. Dunst talked to the overnight clerk, and he said he never saw anyone use the pay phone."

"Do you think the clerk really didn't see anyone or he *conveniently* didn't see anyone?" I asked.

"Could go either way," Lance said with a shrug. "But if I were forced to choose, I'd say he conveniently forgot. He serves a rougher clientele, and if word got out that he'd snitched…"

"He'd either lose business or his life."

"So no cell phone, huh?" Lance asked.

"Nope. His son said he carried one, and then tried calling the number from his home phone. It rang, but no one answered. He claims Mr. Schroeder has one of those find my friends apps on his phone, and he's connected to his father. He can tell us where the phone is."

"And?" Lance asked.

I snorted. "He can't find his own phone. Said he'll call me as soon as he locates it."

"Do you think he'll call you?"

"Yeah. Although Darren didn't seem all that shocked his father was murdered, he still wants to know who did it."

"So he can thank him," Lance said with a sardonic grin.

I couldn't deny that. Darren hadn't been all that shaken up over the news. "There's a chance Schroeder's phone is in his house, and we'll find it once the damn judge signs the search warrant. In the meantime," I said, "I'm getting a subpoena to request the cell phone carrier tell us the last place his phone pinged. The good news is that when Darren called Schroeder's phone, it *did* ring. It hasn't been turned off or died. So if Darren can find his own phone—which didn't ring when I called it—we have a good chance of tracking the vic's phone down before we get the records."

"Unless Schroeder's phone dies first," Lance said. He lifted a hand, gesturing loosely to the crime scene. "You want me to stay here on guard?"

I rubbed the back of my neck. I didn't want to release the crime scene, which meant we needed to keep an officer stationed on the premises and constrict the crime scene tape to the front door. "Nah, I'd rather you come on some interviews with me and help me go through Schroeder's house…if the damn warrant ever gets signed."

He knew far more about Schroeder than I did. Sometimes that could color a person's perspective, but in this instance, it might help me narrow down the suspect list from most of the town to about a hundred or so.

My phone vibrated in my pocket, and I wasn't surprised to see the police chief's name on the screen.

"Langley," I said as I answered.

"Tell me you've got something," Chief Jefferson Porter snarled in my ear. "I've got a town of freaked-out citizens because no one knows *what the fuck is going on*."

"You think they'll be less freaked out when they find out a man's throat was slit from ear to ear a few blocks from the town square?" I asked, incredulous.

"No, but the rumors are swirling, Noah. We've got to tell them something. You got any suspects yet?"

"Yeah," I quipped. "About half the goddamned town."

"Not helpful."

"Tell me about it. Everyone hated the old bastard. Even his son."

"Is he a suspect?" the chief asked hopefully.

"He's a person of interest, but officially, no. I don't think so. He didn't give me that vibe, and he supposedly has an alibi. I'm about to check it out."

"I need more than vibes, Noah. I need you to close this case. I need your proven close rates."

"With all due respect, sir," I said, trying to keep my cool. "My instincts contribute to my success rate."

He was silent for a moment, then said, "Your future here at the Cockamamie Police Department depends on you solving this murder, Detective Langley. And you better hope you have something to tell the public at our news conference at six. You'll be the one to give them an update."

"What?"

"Be here at the station a half hour early so we can get our story straight," he barked.

"You mean go over for a debriefing?"

"Same difference." Then he hung up.

Lance cast me a wry look. "Sounds like you were talking to the chief."

"Press conference at six," I said, stuffing my phone into my pocket. Propping my hands on my hips, I stared at the dried blood on the concrete floor. "We've got to figure out what to tell the public. Apparently, they're losing their minds."

Lance shrugged. "As is the way of things in a small town. The chief's right. This isn't Atlanta or Memphis. People won't forget about it and move on until we catch the killer."

"We won't be telling them the cause of death," I finally say. "No need to stir up more panic. We'll just tell them we found the murder victim in an abandoned business on West Walnut. In the meantime, we'll check out the son's alibi for last night and see if he located his phone. He says he spent the night at home with his wife. I say we go have a chat with her while we wait for that warrant."

Chapter Seven

Noah

Darren's wife was an ER nurse at the Cockamamie Hospital, which was more of a glorified emergency room with a few hospital beds for locals who came down with the flu or had a baby. From what I'd been told, most critical-care cases were sent off to Wayfare County Hospital in Knobnoster, the largest town in the county, which wasn't saying much.

When we showed up at the reception desk, a blond woman in pink scrubs was leaning over the receptionist's shoulder, pointing to something on her computer screen. She stood upright before we had a chance to introduce ourselves. "You're here about Martin, right?

I took note of her name tag. "You're Sherry Schroeder?"

"That's me," she said, tossing her long ponytail over her shoulder. She looked a good decade or so younger than Darren. A grin spread across her face as she eyed me. "Kind of wimpy shiner there for the ER. You want me to get you an ice pack for that?"

I lifted my hand to my cheek. There was a dull ache on my cheekbone, but I'd forgotten about it. Mostly.

"No," I groused, snippier than I'd intended.

But Sherry didn't seem to take it personally. She chuckled, then said, "I'm taking a break, Maria." Gesturing for us to follow, she walked around the reception desk and through the door to the waiting room. "I suppose you have some questions, so let's head into the patient quiet room."

She led us to a private room that looked like it was used for family members who were receiving bad news. After Lance and I introduced ourselves, she said, "Darren called and told me about Martin. Can't say I'm all that broken up to hear about his demise."

Lance's brow lifted, giving me a look of surprise.

"What?" she said, putting some coins in a vending machine and getting a can of Coke. "He was a mean old bastard. I'm surprised no one offed him before now."

I pulled out my phone and turned on my recording app. "Can you think of anyone who might've been particularly motivated?"

She scoffed as she popped open the top. "Are you asking if *I* did it? No, and neither did Darren. We were together last night, and we had friends over from about six until about ten. I can give you their names and contact information, if you like. After that, we went to bed, and I got up at five to get to work by six." She took a sip from her can. "I work twelve-hour shifts. I left Darren in bed."

"Did your father-in-law have any arguments or disputes with anyone lately that you know about?"

She shook her head. "None that I'm aware of, but that doesn't mean there weren't any. Darren and I didn't have much to do with him. He treated Darren like crap, and I was sick of it."

"Why didn't Martin and Darren get along?" I asked.

"Because Martin was a first-rate asshole?" she said bitterly. "He was always a bastard, but he got ten times worse after Mildred died." Then she added, "Mildred was his wife. She died seven years ago. Breast cancer."

Darren had told me much the same thing, but it was always good to see if their stories matched. "When did he retire from teaching?"

"A year before that," she said. "That contributed to his bitchiness too. I think he was bored, and stirrin' up shit provided entertainment. I finally said we weren't playin'."

"Did he have any hobbies?"

"You mean other than bitching? Yeah, he liked to fly his drone."

"He had a drone?" I asked in surprise.

"Yep. Got in trouble a few times for flying it over people's houses and such. He always was a snoop."

"Did he have any close friends?" Lance asked.

She turned to him in surprise. "Friends?" She barked a laugh, then took a drink from her can of Coke. "You have to be a friend to have friends, and Martin Schroeder was only out for himself."

"Was he in any clubs or organizations?" I asked. "Go to any meetings?"

Her brow shot up. "You think the old bastard had a social life? Not a chance. But he did go to the VFW hall sometimes. Liked to play bingo occasionally, then complain when he didn't win." Her mouth twisted to the side, and she tapped her chin with her index finger. "Now that I think about it, he may have accused them of rigging the games one too many times. I think they banned him."

"He was a veteran?" Lance asked.

"'Nam," she said. "Darren always wondered if that's why he was such a son of a bitch, but Martin's brother claimed he was always like that."

"Does his brother live around here?"

"Nope. He died a good ten or twelve years ago. Heart attack." She sighed. "They say the good die young."

"Any other living relatives around?" I asked. "Besides Darren?"

"Nope. Martin's parents are dead. His wife died, probably to escape her hell on earth, and his brother's gone. The only one left is Darren, and like I said, we didn't have much to do with him over the past few years."

"One more thing," I said, "and then I'll let you get back to your shift. Did your father-in-law have a girlfriend? Was he seeing anyone romantically?"

She stared at me in disbelief, then burst out laughing. "This is a joke, right? Because there's no way in hell a woman would be stupid enough to put up with his shit."

"What about the strip club?" Lance asked.

Grinning, she shook her head. "He's too damn cheap. He'd never pay those prices for drinks, and last I heard, they had a two-drink minimum."

I could see that Lance wanted to ask her how she knew that specific information, but he kept it to himself. As he should. It wasn't illegal to frequent the strip bar, and it wasn't any of our business if Sherry Schroeder did.

I turned off my recording app. "Thank you for your time, Ms. Schroeder. This has been very helpful. We'll keep Darren updated on the investigation when we can. In the meantime, if you have any questions, feel free to give me a call."

I handed her a card as my phone vibrated in my hand. "I've got to take a call, but if you could give Officer Forrester the names and contact information for the friends who visited you last night, I'd appreciate it."

"Of course."

I pressed the phone to my ear and walked out of the room as I answered, "Langley."

"The warrant's been signed," Sergeant Miller said. "You're good to go. Sending it to your email now. CSI should be there within the next half hour or less, and Finnegan's got the house taped off. He's there babysitting, waiting for you or CSI to get there."

"Thanks." I estimated it was only a five-minute drive to Schroeder's house. If we beat the team, we'd be able to examine the house before they started collecting evidence. Then Lance and I could start interviewing the neighbors.

Lance and Sherry emerged from the room a moment later, and as soon as she headed off to continue her shift, I filled him in on the warrant. We got into my car, deciding to leave his in the hospital parking lot for now. Just as I was about to pull out of the parking space, I got a call from Darren Schroeder.

"Detective Langley?" he said when I answered, taking the call through the car's Bluetooth connection. "I wanted you to know I found my phone, and I've found the location of my father's phone."

"You did?" I asked, exchanging a look with Lance as I put the car back into park. "Can you tell me where it's located?"

"This is going to sound strange, but it looks like it's in the parking lot of the Piggly Wiggly."

"Someone could have tossed it into a dumpster," Lance murmured.

"No," Darren said. "It looks like it's in the parking lot. Maybe in a car, or someone could have just tossed it out the window? I can send you a pin of the location. It hasn't moved since I found it."

"That would be great," I said. "Thank you, Darren."

"Yeah," he said. "No problem." Then he added, "Look, my dad was a real asshole, but he was still my dad. Now I don't have anyone except for Sherry." He paused, and when he spoke again, his voice broke. "Just find out who did it, okay?"

"I'll do my best," I said before I hung up, hoping like hell that my best was enough. I turned to Lance. "I need to go meet the CSI team and take a cursory look at the house before they get to work. Why don't you head over to the grocery store and keep an eye out for the phone? I'll send you the pin once Darren sends it, then come help you look."

"Sounds good," Lance said, reaching for the door handle. "I'll let you know what I find."

Chapter Eight

Maddie

Linda and Aunt Deidre were in the middle of an argument when I walked through the front door.

"Give me back my wallet!" my aunt shouted.

"For the tenth time, Miss Deidre, I didn't take your wallet," Linda said with a tone of forced patience. She looked exasperated.

"Aunt Deidre?" I called out from the entrance to her living room. "Is there a problem here?"

"That woman stole my wallet!" she accused, flinging her finger toward the middle-aged woman who had become her daily caretaker.

I looked at Linda, hoping she could see the sincere apology in my eyes. "Aunt Deidre, I'm sure she didn't take it. You probably just misplaced it."

"It was in my handbag," my aunt said, her purse looped over her outstretched arm. "And now it's not."

"You didn't have that handbag the last time you went out," I said. "You had the black one."

"I most certainly did not," my aunt insisted, her voice rising in indignation. "I had *this* one."

She was holding up a crisp white purse, so even if she'd gone out with Margarete or someone else without my knowledge, I knew there was no way on God's green earth she'd taken that bag. Aunt Deidre always packed away all of her white clothing and accessories the day after Labor Day. Uncle Albert used to mark it down on the calendar, declaring it the real first day of fall.

"Aunt Deidre," I said softly as I walked over and led her to the sofa. "Why don't you have a seat for a few moments while I interrogate Linda."

"Good idea," she said with a vicious look. "And if you need help torturing her, let me know."

I smothered my gasp and motioned for Linda to follow me into the entryway.

"Linda," I said as soon as we were both around the corner. "I am so, so sorry. I'm not *really* going to interrogate you, obviously. I just said that for my aunt's benefit." The last thing I needed was for Linda to quit. I held up the paper bag containing the cinnamon roll and the lemon bar. "I came bearing gifts."

She took the bag and peered inside, then looked back up at me. "You don't have to worry, Maddie. I'm not quitting."

My shoulders sagged with relief. "Thank God."

"I'm sad to say, this isn't all that uncommon with dementia patients. They tend to become paranoid at times and..." She seemed to be searching for the right word. "Unlike themselves."

While I knew all of this from my talk with Dr. Snyder two months ago, knowing something and accepting it were two very different things. Some days I felt like I was living in an alternate universe, one in which my aunt was only a few steps removed from herself. It was unsettling and ungrounding. Days like today really brought home the reality of our situation. "Aunt Deidre would be *horrified* if the real her knew she'd accused you of stealing her wallet. Or that she'd been downright rude."

Linda placed a hand on my arm, giving me a sad smile. "Maddie, this *is* the real her now. No, she's not like the woman you knew, but this is her too. Her disease has just screwed up her neurons." Her mouth twisted to the side. "You know it's only going to get worse."

I cast a glance at the woman who had taken over for my mother. Truthfully, she'd been an integral part of my life long before my mother's death. Aunt Deidre and Uncle Albert had never been able to have children of their own, so they'd spoiled me with attention and affection. The woman sitting on the sofa, frantically searching her completely empty purse, was not the woman who'd been like a second mother to me. The woman on that sofa was a stranger.

"This disease is not for the faint of heart," Linda said sympathetically.

"Thank goodness she doesn't realize what she's doing half the time," I said, tears welling in my eyes. "She would hate to know she was so rude to you. I mean it, Linda. It would devastate her. She's one of the sweetest women I know."

"Yes, it's hard for her," Linda said, squeezing my arm. "But I was talking about *you*."

I turned to her in surprise.

"Maddie, I know you left your life behind to take care of her. You lost your own support system in the process, not to mention you just lost the uncle who was like a father to you."

I gasped in surprise. How had she known that?

Sympathy filled her eyes. "Deidre has her good moments. She's told me about your childhood. Your mother's death."

I looked away because I was tired of thinking about my mother's death. I'd thought more about it in the last few days than I had in years.

"There are support groups for family members of loved ones with dementia," Linda said. "I can bring the information for you tomorrow."

"I don't know," I said with a grimace. "I'm not sure I want to sit in a circle and complain about my aunt."

She released a small chuckle. "It's more than that, Maddie. Just consider it. You could talk to people who are going through the same thing. It could be more helpful than you realize."

Pushing out a sigh, I said, "I'll think about it."

"That's all I ask," she said, then leaned closer, lowering her voice. "You're doing great, and hopefully things will even out soon. People with dementia don't handle change well, and there's been a lot of upheaval in Deidre's life. Not only did she lose the love of her life, but she also lost her caretaker. Once she gets used to the new normal, hopefully she'll even out and have more good days than bad."

"Thanks, Linda."

She tilted her head, her smile tight. "About your grocery store trip..."

"I know," I said. "I don't think she's up to it."

"She's dead set on going, but I think it's your call. Maybe go in and get a few items. Don't make it a full shopping trip."

I nodded. I knew what happened when Aunt Deidre got dead set on something and anyone tried to stand in her way. A month after Uncle Albert died, she'd insisted that she needed to go to church even though she had a cold with a fever. When I told her she needed to stay home and rest, she grabbed the keys to Uncle Albert's car, snuck out of the house, then crashed into a tree two blocks away. Nothing had looked familiar, and she'd been distracted, trying to figure out which way to go.

Uncle Albert's car had been totaled. I'd sold it for scrap metal, so she couldn't escape with it now, but she might try to find my keys and take mine or, worse, try to walk to the store and get lost.

"I think it's safer if we make a short trip," I said reluctantly.

"Good luck," Linda said as she picked up her purse from the hall tree, then pointed to another purse next to it. "I suspect Deidre's wallet is in there, but she never gave me a chance to show her."

I reached for the purse and dug inside. Sure enough, I found her wallet, stuffed with enough coins that it had to weigh five pounds.

Linda let herself out the front door while I headed into the living room and held up the missing wallet. "Look what I found."

"You frisked it off her," Aunt Deidre said with approval. "Good girl."

"No, Aunt Deidre. It was in your purse on the hall tree. Just where you left it."

"That evil woman must have planted it there," she said, getting to her feet. "But there's no time to spare. We've got to get to the Piggly Wiggly."

"Do you remember why we're going?" I asked.

"Of course I do, you impertinent girl," she said as though I were six years old. "We're getting a chicken so I can fry it up for my niece."

My heart sunk. "Who do you think I am?"

Her eyes narrowed as she searched my face. "You look familiar…"

"I'm *Maddie*, Aunt Deidre. Your niece." When she looked confused, I added, "Andrea's daughter."

She laughed, waving her hand. "Oh no, you can't be Maddie. She's a little girl. You're a grown woman."

While my aunt had been confused before, she'd always known who I was. This was the first time she hadn't recognized me. The ground beneath me felt slippery and unsettled. The one constant I could always count on was my aunt and uncle's love and support. Now Uncle Albert was gone, and Aunt Deidre didn't even recognize me.

I'd known this would happen. I'd known it was inevitable. But now that it was here, it felt like a kick in the gut. It took me a second to catch my breath. "It's me. I'm all grown up, Aunt Deidre."

"Don't be ridiculous," she said with another wave of her hand, then headed for the front door. "Andrea's bringing the dear over for dinner, and she loves my fried chicken." She stopped at the door and turned back to me. "I need to get my secret ingredient, but I can't tell you what it is."

I was having serious misgivings about taking her out of the house, but I hoped that seeing something familiar—like the grocery store she'd been shopping at for decades—might help bring her memory back. Still, I planned to heed Linda's advice and stick to a few items.

My aunt insisted on riding in the back seat, which reminded me of my last Uber passenger. As soon as we got home, I'd have to call the police. What I knew wasn't so earth-shattering it couldn't wait until then.

I was glad Aunt Deidre's olfactory nerves weren't working because that awful rotten egg smell had lingered a bit, but at least it wasn't as bad as it had been while Marty the Man was in the car. When we got home, I planned to leave the doors open and maybe scrub the seats with a baking powder paste, like Ernie had suggested.

I couldn't stop worrying that *he* might have been the victim. Truthfully, I was much more concerned for his safety than Marty the Man's. If that made me a bad person, so be it.

My aunt dozed off during the drive to the Piggly Wiggly—which was the last place I wanted to be given the whole Peter McIntire situation. The last thing I felt like doing strolling down memory lane after the day I'd had. Still, it was Aunt Deidre's favorite store, and she needed familiar things right now, so I'd have to suck it up.

I parked in the back of the lot, away from all the other cars, figuring we could both use the walk. She stirred when I opened the back door, then squinted up at me.

"Maddie?" she asked in confusion.

Relief washed over me. It felt like my world had been set to rights. For a short while, at least. "Yes?"

"What on earth am I doing in the back of your car?"

"You wanted to pretend to be one of my Uber clients," I said with a forced laugh as I helped her out. "We're at the grocery store." I waved to the building. "See?"

"We're getting chicken for dinner," she said, still looking confused, like she wasn't sure how we'd gotten here.

"That's right," I said. "And I know I promised you a full shopping trip, but I've got a bit of a headache, so I was hoping you'd be agreeable to shortening it a bit."

"Oh, you poor dear," she said, lifting her hand to her cheek. "I'll make you some ginger tea when we get back to the house. It always worked wonders for Andrea when she got her headaches."

"Thanks, Aunt Deidre." I covered her hand with my own. It hit me like that punch I'd accidentally dealt the detective that she was all I had left of my family...and I was slowly losing her too.

"Now let's get this shopping trip done so I can get you home and take care of you." She turned and headed for the entrance to the store.

I followed her, still recovering from my emotional whiplash. Once inside the first set of sliding doors, my aunt grabbed a cart and steered it through the next set of doors into the store.

"Good afternoon, Miss Deidre," one of the young cashiers called out from a register close to the entrance. "I haven't seen you in ages."

My aunt stopped and placed a hand to her chest. "I know. I haven't been feeling myself since Albert's passing."

The cashier smiled at her with a sympathetic look. "We all miss him. We've missed you too. I hope you'll be coming in more now that you're feeling better."

Aunt Deidre looked at me with a questioning glance, and I

turned to the cashier and said, "Now that things are getting settled, we'll be in more."

Both women looked relieved, and I felt terrible for not bringing her here sooner. She had friends everywhere—including the grocery store—and by keeping her home, I'd kept her from people who cared about her. What if I'd made things worse?

I couldn't deal with the guilt today.

"Did they put tubes in poor little Colton's ears?" Aunt Deidre asked the woman.

"A couple of weeks ago. So far, so good."

My aunt nodded her approval. "That'll do the trick." Then she started to push the cart toward the produce section, whispering, "Her son had multiple ear infections. They were talking about putting in tubes."

It was crazy to me that an hour ago she'd been a paranoid woman I didn't recognize, a woman who didn't recognize me, but now she was acting like herself. Was it because I'd brought her somewhere familiar?

I'd intended to keep the trip short—both because of the handbag incident and because I was becoming more and more anxious about talking to the police—but she was obviously thrilled to be there, and I had no intention of taking this happiness from her. She had already lost so much. She wandered up and down the aisles, getting food from our list while I trailed behind and marveled that she knew where everything was and the names of every employee. Her doctor had warned me that the memory slippage would be fluid at times, her cognizance shifting by the second, but this felt bizarre.

We'd picked up everything, including a few extras like ice cream and bagels, so I suggested we head for the checkout.

"Oh, not yet," she said with a laugh, like I was ridiculous to suggest it. "We haven't gotten the most important ingredient for the fried chicken."

I peered into the cart and took a quick inventory, not seeing anything missing. "What's that?"

She tapped her chin, her brow furrowing. "I don't remember, but let's walk around and I'm sure I'll know it when I see it."

That didn't sound like a good idea. My anxiety about talking to the police was nearly choking me, and I just wanted to get it done. I'd planned to call the nonemergency number, but if Ernie or Marty the Man really had been the victim, I suspected a call wouldn't cut it. This was going to require a full-blown interview. I couldn't bring Aunt Deidre with me, so I either needed to get Margarete to stay with her or get the police to come to Cabbage Rose House.

But I could also give her a few more minutes. I hadn't seen her enjoy anything this much since she beat Margarete in a rousing game of Scrabble. "One more quick walk through, then we leave, okay?"

"Is your headache worse?" she asked, concern filling her eyes.

"What? No. It's the same. I'm just tired."

She bobbed her head, seeming to understand. "It's your time of the month, isn't it, dear?"

"I'm just tired from work. The coffee shop was packed today. Something happened down in the Bottoms."

She stopped to look up at me. "What do you mean?"

Should I tell her? I didn't want to upset her, but all she had to do was ask someone walking past us and she'd find out the truth and likely a bunch of grisly speculation. Better if she heard it from me. "There was a murder."

She gasped, placing her hand on her chest. "A murder?"

"Everyone was talking about it. It made for an exhausting day."

She got a faraway look in her eyes. "I knew someone who was murdered." She tapped her finger on her chin. "I can't remember who."

For some reason, forgetting about my mother's death was worse than not recognizing me. I stared at her in shock, but she didn't seem to notice. In fact, she'd moved on.

"Then we'll be sure to get you home as soon as I find..." Her lips pressed together, then she shook her head. "It's right there on the tip of my tongue, but it just floats away."

I quickly pulled myself together. This was only the beginning. I better learn to suck it up now. "That happens to me too," I said, forcing myself to sound cheerful. "It's for the chicken, you say? Is it a spice for the breading?"

She considered it for a moment, then said, "No, but that's close."

We walked through the produce department again, then down the canned goods aisle.

"You should have a dinner party," my aunt suddenly said, and for a moment, I thought she'd slipped back into her dementia.

"Oh yeah?" I asked with a laugh. "And who would I invite?"

"All your old friends from school. Like Peter McIntire."

"*What?*"

"Hi, Peter," she said, glancing over my shoulder. "We were just talking about you."

My stomach sunk, and I turned around to face a very handsome man dressed in a light blue button-down shirt with rolled-up sleeves and a pair of khakis. His blond hair was neatly trimmed, and his eyes shone with excitement. "Maddie." To my aunt, he said, "Hello, Miss Deidre. I hope you were saying *good* things."

He shot me a wink.

I tried not to cringe. Peter had always known how to butter up the teachers in school.

"We're having a dinner party," my aunt said with a directness I hadn't heard from her since I'd come back to Cockamamie. "For you and Maddie and all your old school friends."

Oh *shit*. "Aunt Deidre—"

Peter's brow shot up as he turned to me in surprise. "You didn't come to the ten year reunion," he said. "I didn't think you were still interested in our friends from high school."

"Actually—"

"Of course she is," Aunt Deidre said. "I was thinking Friday would be good. At seven? At Cabbage Rose House, of course."

"I'm free," Peter said, beaming. "And I'm sure a few of our other friends would be delighted to come."

"I planned on asking Colleen and some of your other friends," Aunt Deidre said. "Is there anyone else you can think of who might be interested?"

Peter kept his focus on me, his eyes locked on my face. His gaze looked innocent enough, but our past made me squirm inside. "No," he said absently. "Not off the top of my head." Turning back to my aunt, his smile cheerier, he added, "I take it you're here for your pickle juice. I've kept it in the back, waiting for you."

Aunt Deidre squealed in excitement. "Pickle juice! That's the missing ingredient!"

Peter laughed. "You haven't been by in a while, but I knew you'd come in at some point. If you lovely ladies are ready to check out, I can grab it and meet you up at the registers."

"You're the nicest boy, Peter McIntire," my aunt said, beaming.

Peter looked at me and winked again. "When I want to be."

Was he alluding to his past—*our* past? In a moment of weakness back in high school, I'd had a hot and heavy make-out session with Peter at a bonfire our sophomore year, but I'd stopped him when he tried to go to second base. He'd called me a tease and a cock tease, then went and made out with some other girl. I'd ignored him after that, but I'd never forgiven him for trying to ruin my reputation later. Because it hadn't been enough for him to call me those ugly names in person—he'd told everyone in school to do it too.

It looked like I still hadn't forgiven him.

Of course, my aunt looked at him and only saw a handsome,

single man who'd remembered her pickle juice. She thought she was being helpful, and I didn't want to tell her otherwise.

I steered both her and the cart toward the front of the store, picking the shortest line, but of course it was slower than I'd hoped. The cashier had barely started scanning our items before Peter showed up with a jar of pickle juice. He handed it to the cashier, then turned his attention on me.

I looked away, furious. No way would I be roped into a dinner party with Peter McIntire, of all people. I'd find an excuse later. I could tell him I was getting a bunion removed or cleaning out the oven.

"Maddie, if I could have a word with you?" he asked in a slightly pleading tone.

"You young people go have a chat," my aunt said with a shooing motion. "I can finish up here."

That seemed like a bad idea for multiple reasons, the most important one being that I doubted I should leave Aunt Deidre alone.

The cashier smiled at me. She looked like she was in her forties, and she had a motherly air. "It's okay. I'll make sure Miss Deidre's all set."

Well, there went that excuse. Then again, maybe it was better to get this cleared up now. Even if I was potentially threatening my aunt's pickle juice hookup.

There was always Amazon.

I flashed Peter a tight smile, then turned back to my aunt. "I'll be right out front, Aunt Deidre."

"I'm fine," she said in exasperation. "Go on already."

"Out front," I snapped at Peter, walking past him toward the automatic sliding doors. I headed out into the crisp November afternoon, then moved several feet to the side so I could still see my aunt through the window. "What do you want?" I asked, looking up at him with a belligerent glare. I could hear sirens in the distance.

"I suppose that good boy comment was a step too far," he said, looking chagrinned.

"You think?" I asked indignantly. I wrapped my sweater tighter around my body. "There will be no dinner party, Peter. If my aunt mentions it again, you will tell her you're busy."

The sirens were growing louder.

"But what if I don't want to be busy?" he asked earnestly. "I was a stupid kid, Maddie. I really liked you and I took things too far."

"You call telling everyone I was a cock tease too far? I had to shove your hand away three times!" I hissed.

He ran his hand through his thick blond hair in frustration. "In my defense, I was *really* drunk. And things were different back then."

"Yeah," I said with a sneer. "It *was* different back then. It was easier to slut-shame and get away with it."

A police car pulled into the parking lot, its lights flashing and its siren blaring, but it cut the siren as it cruised to the back of the parking lot.

That was weird. My car and another police car a row over were the only cars parked there.

The hair on the back of my neck stood on end. The odds they were here for me were ridiculously low, but it was a reminder that I was wasting time with Peter McIntire when I should be talking to the police. Damn that stupid detective for making me lose my nerve earlier.

"Maddie."

I dragged my attention back to Peter.

"Please," he said with pleading eyes. "I was an idiot, but that's no excuse for what I did. I've changed, Maddie. I've learned from my mistakes. If you'd just give me a chance…"

My brow practically shot up to my hairline. "Give you a chance? My mother died soon after that, you asshole, and you *still* gave me grief."

His face twisted. "You're right. I *was* an asshole. I know it. But let me make it up to you."

There was absolutely no way I was letting him make *anything* up to me. His snide comment after my aunt called him a good boy was enough to illustrate that he hadn't changed as much as he claimed he had.

The police car had pulled to a stop perpendicular to my car, which meant there were now two cop cars around it.

Oh shit. This was looking a lot less like a coincidence.

A tall, uniformed police officer stood next to the car that had arrived first. He walked over to the patrol car as two more officers got out. They had a quick exchange, then approached my car.

What the hell?

"You're right, Peter," I said with little heat, my attention divided now. "You were an asshole then, and I don't believe you're any different now. Now, if you'll excuse me..." I started walking at a fast clip toward my car.

Why were police officers surrounding my car? And why did one of them have a crowbar, looking like he was about to bust in my rear passenger-side window? Had they somehow figured out that I'd been in the area of the murder, and they'd come to arrest me? My heart was pounding so hard I could hear it in my ears.

"What the hell do you think you're doing?" I shouted as I approached them.

The uniformed officer from the first car asked, "Are you the owner of this car?"

Looking younger than the other two, he was tall with light brown hair and the hint of a beard, like he'd been too busy to shave.

I wrapped my arms over my chest, hugging myself as a shudder passed through me. Had the credit union sent the police to repossess my car? No, they wouldn't send the police, and I wasn't actually behind on the payments. Yet. That said, having my car repossessed would be preferable than being in the middle of a murder investigation. "I am. Why does it look like you're about to break into it?"

The officer with the crowbar grinned, but it didn't look the least bit friendly. "Police business."

"Do you have a warrant, Officer?" I asked, my hands on my hips, but my arms were covered in goosebumps from fear.

They must have figured out that I'd given Mr. Smelly Pants a ride to the crime scene last night, right before the murder. Maybe someone had seen me talking to Ernie too. Either one of them might have been the victim. But if that were the case, why would they send a police car with sirens and lights? Wouldn't they just want to question me?

"She's right," the third officer said. "We don't have a warrant yet." He was shorter than the others and skinny.

The first officer shook his head slightly as he cast an annoyed look at his mini mob. "We weren't going to break in, but we'd very much appreciate it if you would give us permission to search your car."

"Not until you tell me why," I said, my stomach now roiling. "I have rights, you know."

A dark sedan pulled up behind the police car, and a man in a suit got out and strode toward us. I recognized the dress shirt and tie before my gaze lifted to his face. I couldn't look away from the bruise blooming under his right eye. I'd given him that black eye less than two hours before.

Detective Asshat. Dammit. It was my lucky day.

Had he come to follow through on his threat to arrest me for assault?

He headed over to my car, surprise flickering in his eyes when he saw me.

"Is this your car, miss?"

Well, at least he'd called me miss.

"Why are all of you so hot and bothered about my car?" I

asked with more attitude than intended. Then again, I was still pissed at him for the way he'd acted earlier, not to mention Crowbar Dude looked like he was seconds from going ham on my car windows.

Detective Asshat's eyes narrowed. "We have reason to believe something pertaining to an ongoing police investigation is inside your vehicle. Do you give us permission to look inside?"

"I was planning to go to the police station after our shopping trip," I said, then realized how bad that sounded. Besides, I had no idea if he was here because of Marty the Man. It was all supposition at this point.

"Oh?" the detective asked, his brow rising mockingly. He directed a derisive look just past my shoulder. "After you two lovebirds finished shopping?"

"*What?*" I turned a little to see Peter was standing slightly behind me with a sympathetic look. Crap. I'd forgotten he was there.

"He is not my..." Significant other? Boyfriend? Husband? I wasn't sure what Detective Asshat was thinking, but when it came down to it, it was none of his business. "Never mind."

"Do you give us permission to search your car, Ms. Baker?" the detective asked, his eyes harder than before.

His use of my name proved he'd likely found out I'd given Mr. Smelly Pants an Uber ride, and I knew I shouldn't hold back anything, but his attitude was pissing me off. I was a witness, not a suspect.

"I could tell you no," I said. "I could force you to get a search warrant, but I have nothing to hide, so knock yourselves out." I pressed the unlock button. The car chirped, and the locks clicked.

The uniformed officers from the second car pulled on black gloves, then opened the back doors simultaneously. Crowbar Dude looked disappointed. Looked like it was his unlucky day too.

"Why are you so interested in my car?" I asked the detective.

He looked down his nose at me with a steely gaze but remained silent.

Both officers dived inside, and seconds later, the one on the passenger side got out holding a cell phone in his gloved hand. "Bingo."

A cell phone?

It only took me a millisecond to figure it out. Not only had Marty the Man been the murder victim, but he'd dropped his phone in my car. Or maybe he was the murderer. He hadn't been very nice.

Oh my God. Had I delivered a man to his murder den?

No. From the way the officers were looking at me, he had been the murderee.

Well, shit a brick. I'd dropped a man off to his murder.

I wasn't sure that was any better.

The detective was pulling on gloves as he walked over to the officer. He took the phone and pressed the screen, his jaw set, then turned his steely gaze on me. "Madelyn Baker, we're taking you down to police headquarters for questioning in a murder investigation."

"What?" I screeched. I wasn't surprised they wanted to talk to me, but the way he said it made it sound like he was ready to book me on murder charges.

"Murder?" Peter shouted.

"What's going on?" Aunt Deidre said behind me, sounding alarmed.

I knew I should have gone to the police station sooner. *Dammit.*

How was Aunt Deidre going to take all of this? Not well, I suspected, especially since she couldn't even talk about my mother's murder. When she remembered.

How much worse could this day get?

One thing was clear. I needed to protect her. "I'll be happy to answer any questions you might have," I said, trying like hell to be polite and appear calm. "But let me make arrangements for my aunt first."

Who was I going to call to pick her up? Margarete was at the top of the list, but I wasn't so sure Detective Antsy Pants would wait.

"I'll make sure she gets home," Peter said, wrapping an arm around her back.

"What's going on?" my aunt asked, confusion and fear clouding her eyes. The purse hanging from her arm shook from her trembling.

"There's nothing to worry about," I said confidently, taking my aunt's hand. I gave her a tight smile. "I just need to talk to these very nice police officers about a man I gave a ride to, okay?"

She gave them a dubious look, then turned back to me. "I think you should call a lawyer."

"I don't think that's necessary," I said. "I had already planned to talk to the police after we finished shopping. I'll tell them what I know and then be home to help make fried chicken." I arched a brow in a mock stern look. "But don't start without me."

She scowled. "I'm not a baby, Madelyn. I'm still capable of doing things on my own."

"I'll look after her," Peter said reassuringly.

I wasn't exactly thrilled Peter was my savior here, but beggars couldn't be choosers. "She can't be left alone," I said. "I'll call our neighbor to come over and look after her until I get home."

"That might be a while," one of the uniformed officers said with a smirk.

Peter shot me a worried look.

"Officer Davens," snapped the officer from the first police car.

The smirking cop sobered, but his comment had me plenty worried. Maybe they really *did* think I had killed Marty the Man?

"Her neighbor's name is Margarete," I said to Peter, my voice shaking slightly. "She lives next door."

Peter nodded, his eyes wide with concern. "Your aunt is right. You should probably get a lawyer."

"I don't know any lawyers." Nor could I afford one.

"Not true," Peter said. "You know Burt Pullman from high school. He's a defense attorney now. Call him."

I nodded, then pulled my aunt into a hug. "Peter's going to take you home; then I'll have Margarete come over. I'll be back before you know it." I dropped my hold on her and turned toward my car, but the uniformed officer who had seemed to take charge blocked my path. His name tag said Forrester.

"We'll have you ride with us, miss," Officer Forrester said kindly.

"Am I under arrest?" I asked, squaring my shoulders as I sized him up with an indignant glare. His kindness could be a trick. I'd seen *Making a Murderer*. Twice.

"No, miss," he reassured me, "but we *will* need to impound your car."

Well, shit. I *really* needed my car. *"Why?"*

He was quick to respond with an apologetic smile. "I'm not at liberty to say, but I assure you we'll take very good care of it. In the meantime, we'd like to bring you down to the police station to ask a few questions about the phone."

It didn't seem like I had a choice, so I nodded in agreement. I had no idea how I was going to get home, but I'd worry about that part later.

Chapter Nine

Noah

"What do you think?" I asked Lance.

We'd put Ms. Baker in an interrogation room, then headed into the observation room to watch her for several minutes. She was sitting stiffly in her chair with a worried expression on her face. She wasn't wearing the knitted hat from earlier, so her hair hung down in rich dark waves, not quite black, to about six inches past her shoulders. She was wearing a long-sleeved black T-shirt and jeans. I'd thought she was cute on the street corner, but I hadn't given her looks enough credit. She was pretty, *really* pretty. No wonder the guy she was with had looked like he couldn't wait to get her home and fuck her.

I was pissed, although not necessarily at her. Lance had gone to the pinned location of the phone and realized there was only one car in the vicinity. Having determined the phone must have been inside the car, he then called in his location to dispatch and ran Ms. Baker's license plate. Officer Davens had heard the call and taken it upon himself to show up, lights blaring.

How the fuck was I supposed to solve this case when I was surrounded by idiots, present company excepted? Maybe I was being too harsh. Truth was, things were progressing with the case, and I was feeling more grounded. I hadn't had a major crisis with judgment calls. Sure, we didn't have many leads yet, but they would come. I'd make damn sure they did.

Lance sighed and leaned his shoulder into the wall. "She didn't do it."

"You sound pretty certain of that," I said, my irritation rising.

"Well, first of all, look at her. You think she's capable of slitting someone's throat?"

"You can't make assumptions like that," I said, annoyed.

"The guy had fifty pounds on her easy."

"More like seventy-five," I admitted grumpily.

"The only blood in the room was around the victim and the drain," Lance said, moving away from the wall. "Based on the angle of the blade, we're either looking for a seven-foot-tall suspect or someone strong enough to get him from behind. She's what? Five-four? Five-five?"

Scowling, I pulled out my work phone and scrolled through the images I'd taken earlier, then held a photo up for Lance to see. "When he was found, he was lying on his side, his knees bent. He could have been forced to kneel."

He gave me an incredulous look. "Why do you *want* to pin it on her?"

"I don't. I just want to be thorough."

"Maybe so, but there's no denying you have something against her."

My mouth twisted to the side. It was going to come out in the interview, so I might as well tell him now. "She's the one who punched me."

"Out on the sidewalk?" he said, his eyes widening. Then he burst into laughter. "You're kidding."

"Do I look like I'm kidding?"

His laughter died down, but his eyes lit up with amusement.

"So you want to charge her with murder because she accidentally gave you a shiner? I thought you were a better cop than that."

My back stiffened. "Of course I don't want to charge her for murder because she punched me. But I also don't want to make assumptions before we collect more information. She had Martin Schroeder's phone, and she was hanging around the murder scene. We need to know why."

During the ride to the station, she'd made a call. I'd figured it would be to her attorney, but instead it was to some woman named Margarete, whom she'd asked to go over and sit with her aunt. After that, she sat in silence but didn't hesitate to give me glares every time I glanced at her in the rearview mirror.

She didn't look like the kind of person who'd hang out with someone like Martin Schroeder, but like I'd told Lance, I couldn't make assumptions. Maybe she was a friend of the family. Or one of his former students. Or...*shit*.

"Do you think she's his mystery girlfriend?"

Lance burst into laughter.

"It was a serious question."

He finally settled down and motioned to the one-way mirror. "Are you shitting me? Look at her."

"I can see her perfectly fine."

He gave me a long look. "I know you're the seasoned detective and all, and you're trying to keep your options open, but come on." He tilted his head, and a lazy grin spread across his face. "I'll bet you a thousand bucks she's not his mystery fuck buddy. Hell, make it five."

I scowled. There was no way I was taking that bet, but I'd seen stranger things. "We'll keep the possibility in mind while we question her."

He shuddered. "*You* do that. I'm going to keep my mind unsullied by such disgusting images." Then he winked and laughed again. "Any word on Schroeder's phone?"

"The crime lab has it, and last I heard, Schroeder's son thought he knew the password. They'll let us know if they get it unlocked." I was eager to check out Schroeder's house, so I reached for the door. "All right. Then let's go talk to her."

"You're not going to let her stew for a bit longer?" Lance asked.

"You think she's innocent, so what's the point?" I snapped, but dammit, I suspected he was right about that. This case couldn't be *that* easy. But I had a press conference in about an hour, and so far I had bupkis to tell the chief or the public.

I stormed into the interrogation room with Lance on my heels.

Ms. Baker jumped in surprise when the door flew open, but then she fixed a glare on me as I sat down. Lance stood by the back wall.

I opened my notebook and clicked my pen, the sound echoing off the walls in the small room. "Ms. Baker, I'm Detective Langley, and this is Officer Forrester." I gestured behind me. "We need to ask you a few questions, but first I have to read you your rights and inform you that we *are* recording this interview."

She crossed her arms over her chest, shooting daggers at me, but nodded.

I quickly spouted her Miranda rights, then asked, "Can you state your name?"

"You already have my name," she spat fire blazing in her eyes as she sat up straighter. "You just called me by my name at the Piggly Wiggly."

I released a sigh and rested my hand on the table. "Ms. Baker, this will go a lot faster if you cooperate."

She lifted her chin, outrage flashing through her eyes. "This will go a lot faster if you stop asking questions you already know the answers to."

Lance snickered behind me, and I glared at him over my shoulder.

"*Ms. Baker*," I repeated, drawing her name out, "I need you to state your full name for the official record."

"Madelyn Nicole Baker."

"Address?"

She rolled her eyes but proceeded to give me her identifying and contact information.

"Do you know Martin Schroeder?" I asked, watching her carefully.

She looked confused. "The high school chemistry teacher?"

That was highly suspicious. The man's phone was in her car, yet she was pretending not to remember him?

Then her eyes widened. "Oh my God, I knew he looked familiar. I had him my sophomore year, but he used to have a handlebar mustache and more hair." Shaking her head in frustration, she looked up at Lance. "Can I just tell you what I know? I really need to get home to my aunt. She has dementia, and I'm worried this is going to give her a spell."

I turned to Lance, who gave me a questioning glance, and then I gave one sharp nod.

Lance took a seat beside me, resting both forearms on the table. "Madelyn—"

"Maddie," she said. "My friends call me Maddie."

"Maddie," he continued in a warm voice. "We'd love for you to tell us what you know."

She pushed out a breath, relaxing a little. "Well, you see, I moved back to Cockamamie a couple of months ago, after my uncle died. As I already mentioned, my aunt has dementia and he was her caretaker, so I quit my job in Nashville and moved here to take care of her."

"What did you do in Nashville?" Lance asked, acting like they were on a coffee date and he was getting to know her. Something tightened in my gut at the thought. Was I pissed that he was easily getting information out of her that I couldn't? Yeah, that had to be why I was so unsettled they'd struck up an easy rapport.

"I was a middle school librarian," she said with a wistful smile that caught me by surprise. It was the first sign of vulnerability I'd seen from her.

"Rough age," Lance said with a laugh.

"Agreed," she said, her eyes lighting up. "It helps if you realize they're in a state of limbo—no longer kids but nowhere close to being adults either. They can act like little shits, but if you get to know them well enough, they're just kids trying not to get swallowed up by the sharks swimming around them."

"Who are the sharks?" I asked, unable to stop myself.

Her voice turned hard. "The secret is that they're all sharks. Some of them just don't know it."

"Interesting theory," I muttered.

Her green eyes turned fiery, and then she gave her attention to Lance, gracing him with a half-smile. "I loved my job, but my Aunt Deidre needed me, and she and my uncle took me in after my mother died..." Her voice trailed off. "Let's just say that I needed a change, so I quit my job and moved back to Cockamamie."

"Just like that?" I asked, brow raised.

"Just like that," she shot back.

"You say your mother died?" Lance asked in a sympathetic voice. He really excelled at the good cop role. I'd have to remember that for future reference.

"She was murdered," she said, holding his gaze even though I could see she wanted to look away. "Here in Cockamamie. I'm sure you heard of it. It was big news."

"You're Andrea Baker's daughter," Lance said, sitting back in his seat. He pushed out a heavy breath. "Maddie, I'm so sorry."

My interest was piqued. What was it about her mother's case that made her presume Lance knew about it? Moreover, she was clearly right.

"It was a long time ago," she said, looking away. "But might as well mention it, as it would likely come up anyway."

Lance nodded, encouraging her to continue.

"So I came back to Cockamamie," she continued, "to take care of Aunt Deidre, but it's a small enough town that there's not a huge need for librarians, let alone in middle schools. So to make ends meet, I've been working at a shop downtown and driving for Uber Last night I picked up a passenger from the industrial park outside of town and drove him to West Walnut Street. His name on the app wasn't Martin Schroeder though. He called himself Marty the Man."

"Did you notice anything unusual about Marty the Man?" I asked.

Her brow lifted. "Other than his obnoxious name? Yeah, plenty. First of all, it seemed odd that he needed to be picked up that late at the industrial park. There's not much going on out there, and second, he wasn't ready to leave when I got there. After about five minutes, I sent him a text telling him I was about to leave without him, and then he hightailed it out of there looking like someone had set hound dogs loose on him. He asked me to hurry and kept looking out the window as though he expected someone to be following us." She looked like she was going to be sick. "He's the murder victim, isn't he?"

Lance turned to me with a questioning glance, and I nodded. "Yeah," he said quietly. "Martin Schroeder is the murder victim."

Her eyes turned glassy, and she looked away before taking a deep breath. She wasn't acting like someone who'd murdered the man in question, but for all I knew she was a good actress.

"Did anyone follow you?" I asked in a no-nonsense tone, pissed at myself. All I had to do was show her a little kindness and she'd be more than willing to answer my questions, as evidenced by her attitude with Lance. So why couldn't I get over myself and do it?

She turned her fierce gaze on me. "No."

"You said you dropped him off on West Walnut?" Lance asked.

"That's right," she said, her tone softening. "I only figured out today that it had previously been a butcher shop. But he was nervous, so he asked me to drive around the block. He was pissed that the app charged him more. In fact, he'd asked me to make another stop first, then changed his mind when he found out it would cost him more money."

"Did he say where he wanted to stop?" Lance asked.

"No. We weren't far from the industrial park, so it could have been just about anywhere. Oh!" Her eyes lit up. "There's one more thing, although I'm not sure how important it is."

Lance leaned closer and said encouragingly, "Why don't you let us be the judge of that."

The hint of a smile lit up her eyes, but it disappeared just as quickly. "He had a brown paper bag with him—like a lunch sack—and it smelled disgusting."

"A lunch sack," Lance repeated.

"Yeah. It smelled like rotten eggs. In fact, he waved his hand next to my face, and I thought I was going to throw up. It didn't seem to bother him, though." She shifted in her seat. "In any case, he got out after I drove around the block, but he didn't look thrilled to be there."

"Did you see anyone else?" Lance asked.

Her mouth twisted to the side, and she took a moment before she said, "A couple of people. There was a guy at the gas station across the street. He saw Mr. Schroeder get out of the car and walk up to the building. He was younger. Maybe late twenties to early thirties." She hesitated, then added, "And a homeless man sitting in front of the building next door. Ernie Foust. Older man with a scruffy beard. He told me not to stick around because bad things happened in that area."

"Did you talk to the homeless man from inside your car?" I asked.

She hesitated again. "I got out."

There was definitely something more to her story. "Why did you get out of the car?"

She glanced down at her hand on the table, then back up at Lance. "I saw him sitting there against the building and got out to check on him. I offered to get him food or take him to the homeless shelter, but he said he had food and didn't want to go to the shelter. I guess people have been stealing the residents' things." She drew in a breath and steeled her gaze on me. "Did you know about that? What kind of lowlife steals from homeless people? What are you doing about *that*?"

"How about I drop this murder investigation and get right on it, Maddie?" I smirked.

Her instant scowl suggested she didn't appreciate the attitude. "That's *Madelyn* to you."

She turned back to Lance.

"Is there anything else you can think of?" he asked. "Anything at all, even if you don't think it's important."

She was silent for a few moments, staring at the table before she glanced up. "He didn't go inside on his own. I don't think he could get in. He knocked on the door and waited for someone to open it."

"Can you describe what they looked like?" Lance asked.

She shook her head. "No. I didn't see who let him in. The door just opened a crack, and he slipped inside."

"You waited for him to go in before you left?" I asked flatly. "Do you usually do that with your passengers?"

She stared at me with a deadpan face. "When you drop people off at their houses, are you suggesting you don't wait, Detective?"

Her question caught me off guard. "I..."

"I take it that's a no." She wrinkled her nose in distaste. "Why am I not surprised?"

Sitting back in her chair, she said, "That's all I remember. Do you have any other questions?"

"What did you do after you dropped him off?" Lance asked.

"I went home to my aunt. We had dinner and then went to bed by ten."

"And your aunt can corroborate that?" I asked.

She suddenly looked nervous. "My aunt has dementia, so there's no telling if she'll remember. But my neighbor was there when I got home. Margarete Jennings. She lives next door."

I wrote down the name. "What about your boyfriend?"

Confusion flooded her face. "How do you know about Steve?"

"He was standing right behind you with your aunt."

After a moment of lingering confusion, her eyes widened. "Peter?" She vigorously shook her head. "He manages the Piggly Wiggly. He's not my boyfriend."

Maybe not, but he definitely wanted to be. "So who's Steve?"

Her cheeks flushed with anger. "If you *must* know, he's my ex-boyfriend from Nashville. We broke up when I moved back."

I had a dozen more questions, but just like the questions Lance had wanted to ask Sherry Schroeder, they weren't pertinent to this case and were therefore none of my business.

"We'd like to see records that you were where you said you were," I said more firmly than intended. Obviously, Lance was getting more out of her, and she was giving him information willingly too, but I couldn't seem to ditch the hostility. I would have loved to chalk it up to my concern for the case and the looming press conference I'd be holding in about an hour, but I knew it was more than that, and it pissed me off. I was a professional and took my job seriously. I didn't let suspects get under my skin. So why was I letting her get to me? Because she'd given me a black eye?

If I were smart, I'd leave the room and let him finish the interview. But I'm a stubborn ass, there was no denying it, which was sometimes a great trait in a murder investigation, sometimes a liability.

I stayed.

"Maddie," Lance said softly, "I'm sure you understand how important your eyewitness testimony is to us. You just gave us some invaluable information. But you can see how anyone outside of this room might find it suspect that you dropped him off at the scene of his murder. I'd love to clear your name right away, so if you can show us records that he was your Uber passenger, and where you picked him up and dropped him off, that would be great. One less thing we have to worry about so we can move on to finding out who *actually* killed Mr. Schroeder."

"Of course, Officer Forrester." Her expression softened, and she pulled out her phone and tapped into it. "Here's my app. You can see my history here."

Lance took her phone and studied the screen, then held it up for me to see. Sure enough, her records showed that she'd picked him up at the industrial park at 6:03 p.m. and dropped him off at 6:18 p.m.. Lance started to pull the phone back, but I reached for it and scrolled down.

The charge for the fare was $8.70, but Schroeder hadn't given her a tip. She'd neglected to mention that.

She gave us—or more specifically, Lance—permission to acquire her official records from the company, and then Lance walked her out to the waiting area and ensured she found a ride home.

I was at my desk when he came back.

"Still think she's innocent?" Crossing my arms over my chest, I leaned back in my chair.

He sat on the edge of my desk. "You think she *did it?*"

"No, but she was hiding something," I said. "Something about dropping off Schroeder. Why would she talk to the homeless guy?"

Smirking, he said, "Some people are actually nice, Noah. They want to look out for other people, with no ulterior motive."

"Yeah, not buying it."

"What do you make of the brown bag?" he asked. "A rotten egg smell. Drugs? Meth lab?"

I pressed my lips together. The abandoned butcher shop had long been associated with drugs, both dealing and parties, but Schroeder seemed too old to be part of that scene. Then again, he'd been a high school chemistry teacher. "We need to ask the narcs guy if he's heard about an older guy working with the Brawlers."

I hadn't been in town long, but it was plenty long enough to have learned about the Brawlers, a group of men who thought they ran the town. They were the source for drugs in the area, and there were rumors they'd started cooking their own stuff. Had Schroeder watched too much *Breaking Bad* and decided to become their cook?

Lance picked up his phone and made a call to Mike Dukas, Cockamamie's only narcotics detective. He took notes while he asked questions, then listened with short nods and a few uh-huhs. When he hung up, he pushed out a sigh. "Dukas claims the Brawlers have a cook now, but he's supposedly Colombian. And about forty years younger than our vic."

"How reliable is that information?" I asked.

He made a face. "Pretty freakin' reliable. So does that rule out Schroeder from working with the Brawlers?"

"Not necessarily," I said. "The brown bag with the rotten egg smell is throwing me. No sign of the bag anywhere outside the butcher shop or down the street?"

"No."

"So did the murderer kill him for the contents of the bag? Or did they kill him for another reason and take the bag as a consolation prize?"

"Good question," Lance said.

"Is Madelyn Baker mixed up in the drug world?"

Lance's eyes flew wide. "What? No. You saw her."

"You can't make assumptions based on how people present themselves." I'd made that mistake before, and it had nearly been fatal.

He glowered at me. "No kidding, but you have to admit she

doesn't fit any kind of profile. She doesn't look like a user. She's clean and well dressed. No telltale signs of drug abuse."

"Could be she's early in the game, You heard her. She's working two jobs. Got a sickly aunt. Maybe she thought she could make some fast money. Wouldn't be the first time."

He gave me a hard stare. "Why are you working so hard to make her part of this? Why can't you accept that she was just his Uber driver?"

"Because Madelyn Baker is the only person we can find who saw the man alive last night. For all we know she made it all up as a cover story for his murder."

Lance crossed his arms over his chest and studied me like I'd lost my mind.

I was beginning to wonder the same thing myself. Why *was* I working so hard to tie her to this murder? The fact that I didn't have a ready answer burrowed under my skin and made me itchy. I needed to be on top of my game for this case. I needed to stop thinking about Madelyn Baker...

Still, I couldn't quite shake the thought loose that there was more to her. Was I prejudiced by my past experience? "What's the deal with her mom?"

Lance looked surprised at the abrupt change of topic. "She was murdered years ago. I was in the eighth grade when it happened. Andrea Baker was a high school teacher, but everyone in town knew her. She was one of those people who everyone loved. Anyway, she was murdered in the high school after hours, and the killer was never caught. The town was a mess for a while after that. It's part of the reason I became a cop, if I'm honest. I wanted to catch the bad guys who did things like that."

I turned to my computer and googled Andrea Baker. A whole page of posts came up about the popular English teacher's murder and the lack of suspects.

"Unlike Schroeder," Lance said, "Andrea Baker didn't have any enemies. No one could think of a single reason why anyone would want her dead. Even her students loved her."

I checked the date of her murder and compared it to Madelyn Baker's birth date. "Madelyn was sixteen."

"Yeah, I remembered Ms. Baker's daughter was in high school, and I'd actually heard about her moving in with her aunt and uncle."

"Martin Schroeder was working at the high school at the same time as her mother?" I mused.

"Yeah, he'd been there since the beginning of time." His eyes widened. "You're not trying to connect the two, are you?"

"I'm trying to keep an open mind," I said with a frown. "Madelyn Baker comes back to town and gives a ride to the most hated teacher at Cockamamie High School, who then ends up dead? What if she decided he killed her mother and got her own revenge?"

"You're kidding me," he said in a flat tone.

I pinned a hard stare on him. "Part of being a good detective is keeping all your options open. Madelyn Baker was hiding something from us during her interview. Why did she get out of the car? And if she's not telling us that, what else isn't she telling us? Did she follow Schroeder inside and kill him?"

"There's no way she could have done it," he insisted.

"She could have if she'd drugged him. What if she gave him a drink during the ride? A bottle of water?"

"You're reaching," he said with a look of disappointment that shot to my gut.

He was right. I *was* reaching, which was totally unlike me. I wasn't normally one to strain so hard to make connections. But something told me there was more to her story. I just couldn't put my finger on it, which meant I wasn't reaching far enough. The evidence wasn't so cut and dried that we could mark her off the suspect list, even if I was willing to bet that five thousand bucks she *didn't* do it. Besides, it was clear as day she'd withheld information.

Did I think she'd killed Martin Schroeder? Doubtful, but she hadn't told us everything. Which meant I wasn't done with Madelyn Baker. Not yet.

"I guess we'll just have to wait for the tox screen. In the meantime, pull her mother's case file. While you're doing that, I need to meet with the chief and get my shit together for this press conference."

Chapter Ten

Maddie

It was nearly six by the time I got home. Officer Forrester had arranged for another officer to drop me off at home since they'd taken my car to look for more evidence, but I'd had to wait for her to finish some paperwork first. I couldn't fault Officer Forrester, though. Before leaving me, he'd told me how sorry he was about my mother...and also for how everything had gone down that afternoon. Which was a lot more than Detective Asshat had done.

Aunt Deidre and Margarete were in the living room watching TV when I walked in. Margarete's face was etched with worry.

"Why did they take you to the police station?" Margarete asked. "Is it about the murder?"

"Did they arrest you?" Aunt Deidre asked, twisting her hands in her lap.

"What? No, I did *not* get arrested," I said with a laugh as I took off my jacket, then hung it on the coat rack. I walked into the room and sat on the arm of the love seat. "They just wanted to ask me questions about my Uber passenger last night, because, yes, he was the man who was murdered." I resisted the urge to shudder. "He accidentally left his phone in my car, and they wanted to know where I'd picked him up and dropped him off. You know, the usual stuff they want to know in a murder investigation."

"With police cars and flashing lights?" Margarete asked, fear in her eyes. "Peter told me all about it."

"Well," I said, trying to stuff down my irritation at Peter, "*that* was a misunderstanding. They tracked his phone to my car somehow, and obviously they had to be cautious. For all they knew, the murderers had taken it."

"They think there's more than one killer?" Aunt Deidre asked.

"They didn't say," I said. "I was just speculating. But I'm home and everything is right as rain." I gave my aunt a pleading look. "I'm exhausted, though, so what do you say we save frying chicken for another night? I can heat up some leftovers for dinner instead."

"Oh, no need to do that," Margarete said, beaming. "Peter took care of it."

My stomach dropped. "What do you mean he took care of it?"

"He dropped Deidre off, then came back about a half hour ago to check on you. He brought a lovely ham and some fixin's from the deli case. He said for you to call him when you got home to let him know you're okay."

The last thing I wanted to do was check in with Peter McIntire, but it seemed impolite not to acknowledge him after he'd made sure my aunt got home safely and then brought dinner. Of course, he'd probably been counting on the manners that had been bred into me.

Dammit.

Then I realized I had an out.

"I don't have his number," I said with relief.

"Oh, not to worry. He left it," Margarete said, waving her hand. "He said it was in the note he left on the kitchen counter."

With great reluctance, I headed to the kitchen and found a small envelope on the counter with my name written on it in neat block letters. I'd always found good penmanship to be an attractive trait in a man. Of course, I'd also found it attractive that Steve had always lowered the toilet seat and look where that had gotten me—broke with five years of my life wasted. The envelope flap was open, so I pulled out a note card that had a caligraphy M on the front and read the message inside.

Maddie,

I called Burt, and he said you hadn't contacted him. Miss Margarete gave me your number, which I passed on to him. I made sure your aunt was settled in with your neighbor, and then I left and came back with dinner so none of you would have to think about food. If I can do anything else for you, please don't hesitate to call me. In fact, when you get home, <u>please</u> let me know that you're okay.

Warm regards,

Peter

His number was listed below his name. I sighed, realizing there was no getting around talking to him. I pulled my phone out of my pocket, then decided to take the chickenshit way out and text him.

I'm home safe and sound. They just had some questions about me giving Mr. Schroeder an Uber ride, so there was no need to call Burt. Thank you for taking Aunt Deidre home and for bringing us food.

The little bubbles appeared almost immediately, followed by his message: *Bringing you dinner was the least I could do, and don't even mention taking care of your aunt. But you should still talk to Burt.*

Attorneys charged astronomical fees, but consultations were usually free, weren't they? Still, I'd told the police what I knew. My part was done.

So why was I worried it wasn't?

I grabbed a wine glass and poured myself a drink from the boxed wine in the fridge, then called my best friend Mallory.

"Girl!" she gushed when she answered. "Isn't it dinnertime at the Cabbage Patch?"

"Cabbage Rose House," I said with a forced chuckle, "and the schedule has been thrown off a little tonight."

"It must be if you're calling me now. You've stressed the importance of Aunt Deidre's routine about a million times over." She paused, then turned serious. "Which means something's wrong. What happened? *Oh my God!* Is your aunt okay?"

"Aunt Deidre is fine, other than her accusing her caretaker of stealing her wallet, then carrying a white purse to the grocery store."

"Jeez, she must really be losing it if she wore white after Labor Day."

Mallory and I had been best friends since my freshman year at college, and she had met—and loved—my aunt and uncle during spring and summer breaks.

"And you're not fazed by her accusing her hired help of theft?" I asked.

"It's not unheard of. I've seen a *Dateline* or two."

I sighed. "Linda would never do such a thing, and Aunt Deidre's wallet was in the purse she's been using, but that's not why I'm calling."

"I don't know," she groused. "Aunt Deidre carrying white after Labor Day is pretty disturbing."

I took a sip of my wine and let out a short laugh. "So is being taken to the police station for questioning in a murder investigation."

"*What?*"

I peeked around the corner of the kitchen. The two older women were still sitting on the sofa watching TV, so I slipped across the hall into my uncle's study and shut the door. "It was a nightmare, Mallory."

Then I told her everything. Giving Marty the Man a ride. Giving Detective Asshat a black eye at the crime scene. Being confronted by the police in the Piggly Wiggly parking lot. Going to the police station.

"Sounds like this Detective Langley is a real piece of shit," she said.

I laughed, then tried to take a sip of my wine, only to realize I'd already drained the glass. "That sums him up rather nicely."

It seemed like a damn shame that such a handsome man was an asshole, but wasn't that the way of things?

Silence hung over the line for a moment. "I think I should come down there, Maddie."

"You can't take off work," I protested. "You already used too many vacation days when Uncle Albert died."

"You need me."

I did need her, but I also wasn't going to ask her to take time off without pay. One of us had to be financially solvent. "It's done," I said. "I answered all their questions, and hopefully gave them something useful to find the murderer."

"And what if the murderer is after *you*?" she asked.

I laughed. "Why would the murderer be after me? I don't know anything about them. I only gave Mr. Schroeder a ride."

"Still, this is disturbing," she said. "And murderers have killed for far less."

"You want to come down here so the murderer can get the *both* of us?"

"Of course not," she argued. "We're a team, Maddie Baker. You need me."

Tears filled my eyes. God how I loved this woman, but I loved her too much to put her in any kind of danger—from her boss, not the murderer. Because why would the murderer be after *me*?

"Fine," I conceded because I'd learned long ago that Mallory could see right through me. "I need you, but not to protect me. I

Blind Bake

need you with me. But it's only two more days until Friday, and you can come down for the weekend after you get off work. I can wait."

"I'll call in sick," she said, then fake coughed. "I feel a nasty case of the flu coming on."

"No," I said firmly. "You'll just be sitting around with Aunt Deidre and Linda, listening to them bicker while I work at the coffee shop. I'm off this weekend, so that will work out better."

"I still feel like I should come now," she said wistfully.

"How about this? If something else happens, I'll call and you can come straight away. I'll even call you at work."

"And then I can cough right in my boss's face. You know what a germaphobe she is. She'll send me home right after she douses me in Lysol."

"See? Everyone wins." Especially since Mallory hated her boss.

"I love you, Mads. I miss you terribly."

"I love and miss you too," I forced past the lump in my throat. "I couldn't have gotten through the past two months without you."

"You're a helluva lot better off without Dipshit Steve," she said. "I just hate that it took your uncle dying to get you to leave him."

"Yeah, well…" There was no denying she was right.

"You're too loyal, which is good for me," she said, "but bad for you when assholes treat you like shit. Just listen to me next time, okay? I have a sixth sense about men."

It was true. She seemed to sniff out assholes like a cadaver dog finds dead bodies. "If I ever date again, you'll be the first person the guy meets. Deal?"

"Deal."

"Okay, I need to go check on Aunt Deidre and make sure she and Margarete haven't tried to make fried chicken without me."

"You tell Aunt Deidre to save the fried chicken for when I get there," she said. "I'll skip my lunch on Friday and take off work an hour early so I can get there before seven."

Knowing Mallory was coming filled me with immense relief.

While I'd told her and Margarete and Aunt Deidre that everything was over, I'd seen the way Detective Asshat had looked at me. He wasn't done with me yet.

Chapter Eleven

Noah

The press conference was as dry as burnt toast, just the way I liked them, but it was obvious the chief had expected me to make more of a show of it. I gave them the facts—the victim's name, his previous profession, and where he'd been murdered. Then I announced that we were still following leads and wouldn't be taking questions at this time. The whole thing took about two minutes, tops, which included an intro and a conclusion from the chief.

Yeah, Chief Jefferson Porter was definitely starting to have buyer's remorse over hiring me. At the time, he'd probably thought he was lucky. Or lucky enough. The town had a twenty-two percent close rate, and I had a history of high arrest and conviction rates.

The obvious downside of hiring me?

After the incident that had nearly ended my life, I'd been on desk duty at my old job for the past month—at my own request.

"I know about your last case," the chief had said during my job interview. It could have come across as condescending, but instead it sounded as if he were commiserating. Like he'd had some bad shit happen to him too.

I'd assumed he'd known. After all, he'd talked to my supervisor, but I hadn't wanted to talk about the case, let alone think about it. I never did. So I'd set my jaw and said, "I'm trying to put all that behind me."

"The use of force was warranted," he'd said sympathetically. "You wouldn't be in that interview chair if it hadn't been. Besides, you were gravely injured in the fallout."

"That doesn't bring him back, does it?"

He'd frowned. "You gonna have trouble drawing your weapon if the situation arises?"

"No, sir," I'd replied in all truthfulness. "I would do the same thing again, but that doesn't mean I can't mourn the loss of a life."

In the end, he told me that was why he'd hired me. That I was willing to shoot if necessary, but not eager to do so. Still, I and my close rate weren't going to stop the public—and the mayor—from breathing down his neck.

But that was his problem. I couldn't be sucked into politics. I had one priority: solving the case. After the conference, Lance and I worked into the evening, combing through Schroeder's house. We didn't find anything earth-shattering, but we didn't walk away empty-handed either. Schroeder had lived frugally, his diet consisting of canned soup, frozen dinners, and large quantities of cheap beer. But everything suggested that he had lived and dined alone. One coffee cup was in the dish rack. One toothbrush in the bathroom. Hell, there'd only been one set of pillows on the full-sized bed in his bedroom.

His living room furniture was old and worn, and his TV was at least a decade old. His appliances looked like they'd been purchased in the previous century. There was a lengthy laundry list of needed home repairs, from a leaking toilet to peeling laminate edges on his kitchen counters, to two broken burners on his stove. He had a rotary dial landline—the base black, the handset yellow, and the cord that connected them in avocado green.

Blind Bake

"How long did Schroeder work at the school?" I asked Lance.

"Long enough that he taught my parents."

"Long enough to get a pension?"

"Yeah, I guess."

"How much do you think this house is worth?" I asked.

"A three-bedroom, one-bath ranch? Not much. Maybe a hundred thousand."

I studied the wood paneling in the living room. "He probably bought it decades ago. I bet it's paid off."

"Probably."

"So what'd he spend his money on?" I turned to look at him. "We need to look at his financial records first thing tomorrow." We'd found stacks of bank statements, but we'd also found a small notebook containing his logins and passwords to multiple accounts, including the information for his bank account. "You start combing through those while I attend the autopsy."

"You know one thing we didn't find?" he asked.

I lifted my brow.

"A box of condoms. Where'd the condom in his pocket come from?"

I ran a hand over my head. "Shit. You're right."

We left the house around nine, and as we walked out, my gaze landed on the empty driveway. "Where's his car?"

"He took an Uber from the industrial park to the butcher shop," Lance said thoughtfully. "Maybe he drove himself out there?"

"We'll ask the sheriff's department to go out and check for a white 2010 Chrysler 200, and if it's not there, I'll put out an APB."

With nothing left to do, I told him to go home and get some sleep so he'd be ready to go the next morning.

I let myself into my hundred-year-old house, a two-bedroom, one-bath bungalow, and turned off the security system. The house wasn't much, but it would suffice until I decided if I was staying in this backward town. Out of habit, I hesitated a moment inside the door, waiting for my English bulldog, Sergeant, to greet me, but then I remembered he wasn't here, another casualty of the case gone wrong. My heart ached under the scar on my chest.

Sarge had been my companion for eight years. He'd helped me through so much. When I'd broken up with my last serious girlfriend. Facing my father's disappointment time and again. When tough cases got to me. He'd been my best companion, and I'd gotten him killed.

I grabbed a beer from the fridge and sat in my leather recliner. I hadn't had dinner, but I wasn't hungry.

This case was bringing up all kinds of shit I'd tried to bury. There was no bringing back Sarge. No bringing back Caleb Whitinghouse. No bringing back my naïve belief that I understood the world and the people in it. That I'd made a real difference in that boy's life and he wasn't going to follow his mother into a life of crime.

I flicked on the TV and watched a late-night talk show, feeling old at the ripe age of thirty-seven because I didn't recognize the actress. But she had long dark hair and hazel eyes that reminded me of Madelyn Baker.

Why was I thinking of her?

It was hard to admit I was scared.

I didn't think she had anything to do with Schroeder's murder, but I'd genuinely believed Caleb hadn't been involved in those robberies and the murder of one of the store owners. What if I was wrong about her too? Because my reasons for believing in his innocence were personal and, if I were being truthful—something that was easier to do after I'd downed one beer and moved on to the second—my reasons for wanting her to be innocent were personal too.

When I finished the second beer I got up and turned on my alarm, double-checking the back door before I headed to bed.

I lay awake in the silence, reliving that nightmarish night.

Waking up to a noise in the house and finding Sarge. My confrontation with Caleb. The gunfire.

I'd loved that dog, and I'd loved that kid too. I'd known him for five years, ever since I became his Big Brother. I remembered what he was like then, the skinny, belligerent thirteen-year-old with sandy blond hair and freckles on his nose. His mother had been recently incarcerated, and he'd been scared, new to the foster care system. It had taken me three months to worm my way past his defenses and become his friend. I'd stayed with him through three more foster homes. Helped him with homework. Celebrated tests and hard-won As. When he was seventeen, I'd hung in there through his confusion and anger when his mother was released from prison and went right back to the drugs that had gotten her incarcerated in the first place. I'd helped him find an apartment, taught him how to pay his bills online, and cheered him on when he found a decent job with a future.

And I'd watched it all blow up in my face.

Goddamn drugs were the cause of so many problems in the world, and they'd been Caleb's downfall, just like they'd been for his mother.

So no. I refused to believe that Madelyn Baker couldn't be a drug addict based on appearances. I made that mistake with Caleb and it has cost me. If *he* could fool me, anyone could. Even a gorgeous brunette who took care of her sickly aunt and looked like the girl next door.

But if I couldn't trust my gut, then what did that mean for my future as a cop? What if I'd lost the instinct that made me a good detective?

There was no denying my instincts has led me astray with Caleb, and in the end, he'd accused me of loving my dog more than him. And then I'd killed him.

Caleb had killed Sarge.

What if he'd killed part of me too?

Chapter Twelve

Noah

The next morning, I showed up at the coroner's office a few minutes before eight with two steaming cups of coffee. I'd already been working for a couple hours, including following up on the search warrant we'd requested for the address where Madelyn Baker had picked up Schroeder. I only hoped the judge wasn't in a bowling league or a canasta tournament that would delay our search.

It had been about twenty-nine hours since the body was found, and we'd made little progress on the case, much to the chief's consternation.

The sheriff's deputy hadn't found Schroeder's car the night before, and the APB hadn't turned it up so far either.

The autopsy didn't reveal much new information. The medical examiner was unable to find any ligature marks we might have missed. The tox screen wasn't back yet, though, so we had no way of knowing whether he'd been drugged. Other than the deep slash in his neck, the most remarkable thing about him was his clogged arteries. According to Dr. Mueller, he would have likely died from a massive coronary within the next few years if he hadn't been murdered first.

I thanked Dr. Mueller for his time, then headed to the station and found Lance at the desk I'd had set up for him on the other side of mine.

"Autopsy show anything?" he asked when I slid into my seat.

"Nothing we didn't already know. How's the financial search going?"

He grinned. "Better than what you discovered."

"Oh yeah?" I asked, perking up. "What you got?"

"He received a monthly pension and social security that totaled about forty-five hundred dollars a month. But his checking account only had five hundred and sixteen dollars and his savings had two hundred."

I sat back in my chair and studied him. "We both saw how he lived. The newest electronics in his house were at least a decade old. What was he spending his money on?"

"Well, you were right about the house being paid off. His son confirmed it, and there's no evidence of a second mortgage or car payment. No credit card debt either."

"Did he make any large withdrawals?" I asked. "Make out any large checks?"

"No, but his pension and social security aren't direct deposits. Up until about six months ago, he was depositing two checks every month, then he made a large cash withdrawal of about forty thousand and cleaned most of it out. He didn't deposit any checks after that, just made small cash deposits. Five hundred here. Two hundred there. Stopped using his debit or credit cards to pay for incidentals like groceries and Walmart around then too. Only paid things like utilities and taxes and insurance."

"So he was paying cash for those things."

"Looks like it."

I frowned. "Where was he cashing his checks and why did he stop depositing them?"

Lance shrugged. "Maybe he's one of those conspiracy theorists who thinks lizards are running the banks or some such nonsense."

"Yeah, maybe, but we still don't know where the money went."

"While you were at the coroner's," Lance said, "a couple of uniformed officers canvassed the neighborhood to see if they'd seen anything suspicious going on at his house. They all said Schroeder kept the Chrysler in his garage. No one had seen him leaving the house that day. In fact, the neighbors nearest him couldn't remember the last time they'd seen him, but he turned his house and front porch lights on every night, and they hadn't been on the night of his murder."

"Have they found the homeless guy yet? Ernie Foust?"

"They've checked the homeless shelter and the usual spots where the homeless hang out, but found nothing. The homeless they've spoken to claim they haven't seen him since Monday.

"Is he lying low or is he in danger?" I said.

"To be fair, even if they had seen him, they might not be forthcoming about it. Some of the officers aren't exactly cordial to them."

"You mean they treat them like trash," I seethed, my anger igniting. I'd befriended plenty of homeless people when I was a beat cop, making sure they had food and a place to stay when it was exceptionally hot or cold. Many of them had remembered, and the connections I'd established had proven helpful on multiple cases after I made detective.

Despite what Madelyn Baker obviously thought of me, I hadn't heard that people were being robbed at the Methodist's homeless shelter. If I had, I would've followed up on it. In fact, as soon as I caught a break in this case, I planned to check it out.

Lance pushed out a sigh. "We never used to have any homeless, but the past few years we've gotten more than our fair share. Some of Cockamamie's residents see them as a blight on the town and the cops take their lead."

It was more of a blight that the town refused to take care of their own, but I kept that to myself.

"Any luck unlocking Schroeder's cell phone?" I asked.

"Last I heard about a half hour ago, no. Darren thought he knew the passcode, but it didn't work. They're currently locked out, waiting for the phone to let them try again."

"Shit." I had a feeling that phone would answer a lot of our questions. I also had a feeling we'd never get into it.

We spent the next couple of hours poring over Schroeder's records. A credit search turned up something we hadn't discovered in the documents from his home. Schroeder had recently applied for a twenty-thousand-dollar second mortgage at another bank that was still in the approval process.

"Maybe he was being blackmailed," I said. It had been a throwaway suggestion, but the more I thought about it, the more it seemed to fit. I sat up in my chair.

"Blackmail?" Lance said. "Who would be blackmailing him?"

"The question of the year," I said. I filled out a search warrant for the second mortgage, but that would likely take a few days to go through, though, and we couldn't sit around and wait.

"That slip of paper with the numbers," I said. "What could they be?"

"Not a phone number," Lance said. "Not enough numbers."

"A locker?" I said. "A parking spot? A storage unit?"

"Apartment number?" Lance suggested.

"What about his keys?" I said. "We need to get those and see what they go to."

"I like the storage unit idea."

"You might be on to something. If I remember right, there was a small key that looked like it went to a padlock. Did you see any padlocks at his house?"

"No."

"Let's call around to storage facilities and see if any of them rented a unit to Schroeder."

"If he did, he was paying in cash." He made a face. "What if he was using a different name too, like Marty the Man?"

I frowned. He'd used an alias, albeit a bad one, for his Uber account. There was a possibility he'd used one for a storage unit as well. "So we'll ask for his name and the alias and go from there."

We'd just started calling storage facilities when my inbox dinged with an email.

"Son of a bitch," I grunted when I read it. "You've got to be shitting me."

Lance sat up in his seat. "What?"

"The fucking judge denied the search warrant for the industrial park. He cited insufficient reasons." Frustrated, I pushed back in my chair. "The fact that it was the last known location of a murder victim before he was transported to the scene of his murder seems plenty sufficient to me." I couldn't help wondering if judicial failings were partially responsible for the Cockamamie force's abysmal close rate.

"There's another way to see it," Lance said.

"You mean track down the owner and ask to look?" I shook my head. "What we find might not be admissible."

"But it might be worth checking anyway to see if it points us in the right direction. Especially since the judge won't issue a warrant." A lazy grin stretched across his face. "And I just so happen to know the owner. He's my friend's father. How about I contact my buddy and get permission?"

I scowled for a few seconds, giving it consideration. "It's better than nothing. Give him a call."

Lance called his friend, who promised to have his father call back right away.

I tapped my pen on the desk. "Have you heard anything suspicious going on at the industrial park?"

Blind Bake

"No, but it makes sense that the drug trafficking would move out there since a good portion of the Bottoms is about to be torn down."

I nodded. I'd considered the same thing, but it was a long drive out there and most people preferred their drug deals to be convenient. "All the more reason to check it out. Any chance your friend's father knows this is going on out there?"

"No way. You can't get any more straight and narrow than Bill Newman."

"Then what was Schroeder doing out there? A legit business deal? If so, hopefully your friend's father will be able to fill in some of the gaps, and we can use his interview, warrant or not." I was starting to feel better about the whole thing, but the denial of the warrant was eating at me. It made no sense.

"We still don't know how Schroeder got out there either," Lance asked. "His Uber account has the same email and password as his bank, and his account only shows one ride—the one leaving with Maddie Baker. Nor does the taxi company have a record of anyone being dropped off there at any point yesterday."

"Right. So where's his car?" That part was bugging me. "It's possible he parked it inside one of the buildings, but why would he leave it out there?"

This whole case had too many unknowns to suit me.

I thought for a second, then said, "Let's have Neil Erickson check with the mechanic shops. He can see if they have a white Chrysler 200. Maybe it's in the shop."

"Good thinking," Lance said.

I picked up my phone and called the rookie to give him his orders. Seconds before I hung up, Lance's phone rang.

"Forrester," he answered as I hung up with Neil. After a brief conversation, he hung up, then flashed me a thumbs-up. "Newman says he can meet us there in fifteen minutes."

I hopped out of my chair. "Then let's go."

* * *

We pulled up in front of a long metal building with multiple units. It was one of multiple buildings, most of which looked deserted. A middle-aged man in jeans and a brown work jacket was waiting for us by a sliding metal door at the far right end. He had the air of a guy who didn't take shit from anyone.

I liked him already.

He had a large set of keys in one hand and his other hand stuffed in his jeans pocket. "I've gotta get back to my cow," he said as he walked toward us, staring at us from under the brim of his worn ball cap. "She's turned sickly, and my wife Diane ain't crazy about keeping an eye on her. I've only got twenty minutes to spare."

"Sorry about your cow," I said, darting a look to Lance. "Is this unit rented to anyone?"

"Nope. It's currently vacant."

Newman unlocked the door and opened it, motioning for Lance and me to go in.

We walked across the threshold into a dark space illuminated only by the light streaming through the door from the outside. It looked to be about thirty feet deep and forty feet wide. The walls were metal, the floor was concrete, and it looked completely empty.

"How long's the place been empty?" I asked.

"About six months. A candle company leased it for a couple of years. They moved on to Chattanooga."

"Do you own the whole complex?"

"Nope," he said. "Just this building. The other three are owned by Buster Higgans."

"How many units are in your building?"

"Six. Only three of them occupied. Business is dryin' up in Cockamamie."

I nodded, not surprised. I knew several businesses had closed up shop over the last couple of years. "Any cameras that you know of?"

He shook his head. "Nope. I keep tellin' them to get some, but some are set in their ways."

"How often do you check the empty units?"

"Honestly, not often at all. Not much goes on out here."

"So if someone was runnin' an operation out here, you might not know," I said.

"Ain't nobody runnin' nothin' out here," Newman said.

I flipped a switch, but the lights didn't turn on. "Is the electricity working?"

"Nope. The renters pay for that."

I pulled my phone out of my pocket and turned on the flashlight, panning the light around me. Taking my cue, Lance pulled a flashlight from his toolbelt and turned it on. Its beam was a hell of a lot brighter than mine, and it didn't take us long to realize the place really was empty. Freakishly so.

"Do your tenants clean when they leave?" I asked as Lance and I finished our sweep.

"Yeah. But it's rarely this spotless," Newman admitted.

"Did your previous tenants leave it this clean?" Lance asked.

"Nope. There was some loose trash scattered around."

Lance swung his gaze in my direction, and I knew we were both thinking the same thing. Someone had been using this place, and they'd cleaned up the evidence. Just like at the butcher shop.

Newman's phone rang, and he answered it with a grunt. His conversation was mostly one-sided before he said, "Fine. I'll be right there." Then he hung up. "Gotta go. The cow's starting to lick Diane's purse."

"What?" On second thought, I held up a hand. "Never mind."

"Mind if we stay for a while, Mr. Newman?" Lance asked. "If you leave the key like Detective Langley suggested, I'll return it to you when we're done."

"Why?" he asked, looking skeptical. "There's nothing here."

"Exactly," Lance said. "But we still want to look around."

Newman pushed out a heavy sigh. "Suit yourselves. All I ask is that you don't make a mess with fingerprint dust or whatever else you use for your investigations."

Lance tried to smother a grin. "We promise not to make a mess, and if by chance we do, we'll be sure to clean it up."

Newman removed the key from his heavy ring and handed it to Lance while I went out to my car to grab a flashlight. I lifted my hand to wave goodbye as Newman got into his beat-up pickup truck and drove off.

Lance stood in the open door, his mouth twisted to the side. "So Maddie Baker's story pans out."

I grunted, getting irritated. The mere mention of her name seemed to do that. "Let's go search the unit more thoroughly and see if we can find anything."

We walked back inside, scouring the floor with our flashlight beams, but whoever had cleaned up had been thorough. It was starting to seem like the whole thing would be a bust, and then Lance stopped short.

"I think I found something."

I walked over, not seeing what he'd found until I was next to him. In the beam of his flashlight was a wooden stir stick. Lance removed a plastic bag from his pocket and picked it up by one end.

"There's a name embedded in the stick." He held it up so we could both read it. "Déjà Brew. It's a coffee shop on Main downtown. Have you been there yet? They've got a chai latte that beats anything I've had in Atlanta."

I gave him a dry look. "Coffee's coffee."

He laughed. "You know you sound like you're sixty years old, right?"

"I'm thirty-seven, and I like my coffee black."

"That doesn't surprise me at all." He lifted the stick closer to his face. "Smells like coffee."

"It's a coffee stir stick. What'd you expect it to smell like?"

"Rotten eggs."

I lifted a brow.

"Maddie Baker said he had a paper bag that smelled like rotten eggs. He was a high school chemistry teacher. What if he really *was* cooking for the Brawlers despite Dukas's intel?"

I considered it for a moment. "I've heard of stranger things. You think they were cooking *here*?"

"I don't know," he said with a shrug. "You heard Newman. Someone cleaned this place up better than it had been after the tenants moved out. And Maddie Baker picked up Schroeder from here." He rubbed the back of his neck. "We shouldn't rule it out."

"Agreed. The question is why is that stir stick here? Was Schroeder drinking a coffee when he showed up and dropped the stick? Was it someone else? Does any of this connect back to Déjà Brew? I think we need to go by and check it out."

"Drop me off at the station, and I'll take Newman's keys out to him. Then I'll get back to the storage facility search. *You* can drop by Déjà Brew." Lance grinned. "Maybe get an Americano while you're there."

"And pay five dollars for a cup of coffee on this salary?" I grumped. "No, thank you."

He laughed. "Like I said. Grumpy old man."

Chapter Thirteen

Maddie

The police still had my car, so Margarete loaned me her husband's old Volvo to drive to work the next day, an old sedan that was twice as big as my car. I'd hoped to keep my trip to the police station a secret, but I'd barely taken my position behind the bakery case at Déjà Brew when Chrissy turned to me and blurted out, "Oh my God, did they really arrest you for Schroeder the Groper's murder?"

My mouth dropped open, as did the mouths of several people waiting to be served their morning coffees and breakfast sandwiches.

So much for keeping it on the down-low.

Time to go into damage control mode.

Lifting my chin, I said, "Arrested? Of course not! I was taken to the station as a witness."

"You saw the murder?" asked a customer in line, a middle-aged man with a questionable mustache.

"No," I said, squaring my shoulders, "but I gave Mr. Schroeder an Uber ride to the place where he was murdered."

A roar went through the line as everyone began asking questions at once, some shouting to make sure they were heard.

I cast a quick apologetic look over my shoulder at Petra, who was cooking the aforementioned breakfast sandwiches in the kitchen, fully visible through the pass-through window. She didn't look pissed, thankfully, although I'd never actually seen her look pissed. Nor did she look disappointed, which I would have found more disturbing. Her face was currently devoid of expression, as though she was taking all of this in and trying to decide how to feel about it.

I held up my hands and shouted, "Everyone! Everyone! I'll answer your questions, but let's be orderly about it. You can ask me something when you reach the counter. I'll only answer each particular question once, though, which means y'all need to be quiet so you can hear both the question and the answer. That way, everyone still gets their coffee in a timely manner *and* you get the answers you so desperately want."

Not that I could fault them for being curious. Detective Asshat had held a press conference in time for the evening news, but he'd shared nothing beyond Martin Schroeder's name and the fact that he'd been murdered. The people were hungry for answers, and I'd just declared myself a witness. I was fair game.

People began shushing each other so loudly the entire space reverberated with it, until Petra quieted them by leaning through the opening and belting out a wolf whistle.

The crowd hushed. Then Petra said in a calm, even voice, "This will all go a lot quicker if y'all just listen to Maddie."

Everyone settled down and all eyes turned on me, which was considerably more attention than I was used to. Sure, I'd addressed classes full of middle schoolers, but there's something different about addressing kids versus adults. Middle schoolers can be vicious—but adults are a whole lot more intimidating.

I soon realized that answering questions one-on-one was never going to work, so I decided to take a more direct approach. I took a deep breath, then said in my teacher voice, "For those of you who don't know, I'm an Uber driver on the days I don't work here at Déjà Brew. On Monday evening, I picked up a passenger and dropped him off on West Walnut Street. Then I went home to my Aunt Deidre. I didn't even know the man I'd dropped off was Martin Schroeder. I sure didn't recognize him from when I was in high school. I didn't find out it was him until yesterday afternoon when the police asked me to answer some questions about dropping him off."

"So why did they show up with lights and sirens at the Publix grocery on 23rd Street?" a woman called out.

"First of all, it wasn't a Publix, it was the Piggly Wiggly on Samson Drive. And the lights and sirens?" I waved my hand in dismissal. "It was some renegade cop who'd heard the detective on the police radio and decided to offer his assistance." Sure, that last part was made up, but who was going to contradict me?

"I heard you were taken in handcuffs in the back of a police car," shouted another woman.

I gave her a tolerant smile. "I was taken to the police station by a kind detective and his partner after they collected my car as evidence for their investigation. They are obviously trying to be very thorough and are likely looking to see if Mr. Schroeder left any clues in my car about what he was doing at that location."

"Because they were looking for evidence that you'd killed him?" another woman called out from the back in a snippy voice.

"Do I look like a murderer to you?" I asked in exasperation.

No one said a word for several seconds. Then Chrissy patted my arm. "I don't think you look like a murderer. A blackmailer, maybe, but definitely not a murderer."

I gaped at her.

"All right," Petra shouted. "She told you her story, now get the line moving."

Chrissy and I turned to her in shock. I'd never heard her raise her voice before, and from the look on Chrissy's face, she hadn't either.

We started taking orders again, Chrissy and I working together to get people out in record time.

Our typical morning crowd usually tapered off between nine thirty and ten, but today the crowd just seemed to keep growing. It was obviously great for Petra's bottom line, and the tip jar was fuller than usual, but it was obvious many of our customers, especially the ones who arrived in late morning, were there to see me, the possible Murderess of Cockamamie. Of course, they hadn't heard Petra's speech about only telling my story once, nor had they been there to hear the story itself, and they peppered me with a million questions. A guy had just fired off half a dozen, which I'd ignored, before Chrissy, his pastry in hand, asked, "How did you hear about Maddie, anyway? Did one of your coworkers tell you?"

"What?" he asked, then chuckled. "No. Several people posted about it on TikTok. I guess it's on the town's community group on Facebook too." He made a face. "For the old people."

Chrissy, who was in her early twenties like he appeared to be, shrugged. I took that to mean, *It's all old people have since they don't know how to use TikTok.* Which I took great offense to since *I* hadn't figured out how to use TikTok, and it hadn't seemed appropriate to ask the middle schoolers for a demonstration last year. Then again, I wasn't on Facebook much either.

She started to hand him his pastry, but I grabbed the edge of the bag and held on tight. "What do you mean it's all over TikTok?"

His eyes widened in surprise, possibly because I was coming across as potential murderer, but then he took a deep breath and gave me a pitying look. "TikTok is a social media site where people post videos—"

"I know what TikTok is!" I said in exasperation, but then the implications hit me—

There were videos about me on TikTok. And likely Facebook.

And possibly Instagram and Twitter. Post after post making people think I was a murder suspect.

"Show me."

His forehead furrowed. "What?"

"Show me the videos."

He set the coffee I'd already handed him on the counter and started tapping on his phone. "I can't show you *all* of them. I have an appointment in a half hour."

"How many are there?" I asked, starting to feel light-headed.

"I don't know," he said dismissively. "A half dozen? I saw the first one because I follow @TinatheTerrible and she posted your speech and used the hashtag *cockamurder*. Then a few others popped up. But hers has the most views." He angled his phone so Chrissy and I could see the screen, and sure enough, there I was telling my story.

"It's not so bad," Petra said from behind my shoulder. She'd emerged from the back without me noticing. "You're just speaking your truth."

Partial truth. What would Detective Asshat think when he saw it? Would it make me seem more suspicious?

"Girl," Chrissy said in awe. "You're going viral! It already has ten thousand views!"

I wasn't sure that was viral, but considering the town of Cockamamie only had about twenty thousand citizens…

"Why are you so upset?" Petra asked, studying my face.

"I don't know," I said, barely above a whisper. "I just have a really bad feeling about all of this."

Pressing her lips together, she eyed me with a sage look. "Why don't you take your break. It's been a crazy morning."

I told myself I was being ridiculous. I *had* told the truth…I'd just left certain parts out. It actually seemed likely Detective Asshat would appreciate that I hadn't blabbed about the cell phone. I mean, I'd learned from true crime podcasts that they liked to hold information back. The detective's carefully worded press conference had proven that. He hadn't even released how Mr. Schroeder had been murdered.

So why wasn't I convinced?

Maybe it was the lingering look the detective had given me as I left the interrogation room yesterday. Like he wasn't done with me yet.

I spent ten minutes in the back, downing a glass of water and using the calm app I'd installed on my phone a couple of years ago to help me chill out after a particularly rowdy class visited the library or my principal showed up with a list of books some parent wanted banned. It was a reminder I'd dealt with harder stuff than this and that things could always be worse.

I could be dead, just like Mr. Schroeder.

That thought sent shudders rippling through me. It was hard to believe he was actually dead. How had he been murdered, and why? And what about Ernie? Why hadn't I remembered to make sure *he* was okay?

I went through another cycle of deep breathing and told myself I'd look for Ernie as soon as I got off work. I'd promised to take Aunt Deidre to the Cockamamie Women's Club meeting tonight, but I should have plenty of time to look before I needed to relieve Linda.

The crowd was already growing again as lunch approached, and the next hour flew by. People were still asking questions, but Chrissy and I had reverted to pointing to a sign that Petra had attached to the back of the cash register while I was on break.

Maddie is not taking questions about the murder at this time.

Seeing it had made me smile. Petra was so nonantagonistic that it had likely killed her to write such a thing, knowing she'd make some of her customers unhappy. She'd done it for me anyway. I thanked God I'd found my way into this coffee shop the week after moving back to town. Even though I'd cried through our interview and had a limited schedule and zero barista experience, Petra had taken a chance on me, and I wasn't sure I could ever repay her for that. It only reaffirmed that she was the best boss I'd ever had, even beating out Principal Rowan, which was saying something.

By one thirty, the crowd had cleared out, so Chrissy went to the back to take her lunch break. Petra was cleaning up the kitchen, which meant I was alone behind the counter when the door opened and our next customer walked in.

I was in the process of making a chai latte for a regular who thankfully didn't seem the least bit interested in the murder nonsense, as Petra had taken to calling it, when I looked up to greet the newcomer. My forming smile froze.

Detective Asshat. Thankfully he wasn't sporting a black eye. Only a red mark on his cheekbone.

I handed the latte to the customer, who was staring at me with a look of caution, and I realized a weird half-smile was still frozen on my face. Taking a deep breath, I turned it into a dazzling smile. "Thank you, Amber. You have a nice day."

"Yeah," she said hesitantly. "You too, Maddie."

Which left me alone with the Cockamamie detective standing in front of my bakery case.

I reached over and tried to snatch the sign from the register, but Petra must have used extra-strength packing tape, because it was so firmly attached that only part of it tore away.

Smooth, Maddie. Way to not call attention to the sign.

The detective watched me with a deadpan expression. He was here about those damn videos, wasn't he? Well, I sure wasn't bringing them up. I was going to pretend like I didn't know about it.

But what if he *knew* I knew and he was trying to trap me in a lie? Shit.

I took a breath. This was okay. It was fine. First rule of interrogation was never to volunteer anything. I'd be an idiot to tell him about the videos. Let him bring them up.

I gave him my most welcoming smile. "Good afternoon, Detective A—" I stopped short of saying Asshat. "Detective," I repeated. My smile stretched wider, and I was pretty sure I was doing an excellent rendition of the Joker. I toned it down a couple of notches. "What can I get for you?"

"A medium black coffee."

"That seems about right," I said dryly.

"What does that mean?" he asked with a scowl.

"You seem like the black coffee type."

He arched an eyebrow. "Meaning?"

"I don't know," I said, reaching for a medium cup. "You just seem no-nonsense. No frills." Uptight, although thank God I didn't say that one out loud. It really was a shame. He was far too good-looking to have a stick shoved so high up his ass.

He held my gaze as if we were in a staring contest. "All right then, I'll take an Americano."

I couldn't stop my short laugh. "I suppose it's a good first step if you're trying to develop your palate past gas station coffee."

"I happen to like gas station coffee," he said. Then he grimaced ever so slightly, as if realizing he'd just admitted to liking a drink equivalent to motor oil.

"To each their own, I say." I started to grind the coffee beans into the portafilter.

"You grind the beans individually for every drink?" he asked.

"That's right," I said, watching the portafilter fill with ground beans.

"Wouldn't it be faster if you ground them up in a batch beforehand?"

"I'm sure it would, but there's nothing better than freshly ground coffee." I looked up at him and tilted my head. "Unless your taste buds are dead. Are yours dead, Detective?" I let my voice rise on the end.

He laughed. "I wouldn't be surprised after all the shit I usually eat."

That caught me by surprise, along with the fact that he almost looked like a human being rather than the police robot he'd been on the other occasions I'd dealt with him. Maybe there was a heart in there somewhere after all.

His blue-gray eyes were practically dancing, and I realized Detective Asshat was *really* good-looking. He lacked the arrogance a lot of really good-looking men seemed to carry like an Am Ex platinum card stuffed in their back pocket, but he had to *know* he was handsome. I mean, he was clean-shaven, which meant he saw his reflection in the mirror at least once a day. And yet, he didn't strut around expecting the world to bend to his will because of his looks.

No, he used his badge instead. But that wasn't fair either. I supposed he was just doing his job. But then so had the men who'd investigated my mother's death. One in particular had used his badge to tear up our house and treat me like the loss of my mother meant nothing. Like I was an inconvenience to be dealt with. Like *I* was the criminal for demanding answers about her death.

It occurred to me that although I knew his partner's name, the only name I had for him was Detective Asshat. Then again, Lance Forrester had been two years behind me in school. He'd been a starter on the football team his sophomore year, which I'd remembered because everyone had made a big deal about it. The detective's name? They must have mentioned it in the press conference and during my interview, but I'd been too keyed up to remember.

Why didn't he just ask his questions about the videos and leave?

If he wanted to play games, I could play games too.

The portafilter was full, so I set it on the counter and tapped it down, flashing him a saucy grin. "Well, then. Let's see if we can wake up your taste buds, Detective."

Blind Bake

A hint of a smile tugged on the corners of his lips, catching me off guard. Damn, he really *was* good-looking.

Giving myself a mental shake, I inserted the portafilter into the espresso machine, put the disposable cup underneath, then pressed a button for a double shot. "Are you new around here, Detective? I don't remember you from high school."

He stuffed his hands into his pockets. "Not as new as you."

"I'm not technically new. I was born and raised here, then left for college. Where are *you* from?"

His eyes darkened, and he gave me a look that suggested he thought I was up to something. But he answered me anyway. "Memphis."

"Born and raised there?"

"Yep."

"What brought you to Cockamamie?"

"Work."

So much for a conversation.

Detective Asshat watched me with his eagle eyes that looked bluer today and less stormy. The silence was becoming uncomfortable.

I pressed the double shot button again and let the cup fill with hot water, then met his gaze. "Since you wanted a black coffee, I take it you don't need room for milk."

"No."

The cup finished filling, and I put a lid on it before handing it over to him. "Here you go, Detective."

He pulled out his wallet. "How much?" His gaze lifted to the menu board behind me, and his mouth gaped. *"Four dollars?"*

"It's on the house."

He frowned, then reached into his back pocket for his wallet. "I'd rather pay."

"Oh, it's not just you," I said. "We routinely give our fine Cockamamie officers free coffee."

He pulled several dollar bills from his wallet. "No. I insist."

What was his deal? "You should at least taste it first," I said. "See if it's worth four bucks."

He hesitated, then picked up the cup and started to take a sip.

"Oh, wait! That's—"

He made a face as he jerked the cup away from his mouth.

"—hot."

He plunked the cup down on the counter, anger flashing in his eyes. "Isn't coffee supposed to be cooler after the whole McDonald's coffee fiasco?"

Making a sympathetic face, I grabbed a small cup and scooped it half-full of ice, then handed it to him. "Not when you're making espresso. The temperature has to be between 195 and 205 Fahrenheit," I said, spouting verbatim what I'd been taught.

"So you purposedly tried to burn me?" he asked indignantly.

I stared at him in disbelief. "Are you serious?"

He took several breaths before he finally said, "I need to speak to your manager."

"What? So you can get me in trouble? Petra's the one who taught me how to make espresso."

"So Petra's the manager?" he asked.

"I'm Petra," my boss said from behind me, walking out of the back. "Is there a problem?"

He shot me a dark look, then flashed his badge at her. "I'm Detective Noah Langley with the Cockamamie Police Department."

"What?" I asked in exasperation. "First you haul me in and treat me like a criminal after I accidentally hit you yesterday, and now you're going to arrest me for assault for giving you hot coffee? Do you *always* threaten to arrest people who accidentally injure you?"

"You want to arrest her?" Petra asked, aghast, coming to stand beside me and taking a *you have to get through me first* stance.

"Whoa!" said Detective Asshat, holding up his hands. "No one said anything about arresting anyone. I merely need to ask you a question." He looked my way before returning his gaze to her. "In private."

Petra propped her hands on her hips and glanced from me to the detective, narrowing her eyes. "Come on back to my office." As she said it, she gestured for him to come around the counter. Chrissy was standing in the doorway to the back rooms, and she stepped aside to let them pass, then hurried over to me.

"What is *that* all about?"

I watched as the door to Petra's office closed behind them. "I'm not exactly sure, but that was the police detective who took me downtown yesterday."

"So why is he here now?" Chrissy asked, regarding the closed door.

"I thought he was here about the videos, but then he ordered a coffee and proceeded to burn himself. He was pissed and asked to speak to the manager, and now they're in the back."

"Huh," she said. "Weird."

"No kidding."

His coffee still sat on the counter, and Chrissy pointed to it. "Is that it?"

"Yeah, it's his Americano," I said distractedly. What was going on in that office?

Chrissy snorted. "What idiot drinks an Americano straightaway?"

"Well, in his defense—"

The office door opened, and Detective Asshat held out his hand to Petra. "Thank you for your help, Ms. Villanova." He fished a business card out of his wallet and handed it to her. "If you happen to think of anything else that's helpful, be sure to give me a call at that number."

She took it, holding it between her index finger and thumb as though it was covered in dog shit. "Yeah. You bet."

Detective Asshat headed toward us with a blank expression.

"Those videos weren't her fault, you know," Chrissy said as he passed her.

He stopped short, then turned back to face her. "What videos?"

The blood drained from my face. Did he really not know about the videos? The way he was studying her now suggested this was new information for him.

So why was he here?

I told myself to worry about that later, because I had another fire to watch as it burned down my life.

"You know," she said like he was an idiot. "The TikTok videos."

He shook his head. "What TikTok videos?"

Chrissy pulled out her phone and tapped on the screen, opening the app. "All you have to do is pull up the hashtag *cockamurder*." She typed in the hashtag, and a video started playing. Only it wasn't my speech from this morning. It was of a guy sitting in his pickup truck, his ball cap turned backward on his head.

"Okay, you know that murder?" he said, his face animated as he talked with his hands. "The guy who was butchered in the abandoned butcher shop? Well, the woman on that video, you know, the one who works at Déjà Brew? She dropped that guy off at the butcher shop!"

"She *said* she was there, you moron," a woman droned off screen.

"I know, Savannah!" he snapped. "There's more to it, though. I saw her drop him off!" His eyes bugged out, and then he settled down. "Anyway, she was there on the sidewalk, shouting at that poor old man standing near the front entrance of the butcher shop, telling him he was gonna pay with his life!"

"I did *not* say that!" I protested.

Detective Asshat looked me over none too kindly before returning his gaze to the screen.

"I think she did it, dude. That woman's the Butcheress of Cockamamie."

"Butcheress of Cockamamie?" Chrissy scoffed. "Surely they can come up with something better than that."

Detective Asshat stared at her phone as it started to play a video of me giving my speech that morning. "Hashtag *cockamurder*, you say?"

Chrissy froze, then glanced between us. "Uh…pretend like I never said anything."

"Yeah," said a guy who'd approached the counter without me noticing. "Cockamurder. There's duets and everything."

The detective caught my gaze. "Don't be leaving town, Ms. Baker."

With that, he grabbed his cup of coffee, tossed a five-dollar bill on the counter, and walked out.

Chapter Fourteen

Maddie

Petra, Chrissy, and I all stood frozen for several seconds while panic swept through me.

"What in the hell were you thinking?" Petra asked Chrissy, swatting her arm.

"What? I thought he knew about it already! Maddie said he was asking in the office asking you about the videos."

"He was asking me about a stupid stir stick," she said, then began to chew on her bottom lip.

"A stir stick?" I asked. "Why?"

"Dunno. He had one in an evidence bag and asked me if it came from here. I said it did. It was stamped with our name clear as day."

"Can't the damn fool read?" Chrissy asked.

Petra ignored her. "Then he asked how long we've been handing out sticks like that, and I told him it was a recent thing."

A few weeks, to be exact. She'd switched out the plastic stir sticks for biodegradable wooden ones, and the company had stamped our name on them as part of an introductory deal.

She gave me an apologetic look. "He asked a few questions

about you, Maddie. Like how long you've worked here and whether you're a dependable employee."

"What did you tell him?" Chrissy asked.

"I told him the damn truth," she snapped. Then her eyes flew wide, and she covered her mouth with her hand. "Chrissy. I'm sorry!"

Chrissy took a deep breath and held out her hands as though to steady herself. "It's okay. We've all had a bit of a shock today. It's not every day you meet the Butcheress of Cockamamie." Her lips twitched, and she burst out laughing.

"Not funny," Petra grumped.

"You know what's not funny?" said the guy at the counter. "Waiting two minutes and three seconds for someone to take my order."

Petra nodded toward the register, and Chrissy walked over to take his order. "Maddie. Let's chat in my office for a moment."

Great. Was I about to be fired? I couldn't say I'd blame her.

I followed Petra, my heart hammering in my chest. Despite the fact that I barely made above minimum wage, I actually liked this job. It sure beat working at that convenience store on West Walnut Street.

"Shut the door and take a seat," Petra said as she sat in her office chair.

Oh lordy, what was I going to do? Given my newfound notoriety, I'd be lucky to find another job, let alone one that I liked.

I sat in the chair, with my hands clasped in my lap, preparing for the worst. Petra would hate firing me, so maybe I should help her out. "Look, Petra, I realize how difficult this is for you. You don't have to fire me. If you need me to leave, you can consider this my notice."

"Who said anything about firing you?" she asked in exasperation, then pinched the bridge of her nose and took a deep breath. "I'm not firing you. You're one of the best workers I've ever had, and

I'm sure not holding this nonsense against you. You just happened to be in the wrong place at the wrong time."

"You don't think I did it?" I asked.

She snorted. "Please. I'd believe Chrissy did it before you."

"Well, thank you," I said, my voice breaking.

She waved a hand in the air. "Nothing to thank me for." She turned serious. "The reason I called you back was to talk to you about my visit with Detective Langley."

I nodded. "He asked about the stir stick?"

"Yeah." She was silent for a moment. "Could the dead guy have picked one up in your car and had it on him when he was killed?"

I gave it a moment of thought. "I don't see how. I've never taken one, not that I can remember."

She cupped her chin and sighed. "So why did he come around asking about a stir stick?"

"I don't know, Petra. Really," I pleaded.

"Girl," she said, dropping her hand. "I know you're innocent. I'm trying to figure out how best to help you."

"Thank you."

"Have you lawyered up?"

My eyes widened. "No. I didn't see a reason to. I didn't do anything wrong. I just gave the guy a ride."

"Maybe it's time to consider getting one anyway."

I had a feeling she was right, especially in light of the detective's reaction to those videos.

"Do you still want me to come in on Friday?" I asked.

She made a face that suggested I was crazy. "Of course I want you to come in, and not just because it's good for business." She winked. "I meant it when I said you're one of the best employees I've ever had, although I'll deny it if you leak that outside of this room."

"You tell Chrissy the same thing, don't you?" I teased.

She grinned. "The difference is Chrissy needs to think she's special. I actually mean it with you."

I laughed despite the sick feeling in my stomach. "Thank you, Petra."

"Do you think you can stay later today?" she asked. "We're busier than usual, and Tony can't come in early."

Tony was the high school junior who worked several evenings a week.

I'd really hoped to look for Ernie, but as nice as Petra was being about this whole mess, I couldn't bring myself to say no. "Of course, but I'll need to leave by 4:45. I'll need to relieve Linda so I can make an early dinner and take Aunt Deidre to the Women's Club meeting."

"You still takin' her to that? Tongues are bound to be wagging."

"Only if Aunt Deidre remembers." For once, I was hoping for her dementia to kick in.

"I'd ask you to come in tomorrow and use your acquired notoriety for my financial gain, but I think you need to make an appointment with an attorney instead. You got someone to call?"

"Yeah," I said, terrified it was coming to this. "An acquaintance from school."

"You should call and make an appointment before you go back out front."

"Okay."

"Good. It's settled," Petra said. "You go take care of that and let me get back to my paperwork."

"Thanks, Petra. Seriously."

"It's nothing," she said, waving her hand. "Go on."

I looked up Burt Pullman's number, then called. I mentioned that I had gone to school with Burt and needed some legal advice, and the secretary scheduled me to see him tomorrow afternoon at three.

I didn't feel better when I hung up. If anything, I worried that talking to an attorney would make me look guilty.

Chrissy was anxiously watching for me when I returned to the front.

"Well, she didn't fire me," I said with a sardonic grin.

She snorted. "Of course she didn't. You're good for business." She pointed to the nearly full tip jar. "Look how much money we've raked in today."

"I'm staying until 4:45, so we'll see if we can fill that tip jar up higher." It felt like tainted money, but I was willing to take it anyway. I had too much credit card debt to worry about my pride.

We were still busy, but since I was staying later, I started asking people whether they'd seen Ernie hanging around. Unfortunately, no one had spotted him.

Had the killer seen Ernie and kidnapped him to keep him quiet?

At 4:45, I started to take off my apron. A group of customers who had just walked through the door got upset, but Chrissy told them that I'd be back at eight on Friday morning. I wouldn't be surprised if she put up another sign.

After I left, I drove around downtown, going slowly as I looked for Ernie, but I didn't see any sign of him. Was that the norm for him? I felt bad that I didn't know.

When I got home, Aunt Deidre and Linda were in the living room. My aunt was shouting, "Potato chips!"

I cautiously stepped into the room, pleased to see the two women sitting together on the sofa. "Was I supposed to bring some home?"

Linda grinned. "No, we're watching *Family Feud*."

I heard a ding come from the TV, and the announcer said, "Larissa said marshmallows! Show us marshmallows!" The ensuing buzzing sound announced that Larissa had guessed incorrectly.

"I'm telling you, it's potato chips!" Aunt Deidre said to the screen.

I gave Linda an amused look.

She got up and followed me into the entryway. "*Family Feud* is good for working her memory muscles."

I nodded. It made sense and was obviously a lot less infantilizing than the memory game I made her play.

"Are you still planning on taking her to the Women's Club meeting?" When I hesitated, Linda said, "She's been talking about it all day."

"I was planning on it, but with things..." I stopped. My aunt asked for very little and this was something she'd talked about for weeks. I wasn't going to deny her this because of my own discomfort. "Yes, I'm taking her."

Her shoulders sank with relief. "She told me about the police showing up at the Piggly Wiggly. I was worried you'd avoid the meeting to escape the gossipmongers."

"I'm not looking forward to it," I admitted, "but I know that *she* is. So I'll suck it up and take her."

"At least they'll be nice to your face," Linda said. "They'll just talk about you later."

I could deal with that. "I'd better get dinner started if we're going to make it on time. She's not set on making fried chicken, is she?"

"Nah, she knows there's not enough time. And she remembers that your friend Mallory is coming on Friday. She plans on making it this weekend."

I pushed out a sigh of relief. My aunt was having a good day, and it sounded like she wouldn't fight me on making chicken.

After I sent Linda off for the evening, I told Aunt Deidre I was going to start dinner so we could get to the Women's Club meeting on time.

Pure joy lit up her face. "Thank you, Maddie. I know this isn't your cup of tea, but I do look forward to them."

To say it wasn't my cup of tea wasn't really accurate since I'd never attended any Women's Club meetings. I hadn't been old enough when I'd lived here as a kid, but my mother had actually been the acting president. She'd viewed the club as a chance to do good for the community. I might have found it easier to see it that way too if Aunt Deidre hadn't told me who all was in it, as I was convinced their main priority would be gossiping and not doing good deeds.

"Of course, Aunt Deidre," I said with a smile. "Wouldn't miss it, but I better get started on dinner…"

"Do you want my help?" she asked, eyeing the television a longing. "The next *Family Feud* is getting ready to start."

"You stay there and enjoy," I said with a wave. "I'm going to call Mallory and check in with her."

I decided to make a chicken and rice casserole, and while I started chopping onions, I inserted my earbuds and called my best friend.

"Give me an update," Mallory said in lieu of a greeting.

"Hello to you too," I said with a laugh.

"No time for pleasantries. Cut to the chase."

So I told her about the TikTok videos and Detective Asshat coming into the coffee shop, asking about the stir stick and accusing me of trying to burn him with his Americano.

"Petra's right," Mallory said. "You need an attorney. Stat."

"Peter told me that one of our high school classmates is a defense attorney now. He insinuated that Burt might give me a cheap deal."

"Maddie," she said with a sigh. "Two things that should never be uttered in the same sentence are defense attorney and cheap."

She had a point. "I called his office and set up an appointment for tomorrow afternoon."

"That's a good plan, but in the meantime, we need to take matters into our own hands."

"What are you talking about?"

"You know that dinner party your aunt wanted to put together? I think you should go with it. Have it Friday night after I get there."

I shuddered. "I don't want to have dinner with Peter and a bunch of people I never kept in contact with."

"Maybe not, but they stayed in town after you left. They'll know stuff about Martin Schroeder that you don't."

"And why would I want to know more about Martin Schroeder?"

"Really, Maddie. Do I need to spell it out for you?"

No, it was sinking in like my feet were encased in concrete and I'd been tossed into the Briny River. If Detective Asshat was going to focus his investigation on me, I might have to find the killer myself.

Chapter Fifteen

Noah

As soon as I left the coffee shop, I headed back to the station and looked up the videos, but I spent the entire drive thinking about our exchange. I regretted accusing her of burning me, and part of me was frustrated as hell. I still didn't think she did it, but too many coincidences were piling up around her. Why couldn't that damn stir stick be from Starbucks? The closest Starbucks was nearly an hour away and would have pointed the investigation from her.

It was fairly simple to track down the guy who'd seen Madelyn Baker outside the butcher shop. (It helped that his name—Derek Castle—and his pressure washing business were listed in his profile.) As he planned to be out of town until later tonight for a job, I interviewed him on the phone instead, figuring I could bring him in later if need be.

He'd been filling up his car with gas when Maddie had pulled up to the curb across the street. She'd driven away, only to pull up again a couple of minutes later. An old guy had gotten out, and she'd started to drive away, only to stop and get out herself, shouting at him about not getting a tip. He claimed she'd also shouted something about her life sucking and telling him he'd regret it, whatever *it* was, then looked right at Derek, catching him eavesdropping. He'd gotten into his car but continued to watch her from the front seat as she talked to a homeless man before driving away. In the meantime, Schroeder had gone into the butcher shop.

We really needed to find Ernie Foust.

"You made it to Déjà Brew," Lance said, nodding to the empty coffee cup on my desk as he walked into the room.

I'd meant to throw the damn cup away before he showed up. "You should be a detective," I droned. "Your sleuthing skills are top-notch."

He laughed. "Looks like you took my advice and got an Americano."

"For all you know, this could be a black coffee."

Chuckling, he shook his head. "They serve plain coffee in different cups. Admit it. It's good."

I didn't like that he was right. It *was* good. Really good. "Coffee's coffee, now do you want to hear what I found out or not?"

He held his hands out at his sides. "I'm all ears."

I proceeded to tell him about my trip to Déjà Brew and my chat with the TikTok guy.

"Well, fuck," Lance said with a sigh.

"She's obviously not telling us everything. What would she make him regret?"

"He didn't give her a tip. Maybe that was it."

"Her reaction seems a little extreme over the loss of a five-dollar tip. What if it was over something else?"

He looked skeptical. "Like what?"

"I don't know," I groaned in frustration. "But I *do* know we need to look into her more."

"You don't seriously think she's part of this, do you?" he asked, incredulous.

I wasn't sure what to believe. She didn't seem the type to be involved with something like this, but it was too soon to draw that conclusion. We needed to keep an open mind, which meant I couldn't let it be clouded by personal feelings. One way or the other.

Because frankly, I was caught off guard by how much I *didn't* want her to be involved.

"Who hurt you, man?" he teased when I didn't answer.

Something in my chest lurched at the question, but I ground my teeth to tamp it down. "My personal life has no bearing on any of this."

"Seems to me it does when you're considering someone a suspect based on a bunch of coincidences."

"There is no such thing as coincidences," I stated bluntly, turning in my chair to face him. "And in this profession, sometimes all you have is coincidences until you can find the evidence."

We were both silent for several seconds, neither of us wanting to believe she was nothing more than in the wrong place at the wrong time. But we also both knew her aunt with dementia wasn't a solid alibi, even if we weren't admitting it out loud. She could have left him, gone home to her aunt, then returned and murdered him.

It seemed unlikely, but…I never expected Caleb to break into my house, strung out on meth, and try to kill me either.

"How long ago did Newman's tenants move out of that warehouse?" I asked.

"Three months."

"Before the coffee shop got those stir sticks."

"Yeah," he said but didn't sound happy about it. "We really need to find this homeless guy, Ernie Foust. He might have seen the murderer."

"Agreed. Maybe get Dukas to ask around. He might have some

sources who know him." I tapped my pen on the desk. "Did we get Andrea Baker's file yet?"

We still hadn't ruled out the possibility that Maddie blamed Schroeder for her mother's murder, and that she killed him out of revenge.

"I've put in a request, but they say the file's old enough that it's been moved off-site."

"Tell them we needed it yesterday."

His eyes narrowed. "You think her mother's murder has something to do with this?"

"I don't know. I want to know more about the case, but I can't do that until I get the goddamned file," I snapped.

Lance held up his hands in surrender.

"Sorry," I said, rubbing my forehead. "I'm just a little stressed." I needed to solve this case, and the only leads we had involved Madelyn Baker.

"Do you know who's stressed?" the police chief asked from behind me.

A couple of guys at the desks across the aisle began to smirk.

A cold chill washed through me as I turned to face my boss. Chief Jefferson Porter was a large man in his fifties. While he was tall, he was also stout, and he was constantly hitching his pants up over his rounded belly. My previous bosses usually called me into their office to chew me out, but he'd clearly decided to make my humiliation public.

Chief Porter didn't wait for me to answer. "I'll tell you who's stressed, Noah. *I'm* stressed. There's a murderer on the loose, and you're sitting at your desk *whining*."

Lance cast me an apologetic look, but I didn't respond to Chief Porter. I was sure anything I said would be turned against me.

"Got any leads yet?" the chief asked. "*Any* suspects or persons of interest?"

"We're working on it," I said, "but Schroeder's son and daughter-in-law have alibis that checked out. Even his neighbors' whereabouts can be accounted for, not that they were ever really suspects."

"What about that Uber driver?"

"Madelyn Baker?" I asked in surprise, flicking a brief glance to Lance then back up to my boss.

"If that's her name, yeah," he barked.

"What about her?" I asked evenly, holding his furious gaze.

"Does *she* have an alibi?"

"She went home to her aunt's house after she dropped Schroeder off," I said. "Her neighbor confirmed it."

"And the aunt?"

"She has dementia," I admitted. "But the neighbor swears Ms. Baker's car was in front of the house all night, and she said the aunt's car was totaled and scrapped a month or so ago. Ms. Baker only had access to her own car. The coroner says the murder took place earlier in the evening, and a witness says he saw Ms. Baker drop Schroeder off at about 6:15, which means we have two individuals backing up her alibi as well as the Uber app. The second witness also pointed to a potential third witness, a homeless man Ms. Baker talked to outside the butcher shop. We're trying to track him down to find out if he saw anything."

Chief Porter's mouth pressed into a line, making his already thin lips pretty much disappear. "All I know is we're closing in on forty-eight hours since the murder and you don't have shit."

"With all due respect, sir," I said. "We—"

"Excuses, excuses!" the chief shouted. "Everyone has one, and they're all full of shit." He took a breath, his face splotchy. "You might want to come up with something before you show up to the Women's Club meeting tonight. Those women are piranhas. They'll ask you a million questions."

I stared at him with a blank look. "Women's Club meeting?"

Then it hit me. A month ago, he'd told me I was to be the entertainment for the Women's Club on the second Wednesday in November. And shit, it was the second Wednesday in November. I hadn't been thrilled about the obligation then, and I was less so now.

"Don't tell me you forgot," he barked.

"Nooo," I said, dragging out the word as my brain struggled to switch gears. "I just got distracted by this case. *In fact*, given what's going on right now, I think I should cancel." A dark look crossed the chief's face, and I added, "Or at the very least postpone."

"There won't be any postponing," he bellowed, "otherwise those women will think I'm trying to hide something from them."

"Why don't we just tell them I'm busy trying to find the murderer?" I asked.

Lance snickered.

"Are you shitting me?" the chief shouted. "Have you *met* the women of this town? They would eat me alive."

"Instead, they're going to eat *you*," Lance muttered under his breath, trying to hide his grin under his hand.

"Did you say something, Lance?" the chief asked, turning his wrath on my partner.

Lance sat up straighter and dropped his hand. "Yes, sir. I was saying that while Noah's providing the godly women of this town with crime stats and giving them inside information on the Schroeder case, I'll be interviewing the teachers Mr. Schroeder used to work with." He flashed me a grin.

Asshole.

The chief stuck his finger in my face. "You better make those women happy, Noah. If you pacify *that* group of women, you can get the whole town to settle down. Don't fuck it up."

Then he stormed off to his office.

Was he really suggesting he was okay with me giving them inside information to get them to lower their pitchforks?

I leaned closer to Lance. "So what should I expect from this meeting?"

He beamed. "My nana's a member of the group."

"So a bunch of old ladies?"

He tilted his head to the side. "No... my cousin Dee's in it too."

"I take it's she's younger?"

"In her thirties."

"So a mix of ages. Good to know. And Chief Porter expects me to give them crime statistics? Do you think that's a good idea with the number of cases that have gone unsolved over the past decade or two?"

He laughed. "It's what the detectives typically do at those meetings. The chief sends someone every other year or so."

"Detectives, you say? Maybe we should send a patrol officer instead this year," I insinuated.

He barked a laugh. "Not on your life. Even if the chief hadn't insisted that *you* do it."

It looked like I was stuck going to the meeting, but there was no way I was going to spout off embarrassing crime stats. Given the force's shit solve rate, that would hardly work in our favor.

"Good call about working on the teachers next," I grudgingly admitted.

"It was next on the list," he said, then held my gaze. "I was surprised to hear you defending her."

My back bristled. "Madelyn Baker? I wasn't defending her."

"You didn't tell the chief what you found out about her."

"*Yet*," I said sternly, then sighed. "It didn't seem right to feed her to the sharks, when at best she's chum. He's so desperate for something to tell the public, I'm afraid he'll name her as a suspect." I pushed out a breath of frustration. "My gut tells me she's not directly, but I can't ignore that she keeps popping up in unexpected places, so for now, we'll keep it to ourselves and only present it to the chief if we think there's something actually there."

He looked relieved. "Good call."

"Maybe so, but going to that women's meeting tonight feels like a *bad* call."

His smirk made it clear he didn't disagree.

"Hey," I said, trying to sound good-natured. "Maybe you should come with me, *partner*."

He burst into laughter. "Not on your life."

Chapter Sixteen

Maddie

Aunt Deidre walked downstairs wearing a dress and her pearl necklace. I took one look at her and realized I was underdressed.

Her eyes narrowed as she took in my jeans. "Madelyn."

"I didn't realize it was that dressy," I said. "Mom always said it was a service club, and besides, this is dressy in Nashville." I gestured to my ankle boots and the brown suede jacket I had on over my cream-colored, lightweight turtleneck. Honestly, what I was wearing made me feel better than I'd felt in weeks, possibly months.

"I suppose it will do," she said, reaching for her coat on the hall tree. "But we'll need to look festive for the December meeting."

"Yes, ma'am."

She stopped and looked into my eyes, her face softening with emotion. "You're a good girl, Maddie. I'm very lucky to have you here."

"Aunt Deidre, *I'm* the lucky one," I said with a warm smile.

Her face welled with emotion. "I know what you gave up to come here."

"Ha!" I barked with a grin. "Shows what you know. I was going

Blind Bake

to break up with my boyfriend anyway, and you helped me do that. Now I get to live here rent-free." I'd skewed the order of events to keep Aunt Deidre from feeling any guiltier than she already did.

"You could have moved in with Mallory. You didn't need to give up your job."

I loved when Aunt Deidre had more lucid days, but the drawback was that it hit her hard every time she realized what it had cost me to come here.

"Aunt Deidre," I said gently, holding her upper arms. "There is literally no place else I'd rather be. I needed to come home and lick my wounds after losing Uncle Albert and realizing Steve is an insufferable moron, so thank you for letting me do that. Now, no more maudlin talk. We're off to the Women's Club meeting, where we'll get tons of news to gossip about over the next few days."

She chuckled. "You're terrible."

"But I'm also right. So let's go."

I was still driving Margarete's spare car so we took it to the meeting. I should have asked Detective Asshat how much longer he'd be keeping mine. Probably longer now that he was even more suspicious of me.

We reached the Cockamamie Recreation Center a few minutes before seven, and the parking lot was so full we had to park in the lot on the side of the building.

"Looks like a big turnout," I said as we started walking toward the entrance.

"They're probably here to gossip about the murder. Let's hope they haven't heard about the Piggly Wiggly incident." She smiled at me, her eyes twinkling. "Although I know Peter has been discreet."

I wasn't so sure about that. He'd loved spreading gossip back in high school—something I knew from personal experience—but I was willing to let it go since he'd been undeniably helpful lately. I'd called Peter right after I'd hung up with Mallory and asked if he'd help me gather some of our old classmates together for Aunt

Deidre's dinner party, but he'd insisted it would be better if he hosted it and made it an informal cocktail party. "You have enough on your plate, Maddie."

I felt like I'd gone back for seconds on my responsibility plate, but I also worried about being beholden to Peter McIntire. He may have been acting like he'd changed, but I didn't trust him. Still, the new plan had its merits. If the party got too intense, Mallory and I could just leave. If Aunt Deidre and I hosted it, I'd be stuck there.

"Well, thank you, Peter. I very much appreciate it," I'd said.

"Don't mention it. Everyone will be excited to see you."

I only hoped their excitement wasn't tied to my notoriety. It wasn't the first time I'd dealt with notoriety. I'd been under a microscope after my mother's death—everyone in town watching me closely to make sure I was okay. But how could I be okay after my mother was brutally murdered? How could I be okay, knowing the last words I'd said to her were that the people in this town meant more to her than I did and I was sick of it? I'd told her that I was going away to college and never coming back. I'd mostly lived up to that last part, because the guilt of coming home had been sometimes too great to bear.

Of course, no one knew my parting words as my mother had gone out that night. They never knew we'd argued. Strangely enough, no one had ever asked about our last moments together. Not even my aunt and uncle.

"You're sure we can't talk Peter out of his cocktail party?" Aunt Deidre asked, sounding disappointed. "Dinner *would* be nice."

"He has his heart set on it, but why don't we plan a dinner party for you and *your* friends?" I suggested. "Like the ones you and Uncle Albert used to have when I was a kid." My aunt and uncle had been known for their monthly dinner parties. I'd witnessed more than a few from behind the upstairs banister, because my mother and I would sleep over those nights after the adults had their fun. Those were such happy memories, and I could only imagine they were part of the reason she'd wanted to host one of those parties for me.

"Oh," she said, waving her hand. "Those days are long past."

"Maybe so, but if you want to entertain, we can make it work. Especially if we have it this weekend while Mallory's here. We could host it Saturday night. What do you say?"

A yearning slipped into her eyes. "It's such short notice..."

"So maybe we'll keep it small this time. We'll have a bigger one in December. We'll even decorate the house for Christmas like you used to when I was a kid." When she was silent, I added, "But only if you want to. We'll only do what makes you happy, Aunt Deidre."

She stopped walking and turned to me. "You are such a blessing, Maddie."

"I don't know about that." I definitely didn't feel like a blessing, but I also didn't want to argue the point in the recreation center parking lot. "But I know life's too short for us not to make the most of it."

A smile lit up her face. "Then a dinner party it is. I'll work on the guest list while Blair Simpson goes over the minutes from the last meeting." She rolled her eyes. "She takes *very* thorough notes but reads them in the *dullest* monotone."

Seemingly cheered, she linked her arm through mine and started for the door again.

It felt good to see her act more like herself, and I let myself bask in it a little as she led the way into the rec center and started introducing me to the other members. They were all in dresses and heels, and I made a mental note to shop for more dresses if I was going to start attending on a regular basis. I got several disapproving looks for my jeans and ankle boots, but a few of the younger women seemed more excited, as though they'd been waiting for the first renegade and now they felt free to bust open their own closets before the next meeting. Soon Aunt Deidre was off talking to her old friends, leaving me to fend for myself, not that I minded. I loved seeing my aunt so animated and excited.

Simone, an old high school classmate, saw me standing alone and approached, excited to see me. After I told her why I'd moved back, she spent the next five minutes telling me about her life. She was a stay-at-home mom with three kids, all of whom were "absolutely brilliant." She provided multiple examples of their brilliance, including her eight-year-old son, Ray, who had just won a class spelling bee with the word potato.

"You know," she said in a very serious tone. "The ending is *very* confusing. Is there an *e* at the end or no *e*? Even Bob Pheasant got it wrong."

I stared at her in confusion. Then it hit me. "Oh! I think you mean Dan Quayle."

She wrinkled her nose. "Same difference. In any case, we're considering putting little Ray into the gifted program."

Marsha, another former classmate, had approached us during Simone's overexcited tale about little Ray. From the way she was rolling her eyes, I felt sure she was going to make some pronouncement about little Ray, but instead she said, "I can't believe Martin Schroeder is dead."

The last thing I felt like talking about was driving the man to his death, but Simone surprised me by saying, "*Honestly*, I can't believe no one killed him sooner."

"You know, I saw him about a week ago," Marsha said, lowering her voice and leaning in close. "He was coming out of the hardware store with a cart full of stuff. The cashier asked him if he was having a rat problem, and he snapped at her, telling her to mind her own business."

"What a weirdo," Simone said, curling her upper lip.

"You know, Maddie," Marsha said, "Colleen works at the hardware store. Weren't you two besties in high school?"

"Yeah," I said, yet like everyone else I'd gone to school with, I'd lost touch. But something else she said caught my interest. "Did he have rat traps?"

"Poison. That along with a whole bunch of other things. Even a hacksaw. What's Schroeder gonna do with a hacksaw?"

"Nothing now that he's dead," Simone said with a shudder.

She was right, and even though he'd never been a pleasant man, it still felt surreal knowing I was one of the last people to have seen him alive.

"If I could have your attention, please," a woman called out.

We all hushed and turned to the front, where an impeccably dressed woman who appeared to be in her fifties called out, "Ladies, it's well past seven thirty. I suggest we get this meeting started. I hear there's a cold front moving in and possible snow flurries. We don't want to be caught unawares."

She looked vaguely familiar. If she'd been in the Women's Club long, I might have known her through my mother. In any case, I'd seen the forecast, and while it had called for cooler temperatures, there'd been no suggestion of snow. But her announcement had the desired effect, because everyone migrated to the folding chairs arranged in the middle of the room, their voices dropping to a low murmur as they sat down.

"Who is that?" I asked after Aunt Deidre and I had taken a seat next to the aisle, toward the back. There was no denying the woman at the front of the room both dressed for the limelight and basked in it. Her blond hair hung to a little past her shoulders, long and straight with lengthy fluffy bangs swept to the side. She wore a cream-colored sweater dress and a chunky brown suede belt and coordinating knee-high boots. I hoped to God I looked like her in about twenty years but doubted I had the sophistication to pull it off. She had a hard look in her eyes, though, like she loved being in charge and she expected everyone to do her bidding.

"Everly Barton. The president."

"Barton...the name sounds familiar."

"She was friends with your mother." My aunt tilted her head, then added, "But not close friends." That made it sound like they'd been frenemies, which wasn't all that surprising. This town took the term two-faced to whole new levels. Or at least it had when I'd lived here.

"Oh."

"She's not from Cockamamie. She met Garrett at the University of Tennessee, and he brought her here as his bride when he returned home to join his father's law firm."

The disapproval in her tone made me chuckle. "Which part offends you? That she's not from Cockamamie or that she exists?"

"Madelyn," she scolded under her breath, then leaned closer, whispering, "She's a dreadful, spiteful woman."

"I'm shocked," I whispered in jest as I pressed my fingers to my chest. "She seems so warm and open. Just look at the way she's watching her subjects like she's trying to figure how to reinstitute serfdom."

Aunt Deidre broke into giggles, which earned her a disapproving look from Everly.

"You're going to get us kicked out," I whispered. "Behave yourself, Aunt Deidre." Which brought on another burst of giggles from my aunt, because when she wasn't in the throes of her dementia, Deidre Saunders was usually a proper lady.

Several people glanced back at us, so I lifted my hand and waggled my fingers, mouthing, "Hi."

So much for trying to keep a low profile.

"Ladies," Everly said disapprovingly. "If we could settle down." She may have used an all-encompassing *we*, but her gaze was firmly on me. Looked like Everly might be skipping the frenemies stage with me and moving straight to tenuous tolerance.

I crossed my arms under my breasts. She didn't scare me.

A bright smile lit up Everly's face. "I realize we usually introduce visitors after we've called the meeting to order, but I think we should get this particular introduction out of the way." She gestured back to me. "Everyone, Deidre Saunders' niece, Madelyn Baker, is here visiting with us *tonight*."

I waved again, but an uncomfortable feeling settled over me as I got the message loud and clear—I wasn't welcome here.

Too bad I didn't like being told what to do.

Everly Barton didn't even know me. Which made it all the more interesting that she knew my name, as we'd yet to be introduced. Did she know me because of the TikTok videos? Everly Barton didn't fit the TikTok user profile, although she could have heard through gossip. She also could have known of me through my mother or through Aunt Deidre, of which the latter seemed more likely. No matter how she knew of me, it was pretty apparent she hadn't liked what she'd heard.

My aunt's body stiffened, and I realized she'd picked up on the insult too. One more instance when I selfishly wished her dementia would sweep away her hurt.

Everly called the meeting to order, then made a motion to the secretary to write down the names of the members who were present. Once that was done, she asked the secretary to read the minutes from the last meeting.

Poor Blair looked frazzled by the multiple things being asked of her, but she stood and cleared her throat as she stared down at her open leather-bound folder. She read the minutes, which took about ten minutes, then call for the votes to approve them. Meanwhile, Aunt Deidre had pulled a small notebook out of her purse and begun making a list of guests to invite to dinner, apparently tuning out all the nonsense around us.

Everly moved on to new business, which included several committee chair reports about their Christmas fundraiser for decorating a giant Christmas tree in the town square and the upcoming Christmas meeting that would be held in Everly's home.

Finally, Everly said, "If that's all the unfinished business, can I get a motion to adjourn the meeting so we can move on to the program?"

"But we're supposed to have refreshments first," a woman called out. "My pumpkin cheesecake bites will soften up too much if we wait much longer."

Everly's lips pinched into a sour pucker. "An officer from the police department needs to give his crime report so he can get back to the station. I *reluctantly* agreed to let him go first." She lifted her chin. "He's a *very busy* man." Only her tone suggested he wasn't. She seemed to do that a lot.

I'd had enough police interaction the last two days to last me a lifetime, and I considered fleeing to the restroom to kill ten minutes of a boring police report, but it would have been obvious I was leaving, and I didn't want to attract any more attention than I already had. I pulled out my phone, planning to scroll through Instagram until the program was done.

"I motion we adjourn the meeting," Pumpkin Cheesecake Bites lady pouted.

"I second," another woman said.

"All in favor?" Everly said in a tight voice. The room filled with ayes. "All opposed?"

I resisted the urge to call out.

"The November meeting of the Cockamamie Women's Club has officially adjourned. Now I'd like to welcome Officer Norman Langley to give the Cockamamie Crime Report."

Polite applause filled the room, but alarm bells were pinging in my head.

Officer Langley?

Wait. That name was familiar, but why? What was the name of my detective nemesis? I couldn't be that unlucky, could I?

But I was just that lucky, it turned out, because Detective Asshat himself stepped through the double doors that led to the kitchen, dressed in the suit he'd had on earlier. He tugged a folded-up exercise mat behind him as he headed toward the front of the room. "I'm going to need a moment to set up."

"Set up?" Everly asked in a near panic. "What on earth do you need to set up *for*?"

He didn't answer, just carried the mat to the front of the room, spread it out, then headed back to the kitchen.

What was Detective Asshat up to?

Everly's face reddened.

"Do you think Officer Langley needs any help?" purred a woman on the other side of the aisle as she fanned herself.

"Maybe I should do something naughty so he'll arrest me," said an older woman who seemed far too excited at the prospect.

Aunt Deidre looked up from her list and caught sight of the detective as he stepped through the double doors again, holding a second exercise mat. "I've seen him before."

I leaned in close to her and whispered, "He was one of the officers who showed up at the Piggly Wiggly. He was sweet enough to offer me a ride to the police station."

"And a ride home," she said.

That had been Officer Forrester, and I was embellishing Detective Asshat's kindness—okay, I was flat out lying—but I didn't want to upset her. "That's right."

She smiled. "He'll find who killed that awful man."

I turned to her in surprise. "You knew Martin Schroeder?"

"Of course. Well, I knew *of* him," she said, wrinkling her forehead in distaste. "He was positively awful to your mother. Such a vulgar, vile man."

"What?" I stared at her in shock. Vulgar and vile? What had Martin Schroeder done to my mother?

I was just about to ask her when Everly cleared her throat. "Without further ado, let me introduce Officer Norman Langley."

The detective was still carrying the second mat to the front, and from the look on his face he'd obviously gotten the message he was as welcome as a cockroach crawling out of a Thanksgiving turkey.

Looked like we had *one* thing in common.

He spread out the second mat, then started to take off his suit jacket. "Good evening, ladies. I'm *Detective Noah* Langley. And instead of giving you a stuffy report, I thought I'd offer you something much more useful—lessons in self-defense."

Then he smiled.

Sweet baby Jesus. It was dazzling.

The room fell silent not only because of that smile, but because of the way his shirtsleeves clung to his muscular arms.

Or maybe I was projecting. God knew the view had stunned *me*.

Detective Asshat worked out.

"But you're *supposed* to give a report," Everly snapped, then realized how she sounded and quickly formed a big, fake smile. "That's what the officers have done in the past."

"Well, I'm here to shake things up, Evelyn."

"*Everly.*"

A knowing look crossed his face, and then he turned to the audience. "I'll need a volunteer to help me demonstrate some self-defense moves."

I expected half the room to jump out of their seats and rush forward, and while some of the women looked eager to do just that, they all remained seated.

"No one?" Detective Asshat asked. "Don't be shy."

"The problem, *Officer*," Everly said snidely, "is that we weren't informed about the change in the program, so none of us are dressed appropriately to be demonstrating *karate moves*."

The detective looked stymied until someone called out, "Maddie's wearing jeans."

My heart lurched. *What?*

"That's right," someone else said. "She's the only one who can do it."

Detective Asshat's face lit up, because obviously he still hadn't figured out that *I* was Maddie. "Then come on up, Maddie. There's no reason to be intimidated."

Intimidated? He wasn't going to know what hit him.

Chapter Seventeen

Noah

A woman stood up, and I nearly fell over.

Well, fuck me blind.

Maddie was Madelyn Baker. How the hell had I not put that together? Although, to be fair, Maddie wasn't all that uncommon of a name. Regardless, I should probably send her back to her seat. I was investigating a murder, and she was currently the only person of interest in the case. Anything that happened could be used against me. Should she have been a person of interest? Maybe? Hell if I knew. I was starting to wonder why I'd ever thought her a potential murderer. And yet, how could I trust my judgment, after Caleb?

The sooner I got this demonstration over, the sooner I could get back to my investigation and clear her of suspicion. Maybe it was best to power through it.

I forced a smile as she walked toward me with a look in her eye that suggested she wasn't intimidated by me in the least. I motioned for her to stand next to me, then turned to the women in the audience, who were watching with rapt attention.

"Ladies, statistics show that one in six women will be sexually

Blind Bake

assaulted in her lifetime—some by someone they know, some by strangers."

"Is that what happened to Martin Schroeder?" asked an elderly woman sitting in the front row. Her hair was snow-white and teased, making it look like she was wearing a cotton ball on her head. "Was *he* sexually assaulted?"

I was staring at her in confusion, uncertain how to answer, when another woman announced, "He said one in six *women* will be assaulted, Viola. Martin Schroeder was a *man*."

"He wasn't a man," Cotton Ball Lady said. "He was a teacher."

A woman sitting next to her, who looked like her sister, nodded. "*Retired* teacher."

"Martin Schroeder was *not* sexually assaulted," I said, which was more than I wanted to say about his cause of death, but I saw no harm in revealing that tidbit of information. "Now, if you're ever attacked, your number one goal should be to get as far away from your attacker as possible. The moves I'm about to show you are intended to buy yourself some time to escape, not turn vigilante and fight your attacker."

Several of the women nodded, and one woman held up her hand.

"Yes," I said, gesturing toward her.

"Aren't you the guy who was on the news last night giving a press conference?"

Shit. "Yes."

"You're much better looking in person than you are on TV," Cotton Ball Lady said.

Several women murmured in agreement.

"Thank you?" I said, trying not to grimace. I needed to get this back on track. "I'm going to demonstrate several moves you can use depending on how your attacker comes at you."

Another woman raised her hand.

"Yes?" I asked.

153

"Is it true Martin Schroeder was gutted like a pig?" she asked in a sweet voice, then batted her eyes.

I took an involuntary step backward. "Uh...we're not releasing details about the cause of death at this time. Now, unless you're asking questions about the defensive moves I'm about to show you, I would very much appreciate it if you could hold your questions until the end."

Several women who'd raised their hands lowered them with sheepish looks.

I drew in a deep breath. This day kept getting better and better.

"There are multiple ways an attacker might approach you. Their main goal would be to subdue you and relocate you to somewhere more secluded. If you're out in the open, they might try to get you into a car or into the cover of some nearby woods."

Several of the women gasped, and Everly literally clutched her pearls.

Too damn bad. This was the real fucking world, and they needed to know how to survive, even if it meant crushing their delicate sensibilities.

"Most men have the advantage of being larger and stronger than you, but that doesn't mean you don't have a chance. You just need to know how to get out of the situation you find yourself in. Your best defense is to cause a scene, and the best way to do that is to scream."

Nervous giggles spread through the room.

"Many women are too embarrassed to make a fuss, something your attacker will count on. If someone attacks you, scream loud and long. Shout for help. Do anything to get attention, because your assailant doesn't want witnesses, and he'll likely run off and leave you behind."

I took a step back toward Madelyn, uncharacteristically nervous about using her for my demonstrations. I told myself it was because she was involved in my investigation. What other reason could there be? It wasn't because of the way her ivory turtleneck clung to her breasts or the way her jeans showed the curve of her very nice ass.

Dammit, Noah. Stop thinking about her ass!

"Sometimes screaming isn't enough," I said, "so you'll need to get out of whatever hold your attacker uses. Now, one common way for an attacker to get you to where he wants you is to grab your hair. Just remember, where he pulls your head, the rest of your body follows." I cast a glance at Madelyn. "Is it okay if I grab your hair?"

It made me feel better that she looked nervous too.

"Sure. I just washed it this morning," she joked.

Several women chuckled, and I almost smiled despite myself.

I stood in front of her but gave the audience my attention. "If someone approaches you from the front and they make you feel uncomfortable, try your best to keep as much distance between the two of you as possible. But if they start to invade your space, don't be afraid to hold up your hands, away from your chest, to help create more distance. Madelyn, hold up your hands and show them how to keep me away."

Her eyes took on a devilish glint, and she grinned as she held up her hands.

"Part of the reason you're holding up your hands is to create that distance, but also to block your attacker if he makes a move." I kept about two feet between us and slowly lifted my right arm toward her ear. "You'll move your left arm sideways to block me and push my arm out to the side."

She thrust her left hand, which connected with my forearm and knocked it aside.

"Good," I said encouragingly. "Don't forget that you can also scream while this is happening. Call attention to yourself. Now, keep me from grabbing your hair."

I reached my left hand toward her head, keeping my gaze on her neck, anywhere but her face. I moved slowly on my first couple of attempts, which she easily blocked. Then I picked up the pace and she did too, blocking every reach and using enough force that I was sure to have a few more bruises in the morning.

"Good. But let's say I sneak past your defensive block and grab your hair." I reached up and grabbed a fistful of her hair on the left side of her head, then turned to face the audience. "See how I can get her to go where I want her." I took several steps toward the kitchen doors, then stopped.

"Madelyn needs to break my hold, hopefully without me ripping out her hair, which means she has to make me *want* to let go. Now, a lot of women might think to kick or knee their attacker in the genitals, which *is* an option, but there's actually a better one —his face. See how we're face-to-face now?" I asked, motioning between the two of us with my free hand. "This is the perfect opportunity for Madelyn to thrust her palm under my chin and snap my head back."

I grabbed her wrist with my free hand and positioned the butt of her hand beneath my chin. "She can also scratch my eyes and cheeks or slam her palm into my nose. Once she does one of those things, there's a good chance I'll release her and reach for my face. This would be her opportunity to break free and run. Now try each of those, Madelyn."

Tightening my fist around her silky hair, I lifted my gaze to her dark green eyes. I felt a kick in my gut even though she hadn't touched me. She stared up at me, her lips parting in surprise, but recovered quickly and went through the motions of each strike—but thankfully stopped short of actually connecting.

I released my hold, and she took a step back. I thought I saw a moment of panic in her eyes, but then it was gone.

Shit. Had she felt a surge of attraction too?

Get over it, Noah. Finish the demonstration and get the hell out of here.

I took a deep breath, then returned to the demonstration. "Now they might sneak up behind you and grab your hair from the back." I grabbed Madelyn's shoulders and turned her away from me, then gripped a handful of her hair. "I could drag her backward, and put her at a complete disadvantage, so her best bet is to face me. Madelyn, turn away from the arm I'm using to hold your hair, but don't swivel at the waist, move with your entire body. Plant your foot behind you and turn to face me, then use the same techniques you used before. Palm to chin. Eye scratch. Nose pound."

She demonstrated each move in rapid succession. It was like she'd done this before.

Had she?

"Okay," I said, putting a few steps between us. "Another move they might try is to approach you from the front and grab your arm. The key here is to break free of the hold, which you can do one of three ways. Madelyn, you grab my wrist and let me demonstrate."

She reached her right hand out for my left wrist, then hesitated before locking on.

"I want to break my attackers hold before she drags me away, and I'm not going to waste time and energy trying to pull her hand off me. See how her thumb and fingers are placed on my wrist?" I said, pointing to her thumb. "This is the weak part of her hold. This is where I'll concentrate my efforts, but again, not by prying at it. I want to pull away from that point. One thing I can do is step to the side and just pivot my arm free."

I took a step back and to the side, wrenching my arm loose "You can also twist your own wrist around theirs to break free, or you can bend your arm at the elbow and pull your hand up. Anything you can do to force them to release their hold." I demonstrated several methods of breaking free from a wrist hold. "Okay, Madelyn. You try."

She looked up at me. "Any particular method you want me to use?"

"Whatever feels natural," I said, then reached for her right arm.

Instead of trying to break free, Madelyn covered my hand with her own and swung her arm inward and up, twisting my arm and forcing me to hunch over. Pain shot through my shoulder. She grabbed my wrist with her free hand and then, keeping my arm extended, pushed me down to the mat onto my knees.

"Your aggressor will try to push up and stand," she said, applying enough pressure on my arm to keep me down on the mat, "but as long as you keep that hold, they can't. At this point, you should scream and try to get someone's attention, because if you let go, they can reach for your legs and bring you down with them. But if there's no one around, you can't maintain this hold all day, so release your hold on their wrist, then plant your foot on their a—I mean butt, and push hard enough that they collapse to the ground."

She released my wrist, pressed her boot onto my ass cheek and gave a good shove as she released my hand. I fell face-first into the mat.

Where the hell had she learned that?

A collective gasp filled the room.

"It's going to take him a few seconds to recover, not only because he has to get up, but because *he* was expecting to take control and now *you* have," she said. "He's in shock. But don't get caught up in your glory, because ten to one he's going to be faster than you and he's going to be pissed as hell. Which means you send him face-first into the dirt and then you *run*. If you're in the middle of nowhere, get in a vehicle—if one's available—and lock the doors. Or run to a nearby house. Or back into the store you just left. You do *not* want to be alone with this man. If you're in public, hopefully his testosterone won't get the better of him and he'll run away. But make no mistake," she said emphatically, pointing at me as I got to my feet. "This man plans to kill you, and likely violate you before he does it, so you need to get the hell away."

The women murmured in shock at her bluntness.

"She's right," I said. "You need to be ready and willing to do *whatever* it takes to get away, because he's not grabbing you to have a nice little chat. Next I'll demonstrate what to do if someone grabs you from behind." Although I was leery of what she would do with this demonstration, a primal part of me was eager to find out.

Her brow lifted in challenge as the corners of her mouth tipped up.

Jesus, why did I find that so fucking hot?

Calm your ass down, Noah. You have fifty or more women in this room who will be eager to report you if you show even the slightest bit of impropriety, not to mention this woman is a person of interest in your case.

Even more so now that she'd shown she wasn't some helpless female.

Shit.

"Okay," I said, moving behind her, trying not to think about the possible implications of her physical prowess. Could Madelyn Baker have gotten behind Schroeder and slit his throat?

She looked over her shoulder and grinned at me. It could have been a malicious grin, especially since I'd been such an asshole during her interrogation and at the coffee shop, but it wasn't. It was almost playful.

There was no way she killed that man.

But was that my gut talking or my dick?

I took a breath to clear my head, then turned to the women. "A lot of aggressors won't be so bold. They're more likely to sneak up on you and grab you from behind. Particularly if you're out on a walking trail where there are trees for them to hide behind. They'll go for the element of surprise. Now, chances are they'll wrap an arm across your upper chest and pin your shoulders to theirs, making it easier to control you. Then they're probably going to lock their hands."

I reached around Madelyn's chest, crooking my elbow around the right side of her neck and grabbing her left shoulder with my hand, placing my left hand over it. I purposely kept my hold loose. She knew more about self-defense than most women did, and something had likely prompted her to learn. Had she been attacked? If so, holding her tightly from behind might make her anxious. Especially since she hadn't volunteered to do this. She'd been roped into it.

But now her hair was in my face, and the scent of honeysuckle and coffee filled my nose as the curve of her ass brushed my legs just below my crotch.

Focus, Noah!

"Your instinct might be to try to run forward, but I've got her pinned. See?" I said as she took a step forward and demonstrated that she was trapped. "That's not going to work. The first thing you're going to do is grab his arm with both hands and hold firmly, because all he has to do is lift his arm a little higher, and he has you in a choke hold." I lifted my arm higher, hooking my arm around her neck. "But if you turn your head slightly, then it's going to be less effective."

Madelyn turned her head, her fingers wrapped tightly around my arm. I paid attention to her breathing to make sure she didn't show signs of anxiety, but she seemed fine.

"He also might grab you from behind and try to pin your arms to your front or sides." I lowered my hold on her and pinned her arms to her sides, holding her tightly against me. "If he's larger than you, all he has to do is pick you up and haul you away." I lifted her off the ground so that her feet were dangling between mine. "You might think this particular situation is hopeless, but you *can* get out of it."

I lowered Madelyn's feet back to the mat. "In either of those holds, you want to start striking backward with one of your hands. Aim for his crotch, but it's okay if you connect with his thigh or abdomen at first. Just keep hitting, and he'll lose his hold on you. Chances are that he'll shift you to the side, giving you the chance to hit him in the groin. He'll drop you, and then you can run away. Okay, Madelyn, you demonstrate."

My arms were around her, linked under her breasts, and I held on tight as she started hitting my leg with the heel of her hand. I shifted her slightly, and she connected with my crotch a few times—without force, thankfully, but I instinctively released her. Rather than step away, like I was expecting, she heaved a soft kick to my thigh. It threw me off balance, and I fell to the mat.

"You want to be sure to buy yourself some time," she said. "You might be tempted to go for the crotch or his gut with your kick, but he'll probably already be holding his crotch, and if you aim there, you're giving him a chance to grab your leg. Better to kick him in the leg as hard as you can, then run like hell."

"Can you do that if he's picked you up?" one woman asked.

"Good question," Madelyn said with an evil grin. "Care to demonstrate, Detective?"

I had to admit I was slightly wary, but I was also curious about what she had planned.

"Sure," I said, getting to my feet.

"Grab me like before and lift me off the ground."

I wrapped my arms around her, wondering if I should have worn a cup for this, then lifted her up.

"If he's carrying you off like this," she said, "you can try to move around to break his hold, but chances are he'll have locked his arms. You need to keep him from moving."

"How do you do that?" Cotton Ball Lady asked.

"By hooking your leg around his. Wrap your ankle around the back of his calf or his knee, and it'll make it harder for him to move. Then use that opportunity to elbow him in the solar plexus or strike him with the heel of your hand. Hit as hard as you can. You want to hurt him. You *need* to hurt him to drive him away."

I lowered her to the ground, impressed.

"What if he has you in a choke hold?" another woman asked. "Will it still work?"

"Detective?" she said, raising her brow playfully.

I stepped up behind her and wrapped my arm over her upper chest and shoulders.

She instantly grabbed my forearm with one hand, then pretended to hit me with the heel of her palm. "This works, but there's actually something more effective."

She turned her head slightly to look up at me. "Ready, Detective?"

"As much as I'll ever be."

The room resounded with nervous giggles.

"I'm going to show you two different things you can try," she said, her hands still wrapped around my arm. "Both of them require you to squat at the knees and lower your hips."

She squatted, and I leaned forward to maintain my hold. "This is an easy move, because your attacker is going to be too stupid to let go, so you can use that to your advantage. He'll have to lean forward to maintain his hold, which will unbalance him. So you push your hips back against him and keep pulling down on his arm, and gravity will win out."

Before I could fully prepare myself, I was flying through the air as she flipped me onto my back on the mat. As I worked to catch my breath, she leaned over me, grinning.

"This," she said, looking up at the women, "would be a good time to stomp on his nose and run the hell away."

The women stared at her in shock.

"Can we see that again?" a younger woman asked. "I want to record it so I can practice it with my husband at home."

"Of *course*," Madelyn said. "I'm sure Detective Langley has no problem with that. I mean, he's here demonstrating so he can help us all be safe. Am I right, Detective?"

"Yeah," I muttered rolling to my side before pushing myself to my feet. "That's why I'm here." So why was I certain she planned to humiliate me?

We resumed our original positions, with me grabbing her upper chest from behind, and she recited what she was doing while she was doing it until I ended up flat on my back again.

"You said there was another way," a woman called out. "Can we see it?"

"Detective?" she asked, holding out a hand to help me up.

There was something about the way she was looking at me that struck me as hot as hell. This was not some helpless damsel in distress. This woman was fierce. And I found myself wondering what she would be like in bed.

Now I wished I'd worn a cup for a completely different reason.

I started mentally tallying the evidence we'd removed from a brutal triple homicide in Memphis a year ago, which was effective as hell.

I took her hand, and she leaned back as she pulled me to my feet.

"So let's say the perpetrator has you in a choke hold, and you can't get the leverage to flip him over your head," she said. "There's something else you can try, but this will take some practice. You'll probably want to watch us demonstrate it a couple of times so you can practice at home."

I wrapped my arms over her chest and whispered in her ear. "A couple of times?"

She laughed, her chest rising and falling under my arm. "You are here to help keep the women of Cockamamie safe, aren't you?"

I pushed out a sigh, and she wrapped her hands around my arm. "So I'm going to pull down on his arm, because I really don't want to let him choke me, and lower into a squat, but this time, he's strong enough to keep me from leaning over. See?"

I leaned back to keep her from tipping forward.

"This is going to take some fancy footwork, which is why you'll need plenty of practice, okay?"

The women bobbed their heads, and a chorus of okays and yeses sounded out.

"I'm in a squat," she said, "but now I'm going to sway my hips to the side and slide my foot behind his."

She slowly demonstrated until her left leg was behind my right one, the top of her thigh pressed to the back of mine. Her right foot was planted several feet to the side. I leaned forward, trying to maintain my hold on her chest.

"Now," she said, her hands still clinging to my arm. "You're going to let go of his arm and reach down and grab behind his knees." She demonstrated as she spoke. "My butt is sticking out behind me and I'm in a deep squat, see? My center of gravity is really low."

In the crowd, a sea of phones were recording us, while Cotton Ball and her presumed sister were taking notes on a notepad.

"Now I'm going to jerk on his legs, which will throw off his balance and make him fall."

So focused was I on her hands touching my thighs, I didn't have time to tense up as she tugged my legs out from under me. Before I knew it, I was whipping backwards as I fell flat onto my back.

"The problem with this move is you're going to end up on the ground with him," she said, kneeling one leg next to my side, one of her hands still on my thigh. "I need to hurt him to give myself time to get away, because unless I've concussed him from dropping his head on the concrete, he's going to reach for me. Now, not only does he want to haul me away to rape me, but he probably wants to hurt me in retaliation for what I just did."

"Can we see that again?" a woman asked.

"Of course," Madelyn said sweetly as she stood and offered me a hand to help me to my feet.

We repeated the maneuver, and again I wound up flat on my

back. When she went to stand, I reached for her arm and yanked her down on top of me, then rolled her onto her back, pinning her arms next to her head and leaning over her with my legs between hers.

The women released a collective gasp.

"Madelyn's right," I said, turning my head to face the audience. "The biggest problem with that move is it can quickly put you at a disadvantage. If I'm a rapist, I've got her exactly where I want her. I could have straddled her hips to subdue her, but between your legs is where a rapist ultimately wants to be."

More gasps.

I glanced down at Madelyn to make sure she was okay. But she was smiling up at me, looking pleased that I'd surprised her.

"While he's got you on the ground, you need to be screaming yourself hoarse," I said. "But he's probably not going to like it, and he's going to try to shut you up. One way to do it is to choke you." I released her hands and reached for her throat. "You can be choked unconscious in less than ten seconds, so you need to react fast. Your first instinct will probably be to reach for his hands and try to pry them off, which is unlikely to work."

Madelyn reached for my hands and tried to pull them away.

"She's going to bring her legs up to my shoulders and lock her ankles behind my head, while pinning my elbows down." Once she'd done as instructed, I said, "Now she's going to lift her hips up, which is going to place unbearable pressure on my elbows, possibly breaking them if you use enough leverage. He'll be in so much pain, you'll have an opportunity to get away."

I looked down at her and grinned. "Okay, Madelyn. Show them how it's done."

As we untangled ourselves to start the move again, I tried my damnedest not to think of doing this move under different circumstances, her naked and willing beneath me.

Blood splatter on the wall.

Twelve-inch butcher knife.

Once again, I reached for her neck, and I'd barely wrapped my hands around it before she burst into action. Crossed her arms over mine. Grabbed my elbows. Forced my elbows down. Wrapped her legs over my shoulders. Locked her ankles. Lifted her hips.

I grunted as pain shot through my elbows, and she immediately released her hold.

"Pretty simple, ladies," she said, still underneath me. "You really should try this one at home with your husbands. It might even spice up your sex lives."

Several women giggled, but Everly jumped to her feet. "I think that's all the demonstrating we need tonight. Thank you, Detective and Mandy."

She politely clapped her hands, then shot us a dark look. The women all started talking at once, comparing notes on what they'd seen.

I realized I was still leaning over Madelyn.

Shit.

"Sorry," I said, getting to my feet and then offering her a hand.

"She got your name right," she said as she wrapped her hand around mine and got up.

"The detective part, which I'm sure was on purpose," I said.

"Only because if you'd had to correct your title to *Evelyn* again, she would have looked like an imbecile."

Grimacing, I rubbed the back of my neck. "Admittedly, purposely calling her by the wrong name wasn't one of my finest moments."

"Funny," she said slyly. "It was the first time I thought you might actually have a soul."

I laughed. "A dark one, I guess."

She shrugged. "If the shoe fits. Not that I'm judging."

The playfulness in her eyes twisted my insides, making me want something I knew I couldn't have.

An elderly woman called her name, the woman Madelyn had been worried about in the parking lot. The aunt who had dementia. Madelyn had given up her entire life to move to Cockamamie to take care of her aunt. Her job. Her home.

But what if she'd done so because she'd discovered something about Martin Schroeder around the time of her uncle's death? Hell, maybe even at his funeral. Then she'd bided her time until she could get revenge.

It was far-fetched and crazy. Yet it was possible. And given all of the coincidences linking her to the case, that slim possibility was all I needed to mark her off-limits.

She sighed. "Duty calls." Then she started to walk away.

Something in me panicked. "Madelyn."

It felt like we were in this stolen moment in time, and once either of us broke it, we'd go back to being Detective Langley and Madelyn Baker, person of interest in a homicide investigation. Which was exactly how it was supposed to be, but something about tonight had poked a hole through the armor I usually wore to guard myself. If I had met her for the first time tonight, I'd have invited her out for coffee or a drink, or at the very least thought of some excuse to get her number. Anything to see her again. Because something told me that Madelyn Baker was unlike any of the women I'd dated before and losing this opportunity might be one of the biggest regrets of my life.

But I'd have to live with that regret, because I was a professional, and I had a job to do, even at the expense of my personal life.

She turned back to face me, her cheeks flushed and her eyes bright. God, she was beautiful. Still, I couldn't let that matter. She couldn't be mine.

"Uh..." I took a breath, swallowing down a wave of loneliness and the urge to ignore my responsibilities to the police force, the town and, hell, even Martin Schroeder, who was, by all accounts, lowlife scum.

Maybe I could ask her out after the investigation.

Only she might hate my guts by then.

I gave her a weak smile. "Thanks for helping with the demonstration."

"Yeah," she said, her own smile fading. She seemed like an intelligent woman. She was sure to have noticed the shift in my demeanor. "I guess we're both doing our part to keep the women safe. I'll see you around."

Maybe sooner than she liked. Especially now that I was going to have to officially interview her about her self-defense training.

Sometimes I fucking hated this job.

Chapter Eighteen

Maddie

What the hell just happened?

I'd meant to teach Detective Langley a lesson about underestimating someone, and somewhere along the way I'd ended up having more fun than I'd had since moving to Cockamamie. Shoot, longer than that. But it was like a switch had flipped inside of him after the demonstration, and he'd gone from acting like a human being back to the robot who had taken me downtown and treated me like a murderer.

An older woman grabbed my arm, pulling me to a halt. "Madelyn. Where did you learn to fight like that?"

"College," I said, trying to catch sight of Aunt Deidre through the crowd of women. What little I could see of her face wasn't a good sign. "I'm sorry," I said, pouring on the charm, "but I need to get back to my aunt. She's not looking well."

"Of course," she said, giving my arm a pat. "But remember that you don't have to do this alone. Many of us want to help. Albert just wouldn't let us."

I gaped at her. "I didn't know that."

"He was a very independent man, that Albert. But a lot of us *do* want to help, Maddie. We love Deidre. Just ask."

"Thank you," I said, genuinely moved. "I may actually take you up on that."

A smile spread across her face. "See that you do. Deidre is a lovely woman and friend. She'd do no less for us."

She grabbed her purse from the chair next to her and reached inside. "This is my card. I'm a receptionist at Bob Parker Realty. I work weekdays, so you can reach me there, but my cell number's on the back."

I took the card and read her name—Connie Smelton—and the phone number for the realty group. A handwritten number was on the back.

"Maybe we could go out for lunch sometime," Connie said. "You, me, and Deidre, although I'm sure a few other women would like to join us."

"I'm sure Aunt Deidre would love that," I said, sliding her card into my pocket. I almost mentioned my aunt's dinner party, but I hadn't seen Connie's name on her list. I'd check with Aunt Deidre first. "It will depend on my schedule at the coffee shop. I only have a couple of weekdays off and every other Saturday."

"You just call and let me know when you're available," she said. "Then we'll work out the logistics. Now you run along to Deidre. She looks a little lost without you."

When I finally reached Aunt Deidre, she was standing next to her chair, anxiety twisting her features.

I stopped in front of her and started to reach for her hand, then stopped. "Aunt Deidre?"

She turned unfocused eyes on me. "Andrea?"

My heart sank. "No, Aunt Deidre. It's me. Maddie."

A scowl wrinkled her face. "Don't be ridiculous. Maddie's a baby." Tears welled in her eyes, and she lowered her voice to a near whisper. "I don't seem to know where I am. Do you know Albert? Can you fetch him for me?"

I swallowed the lump that filled my throat. While I'd been

having fun, my aunt had slipped back into dementia's hold. I wouldn't be surprised if watching me grapple with Detective Langley hadn't shoved her back into its clutches. She had never gotten over my mother's violent murder. Watching me wrestling around had probably been too much for her.

"Albert had to run an errand," I said, blinking back tears of my own. "He asked me to take you home."

"Oh." Her eyes darted around the room as though searching for him. "Are you sure?"

"Yeah," I said, forcing myself to smile. "He was really sorry to be called away. Something about the church building committee."

She seemed to relax at that. "That committee has taken so much more of his time than he was expecting."

"They run him ragged," I said, then reached for her coat on the chair. "What do you say we head on home?"

"That seems like a good idea."

I was helping her into her coat when Everly walked up to us with a stiff smile plastered on her face. "Madelyn, thank you so much for volunteering to help Detective Longhorn."

"You mean Detective *Langley*," I said, more to irritate her than to set her straight.

Her forehead pinched with disapproval. "In any case, thank you."

"Of course," I said. "Anything to help protect the women of Cockamamie."

She started to walk away, then turned back. "You don't expect women to actually do those things, do you?" She spat out the words in disbelief.

"Do I expect them to remember everything they saw? No, it takes practice, but do I hope they remember something that might help them get away from a rapist or murderer? You bet your ass I do."

Everly sucked in a breath in horror, and I had to consciously suppress a snort. If hearing me suggest that she gamble her ass was the most shocking thing she'd heard in ages, then she lived a charmed life.

"If you'll excuse me, I need to get Aunt Deidre home. She's not feeling well."

Everly's gaze narrowed as though she thought I was running off because I'd offended her delicate sensibilities, not because Aunt Deidre was under the weather, but frankly, I didn't give a shit what Everly thought.

I grabbed my coat, not bothering to put it on, then picked up my and Aunt Deidre's things and led her to the exit, waving to multiple women who called out to us, trying to convince us to stay. My gaze shifted to Detective Langley, who'd been ambushed close to the front of the room, surrounded by women peppering him with questions about the murder. He was trying to fold up one of his mats, likely eager to get the hell out of here. Not that I blamed him.

My traitorous brain dwelled on the moment on the mat when I was on my back, and he was poised over me, our bodies inches apart. I tried to shove the image away, along with the tingle spreading through my body, as welcome as a dysentery outbreak on the Oregon Trail. *That's right, think about bloody diarrhea and not the way his eyes filled with lust.*

We headed out the side door to the parking lot. The cold air hit me in the face, and I regretted not taking a few extra seconds to put on my jacket. I led Aunt Deidre over to Margarete's car and opened the passenger door. After she was in, I shut the door and walked around the back of the car, my mind stuck on what the hell had happened on that mat. I'd planned to teach him a thing or two, and instead, I was walking away fully cognizant of the fact that I hadn't had sex in over three months.

I hoped my vibrator was charged.

I started to open my car door when a figure appeared at the

front of the car, someone in a dark jacket with a hood covering their head.

Caught unaware, I released a tiny yelp.

"Don't be scared, Miss Maddie," the figure said, a deep timbre in his voice. "It's me. Ernie. Ernie Foust."

My heart racing, I pressed a hand to my chest. "Oh my word, Mr. Ernie. You scared the crap out of me." Almost literally.

He pulled back his hood some, revealing his shadow-swathed face. While the parking lot had several lights, the closest lamppost wasn't lit.

"I'm sorry. I didn't mean to sneak up on you," he said, his voice shaking. "It's just that I don't want anybody to see me."

I glanced around the parking lot and turned back to him, the meaning of his words sinking deep. "Mr. Ernie, did you see something related to Martin Schroeder's murder?"

He started to say something, then stopped. He took a breath. "There's some bad people in this town, Miss Maddie."

I walked over to him and took his hand, shocked at how cold it was. "Why don't you get in my car, and I'll take you home with us? You can stay the night and get a warm shower and a hot meal."

He pulled his hand from mine, shaking his head. "I can't do that, Miss Maddie. They can't see me talkin' to you, let alone staying with you. I just wanted to warn you to stay away from all of this."

I squinted at him in confusion. "What do you mean?"

"I saw you at the crime scene. You can't be doin' stuff like that."

My heart began to race. "You saw something related to the murder, didn't you?"

He swallowed, his Adam's apple bobbing.

I motioned to the door behind me. "Mr. Ernie, the detective who is working the case is inside. Let me get him and you can tell him everything. He's kind of a shithead, but I know he'll protect you."

He vigorously shook his head. "No."

"Mr. Ernie, you really should talk to Detective Asshat—" I shook my head, "—I mean Detective *Langley*. I'm not his biggest fan, but I can tell he's fair." Although, upon further reflection, I was pretty sure my ovaries were making that judgment call, not my brain.

"No. I've seen what happens in this town when the police say they'll keep someone safe. I'm only here because I think they know about you."

My blood ran cold. "Wait a minute. What makes you think that?" Then again, how could they not? I was TikTok infamous.

"I saw them drive past your house."

"*What?*" I went light-headed as panic hit me hard. "Who drove past my house?"

He swallowed and took a step back. "Just keep goin' on about your life like nothin' happened, and you'll be okay. Make 'em think you don't know anything."

"But I *don't* know anything."

"Exactly. So just keep goin' on like that, and you'll be fine." He moved away, slipping between the two cars parked in front of me. "And don't tell the police about me."

"What?"

"Don't tell them I know anything."

"But I already told them you were there, Mr. Ernie. That you were sitting outside the building next door."

His eyes widened with fear.

"Mr. Ernie," I said, taking a step toward him. "Just talk to Detective Langley, okay? Maybe you can sit in his car and talk to him, and then no one but the three of us will know.'"

He cast a glance at the passenger seat of the car.

"Aunt Deidre is having an episode," I explained, trying to reassure him. "She won't know you, or even if she does, she's unlikely to remember by tomorrow."

His gaze darted to the building, where Detective Langley stood by the open side door, holding one of his mats.

Ernie took a couple of steps backward. "Promise you won't tell anyone about me," he pleaded, sounding close to tears. "They'll kill me if they find out."

"Mr. Ernie..."

"Please, Miss Maddie. *I'm beggin' you.*"

"Okay," I said. "I'll keep it to myself, but do you have a place to stay?"

I was fairly sure he didn't hear the end of my sentence, because as soon as I'd agreed to his terms, he'd taken off toward the back of the building next door.

I stood at the front of the car, watching him run off, not sure I'd made the right decision. Especially once I turned back to get in the car and spotted Detective Langley standing next to his open trunk, studying me.

I gave him a wave, then got in my car and left while he stood in place, watching me drive away. Tomorrow I'd be doing a whole lot more than just talking to Burt Pullman. I was going to find out what Ernie Foust had seen.

Chapter Nineteen

Noah

Of course I was swarmed after our demonstration. Some women wanted updates on the homicide investigation. Some wanted to know if I gave private self-defense lessons. Some just glowered at me, making it clear they either didn't appreciate the demonstration or didn't like outsiders. Probably both.

I wanted to escape. I needed time and space to clear my head. To forget about my ill-advised attraction to Madelyn Baker.

Which would have been easier if she weren't the first person I saw when I carted the first mat out the side door. She was standing in front of a Volvo, talking to a person wearing a hoodie. The hooded figure was slightly taller than her, but just barely, his or her face concealed by shadows and the hood.

Maddie motioned to the building, but the person shook their head. So Maddie tried again, this time motioning to the windshield of her car.

Who the hell was she talking to?

The person turned to face me and took a step back. Maddie glimpsed my way, then advanced toward the hooded figure. They bolted in response, darting behind the building next door. It wasn't a young person's run, more like someone who had a few aches and pains. Someone older?

Maddie turned to face me and waved, then got in her car and left.

What the fuck was that all about?

I put the mat in the back of my car, pondering what I'd just seen. Obviously, she could talk to whomever she wanted. There was no crime in that, but the whole conversation had appeared strained. Like she was trying to convince the person of something. But what? One thing was certain, she hadn't appeared threatened. If anything, the opposite was true.

My fears rose up like a mushroom cloud, engulfing me in paranoia. My gut told me she was an innocent bystander, but my intuition was still suspicious.

You never thought Caleb was guilty either.

But that wasn't entirely true. There had been seeds of doubt. I'd just chosen to ignore them.

I was about to go back inside to get the other mat—and face the gauntlet of women—when something in the empty space where Madelyn's car had been caught my eye. Something small and light colored.

I walked over and found a tan leather glove where the passenger side had been. Had Madelyn's aunt dropped her glove?

I picked it up and stuffed it into my jacket pocket.

After I folded up the second mat, resisting the charms and glares of the women, I stuffed it into the trunk with the other one and headed back to the station to return them. I could return them in the morning, but the sad truth was that I didn't want to go back to my empty house. At least not yet.

I took my time returning the mats and considered going back to my desk and putting in a few more hours of work, but I knew it would be a waste of time. All I could think about was Madelyn Baker. Sure, part of the draw was sexual—I'd felt a chemistry with her I couldn't remember having in a long time—but it was more than that. She intrigued me. She was like a puzzle box I felt compelled to open.

My hand brushed my side, and I realized I still had her aunt's glove. What if I returned it?

It was a little after nine, late for a house call, but I could just drop it off. It was a weak excuse, it was just... maybe it was the murder and everything it had brought up for me, but the urge for some kind of personal connection was consuming me tonight. I knew deep in my marrow that she couldn't be that person, yet I found myself driving to her house anyway.

Having dug up her address from the case file, I pulled up to the front of the old Victorian house where Madelyn lived with her aunt, finding the Volvo I'd seen at the rec center parked in the driveway. The front porch lights were on as well as the lights on the first floor, so I didn't feel like a total asshole walking up to the front door.

I stood on the front porch with the glove in my hand, about to knock on the door, when I stopped myself. This was beyond inappropriate. What the hell was I doing here? Madelyn's aunt had looked upset when they left. What if Madelyn was still trying to get her to calm down? My interruption might make things worse.

I was about to return to my car when the front door opened and Madelyn appeared.

"I didn't take you as the type who'd need to work up the nerve to knock on a door, Detective," she said with a wry look.

I held up the glove. "I found this in the parking lot where your car had been parked. I thought it might be yours or your aunt's."

She stared at me for a long second, then took a step back. "It's cold. Why don't we continue this conversation inside?"

Then she spun around and headed down the hallway, leaving the door open.

I followed, shutting the door behind me. My defenses went up, the hair on my arms standing on end. What if this was some kind of trap? But that was my paranoia talking again.

Chill the fuck out, Noah. I was being paranoid again.

Madelyn disappeared through a doorway, and I trailed after her, finding myself in her kitchen. She was filling an electric kettle with water. "Would you like some tea, Detective?"

"I'm not here on official business," I said. "Call me Noah."

Her brow lifted, and she eyed me curiously before settling the kettle on its base. "Is that appropriate? Calling you by your first name when I'm a suspect in your investigation?"

I gave her a tight smile. "Not really. And you're not a suspect."

"More of a person of interest, then?"

I didn't respond.

She nodded and got two cups out of her cabinet and set them in front of the kettle.

"So tonight..." She tilted one of the cups, keeping her gaze on it.

"Where did you learn to fight like that?" I asked before I could think better of it.

Her head jerked up, her green eyes piercing into me. "I thought you weren't here in an official capacity."

"I'm not," I said softly. "If I were here officially, I'd be asking you who you were talking to in the parking lot, and while part of me is eager to ask, I'm not going to."

"Yet."

"Maybe tomorrow." Or maybe she'd realize that I wasn't out to pin this on her, and she'd trust me with the information. But I was the first to admit that I hadn't exactly built the foundation of that trust bridge. Maybe that's why I was here.

Like I believed that.

No, it was partially true. I wanted her to trust me, but not just for the case.

Maybe I wanted to trust her too.

"I learned in college," she said. "First in a PE course and then I took lessons."

"Because of your mother?"

She pushed out a breath and crossed her arms over her chest. "My mother's murder messed me up for a long time." Her gaze lifted to mine. "And, if I'm honest, I think I'm still messed up."

"You might find this hard to believe," I teased. "But I'm messed up too."

She laughed, then said mockingly, "No! Not the perfect Detective Langley."

I grinned, but it faded quickly. The same weird urge that had sent me here at an inappropriate hour made me want to share my pain with her, maybe because I was hoping she would also share hers with me. "I think we're all messed up to some degree. Some of us are just more messed up than others."

She studied me, her gaze scanning my face, and I felt raw and vulnerable. I wanted to make some wisecrack, asking if I had something on my chin, but I stayed silent. Letting her really see me... because it gave me the chance to really see her too. She had high cheekbones and a small chin. Her lips were full and pink, and I wondered if they were as soft as they looked. Everything about her was lovely, but her eyes were unforgettable. They changed color based on her mood, and right now they were bright as emeralds.

It took everything within me to keep my hands to myself, and it wasn't until her gaze dropped to my abdomen that I realized I'd been strangling the glove that I still held in my hand.

"Sorry," I said, putting it on the counter behind me. "Maybe I should go."

"Or you could stay," she said, but she sounded uncertain. "It's just..." Her gaze lifted to mine again. "If you can just be Noah and I can just be Maddie, would you mind staying for a while? It's been a shit day, and I kind of don't want to be alone right now."

I wanted to walk over, take her in my arms and hold her, and tell her everything was going to be okay, but I couldn't. I wasn't sure everything *would* be okay, at least with her aunt and her life here, and while I wanted to assure her I had no intention of accusing her of murdering Martin Schroeder, I couldn't do that either. Not yet. The professional in me knew better than to do that. The personal part of me though...

Maybe I was misplacing my trust again. That was certainly a fear of mine. But something had driven me here and it wasn't suspicion. There were millions of women in the world, billions even, so why was I here in *her* kitchen seeking comfort? All I knew was that I didn't want to be alone either and, of all the people I knew, for some reason I'd come to her.

Why?

"You're a thinker," she said with a soft smile. "You think too much."

I laughed. "What makes you say that?"

"I can practically see the wheels spinning in your head. You know you shouldn't be here, but you're here anyway."

"Am I that transparent?" I asked, feeling self-conscious.

"No. Let's just say I recognize someone who has lived by the rules their whole life and can't believe they're breaking them." She lifted a brow. "For what it's worth, I still can't believe I let you in."

"Fellow rule follower?"

She made a face. "I told you I'm messed up."

"Following the rules isn't messed up. It's obeying the norms of society."

She laughed. "That's exactly the answer I would have expected from you. And I agree: rules—written and unwritten—are the threads that hold a society together."

"So why is it messed up for you to follow the rules?"

"Because maybe I'm following them for the wrong reasons."

The kettle clicked off and she picked up two metal tea strainers, scooped them into a canister, then dropped them into the cups before adding water. When she finished, she handed one of them to me. "Sugar and honey are in the cabinet behind you. Milk's in the fridge, if you take it the British way."

I lifted the mug to my nose and sniffed. The scent was faint, but I caught a hint of lemon.

"Oh, sorry," she said, shaking her head. "I should have asked you which blend you preferred. It's a chamomile-citrus blend. If you prefer something else like Earl Grey, I can get you that."

"No, this is good."

She walked up to me, so close that for a brief moment I thought she was going to kiss me, but instead she reached for the cabinet behind me. "I take mine with honey."

"Sorry," I said, grabbing the bottle so I had something to do with my hands. "Do you want to sit at the table?"

"Yeah."

I carried my cup and the honey over to the small kitchen table arranged next to a bay window. I sat in a chair and Maddie sat opposite me, placing an empty plate between us. We both doctored our teas and removed the strainers in silence, and I wondered if coming here had been a mistake. Which was laughable because it was *obvious* it was a mistake. The real question was how badly I'd screwed up.

She took a sip, her gaze on me as she lowered the cup to the wooden tabletop. "You know plenty of things about me. Tell me something about you."

"Well..." I sat back, unsure what to tell her or where to start. "I moved here from Memphis about three months ago."

"You were a detective there?"

"I was."

"So why leave a big city like that to move to podunk Cockamamie? I could see it if you were fifty, but you have to be in your mid-thirties."

"Thirty-seven."

"So why Cockamamie?"

"I got tired of all the crime," I said, giving her my standard answer.

She laughed. "If you're tired of crime, you should have changed careers, not zip codes."

I grinned. I'd heard plenty of different opinions to my decision to move, but she was the first person who'd told me that. "Okay, there's not as much crime."

She took a sip of her tea. "Okay, what else?"

"Huh?"

She shrugged. "You *could* volunteer information, you know. This isn't an interrogation."

I cringe, then rub the back of my neck. "I suppose I deserve that. But for the record, I was just doing my job."

She didn't say anything, just waited.

"I have two parents—both living and still married. Their fortieth wedding anniversary is next week."

She smiled. "My aunt and uncle were married nearly fifty. They were in love until the day Uncle Albert died. My dad left my mom when I was three, never to be heard from again. Do your parents get along?"

Her father sounded like an ass, but I kept that to myself. "They love each other, but I wouldn't say they're in love, per se. It's a semi-comfortable companionship."

"Do you get along with your parents?"

"I love my mother, and my decision to move here broke her heart. My father...let's just say it's complicated. He has expectations of me that I never seem to meet. As far as he's concerned, my life has been one mistake after another."

"I'm sorry," she said, reaching over and covering my hand with hers. "That's just wrong."

An electric jolt shot through me from where our hands touched, and my blood all rushed to my groin.

She must have felt it too, because she jerked it away and cupped her mug with both hands.

"Uh..." I felt a need to fill the silence before I did something stupid like lean over the table and kiss her. "I have a sister, Leah. She's two years younger than me, but she's married and has eight-year-old twins. My father approves of her."

"So he's upset with you for not providing an heir?"

I smiled. "No, he approves of her because she's lived her life the way he thinks she should, and I haven't tried to fit his vision for me."

"Hmm..." She narrowed her eyes, studying me intently. "Interesting."

I cocked my head, intrigued. "What?"

"Just that a self-proclaimed rule follower doesn't get along with his father because he doesn't follow his father's rules."

I sat back in my chair and stared at her, dumbfounded.

Concern washed over her face. "Noah. I'm sorry. That was too..."

"Accurate?" Jesus, she was right. How had I never realized that before?

"Noah..."

"Are you sure you weren't a psychologist?" I teased. "You're pretty perceptive for a librarian."

"*Former* librarian," she said with a grimace, then sipped her tea. "Now I'm a part-time barista-slash-cashier and an Uber driver."

"Because you moved back to take care of your aunt?"

"Yeah." She stared into her mug. "But I also broke up with my boyfriend of five years."

Her words were a dose of reality that I didn't much like. Not only was my attraction to her inappropriate, but she'd just gotten out of a long-term relationship. It was another point against us. "He didn't want to come with you?"

"What?" She narrowed her eyes, then released a bitter laugh.

"Oh no, there's no way Steve would have come with me. But for the record, I didn't want him to. I'd stayed with him for all the wrong reasons. Leaving him behind was the best part of leaving Nashville. No regrets, and I hardly ever think of him, which tells you something."

"What were the wrong reasons?" I asked before I could stop myself.

She held my gaze. "I told you. I'm messed up." I was sure that was all the answer she was going to give me, but then she added, "I think..." She paused, then started again. "I was scared of losing him, because then I'd be alone. And ever since my mother died..."

Her voice broke, and I almost told her she didn't have to tell me anything else, but I wanted to know her, and I wanted her to know me. I couldn't for the life of me have explained why, but that didn't make it any less true.

"You have your aunt," I said softly.

"Who is losing her mind, brain cell by brain cell. Yesterday, before we went to the grocery store, she didn't even know me. She thought I was a stranger." She drew a shaky breath. "She's wandered off before and crashed a car, and I'm scared to death I'm not up to taking care of her. But the very last thing I want to do is send her to a home."

"That has to be hard."

"You have no idea." She swiped at the corner of her eye, then looked up at me. "When we were demonstrating tonight...She took a breath. "I think seeing us spar reminded her of my mother's death. I upset her."

It was obvious she blamed herself for that. "Maddie, you didn't mean to. And if I'd had any idea that it would have upset her, I would have sent you back to your seat."

She looked deep into my eyes. "I liked tonight."

Another zap of electricity raced through me, and it took every ounce of willpower not to follow through on my desire to kiss her. A desire, which, if I were being honest, had sparked to life and grown since she gave me that sassy grin on the mats. "I liked tonight too. Maybe that's why I'm here."

But I can't help thinking I shouldn't be. I shouldn't be messing with her emotions. I shouldn't be messing with mine.

"So now you know I'm really messed up," she said with a wry chuckle. "And all I know about you is that you subconsciously break your father's rules." She looked up at me with an intense gaze. "When was the last time you had a serious relationship?"

"A year and a half ago."

"What happened?"

"She wanted to get married but after seeing my parents, I told her I don't ever want to get married. So we broke up, even though we still loved each other. She's already married and expecting a baby."

She grimaced. "Ouch. I suddenly feel like we should be drinking whiskey instead of tea."

I rubbed my chin, giving her a playful grin. "Do you have whiskey?"

Her face lit up. "Nope, but I have some really bad boxed wine."

I screwed up my face.

"Okay," she said. "One more thing to add to the list."

God, she was beautiful. I loved the little sparkle in her eyes when she smiled.

"What list?" I asked.

"My list of things I know about Noah Langley. Number twelve: turns his nose up at boxed wine."

I knew she was teasing, but I was surprised how much I liked the idea of her wanting to know things about me. "And what are in spots one through twelve?"

Her eyes danced. "A woman has to be allowed some mystery."

She was full of mystery, but not in a bad way. I wanted to know everything about her, from how she took her coffee to whether she liked sexy talk in bed.

I wanted to know more about Madelyn Baker, and I wanted it to involve more than chats over tea.

"There's something else," she said quietly. "Something deeper that's messed you up."

I stared at her like a raccoon caught red-handed stealing from a trash can. "You mean dumping a girlfriend I loved and seeing that she very quickly moved on and got the things she claimed she wanted with me isn't enough?"

"Do you think my mother's murder and having a jerk ex was enough to mess me up to this degree?" She shook her head. "There's more to me and my screwed-up psyche, and I know there's more to yours." She gave me a sad smile. "Call it gut instinct because like knows like."

Part of me was tempted to tell her everything—about Caleb, his betrayal, Sarge, all of it. And that was when I realized what a big mistake I'd made tonight. I couldn't tell her any of that.

"I think I should go."

She didn't look surprised, but there was a glimmer of disappointment in her expressive eyes. "Thanks for dropping off the glove."

We both stood, but I made no move for the front door.

"Was it your aunt's?" I asked, stalling.

A grin crossed her face but didn't quite make it to her eyes. "No. I don't know whose glove you brought me, but it's not ours."

I burst out laughing. "So I stole someone's glove?"

"I'd make a citizen's arrest, but I'm worried I'd get tagged as an accomplice," she said playfully.

Her words were sobering. I'd almost forgotten about her role in this case. But while her name kept popping up in my investigation, I knew she wasn't part of this mess with Martin Schroeder. Or at least she hadn't had a hand in his murder.

She walked me to the door but didn't open it. Instead, she looked up at me with a half-smile. "If you decide to steal someone else's glove, you know where to bring it. We could start an underground glove smuggling ring. That would really piss off your father."

I grinned. "I'll keep it in mind." Then, because I felt like I needed to give her one less thing to worry about, I said, "I know you didn't kill Martin Schroeder."

"I know," she said softly.

I narrowed my eyes. "How do you know that?"

"If you thought I'd killed him, you wouldn't have sat at my kitchen table drinking tea."

She had a point.

"But you think I know more than I've said," she continued. "Especially since you saw me talking to that man in the parking lot tonight."

So she'd been talking to a man. I'd suspected, but confirmation was good. "So why don't you tell me everything you know?"

She opened the door and let me pass. I stepped outside before looking back for her answer. She looked thoughtful, as though weighing whether to tell me, but finally she said, "Because some secrets aren't mine to tell."

"Do you know why Martin Schroeder was killed?"

She suddenly looked exhausted. "I have absolutely no idea. Nor do I know what was in his bag or why he went to the butcher shop or why he was at the industrial park."

Watching her closely, I went over the items she'd listed and realized she'd missed one part of the mystery. Was it intentional? "But you do know where Ernie Foust is."

Something flickered in her eyes. "I can assure you that at this moment I have no idea where Ernie is."

She wasn't going to tell me anything else, but she had told me something. Then a new thought hit me. "Maddie, are you in danger?"

Indecision wavered in her eyes before she said, "I have no reason to be in danger."

I wasn't sure I believed her, but I also didn't know what to do about it. Ask to sleep on her sofa? No, that was a terrible idea, because if she gave me the slightest indication that she wanted more than tea and conversation, I wasn't sure I'd be able to resist her.

I pulled out my personal phone. "Give me your number."

"Don't you have it in a file somewhere? I mean, you knew where to find me."

I held her gaze. "I'd rather get it from you."

"Okay."

I pulled up my contacts and added her number, then sent her a text. "Now you have my number too. If you ever feel like you're in danger—"

"Then I'll call 911," she said, looking sad. "I also know this has to be a secret. I can't tell anyone you were here. It could get you in trouble. Right?"

"Maddie..." She was right. About all of it. But that didn't mean I had to like it.

"I'm still a person of interest in your case," she said softly, leaning into the doorframe. "Not to mention, I think you've got some things to work out, and frankly, so do I. Because here's the thing, Detective Langley." She held my gaze. "I don't want to be your next mistake. We both deserve better than that." Then she stepped back and closed the door.

Chapter Twenty

Maddie

I'd been terrified when I'd seen Detective Langley walking up to my front door. I knew he'd want to question me about the figure he'd seen me talking to outside the Women's Club meeting. My first instinct was to send him away, so I wasn't sure why I'd invited him in or made him a cup of tea, or even spilled my guts to him. Or why he'd spilled part of his story to me.

No, that was a flat-out lie. I felt a pull to him like I'd never experienced with any other man. But I couldn't be with him, and honestly, he didn't want to be with me. He was lonely and horny, and I was the most available woman.

Only it had felt like more than that.

But he didn't want to get married or have a family, and both of those things were important to me, which meant it was better this way.

After closing the door on him, I walked back into the kitchen, staring at his cup on the table. Tears sprang to my eyes. I didn't have time to think about my nonexistent love life. I had my aunt to take care of. I really should put some effort into finding a full-time job, and I also needed to work on myself, because I hadn't been lying to Noah: I was still messed up. It was obvious he was too.

I rinsed out his cup, then finished off mine and rinsed it out too. Then, and only then, did I check my phone, telling myself that I was just checking to see if Mallory had tried to get in touch, not because I was like some seventeen-year-old girl with a crush.

His text was there at the top of my notifications.

Thanks

That was it. Nothing more.

Thanks for what? The tea? The conversation? For almost being a booty call?

Men.

I was almost annoyed enough to delete it, but then reason prevailed. I added his number to my contacts, telling myself I could call him directly if and when I found out what Ernie was so scared of.

Mallory had texted, wanting an update about the Women's Club meeting, but I'd also missed half a dozen texts from Peter.

Oh jeez. How had I forgotten about Peter?

Peter: *8 people have RSVPed yes*

Peter: *Do U like red or white wine?*

Peter: *The party is starting @ 8*

Peter: *I figured that would give you time to get your aunt settled. And also in case your friend is running late*

Peter: *Plus I won't have to feed people*

Peter: *Are you there?*

Peter: *Wear a red dress. I'll wear a red tie*

Peter: *Also, wear heels, preferably stilettos*

Peter: *Are you there? We really should talk about creating a signature cocktail*

I was trying really hard not to be annoyed at his persistence, because he *was* going out of his way to throw me a party, but this didn't feel informative, it felt borderline controlling.

Only so he can get in your pants.

Probably, but it was a whole lot more than he'd offered back in high school.

The pickings are slimmer now.

That was probably true too, but I had no intention of letting him get anywhere near my pants, let alone my panties.

Still, he was throwing a party, even if he was being sort of demanding of my time and attention, and he'd gone out of his way to help me and Aunt Deidre. Besides, plenty of people were gossiping about me. This might give me a chance to do some damage control for Aunt Deidre's sake.

Me: *Sorry for the late response. Rough night with my aunt. That all sounds great. Let me know if I can help.*

A text bubble appeared immediately in the chat window.

Peter: *Maybe come early to help set up. Say 7:30?*

The last thing I wanted to do was spend a half hour alone with him, although I was somewhat comforted by the thought that Mallory would be with me..

Me: *I'll see what I can do.*

I pushed out a sigh of relief. While I felt bad that I was using him to get access to our old classmates, he was the one who'd insisted on hosting the party. My aunt had been perfectly willing to host a dinner at our house.

When I went to bed and my head hit the pillow, my mind drifted to Noah sitting across the table from me, looking like he was about to kiss me. Noah, hovering over me, his body pressed against mine in ways that lit my nerve endings and imagination.

But I pushed those thoughts away. There were more important things for me to consider, like the fact that a man was dead and the only other person who'd watched Mr. Schroeder go into the building was now in hiding.

Should I have broken my promise to Ernie and told Noah what I knew?

Part of me had wanted to. But Ernie was running scared, and the last thing I wanted to do was make his situation worse. If he really did know something, I needed to find him and convince him to tell the police. Not only would it help get a murderer off the streets, but it would hopefully get me off the persons of interest list.

I kept worrying it over late into the night, but when I finally did close my eyes and drift off, I dreamed of Noah, his body hovering over me, his lips inches from mine. Only in my dreams, I didn't stop him.

* * *

When I woke the next morning, I was exhausted and sorer than I'd expected. I wondered how Noah was feeling and a wicked smile spread across my face. At least he'd have something to remind him of me throughout the day. Of course, that wasn't necessarily a good thing. While I did believe he accepted I hadn't killed Mr. Schroeder, he still had to follow the evidence, and so far, from what I knew, most of the evidence centered around me. A stolen glove, tea, and our explosive chemistry didn't change that.

I was tempted to sleep in, but my meeting with Burt Pullman was at two, and I had a prescheduled Uber ride at 8:20 this morning, plus I needed to find Ernie in between both. I took longer in the shower than usual, coming up with a plan. I'd go downtown and ask around to see if anyone had seen Ernie that morning, and then…?

I didn't really know what to do after that. I'd figure it out once I found him.

After I dried my hair and got dressed in a pair of jeans and a black sweater, I found my aunt in the kitchen. She was sitting at the table, holding a cup of coffee as she stared out the window overlooking the street.

It was hard to believe that Noah and I had sat at that table less than twelve hours ago. Had I imagined it all? The two mugs in the sink proved that I hadn't.

But then something else stuck out at me. Aunt Deidre was in her bathrobe. She never left her room undressed. Was she feeling unwell?

"Are you feeling okay, Aunt Deidre?" I asked, grabbing a thermos from the cabinet above the coffee maker.

She didn't answer as I poured coffee into the cup. The longer she was silent, the more the fear in my chest grew.

"Aunt Deidre?"

She must have heard the anxiety in my voice, because she finally craned her head a few inches to face me. "Don't worry, Maddie. I'm fine."

Then she turned to look out the window again.

She was far from fine, and she was scaring me, although I had no idea why. I added cream to my coffee and carried it over to the table and sat across from her.

"Aunt Deidre, what are you thinking about?"

"Albert." She continued looking out the window as a tear rolled down her cheek.

I reached a hand across the table and covered hers. "I miss him too."

Pressing her lips together, she gave a firm nod.

"Is that what you're thinking about? That you're missing him?"

"Among other things."

"I'd love to talk about him if you want to. After Mom died..." My throat tightened, and I swallowed, hoping to relieve the pressure. "After her funeral, no one wanted to talk about her."

Aunt Deidre turned to face me.

"I know part of it was because of the way she died. It scared people. But she was my everything, and she was gone, and it left a gigantic hole in my heart. It was like a vacuum, sucking all the joy and happiness that I'd had, leaving only..." I struggled to find the right word.

"Emptiness," Aunt Deidre said softly, looking down into her coffee cup as if the word had been written there in whipped cream.

"Yes," I whispered. "Emptiness." But that wasn't the right word either. What I'd experienced had been deeper and more painful than that. More unceasing.

She looked up at me, her eyes glittering with unshed tears. "We thought talking about her would remind you of the terrible thing that had happened to her. We didn't want you to dwell on it."

"But we didn't talk about our good memories either, Aunt Deidre. All I had to dwell on was what happened to her."

Aunt Deidre's chin quivered. "Oh, Maddie. We failed you."

I shook my head forcefully. "No. You did what you thought was best, and that's all any of us can do. Besides, you and Mom were close, and you lost her too."

She nodded but didn't answer. Then again, she didn't need to.

"Thank you for taking me in," I said softly. "I don't think I ever thanked you for that."

Her eyes widened, and she looked taken aback. "We never expected your thanks, Maddie. *Of course* we took you in. We loved you. *Love* you. If anything, you did me a favor, giving me something to focus on other than Andrea's—"

I nodded. She didn't need to finish the sentence. But since we'd broached the subject, I decided to ask her another question I hadn't dared to ask for years. "I know they never found out who killed her, but do you know if they had any leads?"

"No, but they rarely told me anything. They said it was still an active investigation and the information wasn't available."

"I thought detectives usually kept the family informed about the case." Of course, Detective Bergan had never kept *me* informed. He'd always told me I was a minor and needed to talk to my aunt or uncle. I'd taken him at his word, waiting until I was eighteen to call him again, at which point he'd ignored my attempts to reach out.

"Maybe in other places, but not here."

Or at least not with Detective Bergan.

"What *do* you know about the investigation?"

"Honestly? Not much. Albert, as much as he loved me, thought he could protect me from the big bad world. He told me he'd prefer to listen to the ugly truth first, then retell it to me in a more palatable way. The thing is, there just wasn't much to hear if you scraped the ugly truth away. She was raped and murdered. You can't get much uglier than that."

"She was strangled. That's what the papers said."

Releasing a bitter laugh, my aunt said, "Albert hinted there was so much more to it than what the papers said."

"She didn't die from strangling?"

"I think she ultimately did, but that wasn't her only injury."

I sat back in my seat, struck with the horror that she'd likely suffered. I'd always hoped it had been quick, but from what Aunt Deidre was saying...

Why hadn't I known? It wasn't unusual for the police to keep details from the public, but this was personal. If they'd held back to protect me, it hadn't worked. The not knowing hadn't stopped my mind from filling in details, usually late at night when I lay awake in the dark.

"I'm sorry," my aunt said, then sighed. "We shouldn't be discussing such morbid things. Your mother is gone and buried. We need to leave it all in the past where it belongs."

So why did it feel like the past kept rising up to haunt me?

"Good morning," Linda called out as I heard the front door open.

"Good morning," I called back, keeping my focus on my aunt's face. "Are you sure you're okay?" I asked, barely above a whisper.

"I'm fine," she said with a soft smile. "You head on off to work."

Linda walked into the kitchen, shock covering her face when she saw Aunt Deidre in her robe. "Is everything okay?"

Aunt Deidre lifted her chin, steely-eyed. "Just fine. Maddie was getting ready to head off to work. Isn't that right, Maddie?"

I hesitated, keeping my gaze on my aunt's face, but she continued to look at her home health aide.

"That's right," I finally said as I got up from the table. "I'll get out of you ladies' hair." Then I picked up my to-go mug, grabbed my coat and purse, and headed out the front door.

Margarete was in her yard, bent over as she picked up her newspaper, and I realized I hadn't made any arrangements yet for someone to sit with Aunt Deidre on Friday night.

"Good morning, Margarete," I said, walking over to the shrubs that separated the two properties, although there was a gap close to the house that they used to travel back and forth to each other's properties. "I'm sorry I'm still using your car. I plan to call today and ask the police if they're done with mine yet."

She straightened and turned to face me. "Don't you be worryin' about getting that car back to me. Pincher's not driving it, and I have my own. Truth be told, I should sell it and stop paying insurance and taxes on it."

"Well, I definitely want you to know how much I appreciate your generosity, and I don't want you to think I'm taking advantage of you." I grimaced. "Especially after I ask you whether you're free tomorrow night."

She let out a hearty laugh. "I never think you're taking advantage. But I *do* have plans tomorrow evening. I'm having dinner with Brick and his family. Do you need help with Deidre?"

Well, crap. I should have done a better job of thinking this through. "Yeah, but I'll figure out something else."

"If you get in a pinch—"

"Don't you worry about it, Margarete," I said fondly. "I have other options."

She looked intrigued by my statement, like she was wondering what those other options might be, and in fairness, I was wondering myself. But then those women at the meeting last night came to mind. Would Aunt Deidre mind them dropping by in the evening for a social call? Or would she recognize it for what it was? Glorified babysitting. I knew it was insulting and humiliating for her, yet there was no way around it other than me staying with her 24/7 (not possible) or putting her in a residential care center. Also not an option at this point. I'd figure it out as the day went on.

"Say," I grimaced, hating to ask, "do you mind if I use your car for an Uber ride I have prescheduled today?" I held up my hand. "It's just one run this morning."

She made a pensive face, then shrugged. "I guess it's all right."

"I promise to be very careful with it."

Her face softened. "Of course you will, Maddie. You're always careful."

I wasn't sure how careful it was to track down a man who claimed to have a murderer after him, but I didn't feel the need to volunteer that information.

I got in the Volvo and headed to the gas station to fill up the tank. Then I opened my Uber app, entered the information for Margarete's car and went online to make sure the Uber rider hadn't cancelled. I couldn't help wondering if *I* should cancel. What if she freaked out about being driven by the Butcheress of Cockamamie?

There weren't a lot of people who used Uber in Cockamamie, and sometimes I had to wait an hour or more before a ride came through, but there also weren't many drivers, so if I cancelled I might be leaving Eleanor B. high and dry.

I decided to give it a try.

Eleanor B. was a sweet elderly woman, who'd been waiting for me outside of her house in a bright purple coat. She didn't drive anymore, so her son usually took her to her doctor appointments, but she'd discovered that driving apps could help when he couldn't. She was very chatty and filled up the time. Thankfully, she didn't seem to know about my notoriety. At least it gave me a ten-minute break from dwelling on my own issues. After I dropped her off at the clinic near the edge of downtown, she asked if I could pick her up in an hour. I hesitated, but she told me I was the first driver she'd felt truly comfortable with, so I assured her that I planned to be in the area and would be watching for her notification.

We'd passed a group of homeless men on the corner of Cherry and Vine, so I returned to that area and parked by Déjà Brew, which was nearby, before going to meet them. I decided to head to the coffee shop.

Chrissy's eyes widened when she saw me in line, several people back, but she kept on making drinks while Cynthia, the other part-time daytime employee, manned the cash register. I could hear her using some hokey lines on the customers.

"Ho ho ho! You want a cup of joe?" she asked the man in front of me.

Chrissy caught my eye and made a gagging motion.

When I reached the counter, Cynthia greeted me with a grin. "Just couldn't stay away, could ya?"

I laughed. "Something like that. I need a carafe of coffee and several cups. Say… ten?" I eyed the bakery case, then glanced up at the pass-through window to the back. "Do we have any day-old pastries back there?"

"Whatcha need 'em for?" Petra asked, her head popping up in the window.

"It's chilly today, so I'm taking coffee to the group of homeless men down the street. I thought I'd bring them breakfast too."

Petra beamed. "You come on back and take what you want. And don't charge her for the coffee, Cynthia. We're calling this community outreach."

"If I tell you I'm giving my latte to a homeless person, will you give it to me for free?" the man behind me asked.

Chrissy laughed, then stopped abruptly, leveling her gaze on him. "No."

He shrank back a half step.

"I'll brew a fresh pot for you while you get the pastries," Cynthia said, then reached for the coffee filters.

I headed in back and grabbed a box, and began to fill it with croissants, muffins, and a few bagels.

"What brought on this spurt of altruism?" Petra asked while she fried an egg for a breakfast sandwich.

I cringed, feeling guilty that I hadn't done this sooner and without an ulterior motive. "Honestly, I'm hoping to find the homeless man I saw outside the butcher shop when I dropped off Martin Schroeder."

She gave me a puzzled look.

"I just want to make sure he's okay." Then I added, "He refused to go to the homeless shelter when I offered to take him, and well, it's cold outside and I can't imagine spending the night outside in this weather, so I figured I'd bring him coffee. And his friends might be cold too, so I'm bringing them coffee, because it wouldn't be right to just give some to him."

"You have a soft heart, Maddie Baker. Don't let anyone take that from you," Petra said with a warm smile, then nodded to the box I'd been filling. "Maybe we should make this a regular thing. Giving coffee and pastries to the homeless."

I frowned. "Some people equate them to pigeons. A nuisance."

She held up a hand in a no-nonsense manner, her expression turning steely. "Well, people who think that are terrible human beings, now aren't they?"

My heart swelled. "Thanks, Petra."

She nodded again, and I went up front to check on the pot of coffee. While I waited, I helped fill a few orders, figuring it would pay for the coffee and cups I'd be taking.

A young woman stood at the counter, staring at me in wonder. "It really *is* you."

I gave her a confused look. "Excuse me?"

"You're the woman who took down that guy."

"What?" Oh, God. She thought I was the Butcheress of Cockamamie. "I didn't kill Mr. Schroeder. I merely dropped him off at his Uber destination."

Her eyes widened. "Oh my God! You're *that* woman too? Wow." Shaking her head, she said, "No, not that. I was talking about you kicking that Officer Langmore's ass."

The cold realization of what she was talking about hit me like a Mack truck.

Oh crap. Did someone take a video of that? Uh, yeah. *Many* women had taken videos last night. Shoot, I'd *told* them to.

I plastered on a smile. "What can we get you today?"

Placing both hands on the counter, she leaned forward, eagerness in her eyes. "Where did you learn to do that?"

"Um, a self-defense class."

"Here in Cockamamie?"

"No, in Knoxville."

Her face fell. "Oh." Then she brightened again. "Do *you* teach classes?"

"Me?" I asked with a laugh. "No."

"That's too bad." She took her order and walked away, looking disappointed.

"You need to play that shit up," Chrissy said over her shoulder to me. "This could be lucrative for us."

Sometimes Chrissy seemed far too interested in the success of the coffee shop for someone who was just an employee.

"Do you even know what she's talking about?" I asked.

"Hell, yeah," she said with a grin. "Good thing I've never pissed you off."

I groaned, shaking my head.

"Seriously, girl. Maybe we should offer self-defense classes."

"Here at the coffee shop?" I asked doubtfully.

"Sure, why not? More of that community outreach stuff Petra's always talking about."

I put a hand on my hip as I gave her the side-eye. "So what's in it for you?"

She grinned. "I'll take a cut for helping set it up, of course."

"So we'll charge for them?"

"Hell, yeah," she snorted. "We don't work for free."

The pot finished brewing, so I filled my cardboard carafe with coffee, then grabbed cups, stir sticks, sugar, and creamer, placing them into a bag. Then I left in a hurry before Chrissy tried to get me to demonstrate flipping someone over my back.

Juggling the bag, the box, and the carafe, I headed down the street to the corner next to the trophy shop where I'd seen the group of homeless men earlier.

There were five of them, and they looked nervous as I approached. I wasn't surprised Ernie wasn't with them. He'd made it very clear he was hiding from something, and this was a recon mission.

"Hi," I said cheerfully, "I'm Maddie, and I brought y'all some coffee and pastries."

"Why?" said one of the younger men. He was rough-looking with a dirty face and scraggly beard. He looked like he was in his thirties.

One of the older guys elbowed him in the side. "Don't be rude, Roscoe." Then he turned to face me. "Why, that's right kindly of you, Maddie. We sure do appreciate it." He had a long white beard and bushy white eyebrows and hair to match, making him look remarkably like Santa Claus, only he didn't have a big belly. "I'm Hermie."

"Hi, Hermie," I said. "Nice to meet you."

Two of the other men looked eager to see what I'd brought them, but a middle-aged man scowled, eyeing me with as much distrust as Roscoe.

I awkwardly opened the lid to the pastry box. "Help yourselves, gentlemen."

Hermie took the box and passed it around while I got a cup out of the bag. "Coffee? I have cream and sugar too."

I filled up cups and handed them around, and even Roscoe and his skeptical friend took one. Some of the men doctored their coffee, but a few took it black.

As I handed out the last cup, I said, "I don't see Mr. Ernie here."

"You know Ernie?" Hermie asked.

"Yeah. I knew him from school, and then I saw him the other night. He was telling me how bad the Methodist shelter is, so I thought I'd bring y'all some breakfast. But I don't see him."

"I ain't seen Ernie since Monday afternoon," one of the other men said, an older man with red hair. "He said he was goin' down to the Bottoms."

"That's where I saw him," I said. "I offered him a ride, but he said he was supposed to be there. Do you know if he was working for anybody?"

The redheaded guy laughed. "Ernie have a job? Nah, he don't work for nobody anymore, and he likes it that way."

"Why doesn't he have a home?" I asked, realizing I was getting into nosy/rude territory, but I needed to find him. "Doesn't he get a pension or social security?"

"Lost all his money," Hermie said. "On his son. All that money spent on rehab and programs, and then his son OD'd and died. It was all for nothing."

My stomach sank. "Oh no. I'm so sorry."

He let out a sigh. "Anyways, Ernie lost his house and his car, and now he just lives on the streets."

"How long has he been out here?" I asked.

"Couple of years," the redheaded guy said.

"So he probably hates drugs," I said, more to myself than to them.

Hermie nodded. "That's an understatement."

Had he been watching the butcher shop, thinking a drug deal was about to go down?

"Do you know where else he might be?" I asked.

"Sometimes he likes to hang out at the park by the river," the red-haired guy said.

"And sometimes he hitches a ride out to Cock on the Walk," Roscoe said.

Cock on the Walk was a bar at the edge of town. While I'd driven past it, I'd never gone inside. It seemed unlikely Ernie would go there since he didn't have a car and there were plenty of closer places.

I put a hand on my hip and narrowed my gaze. "Are you bullshitting me, Roscoe?"

Several of the men laughed. "She's got your number," one of them said, jabbing him in the side.

He shrugged. "Hey, she brought good coffee, not some gas station bullshit." He turned serious. "If he's hidin', that's where he'll probably be."

"You can't go out there," the redheaded guy said, wide-eyed.

Even Hermie agreed it was too dangerous. But none of them said he wasn't out there.

Why did Roscoe think Ernie was hiding? "Has anyone else asked about him?"

"Ernie?" Hermie asked with a laugh. "No one pays him any mind, let alone asks about him."

I turned my attention to Roscoe. "How does he get out there? It's at least five miles."

"Guess it's one of those mysteries of life," Roscoe said with a grin that didn't quite reach his eyes.

I wasn't sure if he was lying to me or not, but if I didn't find Ernie at the park, I'd be going to Cock on the Walk when they opened. Even if the smug look in Roscoe's eyes suggested it wasn't such a good idea.

Chapter Twenty-One

Noah

I was in a shit mood.

I'd spent half the night thinking about Maddie Baker. Who had she been talking to in the parking lot? Was she in danger? Should I have stuck around to make sure she was okay?

But I also thought about how much I'd liked sitting in her kitchen last night, and what it had felt like to have her pinned beneath me, her legs wrapped around me.

By six, I'd given up and left for work, my aching arms and back a reminder of my whupping...and of what I couldn't have. Because she was right. She deserved better than what I could give her.

I took some ibuprofen for the pain and decided I'd call the city offices when they opened to request a copy of the surveillance video of the parking lot last night. Maybe it would help me figure out who she'd been talking to and what had really happened.

I left my house at seven thirty, on my way to Martin Schroeder's neighborhood to question his neighbors again, when my phone rang with a number I recognized—my sister. I nearly let it go to voicemail, but I'd only be putting off the inevitable.

"Hey, Leah," I answered with my car's Bluetooth.

"Don't *hey Leah* me," was her irritated response.

"What did I do this time?" I grunted as I turned a corner.

"As though you don't know. Why aren't you coming home for Mom and Dad's anniversary party next weekend?'

"I'm on call that weekend."

"So get it changed."

"Can't. The other detective is going on vacation. Booked his flight and everything. Nonrefundable tickets," I lied, but only partially. Max Holmes, the other non-narc detective employed by the Cockamamie PD was on vacation now.

She was silent for a moment. "Dad's promised to behave."

I barked out a laugh. "What did you have to do to get him to promise *that*?"

"It's not important. What's important is that you're here."

"Why? Because it will look bad to their friends if I'm not?"

Once again, she went quiet. Leah had never been a good liar. Too many tells. "Mom misses you."

"Now *that* I believe."

"She says she'll never get to see your babies."

I laughed again. "I don't have any babies and never plan to. So she's got nothing to worry about on that front."

"Come on, Noah. Surely you can put your feud with Dad away for one weekend for Mom's sake."

"Good try, Leah, but it's not happening. Even if I wanted it to. Gotta work."

"I can't believe you," she accused. "You're not the only one who got hurt by what went down, you know. Mom was beside herself with worry when you were unconscious for three days in the ICU. She was there for you, Noah. And so was I. So why are you punishing *us*?"

She was right. Mom and Leah had been devastated, but my father had blamed me, telling me a good cop would have seen the signs that Caleb was a bad seed. As though that boy had been a crop with a locust infestation. He'd recently retired a lieutenant from the Memphis police, only a few years ago, and now taught criminal justice courses at a community college, which gave him even more time to be judgmental of me and my choices.

"I'm sorry," I said, softening my tone. "I love you both, and I'm more grateful than you know that you were there for me. But I can't come home right now, even if Max wasn't going to California."

"Mom hates this," she said, her voice breaking.

"But not enough to do something about it."

We were silent for a few moments, because we both knew it was true. She could tell him to back off with his criticism and expectations, but she didn't, which was the same as condoning it. Because at the heart of it, she thought he was right about Caleb. That I never should have tried to help him and I should have seen the signs.

The kicker was I couldn't help wondering if it were true.

"Hey, Leah," I said, my emotions getting the better of me. "I'm working a big case and I'm pulling up to where I need to be."

"It's not dangerous, is it?"

I released a short laugh. "It's Cockamamie, Tennessee. How dangerous could it be?"

"Just be careful, okay, Noah? Mom couldn't handle it if you got hurt again."

"Don't worry," I said bitterly. "I wouldn't dream of giving Dad another chance to tell me I told you so." Things had gotten too maudlin, so I was quick to add, "I sent them a gift. It should be arriving tomorrow."

"If you change your mind—"

"I won't."

"Well, in case you do, you can stay with me, okay? Your niece and nephew would love to see you. They miss you too."

I drew in a breath, a wave of homesickness washing over me. I'd given up a lot when I left, but regularly seeing Macy and Mason had been one of the hardest sacrifices. "I sent them a gift too. Don't hate me when they open it."

"Oh my God, Noah," she groaned. "You got them those kazoos, didn't you?"

I grinned, feeling a momentary reprieve from the heaviness that hung over me. "I'd hate to ruin the surprise. But there might be something in there for you."

"Is it earplugs?"

Laughing, I said, "I love you, Leah. Kiss your gremlins for me. And Mom too."

"But not Dad?"

"You can kick him in the—"

"Okay," she said with a laugh. "Got it. Be safe, Noah."

"Always."

Only I hadn't always been safe. But she didn't call me on it as we hung up.

I pulled in front of Schroeder's house and took a moment to settle my emotions. Part of me thought I should give all this up and get a job as a high school teacher back in Memphis, or something slightly less insane than hunting down killers.

Maybe I'd consider it after I solved this case.

* * *

Canvassing the neighborhood was a bust. The only new piece of information came from a neighbor who'd suggested the Schroeder's next-door neighbor on the north side might have killed him over mole poison Schroeder had put out, which had gotten the neighbor's dog sick. Schroeder—big surprise—had refused to pay the vet bills. But it seemed highly unlikely since the neighbor was in his sixties and used a four-legged cane after his recent hip replacement.

We'd relinquished control of Schroeder's house at about six last night, so the police guard and crime scene tape had been removed. But while we no longer had official custody of it, I had a key to the front door and permission from Schroeder's son to enter anytime I wanted. I wasn't sure what I thought I'd find since our previous search had been thorough, but if nothing else, maybe it would kick something loose in my brain. Maybe I'd discover something about his mystery woman.

Using the key, I opened the front door and let myself in, then stopped dead in my tracks. The living room furniture had been cut to shreds, the insides spread throughout the room.

What the actual fuck?

I instantly called Lance and barely gave him a chance to answer before I barked, "Get to Schroeder's house."

"Well, good morning to you too," he said with a chuckle. "Why are we searching Schroeder's house again? Come up with something new?"

"Yeah. Someone's ransacked his house."

"Shit," he said, all humor leaking out of his voice. "I'll be right there."

I was standing outside when he showed up five minutes later, looking fresh in his pressed uniform. I suspected I looked like I'd rolled out of bed in my suit and got right to work. Which was basically what had happened.

"How did you discover this? A neighbor call it in?" he asked as he walked over to me.

"I just canvassed the neighbors myself but didn't get anything new, so I decided to go inside the house with the key Darren gave us and see if anything jumped out at me."

"Good call." Then he gave me a sidelong glance. "I've been canvassing too—the blocks around Walnut, looking for surveillance footage."

"The uniforms were supposed to have already done that."

His gaze swept over the house. "They did, and none of the businesses claimed to have anything. But they didn't check two blocks away."

"And?" I prompted.

He turned to me and grinned. "Bingo. Two businesses have cameras pointed toward the street. They said they'd email me files this morning."

I made a face. "Two blocks away might not catch shit."

"But it might," he said, pulling on a pair of gloves. "In the meantime, I guess we'll check out Schroeder's house again, huh? Any sign of forced entry?"

I tugged on a pair of gloves too as we walked up to the front door together. "I saw the furniture ripped to shreds, called you, and headed back out to wait. Thought we should walk-through together before I report it to the sergeant and get the crime lab out here."

I opened the front door and let him inside.

"Wow," he said, walking in and stepping to the side so I could stand next to him and survey the damage. "They did a number on this place, didn't they?"

"Yep."

It looked like a tornado had ripped through it. Every drawer had been pulled out of the cabinets, the contents strewn on the kitchen counters, table, and floor. The upholstered furniture had been slashed, polyester stuffing spread all over the carpet. We walked around a bit and quickly determined the damage extended throughout the whole house. The drawers in the bedrooms had been emptied as well, the mattresses cut and shredded. The back door had been forced open. I didn't see any footprints on the ground, but I'd let the crime lab deal with that.

"They were obviously looking for something," Lance said. "Strange that the neighbors didn't see anything."

"The neighbors are worthless," I grunted. "I just questioned half the block, and every single person I spoke with claimed to have noticed nothing out of the ordinary."

"They called off the guard around six last night?"

"Yeah, which means it happened between 6:01 and 7:50 this morning."

He cast a glance at me. "Got here that early?"

"I would have gotten here earlier if I hadn't worried about waking the neighbors by knocking on their doors. I figured most of them are elderly and would be up by eight."

"Which means many of them would have gone to bed early last night."

"I suspect it must have happened at eleven or later, or someone would have noticed." I pointed to the house across the street. "Mrs. Milton over there knows the mailman comes everyday around 2:20, but yesterday the mail*woman* showed up at three. She also told me the paper boy comes at six. And that the Winchesters two houses down—" I pointed in that direction, "—have a couple over every Tuesday night at seven, but the couple didn't show up for their usual visit two weeks ago."

I turned toward Lance. "She would have seen a car or truck if it showed up before eleven." Then a thought hit me. "Unless the vehicle didn't park in front of the house."

His brow rose. "You mean they might have parked around the block?"

"Less suspicious that way. Sneak along the houses, then enter through back."

"We need to go back to the neighbors and ask if their homes have surveillance."

"The Murrays, Loflands, and Alegars have video doorbells, but they might not know how to access them," I said.

"I'll check, and if they struggle with the access, maybe I can help them out," Lance said with a grin. "Ready to call the crime scene team?"

"Yeah," I said, trying to figure out what the intruder had been looking for.

Lance shuffled his feet, then asked, "You're not going to try to pin this on Maddie Baker, are you?"

I looked up at him in surprise. "She has an alibi last night for up until around ten."

A grin tugged at his lips. "Do I want to know how you know that?"

I made a face. "She was at the Women's Club meeting last night."

"No kidding? You saw her?"

"It was hard for me to miss her." I gestured for him to head to the front door. "Start talking to neighbors. I'll call the crime lab."

He looked like he wanted to ask more questions, but he must've thought better of it, because he checked his notes and headed to the Murray residence.

I called Schroder's son to make sure he and his family hadn't come in and trashed the house after it had been released.

"Hell, no," he said with a grunt. "We were hoping to sell his crap in a yard sale. Now we're getting nothing."

"We have to process the scene all over again," I said. "It might be tied up longer this time. There's more to sort through."

"Do what you want with it," he said. "If there's nothing worth selling, might as well set the whole thing on fire."

A half hour later, I was sitting in my car in front of Schroeder's house, filling out the form for a new search warrant for the house on my laptop. The passenger door opened and Lance got in, carrying his own computer.

"Find something?" I asked.

"Did I ever." He opened his laptop, revealing a video window in the center of the screen, and pressed play. I leaned in closer to get a better look. The video was dark—obviously taken at night. But the camera was pointed to the left of Schroeder's house. The street was empty, but then a dark four-door sedan appeared on the screen, coming from the right and crossing in front of the house, its brake lights blinking on as it passed Schroeder's house. He stopped the video.

"What time was that?"

"The time stamp is 1:12. The car comes back around ten minutes later." He pressed play and the car appeared again, this time coming to a stop in the middle of the street in front of Schroeder's house for several seconds before moving on.

I could see a blurred movement next to the car. "Stop the tape," I said. "Back it up five seconds and watch the far side of the car."

He did as I said and, sure enough, a blurry figure appeared and then darted to the left, off-screen.

"Someone got out of the car," I said.

"But the interior light didn't come on."

"They purposely turned it off. Does the car come back?"

"Yeah, about a half hour later." He pressed play again, and the car pulled up in front of the house. This time it was more apparent a person was getting into the car.

"The Alegars are on the opposite side of the street. Did you get video from them?"

"Not yet. They said they need their son to come pull it. He supposedly has the login information."

I nodded. "What about the Loflands?"

"I have theirs too. It shows the car, but their cameras didn't capture the car stopping."

"Let's have a look."

He pulled up the video. There was a streetlight at the edge of their property, so we got a better view of the car when it drove past.

"Looks like a Kia Optima," Lance said, then added, "My sister has one."

"The paint is dark. Black or dark blue?" I asked.

"Kia didn't have a dark blue when my sister got her car a few years ago."

I turned to him, impressed. "So we're probably looking at a black car, then?"

"Yeah. Maybe we can find some footage at the end of the street that has the license plate. This street dead-ends onto Wolverton. I'll check with the homeowners over there." He didn't wait for me to respond, just got out, tucked his laptop into his bag, and headed down the street.

By the time I finished filling out the warrant and turned it in, a patrol officer had arrived to help secure the scene. I got him set up, then called the rec center and asked them to send me the surveillance tape from the exterior cameras from the night before. I'd just hung up when Lance came back, looking pleased with himself.

"You got something?"

"A partial license plate and a partial view of the driver."

"No shit," I marveled, walking over to my car. "Let me see."

He set the laptop on the hood of my car, and I leaned in close to help eliminate the glare on the screen. Sure enough, I could make out a couple of numbers and a letter on the license plate. And the driver was partially in view, or at least we got a good look at his bushy beard.

"This is great," I said, excited we finally had something substantial to work with. "You start a search on the license plate." It made me feel slightly better about what I was about to say next. "One more thing. We should probably bring Madelyn Baker back in for questioning."

I'd wanted to let it go, but the only reason I could come up with for doing so was because I liked her. Which was exactly why I'd never questioned Caleb, even though my partner suggested I should. I couldn't let my personal feelings interfere with my investigation. Never again.

His eyes widened. "I know this time stamp is well outside her alibi with you last night, but you can't seriously think she was in that car."

I hadn't even considered that, but he was right. It seemed highly unlikely. Still, I couldn't ignore the other things I'd noticed last night. "No, but I saw her after the meeting. She was talking to someone in the parking lot. Someone who looked like they were trying to conceal their identity with a hoodie. And that someone took off as soon as they saw me."

"Could have been anyone," he said with a frown.

"Could have been someone connected to this mess, possibly Ernie Foust," I said, not any happier about it than he was. "There's one more thing: instead of giving my report, I demonstrated some self-defense moves, but stupid me didn't consider that the genteel women of Cockamamie would all be wearing dresses to their meeting. Madelyn Baker was the only one wearing jeans. So she was the volunteer I used for my demonstration."

He continued to watch me without offering a word, and I suddenly felt clammy.

"She knew how to protect herself. More than the average citizen."

His eyes lit up with amusement. "I heard she kicked your ass."

My eyes narrowed. "You knew?"

"My cousin called me after I talked to the neighbors at the end of the street." Sobering, he added, "You're thinking that if she could kick your ass, then she could easily take down Schroeder."

"She didn't kick my ass."

His grin returned. "That's not what the video showed."

I groaned. "There's video?"

"Yep. Several of them, from multiple angles. All showing her kicking your ass." Turning more serious, he added, "What possible motive could she have had? Because I'm not buying that she just snapped over a tip, or lack thereof."

"I'm not saying she did it. But we have to follow up on what I saw," I snapped. If I failed to investigate all leads, including how Maddie knew self-defense, the murderer's defense attorney could attempt to get the case thrown out. All it took was one qualm to give a jury reasonable doubt.

There was a reason I had high close rates. It was because I dotted every *i* and crossed every *t*. Maddie just seemed to keep getting caught up in this mess.

"You're not trying to tie this to her mother's murder, are you?"

I turned to face him. "What the hell are you talking about?"

"I spoke to a few of the teachers Schroeder worked with. Everyone couldn't stand the man, but one woman mentioned that he and Andrea Baker had a disagreement about a year before she was murdered."

I took a second to let his words sink in. "*What?* Did we ever get her file?"

"No, not yet, unfortunately."

Had Martin Schroeder been a suspect in Andrea Baker's murder? Did Maddie know that?

Fuck!

"What's taking you so damn long to get it?" I growled.

He hesitated, then sucked in a deep breath before he said, "They can't find it."

"What do you mean they can't find it?" I said, my irritation growing. "Was it listed as a cold case?"

"No. It was still considered an active investigation, but it never got entered into the computer system."

"Then how the fuck could it be considered active?" I demanded, becoming livid. "Someone needs to be looking into it for it to be considered active. You're telling me there was just a paper file floating around, and it's gone?"

He held up his hands. "Hey, don't shoot the messenger. I only know what I've been told."

"Who was the investigator?"

He made a face. "Howard Bergan."

"The same Howard Bergan who has dementia but continued to work until they found him stumbling around naked in the Piggly Wiggly six months ago?"

The man I'd replaced.

"That would be him."

I released a string of curse words that was excessive, even for me, before I snarled, "Okay, so an interview with him would be unreliable. So who else worked the case?"

"Honestly, I don't know if anyone else stepped in after the initial investigation," he said. "Howard was pretty territorial. I didn't even know the investigation was still considered open until I started looking for the file."

"Then we'll have to take our chances speaking to Bergan."

"Yeah, good luck with that. From what I hear, he's gone downhill since they put him in St. Vincent's Village."

"We're gonna talk to him anyway." I cursed another blue streak. This whole damn town was ass-backward. What the hell was I doing here?

Straightening it up. But some days I got tired of slogging uphill. Moving back to Memphis was looking better and better.

"We've got to figure out our priorities," I said. "Obviously, finding who trashed Schroeder's house is at the top of the list. You look into the license plate. We can't do anything else in the house until we get the new warrant signed, so I'll head to downtown Cockamamie and ask around about the homeless guy."

The more I thought about it, the more likely it seemed that Ernie Foust was who Maddie spoke to in the parking lot. She'd definitely talked to him outside of the butcher shop.

Lance looked surprised. "The uniformed officers already asked around. No one knew anything about him or where he is."

"Maybe they didn't know how to ask," I said.

"Or he might be dead," Lance said grimly.

"True," I conceded. Which meant Maddie could be in real danger. Rubbing the bridge of my nose, I sighed. "At some point, we'll also need to question Maddie again."

"I still think it's a waste of time," he said. "Especially with this new lead."

"You have to look at all the possibilities, Lance. That's the way you avoid convicting the wrong person. Or giving the defense a reason to throw out the case."

He met my gaze, looking sullen. "If bringing her in will help clear her name, I'm all for it."

"Then we're on the same page," I said. "After you look up the license plate, you can drop by Déjà Brew and tell her we need to talk to her again." Then I added, "Set it up for later this afternoon, for after she gets off work. No need to make it inconvenient for her."

"Chickenshit," Lance grumbled.

Little did he know.

Chapter Twenty-Two

Maddie

By the time I got back to Margarete's car, it had been nearly an hour since I'd dropped off Eleanor at the clinic. I got in and switched on my Uber app, letting the car warm up. Thankfully I didn't have to turn down any ride requests while I waited the several minutes for Eleanor's request to come through. I accepted and headed that way.

Eleanor was standing outside on the curb, her bright purple coat a cheery contrast to the gray building behind her.

I parked and got out to help her in the back. "Hello, Miss Eleanor. Did everything go okay?"

"My doctor put me on a new medicine for my arthritis," she said as she got into the back. "I hope it's not too expensive."

"Surely your insurance will cover it."

"They didn't cover the last one."

I shut her door and got into the driver's seat, turning around to face her. "You know, there are resources to help with medication. Did your doctor or pharmacist tell you about them?"

"No..."

I frowned, hating that she had to worry about affording something she needed. "Would you like some coffee, Miss Eleanor? I have a carafe here with cream and sugar."

"Well, aren't you a delight?" she said, her voice cracking. "I'd love some."

I poured some into a cup, then added her cream and sugar and topped it with a lid before handing it back to her, coming to a decision. "Do you need to go to the pharmacy?" I asked. "You set your house as your destination."

"I do, but I only have so much money for Uber rides," she said with a grimace. "Not that I don't like riding with you, Maddie. But I can't afford to make two trips, so I'll have my son pick it up for me when he comes next weekend." She looked like she wanted to say something else but wasn't sure she should. "Not all drivers are as sweet as you."

Had some been unpleasant to her? "I'm so sorry. You can refuse a driver, you know."

She smiled. "I wish I could always get you."

"I only do this on my days off from Déjà Brew," I said apologetically. "But how about I give you my name and phone number, and you call or text me directly instead of using the app?"

"Really?" she asked, her eyes wide with gratitude.

"Really." I cancelled the ride request on my phone. "In fact, we're off the clock. Let's go get your prescription filled."

"Oh, Maddie, I can't let you do that."

"Too late. Already done. Now which pharmacy do you use?"

"Stephenson Pharmacy, on 33rd and Vine." She reached into her purse. "Don't you need to make money? I can pay you."

"Nah," I said, putting the car into drive. "I need to go to the pharmacy anyway," I lied.

I headed in that direction while Eleanor told me about her doctor's visit. The clinic had gotten a new doctor, and she wasn't sure she liked him.

"He seemed to be in such a rush," she said. "Everyone is in such a rush nowadays."

"That's true," I admitted.

"You know, when one of my friends was killed, I learned how to live in the moment. It was such a devastating loss." She tilted her head and looked at me. "You may have had her as a teacher. How old are you, dear?"

The blood rushed from my head, and I gripped the steering wheel to ground myself. "Are you talking about Andrea Baker?"

"Yes! So you *did* have her?"

I could tell her I was Andrea's daughter, but things might get awkward. She might also clam up, and I suddenly wanted her to talk. My conversation with my aunt earlier had fired up my need to talk about my mother. "I did. She was a great teacher."

All true.

"She was one of those really special people," she said. "Her students could come to her with any problem, and she'd always find a way to help them." She smiled at my reflection in the rearview mirror. "Kind of like you're helping me now."

"Oh," I said, waving my hand dismissively. "This is nothing."

"You know, Andrea used to say the same thing." She searched my face. "You kind of remind me of her."

I swallowed. I'd heard I looked like her, but this was the first time anyone had suggested I behaved like her. I had so many conflicting thoughts about my mother, it made my stomach cramp.

"She was a remarkable person," I finally said.

If Eleanor noticed my delayed response, she didn't let on. Instead, she stared out the window, lost in her own thoughts. "She definitely was."

Taking a deep breath, I pushed forward. "I can't believe they never found her killer," I said, keeping my gaze on the road and my tone light.

"I'm not sure how hard that stupid detective looked," she said. "A few of us teachers gave him a list of possible suspects."

I caught a glimpse of her in the mirror, my heart thumping hard in my chest. "Really? Who was on the list?"

"There was a student who was failing in her class, and his father was furious. He was heavily involved in sports, and failing him interfered with that."

"Do you remember who the student was?"

She frowned. "No, but I couldn't really tell you even if I remembered. Student confidentiality, and all."

"Of course," I said, wondering how I could find out. "Who else?"

"Well, the boy, of course. And another teacher. The two of them clashed on more than one occasion."

"Which teacher?" I asked. Then, worried she'd withhold the person's name, I decided to help her out. "Oh my goodness, was it Martin Schroeder? He was a *terrible* teacher and an even worse person."

She frowned again. "It seems wrong to speak ill of the dead."

"So it was him?"

"They were known to clash in a staff meeting or two."

"That hardly makes him a murder suspect," I said, then forced a laugh. "With that criteria, if my old boss was murdered, half the building would have been suspects." That was a lie. Everyone had loved my principal.

"I suppose," she said. "But this seemed different. More personal."

I took a second for my light-headedness to clear. Hadn't the police said the attack had seemed personal?

"Was his name the one y'all gave the police?"

She pursed her lips. "He seemed to really dislike her, and he was *very* upset that she got a grant for the English department while the school district refused to give him more money for the science department. He resented her for it, even though he could have applied for a grant himself and didn't. Still," she said thoughtfully, "I would hate to think he hurt her, but..."

My mouth went dry. "It could have been possible?"

"Maybe," she conceded with a sour look. "But I prefer to think of the good she did, not how she died. She had a daughter. I wonder how she's doing. I lost track."

I worried she was getting closer to putting two and two together, so I asked her about her son and his family, and she bragged about her grandchildren until I pulled into the pharmacy parking lot.

I made sure she could afford her medication before I browsed the store, trying to find something I actually needed. I bought a package of toothbrushes to back up my story that I had planned a trip to the pharmacy too. Then I drove her home.

"You really need to let me pay you, Maddie," she said, reaching into her purse.

"No, that's fine," I said, giving her a warm smile. "You've helped me more than you know." I handed her a business card so she could call me if she needed a ride in the future, knowing full well she'd figure out who I was.

"How in the world did I help *you*?" she asked in surprise as she took the card.

"It was good to talk about my mother. I hadn't talked to anyone who knew her as a teacher in a long time." I was grateful for her memories—and for the information that hadn't been filtered to protect me. I knew people had been careful about what they shared, worried about upsetting me.

She studied me, then looked down at the card. Her gaze jerked up as she gasped. "Maddie. Maddie Baker." Her eyes flew wide with horror. "I never should have said anything. I'm *so* sorry."

Which was exactly why I didn't feel any guilt over the duplicity. Mostly no guilt. I reached into the back seat and patted her leg. "Please, don't be sorry! I'm grateful you shared. And besides, I asked. So thank you for telling me what you know."

Tears filled her eyes. "Your mother was a wonderful woman, Maddie. The world is a little darker without her shining light."

"Thank you." I got out to open the door for her, and she gave me a long hug.

"You know, if you want to talk to someone who knew her as a teacher *and* a friend, you should talk to Dawn Heaton. They were best friends in the school."

I hadn't thought of Mrs. Heaton in years. "Thanks, Miss Eleanor. I will."

When she turned to go inside, I called after her, "Did *Mr. Schroeder* have any friends within the faculty?"

She stared up at me in surprise. "What?"

"It's just that I was the person who dropped Mr. Schroeder off at the butcher shop, only I didn't recognize him. I think the police are having trouble tracking down clues, so I thought I might bring them a list of people they could talk to."

"Martin have friends?" She released a bitter laugh. "Adversaries? Plenty. But no friends that I know of." She paused in thought. "But he *did* eat lunch with the department head enough times that I'd considered them friendly. Adam Brant. He's still teaching there. Close to retirement. I'm not sure if they still were in contact, but you might give his name to the police."

"Thanks, Miss Eleanor. I definitely will." But not until I talked to him first. The last time I checked, school got out at two thirty. I'd go to my two o'clock consultation with Burt, then drop by the school afterward.

Eleanor headed into her house, and I took a deep breath, unsure how I felt about her revelations about my mother and even less sure of what to do about it.

Could Martin Schroeder have killed her? Was he truly capable of killing someone in such a horrific way, only to show up at school the next day as though nothing happened?

Chapter Twenty-Three

Noah

I drove downtown, trying to figure out the best way to introduce myself to the group of homeless men that usually hung out on the corner of Cherry and Vine. In all honesty, I should have made an effort to meet them a month or two ago, before I needed to get something out of them. I was going to be fighting an uphill battle since it sounded like they hadn't had good experiences with Cockamamie's officers.

I parked close to Déjà Brew, feeling a twofold draw to go in. I couldn't lie—my regular coffee now paled in comparison to the Americano Maddie had made me, and the second draw was obvious.

My attraction to her was a problem. Going to her house had only made it stronger.

I ignored the pull and headed down the street toward the group of men lounging outside the trophy shop.

They eyed me with a wary look as I approached.

"We're not causing any trouble, Officer," said a guy with white hair and a beard, holding up a to-go coffee cup.

I wasn't surprised they knew I was a cop despite my lack of a uniform. I'd been told I gave off a cop vibe when I was on duty.

And the badge hanging around my neck was hard to miss. I wasn't trying to hide who I was—they'd never trust me if I wasn't open with them.

I lifted both hands in surrender. "I'm not here to harass you. I just wanted to know if you've seen a man hanging around. Ernie Foust."

A redheaded older man shifted his gaze to the sidewalk, and they all clammed up.

"Do you know him?" I asked, careful to keep my voice friendly.

"Heard of him," said a younger guy with a scraggly beard. He had a shifty look about him and didn't seem as harmless as the others.

"Seen him around lately?"

His gaze narrowed and a sly grin ticked up the corners of his mouth. "He seems to be pretty popular lately."

"Meaning what?"

The white-haired gentleman flung him a dark look, then turned to me. "Ernie's a great guy. Everyone likes 'im."

I studied them closely. They were hiding something. My gaze flicked to the cup in the white-haired guy's hand, and I noticed the logo.

My blood turned icy. "Is that cup from Déjà Brew?"

"We didn't steal it," the redheaded guy said. "She brought it to us."

"Mack!" the white-haired guy snapped.

His eyes widened slightly.

She? *Of course.* Only...why was Maddie actively searching for the other possible witness? Was she just worried about him? Or did they both know something?

"She?" I asked, hoping I was still giving off a friendly vibe. "She brought y'all coffee?"

"So what if she did?" Roscoe challenged. "People can give us food and coffee. It ain't against the law."

"So Maddie brought you food and coffee?" I asked, dropping her name to check their reaction.

"How'd you know it was her?" the redheaded man asked.

"Mack!" White-haired guy snapped again.

"Hey," I said, holding up a hand. "Maddie's not in trouble and neither is Ernie. I just want to ask him some questions about the murder that occurred on Monday night and make sure he's safe. As for Maddie..." I gave them a knowing smile. "I suspect she's worried about him too."

"That's what she said," redheaded guy acknowledged. "We told her to search for him at the park by the river."

White-haired guy looked like he wanted to strangle his buddy.

"Neither of them are in trouble," I assured them again. "Like I said, I just want to ask Ernie some questions." I was about to leave, but it occurred to me that they knew Maddie by name and we'd found a Déjà Brew stir stick at the industrial park space. What if Ernie had been out there with a stir stick she had given him? "Is bringing coffee to y'all a regular thing for her?"

The redheaded guy glanced up at the white-haired guy before he turned back to me. "No. It was the only time." But he looked nervous, like he was trying not to piss off his buddy.

I glanced at Roscoe.

He grinned, but it didn't reach his eyes. "Hey, a pretty little thing like that? How can we not look forward to free coffee from her? I always like me a free taste, if you know what I mean." He winked, then stuck out his tongue and wiggled it.

I resisted the strong urge to drive my fist into his face. I didn't trust this guy and planned to send a uniformed officer to get more information on him after I left. While the other men came across as being down on their luck, Roscoe seemed like trouble. Not to mention he was thinking about Maddie in ways I didn't like. He seemed like the kind of guy who didn't ask for permission.

"My name's Noah Langley," I said, handing the white-haired

guy a card. "I *promise* you that Ernie's not in trouble. If you see him, I'd appreciate it if you'd either let me know or encourage him to reach out to me. He wouldn't have to come to the station. I'd come to him."

He reluctantly took my card. "I'll see what I can do."

"Thank you," I said gratefully. "Now, did you send Maddie anywhere else besides the river park to look for him?"

"Not that I recall," the white-haired guy said.

Roscoe gave me a grin that suggested he had plenty of secrets and one or two of them had to do with Maddie.

Fuck.

I thanked them for their time, then headed to Déjà Brew. She might not have gone searching for him yet. For all I knew, she'd taken them the coffee on her break and planned to go later. I felt an overwhelming urge to check on her, but I told myself I was mostly going in because I wanted another Americano.

I knew I was a liar.

There was only one customer at the counter when I walked in, but a few more were sitting at tables in the dining area. Two women were sitting together, deep in conversation, and a man was working on a laptop, wearing headphones.

A blond middle-aged woman I hadn't seen before was working behind the register, and the goth-looking barista who had told me about the TikTok videos was making drinks. She did a double take when she saw me walk in.

The customer in front of me swiped her credit card, then moved to the end of the counter to wait for her drink.

The cashier gave me a huge grin as I approached. "Hi! Welcome to Déjà *Brew*! I have just what you need, to perk up *you*."

The goth barista rolled her eyes at the rhyme.

"So," the blond woman asked. "What can we get you?"

"I'd like an Americano."

"Sure thing!" she said, her smile growing even bigger. I wondered if she'd had too much caffeine.

I handed her my debit card and she swiped it before handing it back.

"You're a handsome thing," she said, tilting her head to the side. "I haven't seen you around. New to town or just to Déjà Brew?"

"Fairly new to both," I said, glancing behind her as I looked for Maddie.

"Cool it, Cynthia," the barista said. "He's a cop."

Cynthia took a step back, and her smile fell. Had she had a bad experience with a cop or previous run-ins with the law? Hard to tell in Cockamamie.

"Go take your break, Cyn," the barista said. "I've got this covered."

Cynthia practically shoved my receipt at me and bolted into the back.

I tucked my card and receipt into my wallet and moved down the line so I was directly across from the barista.

"Maddie's not here, so you came in for nothing." Her dark eyes had narrowed into a glare.

"So it's Maddie's day off?" I said, glancing in the back again.

"Looks like Cockamamie PD's got their top man on the job," she smirked.

I'd walked into that one.

"She didn't kill that man," she sneered as she handed a drink to the waiting customer. Once the woman was almost to the door, the barista turned to me again, lowering her voice. "If you knew anything about her, you'd know she's incapable of hurting a spider, let alone a grown man. Even if he was a pervert."

I cocked my head. "What do you mean he was a pervert?"

"You seriously don't know?" she asked, shaking her head in disgust. "Some cop you are."

"Yeah, I suck," I said, inching closer to her. "Schroeder was a pervert?"

She pushed out a sigh as she started to grind the beans for my drink. When she finished, she darted me a glance, and seeing that I was still giving her an expectant look, she said, "He liked 'em young. It worked out great since he was a high school teacher." She shrugged, trying to play nonchalant, but I caught the pain in her eyes. "All that power? You should ask the school why he lost his job."

"His daughter-in-law said he retired."

"Yeah," she said with a snort. "Don't they all?"

Shit.

She finished up my drink as I considered the implications. How long had he been molesting students? Did he have a current victim? Is that why he'd had a condom in his pocket? But he wasn't teaching anymore, so where had he been finding his victims? Was he tutoring? And could this be where all his money had gone? What if one of his victims had blackmailed him?

I had *way* more questions than answers.

"Do you know any of his victims?" I asked.

She gave me a hard stare. "You expect me to do all the work for you?"

"So point me in the right direction."

She held my gaze, and suddenly I knew.

Fuck. She had been one of them.

I gave a slight nod in acknowledgement.

"I ain't talkin' to *you* about it," she said. "I already tried that once, but just like I expected, you police don't give a shit."

I leaned closer and lowered my voice. "You reported it." It wasn't a question.

"Little good it did. They called it a 'he said, she said' situation, and I was a girl from the wrong side of the tracks who couldn't be trusted."

No wonder she seemed to hate my guts. I was guilty by association.

"I'm sorry," I said, genuinely meaning it.

"Yeah, well..." she said, staring down at my drink as she made it. "Water under the bridge."

Only I strongly suspected it wasn't.

Dammit. As soon as I left here, I was going back to the station and pulling up anything I could find on Schroeder. Why hadn't her report come up before now? I'd trusted the sergeant to pull any priors, but I hadn't followed up, presuming he'd let me know if he found something.

Fuck.

How many more victims were there?

Suddenly, I remembered Maddie talking about being messed up. She'd said it wasn't just because of her mother's death and her ex.

I swallowed hard. Jesus.

"Did he...with Maddie...?" I let the question hang unfinished.

"Are you asking if he molested Maddie? Hell if I know. It's not like we have a club and compare notes on his techniques."

"I have one more question, and then I promise to leave you alone," I said apologetically. "Do you happen to remember which detective you talked to about this?"

She snorted. "Bergan. Howard Bergan. Real piece of shit."

Anger radiated through me. His name kept popping up and never in a good way. "I'm beginning to get that impression."

She finished my drink and handed me the cup.

I took note of the name on her name tag before I met her gaze. "Chrissy, it's too damn late to help you, but..."

"Save the speech," she said, but she wasn't as gruff as she'd been before. "All I ask is, one, you keep this to yourself. And two, lay off Maddie. She's one of the best people I know. She's doing the best she can, and she doesn't need the stress of worrying you're gonna arrest her for that lowlife's murder."

I couldn't promise the second part, but I gave her a slight nod.

"I'm still sorry," I said. "You're owed an apology."

"Only you're not the one who needs to give it, now are you?" she asked sarcastically.

She had a point.

I thanked her for the drink and turned to head out the door.

"Detective?" she called after me.

"Yeah?"

Her eyes hardened. "No offense, but I hope you're shit at your job. Whoever offed him did the world a favor."

I was beginning to suspect she was right. I also realized I needed to get her alibi. But I'd save that for later. I had something more pressing to do.

I called Lance as soon as I walked out the door. "No need to drop by Déjà Brew," I said as soon as he answered. "Maddie's not working today, but I found out something else. Schroeder molested at least one of his students."

"*What?*"

"I know of at least one student who reported it." I considered how old she looked and did some quick mental math. "It probably happened about eight to ten years ago. A woman named Chrissy. I don't know her last name, but obviously it might be under Christine something. Pull her report and anything else you can find. I'm not sure why it wasn't pulled in the first place," I spat out, getting angrier by the minute."

"Noah," he said slowly. "There isn't anything on him for molestation."

"What are you talking about? Of course there is," I insisted. "I just spoke to one of his victims, and she told me Bergan handled the case but nothing came of it."

Lance was quiet for a long moment. "Noah," he said softly, "I'm telling you, there's nothing. We looked for priors. He was clean."

So the sergeant hadn't screwed up after all. The implications of what Lance was saying sunk in. "Fuck. Fuck. *Fuck.*"

Not only was the Cockamamie police force inept. They were also corrupt.

This changed everything.

"We're not discussing this at the station. Meet me at the riverside park by the playground. There's something I need to do first, so wait for me."

Chapter Twenty-Four

Maddie

The park looked pretty deserted, but then again, it was a cold, cloudy, late Thursday morning, too chilly and damp even for the mothers who often used the playground at the front of the park to entertain their children. I hadn't been out here in years—probably since I'd been in high school—but the playground was visible from the highway that ran past it.

I turned down the road leading to a small boat ramp and picnic area. Although I wasn't sure where the homeless would congregate, that seemed like a logical place, especially on a cold day. The picnic area would provide a roof and a windbreak.

Sure enough, there was a small group of people huddled around a grill where they'd built a fire. The coffee probably wasn't very hot anymore, but I decided to offer them some anyway. I couldn't offer them any pastries because the other men had eaten them all.

I got out, carrying my carafe and the bag full of cups and fixings. They gave me a wary look as I approached.

"Hi!" I said cheerfully, making sure I had a bright smile. "I'm Maddie. Would you like some coffee? I'm not sure how warm it still is, but..."

None of them answered.

I continued to approach, feeling more anxious than I had with the other men. Unlike the corner of Cherry and Vine, here there were no potential witnesses or anyone to intervene if anyone tried to hurt me. There was but the two men and two women huddled around the fire, staring at me with distrust and hostility.

"I don't intend to cause any trouble," I said, slowing my approach. "All I want is to find Ernie Foust."

"And you think that coffee is enough of a bribe for us to sell out our friend?" one of the women sneered. She wore a dark gray stocking cap and a red scarf around her neck.

"You wouldn't be selling him out," I said, continuing to get closer. "He came to me last night, telling me he was in trouble. I just want to help him."

The other woman had on fingerless gloves, and she held her hands toward the flames as she narrowed her eyes at me. "You the woman who dropped that son of a bitch off at the butcher shop the other night?"

Did she plan to hold that against me? Either way, I decided it would be more dangerous to lie. "Yeah, that's me. But Ernie was there too. I think he might have seen something. Or at least someone *thinks* he saw something."

A chill ran down my back. It was perfectly reasonable to assume that the same someone might believe I'd seen something too if I continued searching for Ernie. These people seemed protective of Ernie, though, and I doubted they'd say or do anything to get him, and therefore me, in danger.

"We don't know nothing about nothing," one of the men piped up. He had a long, dirty black dress coat that looked far too big for him.

"I don't expect you to tell me anything other than where you think Ernie might have gone."

None of them said a word.

So maybe they needed more convincing.

I set the carafe on a picnic table and started to fill a cup. The brown liquid let off steam in the cold air. "Do you guys ever go to the Methodist homeless shelter?"

"Not if we can help it," said the man in the coat.

"Ernie told me that he didn't like to go there because they stole his things."

"That's right," the fingerless gloves lady said.

"What do y'all do for food?" I asked, setting the nearly full cup on the table. I covered it with a lid to keep it warm and started to fill another.

"There's a soup kitchen on Vine," the woman with the red scarf said, eyeing the cup of coffee on the table.

"But that's about a mile from here," I said.

"We walk," one of the men said.

I finished filling up the cup and held it up. "Do y'all take cream or sugar? I have some in the bag."

"Both," said the woman with the scarf.

"Marge!" the other woman protested.

"Hey!" Red Scarf Lady said. "It's free coffee. Even the Methodists give you shit coffee before they steal your stuff."

"I'm not here to steal your stuff. I'm just looking for Ernie." I offered them a friendly smile. "And this is *good* coffee. It's not much, but it might help warm you up."

Marge—the red scarf woman—walked over and I set the cup on the table. "Cream and sugar?" She nodded, and I asked, "How many of each?"

"Four each."

"Perfect. Let me doctor that up for you." I reached for the cream containers and started dumping them in.

"What are you, our hostess or something?" one of the men behind me sneered.

It was intended as an insult, but I decided to ignore it. If the homeless shelter was stealing their things, then they had every right to be distrustful.

I added the sugars all at once, gave the cup a good stir and handed it to Marge. "No. I work at the coffee shop downtown— Déjà Brew."

"So it *is* good coffee?" the woman with the fingerless gloves asked. She was still by the fire, but there was a hint of longing in her voice, and she was eyeing Marge as she took a sip.

"I'd forgotten coffee could taste so good," Marge practically purred.

The woman with the red scarf hustled over. "I like mine with two creams only."

"Let me fix that up for you," I said, filling another cup and adding the cream. After I handed it to her, I glanced over at the fire. "Gentlemen?"

"Oh, hell..." the guy with the long black coat said. "Black."

I picked up the cup with the lid and handed it to him.

"What about you, sir?" I asked.

The lone holdout still stood next to the fire, and the harsh look in his eyes told me he didn't like being put on the spot.

"How about I just put a cup on the table, and you can get it later if you want?"

"Don't treat me like a child," he snapped, his voice full of rage.

I turned to face him, holding his gaze. "I apologize if that was how it sounded, but I meant no disrespect, sir."

"People think we're worthless just because we're facing some tough times , but we're not," he said. "I used to have a job. I used to have a family." His voice broke.

I wanted nothing more than to go over and give him a hug, but that was the last thing he wanted from me.

Blind Bake

"There ain't no jobs here in Cockamamie, but you gotta have a car to get over to Hyacinth, where the canning factory was hiring. And I ain't got no car. It broke down, and I'd done maxed out my credit cards, so I couldn't get it fixed. And then I fell behind on the payments. My wife left me. And then I lost my house because I couldn't pay the rent..." His voice trailed off, and his cheeks flushed. It was obvious he hadn't meant to share so much. "I ain't trash."

I walked over to him, blinking back my tears, and stood in front of him. "No, Mr....?"

"Dittmar. Sam Dittmar," he said fiercely.

"No, Mr. Dittmar," I said, practically gritting my teeth to keep from breaking down. "You are *not* trash. You are a person worthy of respect."

How had these people gotten to this state? I'd encountered nine homeless people in a town of twenty thousand, but it seemed like nine too many.

"Other than the homeless shelter, are there resources for y'all?" I asked, turning to face the others.

Marge shook her head. "Not really. Some of the businesses give us leftover food out of their back doors. And the Piggly Wiggly gives us food."

"The manager is pretty nice," the fingerless glove woman said.

I blinked in surprise. "Peter McIntire?"

"Dunno his name," Fingerless Gloves Lady said. "But he gives us full meals in to-go boxes from their deli. Hot meals. Rumor has it he even gives some people odd jobs here and there."

I let her information sink in. Peter McIntire was feeding and employing the homeless? Maybe he *had* changed.

"Some of you are likely on social security," I said, taking in their ages. "How do you get your checks?"

"I ain't got my check in years," the man in the black coat said. "Got no address to get it sent to."

"But you can have it direct-deposited."

"The bank closed my account 'cause I ain't got no address."

I couldn't believe what I was hearing. I turned to the others. "And the rest of you?"

They all had similar stories of getting caught in a trap of bureaucracy and red tape, and my anger began to build. Instead of raising money for a stupid Christmas tree in the downtown square, the Women's Club should be trying to help the disadvantaged people in town.

"If you could find an affordable place to stay, would you take advantage of that?" I asked.

"What are you, our fairy godmother?" Mr. Dittmar sneered.

"No," I said, the wheels in my head spinning with ideas. "But I'm good at figuring out how to make things happen."

I was a librarian, and we were taught to be resourceful. I couldn't give them shelter, but I could figure out how to get it. There were grants for such things. You just had to know where to look and how to apply.

For the first time since I'd moved back to Cockamamie, I felt like I had a real purpose other than watching my aunt fade away. Like I could make a difference in people's lives.

Like I was needed.

But how did I make all this happen?

The wind kicked up, and I brushed away the hair that blew into my face. "But let's get back to Ernie. Do you have any idea where he might be?"

They all remained silent.

"Do you think he might have gone back to the Bottoms?"

"Ernie don't go to the Bottoms," the guy in the black coat said. "He don't like it down there."

Yet that was exactly where I'd found him, so either the guy in the black coat didn't know him well or Ernie's presence there was out of character. Roscoe hadn't given any indication that Ernie's presence at the Bottoms was out of the ordinary, but Roscoe didn't come across as particularly trustworthy either.

"Do any of you know a guy named Roscoe?" I asked.

That earned me a few hard stares.

"You don't want to go anywhere near him," Marge said. "He's bad news with a capital T."

"Shady as shit," Mr. Dittmar agreed.

Marge had mixed up her idioms but two of them agreeing about Roscoe's character caught my attention. "What makes you say that?"

"Roscoe isn't just homeless. He's done time," Mr. Dittmar said.

"I'm not even sure he's really homeless," Marge said. "I've seen him get in a pretty pickup truck."

"Roscoe came into town a couple of months ago and took up with the guys who usually hang out downtown," Mr. Dittmar said. "We think he's bidin' his time, but for what? We don't know. We just steer clear of him. You should too."

"Roscoe told me I should look for Ernie at Cock on the Walk."

Fingerless Gloves Lady's eyes flew wide. "Do *not* go there. The Brawlers hang out there."

"The Brawlers?" I asked, confused. "Who are the Brawlers?"

"Only the people who supply most of the fifty-mile radius with drugs. They don't like people messin' with their business, and showin' up there is seen as messin' with their business."

"So why would Roscoe tell me to find Ernie there? Does he work with the Brawlers?"

"Ernie?" the black-coat man asked. "Hell, no. He hates drugs. His son was an addict. But if you're asking if Roscoe works for the Brawlers, I wouldn't put it past him. Helen's right. He's bad news. Stay away from him. And them."

"So there's no way Ernie would be out there?" I asked, and when they all agreed, I said, "Well, is there any other place you think he could be?"

"Nope," the guy in the black coat said.

I propped a hand on my hip. "Are you just telling me that, or do you really not know?"

"Just let it go, girl," Marge said. "I think your heart is in the right place, but you need to let it be."

Maybe she was right, but I wasn't sure I could.

I reached into my pocket and pulled out a couple of my cards. "If you see him, will you please give him one of these and tell him to call me. I'm really worried about him and want to make sure he's okay." I patted the carafe. "I'm gonna leave this here for y'all to finish off. And if any of you need help, you can use that number too. Just give me a call."

Leaving them out in the cold was hard, but I forced myself to turn around and get back in my car. They hadn't seen the last of me. I was going to do something to give them back their dignity, but it would have to wait.

Chapter Twenty-Five

Noah

I headed to the park and drove all the way to the back by the river. The men said they'd sent Maddie out here to look for Ernie Foust, and the homeless tended to congregate in the picnic area overlooking the river.

The playground looked deserted as I drove past, and I wasn't surprised to see a small group of people standing around one of the barbecues by the boat ramp when I pulled up.

I parked in the lot, then started to wander over, noticing the cardboard Déjà Brew box on a picnic table. The cups in their hands bore the same logo.

How long ago had she been here?

I got out and headed toward them, flashing a smile. "Hi."

"We're not doing anything wrong," a guy in a black coat said.

I held up my hands in surrender. I hated that the first thing they expected from a cop was harassment. "I'm not here to bother you. I'm looking for someone you might know. Ernie Foust."

They all remained silent and unresponsive. Almost like they'd expected me to ask about him.

"I know Maddie was already here looking for him." I motioned to the cardboard box on the picnic table. "She's worried about

Ernie, and so am I." Of course, I was only guessing that was her motivation for searching for him, but I couldn't bring myself to consider a more sinister reason.

And look where that got you with Caleb.

I shrugged it off. I couldn't afford to be distracted.

None of them corrected me.

"I take it he wasn't here?"

They remained silent.

Dammit.

"Did you all steer her in a direction to find him?"

"We ain't seen no one this morning," a woman with fingerless gloves called out belligerently, but the man by her side shot her a sideways glance to shut her up.

"You're telling me that box of coffee just magically appeared?" Before they could answer, I held up my hand. "Let me be clear: no one is in trouble here. Not you. Not Ernie and not Maddie. I just need to know where you steered her so I can make sure she's safe."

"She mentioned going to Cock on the Walk," a woman with a red scarf said. "But we tried to talk her out of it."

What the fuck? Why was she planning to go out *there*? "Does Ernie have ties to the Brawlers?"

"We told her he didn't, but..." The woman shrugged. "Someone else told her to look for him out there."

Fuck. I knew without asking that it was that goddamned Roscoe.

"How long ago was she out here?" I demanded.

They returned to their self-imposed vow of silence.

"Look," I said, getting frustrated. "Again, no one's in trouble here, but y'all know just as well as I do that she has no business being out there, so how long ago did she leave?"

"About twenty minutes ago," the woman in the red scarf said.

Long enough to get herself into a world of shit, self-defense moves or no.

I hustled back into my car and headed to the front of the park, ready to call Lance and tell him I'd meet up with him after I went out to Cock on the Walk, but his cruiser was already parked in the lot by the playground.

Rolling down the passenger window, I pulled up next to him. He rolled his window down with a questioning look.

"Get in," I said. "We're making a run out to Cock on the Walk."

His eyes clouded with confusion. "Why?"

"Long story. I'll tell you on the way."

Moments later, he was climbing into my passenger seat, and I backed out of the spot as he buckled.

"Why are we headed out to Cock on the Walk?" he asked.

"Maddie Baker."

He released a loud groan. "Noah, I know you've got it out for her—"

"Maddie's headed out there."

His eyes narrowed. "Why would she go out to the Brawlers' bar?"

"Because a homeless man named Roscoe told her to."

"I think you missed a few steps," he said. "Start from the beginning."

I told him that Maddie and I were both looking for Ernie Foust, but I was always a solid step behind her. And I recapped my encounter with Chrissy, the barista who'd filed a police report with Bergan.

"Surely Maddie wouldn't be stupid enough to go out to Cock on the Walk," he argued.

"She just moved back a couple of months ago, and Cock on the Walk popped up...what, ten years ago? What if she doesn't know how dangerous it is?"

"You're not accusing her of going out there for nefarious reasons?" he chided.

"Linking her to the Brawlers is a huge stretch," I said.

"So why do you think she's looking for Foust?" Lance asked.

"Based on what I'm finding out about her, I suspect she's worried about him."

His jaw dropped, his brow shooting up. "And *you're* worried about *her*."

"Don't make more out of it than it is. I'm protecting a citizen who might be in trouble. Nothing more, nothing less." I played it cool, eager to change the subject. "Sounds like Bergan made the barista's sexual assault case disappear, and now Andrea Baker's file has disappeared too. How many other files have up and vanished?"

Lance stared out the windshield, looking troubled. "Honestly? I have no clue. I've been on the force for eight years and never suspected this sort of thing was going on." Shaking his head, he bit out. "Some cop I am."

Was he telling the truth? It was hard for me to trust anyone, or more accurately, I no longer trusted my judgment, which was a huge liability since sometimes instincts and judgment calls were all I had to go on.

But I'd brought Lance into this and there was no turning back now. I'd just be on alert for signs that he was in on the cover-up.

"I suspect Bergan was really good at covering his tracks, but I doubt he did it on his own," I said. "The question is why he made the cases disappear. With Schroeder, it was probably money. We did wonder if he'd been blackmailed. Maybe Bergan extorted money from him in exchange for making his problems go away."

"But what about more recently?" Lance asked. "Bergan's been out of it for at least six months. Why is Schroeder's money still missing?"

"Maybe the money didn't just go to Bergan. Maybe he was paying off someone else on the force. And the accomplice started charging more after Bergan was out of the picture."

"Yeah, maybe," Lance said, looking like he was going to be sick. "Do you think the chief is part of it?"

Blind Bake

I debated it for a moment, wanting to give him an honest answer. "I'd like to think not. He was concerned about the poor close rate of cases. He's got the mayor breathing down his neck. I think he's on the up and up."

"But we're still having this conversation away from the station," Lance pointed out dryly. "And not in his office."

"Can't be too careful."

This was supposed to be a cushy job. Doing good police work like I'd done in Memphis, but in a safer place. Now I was caught up in police corruption. How the hell had this happened?

"We'll keep this to ourselves until we know who we can trust, and at the moment, the only person I trust in this town is you." At least until he proved himself untrustworthy.

Lance was silent for a moment, then nodded as he turned to face me. "Same."

"Okay, now that we're on the same page..." But I wasn't sure what to tackle next. If there was widespread corruption in the department, we needed to bring in the state police. And yet...there was a chance Bergan had been acting alone, which meant we wouldn't have to rip the department apart, especially since Bergan was supposedly mentally incompetent now. It might also be better to compile more evidence first to present to the state police. Before any potential accomplices found out we were onto them and started covering their tracks.

I let everything churn in my head. "Is Bergan married? Does he still have a house?"

"Are you thinking the files might be there at his house?"

"Maybe. But we'd need a warrant, and we're not going to get one with what little we have." Then a new thought hit me. "Judge Neilson might be part of this. He wouldn't sign that warrant we requested to search the industrial park."

"A judge?" Lance choked out.

"Were Bergan and the judge tight?" I asked.

"I'm not sure. I didn't know Bergan very well. He had an *I'm better than you* attitude."

Why was I not surprised?

"He didn't take to the new guys. And up until he left, he considered me a new guy. From what little I knew about him, though, he was kind of a loner. He didn't hang out with anyone after work. He didn't seem to have many friends."

"So who was his accomplice?"

"Honestly, Noah, I don't know."

What a fucking mess.

"I think we should work together for the rest of the day," I said. "We're going to keep everything close to the vest. We'll give limited information to the chief, and nothing that might alert anyone involved in those missing files. We can't forget one of those cases involves some serious allegations against the vic."

"Or that the other missing file is Andrea Baker's," he said, sounding lost in thought.

"Do you know if Maddie requested the file on her mother?"

"What?" He turned to face me. "No. I looked to see the last time it was pulled, and it was years ago. No recent requests either."

"So she just happened to pick up a man who was a person of interest in her mother's murder?" I mused.

"I thought you'd given up trying to pin this on her," he argued.

"I'm merely pointing out facts. From what I understand, the passenger can't request specific drivers on the Uber app. She had no way of knowing Martin might eventually request a ride. That would rule out premediation."

"So you actually believe it's a case of her being in the wrong place at the wrong time?"

"Yeah, I do. For now." My mind shot back to that shadowy figure she'd encountered last night, and the way she'd instantly launched into a search for Ernie Foust this morning. It seemed to confirm my suspicion about who the figure was. It seemed to confirm my suspicion. "I'm starting to feel more certain that guy Maddie met with outside the rec center last night may have actually been Ernie Foust."

Lance nodded, as if recalling our earlier conversation. "The guy looked homeless?"

I considered his baggy clothes and stooped posture. "Could have been."

"So what...they agreed to meet there?"

"She left early because of her aunt, so I don't think so. Plus, she was gesturing toward the building, like she was trying to get him to come in." Oh shit. "What if she was trying to get him to come talk to me?"

"You think?" Lance asked in surprise.

"I can't imagine the women of Cockamamie would want her bringing a homeless man in to try their pumpkin rolls."

"So let's walk this through. You think Ernie Foust saw something, he showed up last night to tell Maddie, but you came out and scared him off?"

I frowned. "Maybe. I *do* know she's trying to find him. The only reason I can think of that she'd do that—the day after she met someone in the parking lot last night—is because she's worried about him."

We were pulling up to Cock on the Walk, and Lance turned to face me. "You got a plan for this? You know they're not going to be thrilled to see us walking in."

"*You're* not going in," I said, shooting a glance at his uniform. "I'll go in and let you know if I run into trouble."

He gave me a leery look. "I don't think going in alone is a good idea." He took in the three trucks and two motorcycles as I pulled into the parking lot. "I don't see her car.

"Her car's still with the crime techs, but last night she was driving an old Volvo."

"I don't see any Volvos here," Lance said.

"Captain Obvious," I grunted, starting to get nervous.

"Maybe she realized coming out here was a bad idea."

My stomach clenched. "Or maybe they're holding her and moved her car."

"Do you really think they'd do that?" Lance asked.

"You'd probably know better than me, but what if she showed up asking questions they didn't like?"

"Fuck." He pulled his phone out of his pocket. "Let me call her and see if she answers." He started going through his contacts.

I gave him a sideways glance. "You have her number programmed into your phone?"

"I decided to call her to ask her to come into the station this afternoon instead of dropping by the coffee shop." He turned on the speaker, and the phone went straight to her voicemail.

"This is Maddie," her cheerful voice announced through his phone. "I can't talk right now, but leave your name and number, and I'll get back to you as soon as I can."

"Hey, Maddie," Lance said after the beep. "This is Lance Forrester. Would you give me a call back as soon as you get this message? We just want to make sure you're okay. Thanks." He hung up and looked at me. "You know there's every chance she won't return my call."

I parked close to the entrance and got out and took off my jacket, tossing it into the back seat. My shoulder holster and the badge around my neck were both clearly visible, but I still wasn't sure they would be enough to protect me.

I leaned inside. "Get in the driver's seat and be ready to leave when I come out."

Lance looked uncertain. "Maybe we should get some backup."

"I can't call for backup for this, and we both know it."

"Noah, it looks like she's not even here," he pleaded.

But what if she had been? My stomach clenched at the thought. "I still have to go in."

I left the door open with the keys in the ignition, leaving him to walk around and get in the driver's seat.

My heart was racing as I walked through the doors. While I'd heard about this place, I'd never been inside. I had hoped I'd never be forced to, but if there was *any* chance she'd come out here, there was no fucking way I could leave her here.

All eyes turned on me the moment I stepped inside, but it took a moment for my eyes to adjust to the dim lighting. The bar smelled like stale beer, sweat, and car grease. There were a couple of rough-looking guys sitting at the bar in front of me and a woman wearing a short skirt, a tube top, and four-inch black stiletto heels standing between them, leaning into the man to the left. Two older men with biker vests were nursing bottles of beer at a table in the corner.

The bartender wore a black T-shirt. He had a bushy beard and dark eyes and stood behind the bar with his arms crossed over his massive chest. He appeared to be in his forties or early fifties, but his beard made it hard to tell. "I think you took the wrong exit, son," he said with a hard stare.

"I don't want any trouble," I said, slowly advancing to the bar. "I'm looking for a woman."

The bartender grinned, but it wasn't friendly. "If you need help with your love life, maybe you should try Tinder."

The customers at the bar chuckled.

I flashed a tight smile. "I'm looking for someone specific. She's a brunette, long hair. Green eyes. Pretty." Then I added, "She's got a girl-next-door look."

The bartender motioned to the woman standing at the bar with the two men. "You talkin' about Rena?"

Rena turned to face me. Her shoulder-length dark hair was streaked with an unlikely shade of blond. She wore heavy eye makeup, and her lips were painted bright red. I was willing to bet my next paycheck that she was a prostitute.

She batted her eyelashes at me. "I can be your girl, *Officer*."

"While I appreciate the offer, miss, you're not the woman I'm looking for."

One of the men sitting on the stools next to her burst out laughing.

I turned to the bartender. "Have you seen anyone like that this morning?"

He rested his hand on the counter and leaned into it, eyeing me with a bored expression, but the muscles of his arms and chest were flexed. He was ready for trouble. "These are the only people I've seen in here all morning."

"You're sure?"

His brow rose slightly. "You accusing me of lyin'?"

"No, sir," I said, holding his gaze. "Just making sure you didn't forget."

"I think I'd remember someone like that," he said.

"And maybe want to dirty her up some," said the other guy with Rena.

I ignored his comment and kept my attention on the bartender. "If she *does* show up, I'd appreciate it if you'd make sure she leaves in the shape she showed up in."

The bartender's eyes narrowed.

The lot of them could have been hiding her, but I didn't think so. While the bartender wasn't friendly, he didn't look nervous. Just belligerent. And Rena, who appeared to be the weak link of the group, didn't seem guarded or on edge. Just curious.

"What's her name?" asked one of the men at the table in the corner.

I hesitated. I didn't want to volunteer anything they could use against her if she *did* show up, but her first name would probably be okay, and Lance and I would have to find a way to convince her to avoid this place. "Maddie."

"This Maddie got a last name?" the bartender asked.

"That's all you need."

"You want us to call you if she shows up, Officer?" Rena asked.

I pulled a business card out of my pocket and handed it to her. "I'm Detective Langley. You can give me a call on that number."

The man next to her snorted.

I took one last look around the room, then nodded to the bartender. "Thank you for your time."

Then I turned and headed for the door, hoping I didn't get jumped on the way out.

But I got out the door safely, the sunlight partially blinding me as I headed toward the passenger side of the car and got in.

Lance clearly had his concerns too, because he backed up as soon as I got the door closed.

"Well?"

"She hasn't been here."

He headed for the highway, turning toward town. "You're sure?"

"I can't be one hundred percent sure, but I'm sure enough." I dug my phone out of my pocket. "*I'm* calling her."

She probably didn't want to hear from me, but that was too damn bad. The call went straight to voicemail again. Why was her phone off?

After her outgoing message played, I waited for the beep and tried hard to keep the irritation out of my voice. "Maddie, this is Detective Noah Langley. I know you were thinking about coming out to Cock on the Walk, but I'm asking you to reconsider." I took a breath to settle my rising anger. "I just dropped by to make sure you hadn't been *murdered*, so they'll be watching for you now. It would be a very bad decision to pay them a visit." Then, for good measure, I added, "I know I'm not your favorite person, but I'm asking you to call me so I know they didn't actually murder you and hide your body behind the bar and sell your car for parts."

I hung up, still feeling unsettled.

"You okay?" Lance asked, darting a glance at me.

No. I was scared shitless something had happened to her, but there wasn't a damned thing I could do about it. And worst of all, I couldn't tell my partner how freaked out I was.

"Fine," I ground out. "Now that we know she probably isn't dead, let's figure out what to do next. I take it that the teachers you talked to didn't bring up the molestation accusations?"

He shook his head. "They didn't much care for Schroeder, but they said he mostly kept to himself. They sure didn't mention or even hint that he might've been molesting his students."

"We need to swing by the high school and talk to the administration. See if they can enlighten us on the real reason Schroeder was no longer teaching at the school."

"That's gonna have to wait," Lance said. "The warrant came through, and the crime scene guys are on their way to Schroeder's house. We need to head over and meet them."

Chapter Twenty-Six

Maddie

While I was anxious to find Ernie, I wasn't stupid. Everyone had made Cock on the Walk sound like a dangerous place. I needed to find out more about it before I went out there.

Which meant I wasn't sure where else to look for him, which really had me worried.

I started to drive past the hardware store and remembered we needed light bulbs. They would be cheaper at Walmart, but all this talk about the past had jarred my guilt loose. I still felt shame over how I'd left my best friend Colleen behind when I went to college. And Marsha had said Colleen worked at the hardware store. I could afford to pay fifty cents more.

The hardware store was a mom-and-pop shop that had been on the edge of downtown since the 1940s, but like most family-owned businesses in the area, it had seen better days. I hadn't been inside for years, but I knew it wasn't usually busy.

A bell dinged on the door when I walked in, and I smiled at the cashier, who was checking out a younger man in painter's coveralls. She shot me a glare like she expected me to try to shoplift a shovel out the front door.

I saw a display of light bulbs down an aisle and went to investigate. I was wrong, they were a full dollar more, and I was beginning to rethink this purchase, especially since I was losing money from lost Uber rides today.

"What on earth did those poor light bulbs ever do to you?" a young woman next to me asked with a laugh.

I turned to her in confusion, then smiled. "Colleen."

Seeing her was like a trip to the past, but while I was glad to see her, it also hurt.

Her eyes flew wide. "Maddie Baker? Is that you? I heard you were back in town! I can't believe it!" She threw her arms around me and pulled me into a tight hug. "I can't believe you're *here*! In my store!"

I hugged her back, feeling a rush of guilt. I should have called her months ago, but we'd had a falling-out years ago, and I'd been too embarrassed to reach out.

She pulled away, taking in my face. "You haven't changed a bit!"

I took in the dark circles under her eyes along with her crow's-feet. Her light brown hair had a shoulder-length style that looked self-done.

Colleen had found out she was eight weeks pregnant two days before high school graduation. I'd told her that she didn't need to let it change the trajectory of her life, but her mother had convinced her differently. So she'd given up a scholarship to UT and being my dorm roommate to marry John Nichols and become a young bride and mother. I was young and dumb and too self-centered to offer her support. At the time it had felt like she was abandoning me just like everyone else: My father when I was a baby. My mother. And then Colleen. And that she was making a stupid decision I couldn't condone. I'd barely stopped to consider how her life had imploded. By the time I'd realized I'd been a brat, it felt too late to make amends.

She'd made a difficult choice, one she'd thought was right, but looking at her now, I wasn't so sure it had been.

"It's good to see you, Colleen," I said softly, tears filling my eyes.

"Hey, now," she gushed, her voice breaking. "None of that. You're gonna make me cry, and Ashley doesn't like it when I cry during my shift."

"If Ashley is the woman working the register," I said, "then I'm not surprised."

Colleen giggled and, lowering her voice to a whisper, said, "Ashley is the owner's daughter, and she takes her job *very* seriously."

"How's that paint comin', Colleen?" Ashley shouted from the front.

My brow lifted. That didn't sound very professional.

Colleen thumbed toward the counter behind her, giving me an apologetic look. "I gotta mix some paint."

"Lucky for me, I was gonna pick up some paint," I said, wondering what in the world I was going to do with a gallon of paint.

She smiled. "Then you've come to the right place." She leaned closer and whispered, "Although, as a friend, I feel obligated to tell you that you can get it cheaper at Walmart down the road."

"I think I'm good with getting it right here," I said.

Her smile brightened. "Well, alrighty then. Do you need help picking out a color? What room are you painting?"

What *was* I going to paint? "My room," I said. "I think it needs a change." Only after I said it out loud did I realize it was true. It was still decorated the way it had been when I moved in with my aunt and uncle back in high school. It wasn't juvenile, but it was time for a change.

"Is it still done in pink and white?"

I stared up at her. "You remembered."

Her face fell. "Of course I did. I spent endless hours in that room." A wistful look fluttered across her face. "I remember everything."

Shame washed through me, making my face hot. "Oh, Colleen ..." I started, a tear sliding down my cheek. "I'm so, so sorry."

She stared at me in horror, then shot a worried glance to the front. "Ashley," she yelled. "I'm taking a short break."

"Don't you need—"

"I *said* I was taking a *break*!" Colleen shouted.

I stared at her in shock.

She grabbed my arm and dragged me to the back of the store, through a large storage area and then out to a small lumber yard, where a man was climbing into a forklift, music blaring. She gave him an exasperated look before dragging me to the side of the building so that we were standing in the parking lot.

I'd been too caught off guard to wonder why she was dragging me outside, searching for privacy, but now it occurred to me that she was about to tell me off. I squared my shoulders, prepared, because frankly, I deserved it.

But her frustration bled away, leaving her looking tired and far older than thirty-four. "Maddie, I forgive you."

"Just like that?" I asked in disbelief.

"Of course just like that."

I shook my head.

"We were stupid kids. We thought we knew the way of the world, but we didn't know shit." The wind gusted, and she crossed her arms over her chest, wrapping her fingers around her thin arms. At least she had a long-sleeved T-shirt on. "I'll be honest, it took me a while to totally understand, but havin' kids'll do that to you."

I stared at her in confusion.

"Maddie, I have kids close to the age we were then." She laughed and hugged herself tighter. "Lordy, do I have a better understanding now."

She had kids in high school? But of course she did. She'd had

Blind Bake

her first babies—twins—at eighteen. Which would make them sixteen now.

"I see so much of you in Savannah it's not even funny," she said with a laugh. "She thinks she knows better than everyone else. That the answer to life lies outside these city limits." She frowned. "Which is why I haven't told her you came back. Gotta let the girl have her dreams."

I stared at her in confusion.

"She knows my best friend left to go to college while I stayed here to have a family. She thinks I'm a moron, so *you're* her role model. Her road map to freedom. I can't take that from her."

"Colleen..." My voice broke.

"No," she said in protest, holding up a hand and turning fierce. "Don't you dare feel guilty. I want her to have that hope. I want her to escape this stupid town." She took a long, slow breath, looking like she was close to breaking down. "And I hope to God she doesn't get sucked back in like you were." She shook her head. "This place is a fucking black hole."

I stared at her, unsure of what to say or do. I'd wanted to know what had happened after I left, but suddenly I wasn't so sure.

"You want me to leave you alone," I said.

"Yes." Tears filled her eyes. "Seeing you hurts too much."

"Oh, Colleen..."

She shook her head. "I made my decision. Life's too short to have regrets."

And yet she looked like she was full of them.

"Colleen, I don't want to leave it like this."

"Messy?" she asked with a laugh. "That's life, Mads. You never could deal with that. Guess some things never change."

She started to walk away, and I wondered what the hell had just happened.

"You think my life has been perfect?" I shouted after her. "You think I haven't dealt with life, Colleen? I gave up my life to come back and take care of my aunt. My father walked out when I was a baby. My mother was *murdered*! Do you think that's *perfect*?"

She'd stopped to face me, a mixture of pity and irritation on her face. "I never said perfect, Maddie. But when you look at it, that's the root of your problem. You want everything to be perfect, but life rarely is."

She started to walk away, then stopped for a full second before turning at the waist to face me. "You know, everything isn't always about you."

I gasped, but I supposed I deserved that too. I had made likely the most traumatic experience of her life about me.

She stopped and turned around to face me. "How'd you know that I worked here?"

I ran a hand over my head. "Uh...Marsha. I saw her at a Women's Club meeting last night."

Releasing a bitter laugh, she slowly shook her head. "So you go to those now?"

My defenses rose. "I took Aunt Deidre. I think they're full of shit. Raising money for Christmas decorations for the square when there are people living on the street? Yeah, no thanks, so don't get judgmental on me."

Some of her hostility faded.

"How'd my name come up?" she asked, crossing her arms over her chest. "She gloating that she has a fancy-ass job at the doctor's office while I mix paint?"

"No," I said. Jeez. Did people trash-talk her? "She was telling me about Martin Schroeder making a weird purchase last week. She also let me know you worked here."

She nodded, and since I was curious, I asked, "Did you see him come in? Did he buy rat poison?"

"What? Why are you asking?"

"I guess because the police keep questioning me since I was the one to drop him off at the place he was murdered." I laughed, but it was brittle. "You may work at a hardware store, but I work part-time at Déjà Brew and Uber on my off days so I can pay my bills. I gave Mr. Schroeder an Uber ride." Then I added, just to be clear, "I didn't kill him, Colleen."

She shook her head as though trying to clear it, then drew in a breath, wrapping her arms over her chest again. "Of course you didn't do it. That's the stupidest thing I've ever heard." Then the barest hint of a smile appeared. "And I have three teenagers in my house—two of 'em boys—so I'm exposed to stupid on a regular basis."

A lump filled my throat, and I tried to smile back.

She ran a hand over her head. "I remember him coming in. Ashley rang him up, but I was getting ready to take over the register so she could take a break. A bunch of other people have come in since then, and my memory's not what it used to be, but I remember thinking it was odd."

She pushed out a breath and looked up at the sky. "He picked up some rat poison, a bundle of rope, the thick kind you use to tie stuff down in your truck and such." She made a face. "He also got a hacksaw and some PVC pipe. Miguel asked him if he was gonna work on the pipes in his house, and Mr. Schroeder told him to mind his own business, only plenty of cuss words were used. He also got a padlock, the heavy-duty kind. You know, the kind you use on sheds or storage units if you don't want someone to use bolt cutters to cut it off." She frowned. "He also got a welding torch, only he didn't know how to use it, and Miguel had to show him. Nearly took Miguel's head off when he asked what he'd be welding so he'd know which supplies to recommend. Mr. Schroeder told Miguel he only needed to know how to turn it on and off."

"That's weird."

"You have no idea. And he paid cash. After he left, Ashley complained that the money smelled disgusting. Sweat and some chemical smell."

"If I gave you the name and number for a police officer, do you think you could call him and tell him what you just told me?"

She made a face. "I don't know, Maddie. I don't really want to get involved."

"It's Lance Forrester," I said. "Remember him? He was two years behind us. He's been so nice to me through all of this." When she hesitated, I added, "You can have Miguel or Ashley call them."

"Why don't you tell them to come talk to us? Don't they know about it?"

"I have no idea, but it seems weird enough that it might be important." She made a face again, and I couldn't help wondering why she didn't want to talk to the police. Maybe she'd had a bad experience. Plenty of people had been scared off from voluntarily talking to them. "It's not like it's gonna prove you didn't do it. Just that he was a weird old perv."

"That's okay," I said, disappointed, but she was right. It didn't clear my name. I'd see if Noah or Lance were interested, and I could point them toward Marsha, if need be. "You just think about it."

She turned to go back inside, then glanced back at me. "I hope things work out, Mads."

"Yeah," I said. "For you too."

I got in my car and leaned my head back on the headrest, closing my eyes as the past ten minutes replayed in my head.

My soul felt dirty, like no amount of soap or apologies would make it clean. Colleen had accused me of a lot of things—most of which were likely true—but it was going to take some time to unpack it all. Repairing our relationship had waited for sixteen years. It could wait a little longer.

Not that Colleen seemed eager to fix it.

A rap on my window made me jump, and I turned in fright to see who was trying to get my attention. A woman I didn't recognize was bent over, her nose nearly touching the glass. Her face was covered in grime, and it looked like she was wearing multiple layers of clothes. Her hand was on a filing car cart behind her, piled with black trash bags. She didn't look all that excited to see me, even though she was the one who'd rapped on my window.

I guessed it was *kick Maddie to the curb* day.

I rolled the window down a few inches and waited.

"I hear you're lookin' for Ernie," she grunted with a scowl.

I narrowed my eyes. "Who told you that?"

Shaking her head in disgust, she cast a glance toward Main Street. "People talk."

Which wasn't good news for me or Ernie, if he was really hiding from someone scary.

"Yeah," I admitted. "I'm looking for him."

Her hard dark eyes locked on mine. "He wants to be left alone, so you need to leave him alone. You're causing him enough trouble."

"How am I causing him trouble?"

Her glare darkened. "Just leave him the hell alone. *Or else.*" Then she spat on my window, making me glad I hadn't rolled it down all the way.

I rolled it back up, and started my car, groaning when it was slow to turn over.

So what did I do now? I wanted to talk to Dawn, but school wasn't over until 2:30, and it was about 12:30 now.

I grabbed my phone to see if Mallory had texted about the weekend and saw I had several missed calls. I hadn't taken my phone off do-not-disturb after picking up Eleanor this morning. I had three voicemails, one from a number I didn't recognize, two from people in my contacts—Noah and Linda.

While the call from Noah was concerning, it was the voicemail from Linda that sent me into a panic. She *never* called me unless something was wrong.

I pulled up her voicemail first.

"Maddie, I don't want to alarm you, but Deidre's gone. She's not in the house, and the back door was open. I think maybe you should come home."

My blood ran cold as I called her back. "Did you find her yet?" I asked the moment she answered.

"No," she said, sounding scared. "I can't find her anywhere."

"Okay," I said, trying not to panic, but I'd blown past panic and was running headlong into hysteria. "I'm on my way home."

Chapter Twenty-Seven

Maddie

Linda was frantic when I arrived, standing on the front porch with her phone in her hand. "I don't know what happened. We had just eaten lunch, and she said she was feeling poorly, so I told her to lie down in bed. Truth be told, I was worried about her. So I checked on her after lunch, and she wasn't in her bed or anywhere else. And then I found the back door open. I could swear it hadn't been like that earlier, when I was cleaning up. I think she might have slipped out while I was in the powder room."

That sounded odd. Aunt Deidre usually wasn't sneaky when she went out. She just wandered off.

"But when I couldn't get a hold of you, I called the police," she said, tightening her grip on the phone. "They're on their way."

I nodded. While they didn't need any more reminders that I existed, and I wasn't thrilled they were coming, Aunt Deidre was my priority. I'd suck it up and deal with it if they helped bring her home.

"Okay," I said. "What was she wearing? She had on her robe when I left this morning."

"She was wearing a pair of dark brown slacks and a light pink cardigan twin set with pearls." Her chin trembled. "Maddie, she didn't take her coat."

It was in the low forties with cold gusts of wind. She'd be feeling that pretty quickly. "How long has she been missing?"

"Almost an hour."

A new sense of panic hit me. "I'm going to go on the Nextdoor app and post about it there. See if anyone has spotted her. You watch for the police." I glanced at the house next door. "Have you told Margarete?"

"She's not home. That was the first place I checked."

"Okay. Good." But it *wasn't* good. I was terrified my aunt was lost and scared and freezing to death.

Grabbing my phone, I opened up the neighborhood app, then made a post about Aunt Deidre and included my phone number. By the time I'd uploaded a couple of photos, a police car was pulling up to the front of the house.

Linda went out to meet the officer in the front yard, but I hurried upstairs and did a quick sweep. There was a possibility that Aunt Deidre had been confused and gone into another room or bathroom, but I found no trace of her.

I headed back downstairs as an officer walked through the front door with Linda. Thankfully, he wasn't someone I'd encountered in the whole Mr. Schroeder mess. He said he'd take Linda's statement first, so I excused myself to go check out the basement. It was an unlikely place for her to have gone. The stairs were steep, and she hated using them. Uncle Albert had been in charge of the laundry for years until they'd added a laundry room to the first floor.

The basement was dark and empty, just boxes piled up against the stone basement wall along with some discarded furniture—a small table and a rocking chair. No sign of Aunt Deidre.

I went back up and out the back door, looking around the yard for any sign of her or where she might have gone. There was a single-wide, unattached garage at the back of the yard. It had a rickety garage door with no opener, one of the reasons I didn't park my car inside it. The other reason was that it was full of stuff my uncle had accumulated over the years. There wasn't room for a car.

But now I noticed the side door was open.

"Aunt Deidre?" I called out as I walked over to the door. No one responded, but I kept moving until I reached the entrance. I lingered there a moment, letting my eyes adjust to the dimly lit space. Uncle Albert's lawnmower and power tools filled the space, along with more discarded furniture. "Aunt Deidre?"

She still didn't respond. Just as I was about to turn away, something caught my eye—an empty food storage container that had held the remains of our leftovers from the other night, along with a fork.

Had Aunt Deidre brought a snack out here?

"Maddie?" Margarete called out, and I went back outside to find her in her backyard, wringing her hands. "Linda said Deidre's missing."

I hurried over to her, and she gave me a hug. "I searched the house from top to bottom and just checked the garage. She's not there, but it looks like she ate some leftovers in there earlier."

"Maybe she carried them out this afternoon," Margarete said, patting my arm. "And then wandered off. Linda has nearly finished giving her statement. The police officer wants to speak to you next."

"Okay." I followed her inside, trying to quell my anxiety. When Aunt Deidre had wandered away before, she'd been upset about not going to church. I needed to ask Linda if something had set her off this morning.

An older officer was sitting at the head of the dining room table, taking notes in a notebook, while Linda sat in a chair on the side. He glanced up as Margarete and I entered the room. "Hi, I'm Officer Summit. You must be Deidre's niece."

"That's right," I said, taking a seat opposite Linda. Margarete took the chair next to me, clinging to my hand.

"Has your aunt been acting unusual lately? Out of sorts?"

"She has dementia, so unusual is the new normal," I said, trying to keep from letting my fear take over. Talking to him made this all too real. "She hasn't been herself for years."

Officer Summit gave me a kind smile. "I know you're scared and worried, but we already have two patrol units driving around looking for her. I just figured we might be able to narrow our search if we have a better idea of her frame of mind."

Tears filled my eyes. "She's worried about me, of course. The whole Martin Schroeder thing has her upset."

Confusion covered his face. "Why would she be worried about Martin Schroeder?"

Did he really not know? Did police officers not gossip around the water cooler?

"My involvement," I said. "I was the Uber driver who picked him up from the industrial park and dropped him off. But he left his phone in my car, and then the police showed up at the Piggly Wiggly while my aunt and I were out shopping. Well, that upset Aunt Deidre. Especially when they took me to the police station. Then this morning she came downstairs and was drinking coffee in her bathrobe."

Margarete gasped. "Oh my."

Officer Summit looked confused. "I take it that's a big deal?"

"She would never leave her room without putting her makeup on and getting fully dressed," Margarete said emphatically.

"Agreed," Linda said with a grimace.

"How was she after I left?" I asked, directing my question to Linda.

"She was quiet all morning, and like I mentioned when you got home, she wanted to lie down after lunch. She seemed preoccupied. Worried."

"About her niece?" the officer asked.

Linda looked uncertain. "Maybe. She never said one way or the other. It was just my observation. She could have actually been confused or muddled, only she seemed more present this morning than she has lately."

"With me too," I said. "We talked this morning before I left, and she didn't seem confused or disoriented. She was more with it than she has been in quite a while."

Officer Summit was quiet for a moment as he wrote things in his notebook. He glanced up. "Before she got sick, was there anywhere she liked to go to if she needed to get away to think? Take a walk to the park? Or anyone she'd go to for advice, like a friend or clergyman?"

"She would come to me," Margarete said, then looked alarmed. "But I wasn't home. What if she went looking for me?"

"Only she didn't seem confused," Linda said.

"But sometimes sleeping resets her mind," I said. "Maybe she dozed off and woke up confused?" It was the only thing I could think of because I couldn't imagine her walking away without letting me or Linda know. She'd know we'd be worried sick.

I picked up my phone and checked the Nextdoor app to see if anyone had responded. I gasped when I read a comment. "Someone thinks they saw her walking toward downtown."

Officer Summit perked up. "Do they mention which street?"

"Rosemary and Third." I stood. "I'm going to go find her."

Officer Summit gave me a kind smile. "Now hold on. Let me tell dispatch and they can get cars over there faster than you can reach her." He picked up his phone and made a call, relaying what I'd discovered, then hung up. "Okay, they're sending a unit over in that direction. We'll find her, Maddie. I promise."

"You're not supposed to promise things," I said. "In case you can't follow through."

He laughed. "Someone's been listening to true crime podcasts, but in this instance, I have no problem promising. We'll find her.

You just sit tight, and once we have her, we'll bring her straight home. Which is all the more reason for you to sit tight."

What he said made sense, but it was hard to sit here and do nothing. "Would anyone like coffee? Tea?"

"I'll take a cup of tea," Margarete said, but Linda shook her head, looking worried.

"This isn't your fault, Linda," I said. "She's run off on me before."

"If I had known…"

Margarete gave her a sympathetic smile. "Deidre always did have a mind of her own. There's no holding her back once she gets something in her head."

"Officer Summit?" I asked.

"I'll come help you," he said, getting out of his chair.

I got up and went into the kitchen to fill up the kettle, Officer Summit following behind me.

As I filled the kettle with water, I couldn't stop thinking about what Margarete had said. What if Aunt Deidre continued to run off after this? I couldn't lock her in. That brought up a whole host of other dangers like the possibility of a fire. But running off was also unsafe. Was I going to have to consider putting her in a more secure facility? It would kill her.

"She's going to be okay, Maddie," Officer Summit said softly.

I turned off the water, then set the kettle on its stand. "I hope so."

"I'm acquainted with your aunt and uncle, you know," he said. "But I knew your uncle better. He helped with my Boy Scout troop. He didn't have a son, but he volunteered anyway and kind of stepped in for the boys whose dads weren't around much. When I was in my teens, he was always there for me. And then when I joined a men's prayer group a few years ago we connected again. Always lending people a hand."

"Uncle Albert was a special person," I said, turning so my butt rested against the counter. "They both are."

I studied him, guessing that he was in his late forties. If I was right, he would have been in his twenties at around the time my mother was killed. There was a good chance he was on the force at the time. Maybe he would have some answers. Maybe, because he'd cared about my uncle, he'd see fit to share them.

"Did you have anything to do with my mother's case?" I asked.

He looked startled by my question.

"I'm presuming you may have been part of the force when she was murdered."

He gave me a tight smile. "I was a rookie. I helped lock down the scene, but I wasn't part of the investigation."

"What do you think of Detective Bergan?" I asked. "Is he still on the force?"

"He retired about six months ago. They replaced him with a new detective from Memphis."

Good riddance, as far as I was concerned. Then the meaning of his words sunk in. "Detective Langley."

"That's right." He grimaced. "I guess you talked to him when he interviewed you about dropping Schroeder off at the butcher shop."

"I did." The kettle was starting to boil, so I grabbed two cups and decided to make a pot instead of two cups. I retrieved the pot from the cupboard and filled the tea strainer accordingly. "Would you like some tea?"

"No, thanks. Never did like it much."

"Coffee?"

"Oh, no," he said. "I'm good."

"Officer Summit," I said, dropping the tea strainer into the ceramic pot. "Since Detective Bergan retired, does that mean my mother's case is closed?"

"Oh, no. A case is never closed until it's solved."

"But it's been nearly twenty years. I can't imagine anyone is still looking into it. Does that mean it's a cold case?"

He grimaced and rubbed the back of his neck. "Honestly, I don't know."

"How would I go about getting a copy of the file?" I asked. "Can I just request it? Or will I have to fill out a Freedom of Information request?"

He gave me a sympathetic look. "Why all the sudden interest?"

"I don't know. I guess this murder brought back a lot of memories. So has coming back home. I left after high school and rarely visited."

"I do recall Albert mentioning that at the prayer group," he said.

"Whenever I asked Detective Bergan for information, he always blew me off. I hardly have any information about what happened to her. I would really like some answers."

"You don't want to know, Maddie," he said sympathetically. "Trust me. I saw her…" He swallowed. "You need to let go."

I stared at him in shock. "What did you see?"

He shook his head. "Things no daughter should know about their mother. You need to let this go. But if you like, I'll do some asking around about the status of the case. While you don't need to know the horrific details, I understand your need for justice."

I knew he was trying to protect me, but I was a grown woman. It was up to me to decide what I could handle or not, but I appreciated that he recognized my need to find whoever hurt her. I was about to thank him when his phone rang.

He pulled it out of his pocket and answered, "Officer Summit." His face brightened. "They did. That's great news. I'll tell her niece." He hung up, beaming. "They found your aunt."

I closed my eyes, relief making me temporarily light-headed. "Thank God. Where was she?"

"The police station."

"What? You mean someone picked her up and took her there?"

"No, she walked there herself."

"What? Why?"

"I don't know," he said, "but they said someone from the department is bringing her home now."

"Who's bringing her home?"

"Detective Langley."

Chapter Twenty-Eight

Noah

The crime scene team didn't turn up anything Lance and I hadn't already figured out during our walk-through. Whoever had broken in had likely used gloves, and it was obvious they had been looking for something in particular.

Lance and I went out to sit in my car and discuss our findings, or lack thereof, in private.

"What do you think?" he asked. "Could Schroeder's accomplice in the department have been behind this?"

"Not likely," I said. "Especially since the car that did the drop-off is probably a stolen vehicle from Chattanooga."

While we'd been inside, Lance had gotten a call that the partial plate number and make and model matched a car stolen from Chattanooga two days prior.

"So it's an outside job," Lance said.

"Not necessarily," I said. "We know that someone involved in the ransacking of Schroeder's house was driving a car stolen from Chattanooga the day after the murder, but that doesn't mean they stole it. We still haven't figured out what they were after, but Maddie said Schroeder was carrying a paper bag, right? What if they were after the contents of the bag?"

"Whatever was in there couldn't be much," Lance said. "It was a small bag."

"Money. Designer drugs. A flash drive with information. A phone. Any number of things someone might consider important could have been in there. What we *do* know is that *someone* took it and *someone else* wants it. We just need to figure out who one of the someones is. Then the rest might all fall into place." I turned to him. "The storage units were a bust?"

"No Schroeders. No Marty the Mans. No names that could be linked to Schroeder."

"That we know of," I said.

He lifted a shoulder. "Agreed."

"I think he's hiding something somewhere. Was the paper bag holding a sample? Was it the whole thing?" I turned to Lance. "Is Dukas sure Schroeder wasn't involved with the Brawlers? They have connections to Chattanooga."

"I can ask again."

"No, I'll do it. Let him get pissed at me for questioning him again."

Lance looked queasy. "Do you think Dukas could be part of it?" Lance asked. "The cover-up with Bergan?"

I considered it. "I think you'd be in a better position to answer that. You've been in the department for eight years."

"My gut says no, but honestly, my gut isn't pointing the finger at anyone else either."

"Has anyone quit or retired?" I asked.

He sat up. "Actually. There is." He turned to face me. "Tony Jayson. He retired about three years ago. He's still around here, living in the woods. He was a sergeant."

"So he had the power to help bury cases."

"You want to pay him a visit too?" he asked.

"Yeah, but first I want to visit the school administration and get some actual evidence of the molestations from Schroeder's personnel file."

"You want to warn them we're coming?" he asked.

"Nah. I think we'll surprise them."

I pulled away from the curb and was heading toward the school when Lance got a call.

"No shit," he said. "Thanks for letting me know." He hung up and frowned. "Maddie Baker's aunt is missing."

I sat upright. "What?" An undercurrent of anxiety had been plaguing me since we left Cock on the Walk.

"Apparently, her aunt wandered away from her house. They have a couple of units looking for her in the vicinity of where she was last seen."

It wasn't lost on me that Maddie hadn't returned either my or Lance's calls. My mind drifted to a darker scenario that had my hands tightening their grip on the wheel.

"Has anyone seen Maddie since the group at the park?"

"She's at her house with Officer Summit."

I was surprised by the surge of relief that washed through me. "Okay. That's good."

"I thought you said you didn't think she'd been out to Cock on the Walk."

"I didn't, but it's good to get confirmation." That was an understatement. "I want updates on the situation."

"Okay," he said, tapping on his phone screen.

We drove in silence for a few minutes before Lance got another text. "They found her."

"Where?"

"She wandered into the police station. She was pretty upset. Kept saying her niece is in danger."

I shot him a glance, then whipped my car into a U-turn and turned on my siren. "Tell them to keep her away from everyone. No one talks to her until we get there."

Blind Bake

"Noah, the woman has dementia."

"We're not taking any chances, and I don't want her telling the wrong person what she knows."

We arrived at the station in less than five minutes. The desk sergeant had gotten Maddie's aunt a bag of shortbread cookies from a vending machine, and a female officer was sitting with her in the waiting room.

Maddie's aunt had a blanket wrapped around her shoulders, and she glanced up when we walked in. "I know you both," she said with a scowl. "You took my Maddie away."

I glanced at Lance, then back at Maddie's aunt. "I don't think we've been properly introduced, Ms. Baker. I'm Detective Noah Langley." I motioned to Lance. "And that's Officer Lance Forrester. We're working on Martin Schroeder's murder case."

"I know," she said impatiently. "You two hooligans hauled her away like a criminal."

I squatted in front of her. "That was all a misunderstanding. Maddie has been very helpful."

"Of course she was," Deidre said. "She's just like her mother, and Andrea, God rest her soul, helped everyone. But Baker was my maiden name. I've been Deidre Saunders for thirty-nine years." Her eyes filled with tears. "I lost my Albert, but I still have his name."

I took her hand. "I heard about your husband's death. I'm sorry for your loss, ma'am."

She sniffled and nodded. The female officer handed her a tissue.

"Maddie gave up everything to help me," Deidre said. "And all I've done is put her in danger."

The female officer seemed to be listening intently. I didn't want to have this conversation in the waiting room, and I definitely wasn't taking her to an interview room. "How about Officer Forrester and I take you home?" I suggested.

"But I haven't told you what I need to tell you."

"You can tell us on the way," I said, standing and offering her a hand.

"You don't believe me," she said bitterly.

"No, ma'am," I said. "I never said any such thing. I just think it's best if we continue this conversation once we get you home."

"I don't want to talk about this in front of Maddie. It's only going to upset her."

"Then we'll talk about it without her."

She narrowed her gaze, staring up at me. "Are you going to take me seriously? Because everyone else is treating me like I'm a crazy old woman."

"I'm taking you as serious as a heart attack, Ms. Saunders." I held her gaze. "I just want to continue this conversation someplace more private."

She must have believed me, because she took my hand and let me help her to her feet. The blanket that had been resting on her shoulders puddled onto her seat.

"Where's your coat, Ms. Saunders?" Lance asked.

She started to become agitated. "I had to get to the police station. I didn't have time to go back in the house and get it. And stop calling me Ms. Saunders. That was my mother-in-law. Call me Deidre."

I shot him a glance. Something had definitely spooked Maddie's aunt, but the question was whether her concern was real or fabricated by her disease.

Lance shrugged out of his jacket and wrapped it around her shoulders. "Let's get you out of here, Miss Deidre."

I led her out the front door to my car in the parking lot. After I got her into the back seat, I turned to Lance, who was standing to the side.

"You sure you want to do this at Maddie's?" When I nodded, he released a loud sigh "Okay. You're the boss."

We got into the car and Lance asked, "Have you got the address?"

I didn't need one, but Deidre didn't know that. "It's 1489 Mockingbird Lane," she said with a sigh. "I know my own address."

When neither of us said anything, she said, "I have my good days and my bad. And today's a good day. A *very* good day. Plenty clear enough for me to remember all my regrets."

I glanced at her in the rearview mirror, wondering what was going through her head.

Lance made a call on his phone and spoke to someone, presumably the officer with Maddie, and told him we were on our way with her aunt.

"I hate this disease," Deidre said softly, staring out the side window. "I stole Maddie's life, and now I've put her in danger."

"How have you put her in danger?" I asked, figuring I could start questioning her informally in the car. I'd prefer to do an official interview, but it might not matter. Evidence put forward by a woman who had documented dementia wasn't likely to stand up in court, so it was essentially inadmissible anyway.

Lance got out his notepad and pen.

"She should never have to drive her car around town and pick up strangers. It's dangerous. Albert is probably rolling over in his grave, ashamed that I let her do it."

"For what it's worth," I say carefully, "Maddie loves you very much. She wants to be here. And she knows how to take care of herself. She kicked my ass last night in our self-defense demonstration." I cringed. "Excuse my language."

"I don't remember much about last night," she says, her voice fading. "And I sure didn't know she could do that." She was silent for a moment. "She wanted to take Tae Kwon Do after Andrea died, but I wouldn't hear of it. It wasn't ladylike. I can't help wondering if I should have let her. She felt so out of control, and it was something simple I could have done to restore her peace of mind. Besides, she went and learned it anyway. She just kept it from me."

"I'm sure you did what you thought was best, Miss Deidre," I said. "And I'm sure Maddie knows that."

"But we all know that saying about good intentions," she said, her voice tight. "The path to hell is paved with them."

"You're being too hard on yourself, Miss Deidre," Lance said. "We all make mistakes. Every single one of us. Noah's right. Maddie loves you. She knows you were doing the best you could."

So was that her concern? She thought Maddie was in danger because she was an Uber driver letting strangers into her car? That wasn't exactly something the police could help her resolve, but her mind didn't work normally. Then I remembered what she'd said about not having time to go back inside and get her coat before leaving for the station.

"Why didn't you have time to get your coat, Miss Deidre?" I asked, watching her in the rearview mirror.

"Because that man told me she was in danger, and someone was going to get her."

I jerked the car over to the side of the road, then turned around to face her. "What man?"

"An older gentleman. I can't remember his name. Or maybe he didn't give it." She closed her eyes. "I can't remember now. I think he told me and I forgot."

"Where did you see him?" I asked.

"In the garage behind the house. I went upstairs to take a nap—I've been feeling out of sorts all day—and saw him from my bedroom window. I went down to see what he wanted."

"That was dangerous, Miss Deidre," Lance said. "He could have hurt you. You shouldn't have gone out there alone."

"He looked cold, so I went down to ask him if he wanted to come inside. But he wasn't in the backyard by the time I got out there. I found him in the garage. He apologized for hiding in there." She squinted. "Or I think he did."

"Did he say why he was hiding in your garage?" I asked, wondering if this was a product of her dementia.

"He said he was there for Maddie." She looked up at me in the mirror. "She's in danger."

"Did he tell you that?"

She shook her head, starting to get agitated. "I don't remember." She smacked her hand against the side of her head. "Why can't I remember? This is important!" Another smack.

I unbuckled my seatbelt and got out of the car, opening the back door so I could sit next to her and grab her hand. "That's enough of that. We don't want Maddie to think we're abusing you," I said jokingly, but it fell flat. "Miss Deidre, you're doing the best you can, and that's all anyone can ask."

"But it's not enough!" she protested and started to cry. "I need to protect her! I need to save her!"

"That's our job," I said. "You let *us* take care of that."

She started to sob and wrapped an arm around my neck, clinging to me as she cried into my shirt. I glanced up at Lance, unsure of what to think or even do. We needed to get her home, but I wasn't sure taking a sobbing Deidre home was the best thing for Maddie.

"Lance, why don't you drive, and I'll sit back here with Miss Deidre?"

He nodded and got out, coming around to the driver's side. "You want to head to Maddie's?"

"No," Deidre said, sounding panicked. "She can't see me like this."

Lance gave me a questioning look.

"Are you hungry, Miss Deidre?" I asked. "Lance and I have been working nonstop and haven't had time for lunch."

Her crying slowed and she sat up a little straighter. "I don't think I should be going into a sit-down restaurant."

"No," I said softly. "Of course not. We need to get you back to Maddie. I was thinking we could pick something up. Maybe even bring something to Maddie. What does *she* like?"

That brightened her up. "She loves Big Bob's Drive-In, or at least she did when she was little. She liked their cheese fries and chocolate shakes."

"Okay, then," I said with a smile. "What do you say to Big Bob's, Lance?"

"Sounds like a plan," he said enthusiastically as he pulled out onto the road. "I love that place."

"What about you, Miss Deidre?" I asked. "What would you like?"

"I haven't had one of their burgers for years," she said faintly, as though caught in a memory. "Albert had to stop eating them because of his heart." She looked up at me, teary-eyed. "We were so careful after he found out he had heart disease, but he died anyway." Several tears streamed down her face.

"I'm so sorry you lost him," I said soothingly. "It sounds like you had thirty-nine wonderful years together, but I know that's not comforting when you're missing him so much. I'd give anything to have a relationship like yours."

She smiled up at me through her tears, reaching up to pat my face. "You know, Noah. You're not the asshole I thought you were." Then she added a prim, "Pardon my French."

Lance burst into laughter, and a huge grin spread across my face.

"Don't let that get around," I teased. "I kind of like my asshole status."

"It won't serve you much in the relationship department," she said with a laugh. Then she pointed out the window. "Oh, look. We're here."

Lance pulled up to the drive-through menu board and placed our order—we really had skipped lunch—and then pulled up to the window and we waited.

"Miss Deidre," I said. "Did the man you talked to have a weapon?"

"Oh, no," she said dismissively.

"Did you feel threatened by him?"

"What? No. He was very polite. Said he should have gotten permission to stay in our garage, but he didn't want to scare us."

"Did he happen to say if his name was Ernie?"

She squinted as she thought, then shook her head. "I don't remember. But he looked very familiar. I was sure I'd seen him before."

"Maybe last night," I prompted, which went against everything I had been trained to do in an interview, but I suspected we were working on borrowed time before the details slipped her mind, and I needed to know what she saw. "In the parking lot outside the rec center."

"Maybe."

"That's fair," I said. "So you saw him from your bedroom window. You went out to check on him and found him in the garage. Why did you look in there?"

"I saw him close the door."

"Okay," I said. "And he said he'd been staying there?"

She frowned. "I'm trying to remember. I know he was upset. He told me Maddie is in danger."

"But he didn't say why?"

She shook her head. "I don't think so. But he was so insistent that I got scared. I knew I had to tell the police."

I pulled a card out of my pocket and handed it to her. "Next time, you call me, okay? We can't have you getting lost or freezing to death."

She took the card and looked it over. "Thank you, Noah."

An older teenage boy opened the drive-through window and handed Lance several bags and a drink tray.

"Don't thank me yet," I said, tugging out my wallet and passing a couple of twenties up to Lance. "Wait until you dig into your burger."

We got the food, and then Lance headed to her house. Miss Deidre said she wanted to wait to eat at home, and while the smell of the fries and burgers made my stomach audibly growl, I decided we should wait to dig in too.

My mind settled on the problem of what to do about Maddie. Although I believed Deidre's story, I highly doubted the chief would approve of stationing someone at their house. Especially since the intel had come from a woman with dementia. But I planned to check on the garage. If I could prove someone had been sleeping out there, it might help my case.

Maddie was already running out of the house by the time Lance pulled up to the curb. She opened the back door on Deidre's side, immediately reaching in for her aunt. She stopped short when she saw the Big Bob's bag on Deidre's lap.

"You stopped for *lunch?*" she demanded, her gaze lifting to mine. "I've been worried sick, and you stopped for lunch!"

I held her gaze, recognizing her reaction for what it was. I'd seen it time and again. She needed someone to blame for this, and I was the easiest person to target.

"I told him to stop," Deidre said, sounding exhausted. "I remembered how much you love their cheesy fries and chocolate shakes." She gave her an apologetic look.

Maddie's anger faded, and it was easy to see her guilt setting in.

"Maddie, let's get your aunt inside."

She ran a hand over her head in frustration, but then she sighed. "Yeah. Okay."

Deidre and Maddie walked into the house, Deidre holding the

Big Bob's bag for her and her niece, while Lance and I followed with their drink tray.

"Good guess on telling her that Maddie would be worried about her," Lance said under his breath. "But it wasn't much of a guess since you likely knew it was true."

My heart skipped a beat. Did he know I'd come over here last night? I realized he just thought I'd just presumed. "Yeah."

"What do you make of this mystery guy?"

"I'm not sure yet," I said, "but if I had to guess, I'd say it's Ernie. I definitely plan to look out back. First, let's go answer any questions Maddie might have."

"You've been calling her that all day," he said.

I turned to look at him. "What?"

"Maddie. Up until this morning, you called her Madelyn, but today you're calling her Maddie."

"She told me to call her Maddie."

He grinned. "That's not what she said in the interrogation room. What changed?"

I couldn't tell him about last night, and the way she'd looked at me when she said she wanted us to have tea together as Noah and Maddie, not Detective Langley and Madelyn. "I guess I picked it up from listening to you."

Then I stepped in front of him and entered the house ahead of him.

Maddie stood to the side while two other women got Deidre settled on a sofa and wrapped a throw around her lap.

"Go eat your food while it's hot," Deidre said to Maddie, holding up the greasy bag. "Bring mine out here. I'll just eat it on the sofa."

Maddie looked up at me standing in the doorway. I still had the drink tray. She glanced down at it, then grabbed the food bag from Deidre and told me, "Come with me into the kitchen."

Lance, who'd just entered the room behind me, nodded. "I've got this covered," he said. "Go ahead and fill her in."

Once we reached the kitchen, Maddie set the bag on the counter and took the tray out of my hands and set that down too. "What happened?" she asked, her voice shaking. "How did *you* end up bringing her home?"

I tried not to take offense at the emphasis she put on *you*. "She showed up at the station, Maddie. She said she had to tell the police that you were in danger. She saw a man in your backyard who told her so."

Her eyes flew wide. "*What?*"

"I plan to go check out there in just a second. I wanted to check on you first."

Tears filled her eyes. "I was so scared. I told you I'm bad at this. But Linda, the home health aide, called me and told me she was missing, and I just *panicked*." She looked up at me, heartbreak in her eyes. "I'm going to end up hurting her."

"Hey," I said. "No." I didn't give it any thought, I reached for her, pulling her into my chest and wrapping her up in my arms.

She didn't resist, just sank into me and cried into my chest.

I told myself this was a normal reaction to someone in pain. She wasn't the first person I'd hugged in the course of an investigation, but I couldn't fool myself into thinking it meant nothing. I wanted to stroke her hair and wipe her tears away.

I'd crossed a line I hadn't intended to cross.

I don't want to be your next mistake.

She'd been right. Starting something with her would be a mistake for both of us, so why didn't I want to let her go?

But this wasn't about me, or the things I wanted despite myself. This was about comforting her. "This wasn't your fault, Maddie. You weren't even here. Honestly, it sounds like it wasn't anyone's fault. But you—" I pulled her back so I could look into her face. "*You* are not to blame for this, so don't take ownership of it, okay?"

She didn't answer. She looked like she was about to fall apart, so I hugged her again, and she wrapped her arms around my waist.

I liked her in my arms. I liked that she was turning to me for comfort. I wanted to make her aunt's dementia easier for her, but I didn't have the first clue how to do it.

"She loves you, you know," I whispered into her ear. "I think she would do anything for you. Even walk over a mile in the cold without a coat to get help for you."

"I don't know what to make of that," she said. "I was so scared for her. When I saw the leftover container in the garage, I worried someone might have taken her."

That caught my attention. I set her back again, moving slowly so as not to startle her. I needed her to remain vulnerable. I needed her to talk to me instead of hiding what she knew. "Why would you think someone had taken her?"

Her face froze.

I lifted a hand and swiped back the hair clinging to her damp cheek. Bad idea, but that realization came to me too late. "I want to protect you, Maddie. You and your aunt. Can't you see that? Does this have anything to do with the man you were talking to in the parking lot last night?"

Just like that, the openness in her eyes was replaced by a shuttered look.

I suppressed a groan, because I knew letting her see my frustration was the surest way to get her to shut down even more. "Why won't you tell me?"

"You think I'm involved," she accused with only an ember of heat behind her words.

"No," I said honestly. "I think you're protecting someone. I think you're protecting Ernie Foust."

Her nostrils flared slightly as she looked away.

"Don't you see that telling me is the best way to protect him? You thought asking around about him might have gotten your aunt kidnapped. How bad would you feel right now if that were true?"

She pulled back, putting distance between us, her eyes flashing with anger. "That's not fair."

"Maybe not," I conceded with more bitterness than I'd intended, "but that's life. There's not a damn thing fair about it, and I'm not going to pretend there is. If life were fair, your mother would still be alive. Your aunt wouldn't have dementia." And Caleb wouldn't have imploded both of our lives, but I didn't include that personal note. Her own stack of unfairness was high enough to make my point.

She turned so that her side was facing me, but I could see her mind was whirling.

"I've spent the morning trying to find Ernie too," I said.

Her face jerked to search mine, but I couldn't read her emotions.

"I know Ernie talked to you in the parking lot last night," I said softly. I wasn't one hundred percent on that, but I felt no shame in pretending otherwise. Especially if it convinced her to open up. "I know you've been looking for him because I've been about ten steps behind you. I saw your trail of Déjà Brew cup breadcrumbs."

The corners of her lips turned up slightly, but the almost-smile faded before it could fully form.

"Hell," I said with a deprecating laugh, "I even went to Cock on the Walk to look for you."

Her eyes widened. "Why would you go out there?"

Irritation burned a path down my throat. "Because I know that fucker Roscoe told you to look for Ernie out there, and your friends at the park told me you might be going out there next."

She eyed me with confusion. "So you went to see if I'd found Ernie?"

"No," I said, my frustration building, although I wasn't sure why. Because I didn't want her to know how much I care about her even though I hardly know her? Because I didn't want her to see *my* vulnerability?

I'd made myself vulnerable to Caleb and he had used it against me, first breaking my heart and then nearly piercing it with a bullet.

Jesus, I was fucked up.

"You were looking for *me*?" she asked, starting to get outraged. "It's not against the law to search for someone."

"I was looking for you to make sure you were *okay*," I snapped, hating that I was telling her this. I flung my hand in her direction. "I left you a voicemail telling you to call me and let me know you were safe."

No, I was pretty sure I'd *begged*.

Goddammit. I was losing control, acting like a lovesick preteen. But this woman...

"I'm going out back to check out the garage," I grunted, starting for the back door. But the door was already opening, and a uniformed officer entered the kitchen.

"Already looked," he said. "Nothing out there."

I narrowed my eyes. "Officer Summit?"

"That would be me. You must be Langley. Don't think we've had the pleasure of working a case together." He held out his hand for me to shake.

I gripped his hand, then quickly released it.

"Ms. Baker told me she'd found a Tupperware container of partially eaten leftovers out back, so I went to investigate. Looks like Ms. Saunders took it out back, maybe got turned around and confused, then headed toward downtown."

I held his gaze, my body language more hostile than I intended due to residual anger. "Ms. Saunders said she encountered a man in the backyard. She said he'd been staying in the garage."

Summit shook his head, wearing a friendly smile that seemed to take no note of my unfriendly posture. "Didn't see any sign of that, but of course, you're welcome to see for yourself."

I narrowed my gaze, pinning a hard stare on him. Something about the guy rubbed me the wrong way, although I couldn't pinpoint what. *Shit.* I was probably letting my conflict with Maddie bleed over into my work.

All the more reason to stay the fuck away from her.

I stomped outside and took several deep breaths, trying to calm down, then glanced around the backyard. It wasn't very big. If Deidre had seen the guy from her window, he must have been standing front and center. I turned back to look at the house. Several windows overlooked the backyard, so I couldn't be sure which was hers.

I pulled out my phone and texted Lance.

Go up to Deidre's window and look down into the backyard.

He sent me a thumbs-up emoji, and a minute later, I saw him standing at a window on the right side of the house.

I called him on the phone, not wanting to shout, and when he answered, said, "Is that her only window?"

"Yep."

"Okay. Tell me if you lose sight of me as I walk around." I started to walk toward the opposite side of the yard.

"Officer Summit said no one had been in the garage other than Deidre."

"Yeah, well, that's his opinion, now isn't it?" I grumped, keeping my eyes on the ground, hoping something would jump out at me.

"I wouldn't dismiss his opinion," he said. "He used to be a detective."

I stopped and turned around to face him in the window. "How long ago?"

He was silent for a moment. "He was a detective when I joined the force. I think he transferred back to patrol a couple of years later. But I don't know, Noah," he said. "He's a pretty stand-up guy."

"Perfect cover. How long has he been with the department?"

"He's about to retire."

"Fuck me." I shot a glance at the back door, then marched to the side door of the garage. "Check on him and see what he's doing right now. Keep an eye on him."

"Okay."

He hung up, and I turned on my phone's flashlight, shining it around the space. The garage was full of clutter—a lawnmower, tools, discarded furniture. It was hard to move around the space. If someone had crashed here, I wasn't sure where they would have slept.

I started paying closer attention to the dust on the various pieces, looking for signs someone had moved things around. I finally found it in the back corner. The dirt on the floor looked like it had been displaced, and the dust on the table had been smeared. I traced the path from the corner to the door and found a partial footprint—a sneaker by the look of it.

The door swung open, and Lance appeared in the opening.

"Well?" I asked.

"He told Maddie to call if she thought someone was prowling around, but he seemed pretty convinced her aunt had imagined the whole thing. Then he took off."

"He's a fucking liar," I said, pointing to the print.

"Dammit," he said. "I like that guy." He looked up at me. "So who do you think was out here? Because there's no way in hell Deidre or Summit made that footprint, and Summit wasn't wearing athletic shoes."

"It's too big for Maddie or her aunt. I think it was Ernie Foust," I said. "I think he's been staying in her garage."

"Shit," Lance grunted.

"It fits," I said. "No one knows where he is. Second, from what Deidre said, I don't think he was trying to threaten her. It was more of a warning. Maybe he was staying out here to watch over Maddie." I turned to Lance. "Did he know her before all of this?"

"You mean like a family connection? Not that I know of."

"Any kind of connection at all?"

"I don't know. Maybe we should ask her."

I rubbed the back of my neck. "I think you should do it, but first I need to figure out what to do about the footprint. It would be an uphill fight to get the funds for the crime lab to run the print on a simple B&E, especially since it doesn't look to have involved a B, and Summit would know we're onto him. If he was Bergan's partner…"

"Shit," he repeated.

"Exactly," I said. "So we'll keep this to ourselves for now. I'll take a photo of the print while you go ask Maddie about her connection to Ernie."

"Okay."

He spun around to head out the door, but I called after him. "Lance."

He glanced over his shoulder.

"Tell her not to call him. Under any circumstances. Tell her to call you."

He frowned, studying me. "Not you?"

My heart felt like it was being squeezed by a juicer. "No. She'll be more inclined to call you."

That was a lie, but I had no intention of confessing that.

He studied me for a long moment, then nodded and walked out the door.

Chapter Twenty-Nine

Maddie

I'd gone through so many emotions over the last two hours that I had a massive headache. After Noah had stormed out, Officer Summit told me what he'd found out back—nothing—and Lance proceeded to take a call. He asked me to point out Aunt Deidre's room, then headed upstairs, presumably to check it out.

"Where's that nice young man I talked to in the car?" my aunt asked, eating her hamburger as she sat on the sofa, which was more than a little worrisome. Aunt Deidre was a woman who conformed to the laws of civility, and eating a hamburger on her sofa with a crocheted afghan on her lap in the middle of the afternoon broke several of them.

She stared at me expectantly, waiting for an answer.

"You mean Lance? Officer Forrester?" I asked, rubbing my forehead. I felt like I was living in a parallel universe watching her. Next thing I knew, she'd be ordering a pizza and popping open a beer.

"No. I'm talking about the nice man in the shirt and tie."

"Detective Langley?" I asked in surprise.

Now that I thought about it, it wasn't so hard to believe. Sure, he was rough around the edges, but underneath that gruff exterior he had a heart. He'd pulled back his armor and let me catch a glimpse of it last night...and then again in the kitchen. The way he'd held me had caught me off guard, and I was sure it had surprised him just as much. Last night, I'd told him there was more to his messed-upness than what he'd gone through with his girlfriend and dad. And after our talk just now, I felt even more certain about that. He'd gotten pissed when I'd practically forced him to admit he'd been worried about me. Sure, he made it clear he didn't think we should get involved, but he practically wore a neon sign flashing his issues—commitment, trust, intimacy, just to name a few. The list was probably as long as my forearm.

One more reason to stay far away from Noah Langley.

So why was my heart protesting?

Because it's an idiot.

Lance came back into the living room, hanging around in the background while Officer Summit finished up some notes in his notepad.

"Is everything okay?" I asked Lance.

"Yep."

Officer Summit stood and walked over to my aunt and me. "Now that Deidre's safe and sound, I'll let y'all get back to your day. You've got nothing to worry about, but if you run into any trouble, you be sure to call me," he said, placing a business card on the end table by the sofa. "Your Uncle Albert would want me taking care of you both."

"Thank you, Officer Summit," I said. "Thank you for all your help."

"Just doin' my job."

He let himself out, and I realized Lance had stood at the side, observing the interaction. He slid out back to join Noah, and I paced the living room, probably making Linda and Margarete nervous.

Something didn't feel right. I just couldn't figure out what. Was I just unsettled after my latest emotional upheaval with Noah?

Lance returned to the living room after a few minutes, and I could tell something had changed, because now he seemed more guarded, more rigid. He looked more official now. "I have a couple more questions for you, Maddie, and one for Miss Deidre, but I can just talk to you both here."

I supposed it should be comforting that he didn't want to take me back to the station, but I was still anxious. Why was he acting so official?

Aunt Deidre watched him intently from her cocoon on the sofa, Linda and Margarete still huddled around her like mother hens.

"Okay..." I said hesitantly.

"I'll start with you, Miss Deidre," he said, offering her a warm smile. "Could you tell me what the man in your backyard was wearing?"

She nodded. "Jeans, one of those sweatshirts young people like to wear now. You know, with hoods and no zippers, and a pair of sneakers. I think they were supposed to be white, but they looked like they were a dark gray. Oh! And he had a black backpack."

I stared at my aunt in shock. "Aunt Deidre, are you sure you're describing the guy you saw in our backyard and not the one I spoke with last night?"

She swung her attention to me. "Definitely this afternoon."

She had just perfectly described Ernie's outfit from the night before, which lent weight to Officer Summit's insistence that Aunt Deidre had imagined it all. Unless...was it possible Ernie had followed us home and stayed out in the garage?

I glanced over at Lance. "You heard Officer Summit. He seemed convinced Aunt Deidre made it all up."

"I know what I saw!" she protested, but then she sank back into the cushions as though she was no longer sure.

Lance gave me a long look before turning back to my aunt.

"The man you saw. He was wearing the backpack? Both shoulder straps on?"

She nodded.

"You said you saw him going into your garage, correct?"

"Oh yes," she said, seeming to get her confidence back. "Definitely."

"And then what happened?"

I shot Lance a questioning look. Could he and Noah have found something that Officer Summit had missed? Then a darker fear took root in my head. What if he was trying to prove that I was unfit to take care of her? Aunt Deidre was all I had left. I couldn't lose her too. Not yet. But Noah knew that. I'd exposed my fear to him, and I refused to believe he'd hurt me like that. No, this meant they were taking her claims seriously. Despite what Officer Summit thought.

Aunt Deidre stared up at him, her eyes bright with awareness. "Like I told that nice young detective, I saw the man in the yard and I came down to see if he was okay. Then I found him in the garage. He ate the leftovers, but he was nervous that I'd found him. He said he was there because..." Her voice trailed off and worry filled her eyes. "I can't remember why he was there." She glanced over at Margarete. "Why can't I remember?" Her eyes filled with tears. "It's right there, and it just slips away."

"There, there, Dee," Margarete said. "You've had an exhausting day. Would you like to go lie down?"

"Yes, I think I would."

Margarete looked up at Lance. "Would that be all right?"

"Of course," he said. "But if you think of something else that might be helpful, I'd appreciate it if you'd let us know."

"Of course," Aunt Deidre said as she handed her trash to Linda and then let Margarete help her up from the sofa.

"I'll help her get settled," Linda said, looking lost and upset.

I gave her a quick hug and told her everything was okay, but I could see she was still shaken—and likely worried she might be out of a job.

I knew I should let her do her part, but I felt helpless. Superfluous. I'd nearly lost my aunt, and now I wasn't even helping her to bed. "Maybe I should do it," I said.

Margarete winked at me as she rounded the corner to the staircase. "Don't be silly. That fine young officer still needs to ask you some questions."

Was she trying to set me up?

Only Lance Forrester wasn't the law enforcement officer I was interested in, which was too damn bad since he seemed way less complicated.

Lance shifted on his feet.

"I think I need some tea," I said, heading for the kitchen. What I really wanted was wine, but it seemed wrong to be day drinking after my aunt had just run away.

"Your aunt got you a shake and some cheesy fries," Lance said, following me.

"How could she get those if she didn't have any money?" I asked as I reached for the kettle. I seemed to be making a lot of tea lately.

He nodded to the back door.

Noah paid for food for her and me?

It was yet another layer in a man who kept surprising me.

I filled the pot with water and turned it on. "What questions do you need to ask me, Lance?"

I could see Noah through the back window. He stood just outside the garage door, studying something inside.

Stop thinking about Noah Langley and worry about more pressing matters...like the man who's about to interrogate you.

I turned to face him, giving him my undivided attention.

He stood next to the back door, not exactly a casual pose but not intimidating either. "First of all," he said, "you said the description your aunt just gave matched the man you talked to in the parking lot last night? Can you confirm that?"

Why wasn't Noah asking me all of this himself? "Yes, it's exactly what he was wearing last night, which is why I have to wonder if Officer Summit was right about Aunt Deidre getting confused."

He nodded, not commenting one way or the other.

If he thought she'd imagined it, wouldn't he say?

"Next question: prior to your encounter outside of the butcher shop, did you have any previous acquaintance with Ernie Foust?"

I snort-laughed, finally realizing why Lance was in here and not Noah. Noah had run out because things had gotten too emotional, and he couldn't handle that. He couldn't handle facing *me*. "Oh my God, he was too chickenshit to ask me that question himself."

Lance didn't confirm or deny, just watched me, waiting for my answer.

"Yeah, but I didn't realize it until I got back from dropping Mr. Schroeder off. When I told Ernie my name that night, he said he knew me through my mother. I asked Aunt Deidre about it, and she told me he used to be the high school janitor."

He blinked at me. "What?"

I cocked my head. "Why do you look like you're going to be sick?"

"Ernie Foust was our janitor?"

"Yeah. I sure hadn't remembered him, but then again, does any high school student pay attention to the janitorial staff?"

"No. I guess not." He paused, then said, "I know Officer Summit suggested you call him if you run into any trouble, but Detective Langley wants you to call me instead."

His words sank in like a fifty-pound rock tossed into the Briny River. "I see."

He narrowed his eyes. "I don't know what you're thinking, but I assure you that we're not trying to entrap you or pull off anything devious. We just want to make sure you and Miss Deidre are safe."

That wasn't what I'd been thinking at all. What I had been thinking was that Noah Langley had run out to Cock on the Walk because he was worried about my personal safety, but now he was pawning me off on his partner. What was I supposed to make of that?

"I see," I said again in a stiff tone.

Lance's expression made it clear he didn't believe me, but he wished me a good day and walked out the back door.

Chapter Thirty

Noah

Wearing a grim expression, Lance found me in the backyard. "Well, that went well."

I pushed out a sigh. "Which part didn't she like?"

"It would be easier to list what she *did* like." He glanced over to the garage. "Still want to keep that to ourselves?"

"Yep."

"Get a photo of the print?"

"Yeah. Did you find out if she knew Ernie Foust before all of this?"

"It was more like *he* knew *her*. I guess he was a janitor at the school and knew her mother."

"What?"

"I know, right? Maddie didn't remember him, and neither did I. I also told her to call me instead of Summit if she needs help."

"You think she'll do it?" I asked.

"Honestly, I don't know."

I had a feeling she wouldn't, which scared me more than I wanted to admit. But the best way to protect Maddie was to find out who killed Martin Schroeder and put him behind bars.

"Let's go back to our original plan to talk to the principal at the high school. Then I think we should have another chat with Darren Schroeder to see if he knew anything about his father's extracurricular activities with students. After that, we'll accelerate our plan to stop by Bergan's house and talk with his wife."

"Sounds like a full afternoon. All I ask is that I get to eat my now-cold hamburger, because I'm starving."

We both ate on the way, and even semi-cold the burgers were good. We'd just finished when I pulled into the parking lot and saw students pouring out of the building.

"Looks like school just let out," Lance says.

"No shit," I grumbled as I slowly drove through the mass exodus and maneuvered into a visitor parking space close to the front door.

The school had a buzzer on the outer door to get inside, but we didn't need it. There was still a steady stream of students coming out, and Lance and I were pushing against it like two salmon swimming upstream.

A bored teenager sat at the front desk, staring at her phone. "School's been dismissed, so you don't need to sign your student out," she said, not bothering to look up.

Her demeanor pissed me off, so I said in an official voice, "I'm Detective Langley and this is Officer Forrester. You're just the person we need to talk to."

Her head jerked up, her eyes wide.

"Asshole," Lance chuckled under his breath.

"I didn't do it," she blurted.

I leaned a forearm on the counter, not all that surprised she felt guilty about *something*. "Really? Because that's not what your buddy said."

Her mouth dropped open, and she looked like she was about to pass out from shock.

"Can I help you officers?" asked a woman as she rounded the corner.

I looked up at her. "We need to speak to Principal Posner."

"Uh..." She shifted her gaze to the terrified teen, then back to us. "He's in his office. You can follow me."

I gave the teen a hard stare. "Don't do it again."

"I won't," she said with a shaky voice, staring up at me with wide eyes.

"Then we're done here."

She reached under the desk, grabbed her backpack, and ran out the door.

The woman looked aggravated. "Desiree wasn't done with her shift."

When I didn't answer, she let out a loud sigh and headed toward the back. We followed.

I knew Principal Posner was a man in his early sixties working past retirement—facts I'd learned after moving to Cockamamie—but I'd never met him. When we appeared in the doorway, he was sitting at his desk, on the phone. It struck me that he looked older, more like he was in his seventies, but I suspected it was the result of dealing with the stress of teenagers for thirty-plus years.

He took one look at us, froze for a moment, then said, "Sandra, I'm gonna have to call you back."

He hung up, shifting his gaze from me to Lance and back again.

"Mr. Posner," I said, walking into the room, "I'm Detective Langley, and this is Officer Forrester. We're here to ask a few questions about Martin Schroeder."

He got up to shake our hands, then motioned to the two chairs in front of his desk. "Please have a seat. I was wondering when you'd come by."

Lance's brow rose. "You were expecting us?"

"Well, when a thirty-year teacher gets murdered with no obvious suspects, it doesn't take a brain surgeon to know a detective or two is going to show up."

His statement raised a few questions, but first things first. I pulled out my phone, started a recording app, and set it on the desk. "Mr. Posner, I'm going to record this interview so I don't have to take notes. I'm sure you don't have a problem with that."

He looked like he was going to say something, but then a tight smile stretched across his face. "Of course, Detective."

I let him sit for several uncomfortable seconds before I started. "You said we have no obvious suspects. What makes you say that?"

He gave me a blank stare. "Well, it's obvious. He was murdered on Monday night, and you still haven't arrested anyone. So it stands to reason you're now branching out to his outer circles of friends and coworkers."

"Who were Mr. Schroeder's friends when he worked here?" I asked.

Mr. Posner sat back in his seat, steepling his fingers over his slightly rounded stomach. "Martin had difficulty connecting socially with his coworkers."

I couldn't help snorting. "Is that HR speak for he didn't have any friends?"

He grinned, but it was obvious he was placating me. "Martin was difficult. He didn't get along with most of the other teachers, and they weren't always shy about their animosity."

"And I'm guessing that's your HR speak for saying they got into arguments." I leaned into the arm of my chair. "This might go faster if you stopped beating around the bush and gave it to me straight."

He shot me a glare. "It seems wrong to speak ill of the dead."

"It sounds like there are plenty of people who don't share your compunction, so maybe we should start with you giving us a list."

"Of people who didn't like Martin?" he asked with a bitter laugh. "It would be easier to give you a list of people he got along with."

"Okay," I said. "Give me that."

"Adam Brant. The head of the science department. They often ate lunch together, until Martin retired."

"Does that mean Adam Brant is still working here?" I asked. "He hasn't retired or quit?"

"Oh, no. He's a good fifteen years younger than Martin. I worried Martin would be contrary when I promoted Adam instead of him, but they must have worked out some kind of compromise."

"Was Schroeder a good teacher?" I asked.

He pulled a face and shifted in his seat. "I wouldn't go that far."

"So he was a shit teacher," I said dryly, then added, "Pardon my cursing."

"His classes often had lower test scores on standardized testing," he said, looking uncomfortable.

"Yet he taught here for more than thirty years," I said.

Mr. Posner looked pissed. "I can hear the accusation in your voice. *Why didn't I get rid of him?* Ever heard of tenure, Detective? It makes it very hard to get rid of teachers with poorer teaching styles."

"Shit teacher seems like a shorter, more accurate way to describe it," Lance said. "I had him, so I speak on good authority."

Mr. Posner turned his glare on my partner. "When you're an administrator, sometimes your hands are tied."

"Is that why you let him continue to teach even when there were accusations that he'd molested students?" I asked.

His face paled. "What? Where did you hear that?"

"That part's not important," I said. "The part that *is* important is that I don't hear you denying it."

Mr. Posner squirmed again. "You have to understand that things are different now. People were more tolerant of things people now find offensive. People these days are 'woke.'" He lifted his fingers to form air quotes.

Lance's hands tightened around the arms of his chair. "I think you mean that people decided women didn't have to tolerate sexual harassment and assault."

Mr. Posner opened his mouth and closed it. He took a breath, then tried again. "I understand your frustration, Lance." He gave him a half-hearted grin. "Yes, I remember you. You had quite an arm. Got yourself a football scholarship to UTC."

"I did," Lance said, holding his gaze. I could feel the anger radiating from him. "I nearly flunked out because the teachers here were so bad they didn't prepare me for college."

Mr. Posner's brow rose. "You're blaming your poor academic performance on me?"

"You're the man in charge." Lance pushed out a breath. "But that's water under the bridge. What we're addressing has to do with more than people being 'woke.'"

"Like the administration ignoring the complaints of female students who claimed to be harassed by Martin Schroeder," I said.

Mr. Posner made a face. "I'm not sure what you heard, Detective Langley, but it's not as bad as you think it was."

"When I look at Martin Schroeder's file, which I will as soon as this discussion is over, how many complaints will I find?" I asked.

The principal's face paled. "We've had many teachers come and go throughout the years. It's not like I know what's in *all* of their files off the top of my head."

"So you're saying you've had so many teachers accused of sexual misconduct you can't remember," I said.

"What?" he gasped, flustered. "Of course not!"

"How many teachers would you say have been accused, Mr. Posner?" I asked.

He made another face. "Probably eight or nine." His expression turned pleading. "That might sound like a lot, but that includes the track coach who ran off with a senior." He gave me a pleading look. "But he was twenty-two, and they were in love."

Like that made it better.

"Why did Martin Schroeder stop working here?" I asked.

Mr. Posner looked nervous. "He'd worked here thirty-one years."

"If you're trying to insinuate he retired, just remember I *will* be looking at his file. Was he fired or did he retire?"

"He retired."

"But he retired under duress, am I right?" I asked. "Was it before or after the police investigation into his alleged molestation of a student?"

Mr. Posner leaned forward. "That case went away! Detective Bergan said there wasn't enough evidence to push it forward."

"How many cases were filed with the police?" I asked.

"You'd be in a better position to answer that," the principal spat.

"Humor me," I said.

Swallowing hard, the principal said, "Four." He grimaced. "Apparently Martin was having difficulty with self-control the past year or two of his employment."

"You think?" Lance said in disgust.

"Detective Bergan assured me the cases would never be made public. He said he would keep them quiet to protect the underaged girls. I convinced Martin to retire to keep from bringing disgrace to his family. Plus it would remove him from temptation."

"Jesus," Lance muttered under his breath. "You know what would have also removed him from molesting teenage girls? Putting him behind bars."

I shot Lance a warning look, but I understood his frustration. He was a cop—a damned good one—and this had happened in his hometown, his alma mater, maybe even to one of his classmates, and he'd missed it all. He was pissed as hell at Martin Schroeder, but I suspected he was pissed at himself too.

"Did you work out any kind of deal with Detective Bergan to keep it quiet?" I asked. "Did you do him any favors? Make sure one of his kids got a spot on a team or an A on an important test?"

"What?" he blustered, his face turning red. "I would never do anything like that!"

"So let me get this straight," I said dryly as I leaned forward and tapped on the desk to make my point. "You had no problem letting a pervert sexually assault students, but you draw the line at securing a kid a spot on a team or a good grade?" I leaned in closer. "Sorry, I'm just trying to figure out your line in the sand."

"You don't know what it was like," he protested in a whine. "I was under *so much* pressure."

"Oh, poor Mr. Posner," Lance said mockingly. "You had it so much worse than those girls." His eyes narrowed. "I bet it was partially their fault, right? Wearing low-cut tops and short skirts."

"Try shorts with their ass cheeks hanging out," the principal said bitterly. "Girls these days have no idea how to dress appropriately. Where are their parents?"

I leaned back in my seat, taking a casual pose as though giving his assertion merit. "Maybe a teacher showing them the consequences of their actions isn't such a bad thing," I said. "Better to learn here, in the safety of the school, than out in the real world, where worse things could happen. Right? Like getting beaten up and raped. Better to just get fondled. I mean, what's the harm in that?"

"Right," Mr. Posner said, then shook his head. "I mean no. It was wrong, but it could have been *so much* worse. Many of the girls changed after their situations were brought to my attention. While I don't condone what Martin did, obviously, it all seemed to work out."

I thought about Chrissy at Déjà Brew, and the bitterness she carried with her—would likely always carry with her—and I wanted to punch Mr. Smugass's teeth out.

But there were better ways to deal with men like him.

"What about Andrea Baker?" I asked.

His face paled. "What about her?"

"She was raped in your school. In her classroom. Then murdered."

"That was *entirely* different. She was a teacher and it happened after hours," he said in a rush. "Detective Bergan assured me the act was personal. The students and other teachers had *nothing* to worry about."

"Only they did," Lance said in a cold tone. "Because it was your job to keep them safe and you not only failed, but you turned a blind eye."

The principal shot daggers of hate at Lance, and I knew we'd gotten everything he was going to give us.

"Mr. Posner," I said, "I'm going to need Martin Schroeder's file ASAP. Like within the hour. And I'm also going to need the files on every other teacher who had allegations of sexual misconduct brought against them."

"I'm not sure I can do that," he said. "I have a meeting to go to, and my office staff has left for the day."

I pulled back my jacket to make sure my badge was clearly visible. "Make time, and I'll be sure the prosecutor is made aware of your willingness to help."

Mr. Posner swallowed hard and stood, his chair rolling back and hitting the credenza behind him. "Then let's get started."

Chapter Thirty-One

Maddie

I stood at the living room window and watched Noah and Lance pull away. I should have just come out and told Noah about Ernie last night. They could protect him—and us. The fact that someone other than Ernie might be lurking outside our house was more dangerous than Aunt Deidre wandering off wasn't lost on me either.

Margarete came down the stairs and found me looking out the window.

"Did those fine young officers take off?"

I smiled at her, but it was forced. "You saw Officer Summit leave. I can give you his number if you like. His card is on the table."

She laughed. "I suppose that's a fair shot." Her humor faded as she regarded me. "You look tired. Why don't you go upstairs and lie down too?"

I shook my head. "I'm too keyed up." Then I pulled my phone out of my pocket and saw the time. "Crap. It's after two. I missed my appointment."

"You had an appointment?"

"Yeah." But it no longer seemed important. Noah had let me

know I wasn't a suspect, and while he was infuriating, I believed him. Lance too. They were good guys, doing the best they could to solve the case.

"Maybe you can still make it."

Shaking my head, I said, "No. I can't leave Aunt Deidre right now."

"She's sleeping, and between Linda and me, we've got her covered. You go." She made a shooing motion. "You look like you need to get out of here."

My nerves were getting the best of me, and I suspected I was about to wear out Aunt Deidre's wood floor with my pacing. Still... "It doesn't feel right."

"Poppycock," she said. "Go already. You're getting on my nerves."

It took a bit more convincing, but I grabbed my purse and jacket and headed out the door. By then, it was 2:40, well past an acceptable time to show up late to an appointment, even if I'd planned to go. But if I stayed home, I'd leap out of my skin, so I figured I might as well go out to the high school and talk to my mother's friend.

There were still quite a few cars in the parking lot when I parked, and I didn't have any trouble getting into the building. I hadn't been inside since I'd taken my last final exam fifteen years ago, but it didn't look like much had changed.

Sure enough, the English department was exactly where it had been when I'd gone to school here, but as I headed to the English hallway, my chest constricted, and I took a moment to catch my breath. I was being ridiculous. I'd come back to school after my mother's murder. I'd walked past her classroom every day, multiple times a day, for over two years until I graduated. So why did it feel like this was the first time?

You can do this, Maddie.

I could. I was stronger than this.

I put one foot in front of me. And then another. Twenty steps later, I was outside her old classroom. The door was open, and the light was on, as though the teacher—Ms. Baine, from the nameplate next to the door—had stepped out for a few moments.

It looked entirely different, but I was still transported back to life before her death. Before my world had been shattered. I'd been so mean to her before she left that night. Said such horrible things.

It was hard living with that kind of regret.

"Maddie?" My name, spoken barely above a whisper, by a woman a few feet behind me.

I turned to face her, surprised to see Dawn Heaton. Her dark hair was now streaked with gray, and there were lines around her eyes and across her forehead. She looked older, which was logical—I hadn't seen her in nearly fifteen years—yet somehow I'd expected her to look the same. She and my mother had been close, and she'd tried to check in with me and make sure I was okay—or as okay as I possibly could be—before I went to Knoxville. I was the one who'd stopped communicating. She was a reminder of what I'd lost, and back then I'd been trying to pretend I was okay. I guessed I still was.

"Hey, Miss Dawn."

She shook her head, tears filling her eyes. "You look so much like her."

"How are you?" I asked, uncomfortable. Maybe that was another reason why I had been so earnest about moving away. Because I felt unworthy of the comparisons. My mother had been on a pedestal I could never reach. I would always be in her shadow here.

"I'm fine. Good." She moved closer, reaching for my face and clasping my cheek while she searched my eyes. Was she looking for more signs of her best friend? Was she disappointed that she found me lacking? "How are you? I was sorry to hear about your uncle. I was at the funeral, but there was such a crowd I never got a chance to talk to you."

"That's okay," I said. "It was a pretty busy day."

She gave me a sad smile and dropped her hand, as though realizing she may have reached across an invisible boundary between us. "And how's Deidre? I heard she has dementia."

"Yeah," I said. "That's why I'm back. She can't be alone."

A tear trickled down her cheek. "Andrea would be so proud of you."

I gave her a grim smile. "I'm not sure about that." I took a breath. "But I *would* like to ask you some questions about her."

Her face brightened. "Of course! Do you want to come into my classroom? I was changing a bulletin board. We can chat while I staple."

"Of course, thank you."

I followed her into her room, which was still next door to my mother's. It was bright and cheery, with bulletin boards decorated with book quotes and a large banned-books board with book covers and the names of students who had read them. I grinned. That was so like Dawn. She'd always encouraged her students to be rebellious with their reading.

"What would you like to know?" she asked as she picked up a stapler and started putting up a red border on one of the boards.

I wasn't even sure where to start. *Who might have wanted my mother dead? Did she have any enemies? Did the police do a good job?*

Instead, I found myself asking the question that had been burning in me since about two seconds after I'd found out she was dead. "Do you think she knew I loved her?"

Dawn froze, then turned to face me, horror in her eyes. "Oh, Maddie. How can you ask that?"

"I wasn't..." My voice broke, and I pulled out a chair at the nearest desk and sat down. "I was so mean to her those last few months. She was gone so much, and I was having a hard time."

Peter had made my life hell. But as much as my mother had always insisted I could tell her anything, I hadn't felt like I could tell her about that. I'd needed her anyway. I'd expected her to be a mind reader, and when she hadn't fulfilled that impossible task, I'd punished her for it.

"Maddie," she said insistently. "She loved you so much, and of course she knew you loved her. She was worried." She hesitated. "I'm not sure how much to tell you."

"All of it. I want to know everything."

She walked over and pulled out a chair, moving it in front of me. "She knew something had happened to you, but you refused to tell her, and she didn't want to push."

I nodded. "She was right. Something *did* happen."

She swallowed and reached out, taking my hand. "She suspected that Martin Schroeder was being inappropriate with some of his students, and you had him that year."

My mouth dropped open as I was hit by the implication of what she was saying. "What?"

"She and Martin already didn't get along. He held a grudge because she got a grant for a special unit, and his budget request for some new lab equipment was turned down. He handled it very poorly."

"Eleanor Williams mentioned that to me."

Her eyes brightened. "You've spoken to Eleanor?"

"Kind of accidentally. I picked her up for an Uber ride this morning."

She nodded as though that seemed the most natural thing in the world. "He threw quite a fit. *Everyone* knew about it. Then you were assigned Martin for chemistry, and Andrea was concerned he'd hold it against you. But he was the only accelerated chemistry teacher at the time—awful teacher though he was—and you were determined to take as many advanced classes as you could. So she let it be. But you started to become more sullen and withdrawn that fall. And that's when we started hearing rumors."

"What kind of rumors?" But I already knew. Eleanor had told me, only not in this context.

"He'd always made comments that were slightly inappropriate, but Mr. Posner had always turned a blind eye, and it had never seemed to go any further. Suddenly, we were hearing whispers that he was being physically inappropriate with a student, but we had no idea who. No names or even grade levels were associated with the rumors. For all we knew it was completely fabricated. But one day Andrea overheard two girls discussing it in her class. When she asked them to give her more details, they refused to tell her and said they were just goofing off."

"Do you know who she'd overheard?"

"No." She took a breath. "She took what she heard and the way you were acting..." She held my gaze. "Maddie, did Martin Schroeder...?"

I shook my head vehemently. "No, Miss Dawn. Never. He went out of his way to be hard on me, but he never did anything sexually inappropriate."

She sat back, looking stunned.

"I was upset for another reason." I swallowed. "Peter McIntire groped me at a bonfire after a football game that fall and kept trying to pressure me to touch my breasts. When I finally convinced him no meant no, he told everyone I was a tease and used a few vulgar names that caught on. It earned me a certain reputation for a while."

I released a bitter laugh. "Funny how I felt like my life had been destroyed. And then I found out what having my life destroyed really felt like." I shook my head again. "But I didn't want to tell Mom. I just wanted it to go away, and I knew she'd never let that happen." I barked a laugh again. "The irony is it didn't go away anyway."

She stared at me in silence, but something in her expression suggested she had more to say, that she wasn't just shocked by my revelation.

"Maddie, she planned to confront Martin with her accusations."

My heart slammed into my rib cage. "What?"

"Shortly before her death she said she was going to confront him and make him admit it."

I scooted to the edge of my seat, my head swimming with… hope? Excitement? I'd always hated that her killer had never been caught, but it had made me more sad than angry. I'd trusted that the police didn't have the leads they'd needed to solve the case. But now I was hearing differently. "Is that why she came up to the school that night? She only told me she had to meet someone. Not who."

Her eyes were wide with confusion. "Maddie, she didn't tell me she was going to the school that night."

My hands began to shake. "Do you think she was going to meet Mr. Schroeder?"

Fear filled her eyes. "I don't know."

Could the answer have been here all along? Had the police ignored the solution that was right under their noses? "Do you think Martin Schroeder killed my mother?"

"I don't know," she whispered. "I told that detective investigating her murder that I thought it was possible. A group of us did, Eleanor included. But they obviously never arrested him."

"Did he have an alibi that night?" I asked, my heart racing.

"Honestly, Maddie, I have no idea."

We were silent for several seconds. My mother had thought I was being molested, but instead of asking me, she'd planned to confront the man herself. Would he have killed her for that? I hadn't been a victim. But if there were rumors, perhaps someone else had been. Why had I never heard the talk? Then again, I was toward the bottom of the pecking order. I rarely was included in the school's gossip mill.

"Eleanor said Mr. Schroeder was closest to Mr. Brant. Were they friends?"

"I wouldn't exactly say they were friends, but Adam Brant *did* defend him from time to time."

I jerked my gaze to hers. "Why would Mr. Brant defend him?"

"I don't know," she admitted. "We often half-jokingly claimed Martin had something on him."

They'd been joking, but what if it was true?

Why hadn't Detective Bergan done anything with all this information?

"Do you think Mr. Brant is still here?" I asked, growing agitated.

Her eyes flew wide. "You don't plan to confront him, do you?"

Did I? Common sense told me to call Noah and tell him all of this, but he was in the middle of an investigation, and this felt like ancient history. My mother could hardly have risen from her grave to murder Martin Schroeder out of revenge.

I couldn't help recognizing that if Martin Schroeder killed my mother, that would provide me motive to kill him. I should let this go until they found her murderer, but I was tired of waiting for justice. Maybe it was time for me to get it on my own. If I got more information from Mr. Brant, I could decide whether to present it all to Noah now or wait.

"I don't know. Do you think he's here?"

She worried her bottom lip with her upper teeth as though trying to decide whether to tell me. Finally, she said, "Yes. Most of us stay an hour after the bell on Tuesdays and Thursdays to work with students who need help."

I stood. "Thanks. It was great to see you, Miss Dawn. I'd love to have lunch with you sometime and catch up on pleasanter things."

"Maddie." Worry covered her face. "Maybe you should think this through."

"I'm okay. I promise." Then I walked out of the room.

* * *

Mr. Brant was in his room, standing next to a student who was adding something to a flask of clear fluid that he held over a Bunsen burner. I barely recognized him. Time had not been kind. The older man must have sensed my presence at the door because he turned to face me. "Can I help you?"

I should have gone in with some sort of plan. It wasn't like Mr. Brant was going to admit he knew Schroeder was molesting students or that he'd killed my mother. What exactly did I hope to gain here? I wasn't sure, but I knew I had to face him.

"Can I help you?" he repeated, sounding more on edge.

I'd waited eighteen years to find out what had happened to my mother. I decided I was done waiting. "I'm Maddie Baker." I held his gaze, then added, "Andrea Baker's daughter."

He stared at me and paled, reaching out a hand to rest on the table next to him to support his weight. Something flickered across his face before he turned to the student. "You keep working on the experiment, Paul, and I'll be right back."

Paul looked slightly alarmed but didn't protest as Mr. Brant made a beeline for me.

"In the hall," he grunted.

I walked into the hall, and I could hear Mr. Brant's stomps following me out. I turned to face him, and he came to a halt a few feet away, his face reddened with anger.

"What are you doing here?" he demanded.

I narrowed my eyes and tilted my head. "That's a very interesting reaction to me merely showing up at the entrance of your classroom."

His eyes widened as my statement hit him. He took a breath, but if it was meant to be calming, it missed its mark. When he spoke again, he sounded even angrier. "What are you doing here?"

"You mean in the school? I just dropped by to see some of my former teachers." I decided there was no reason to throw Dawn's name out yet. Let him wonder. "And if you're wondering why I was dropping by to see you? I just wanted to say hello. Same as with the others, but they were much less hostile."

He swallowed hard. "You were never one of my students."

He was acting so guilty over someone he hardly knew showing up at his door. He knew something, and he was terrified I knew what it was.

"I know," I said, keeping my tone even. "But I wanted to say hello anyway. So awful about Martin Schroeder, isn't it?"

He studied me, reminding me of a rat trapped in a corner. What did he know? I wasn't deluded enough to think he'd just admit it. Interrogating him was a job for Noah. But I could get in one last parting shot. Something to make him freak out a bit until Noah and Lance spoke with him.

"You know, I was the one who gave Martin Schroeder a ride to that butcher shop. We had about ten minutes for a nice little chat." I paused and leaned a little closer, lowering my voice. "He told me *everything*."

Mr. Brant looked like he was about to pass out. "I have no idea what you're talking about."

"I'm sure you don't. You have a nice day, Mr. Brant." Then I strode past him and headed for the exit. I'd done what I'd set out to do. I was going home to my aunt.

Chapter Thirty-Two

Noah

Posner made a big show of how difficult it was for him to locate the employment files, until I suggested charging him with interfering with an investigation. Then, miraculously, he produced them within minutes.

Multiple accusations had been filed against Schroeder, but interestingly enough they had all been within the last years of his employment. Whether that was due to him becoming more careless or the girls and their families becoming more *woke*, I couldn't say. Yet. But I planned on talking to his son as soon as we finished up here.

First, I planned to talk to Adam Brant, Schroeder's department head for the last twenty years of his employment. He would know of any accusations and, given Posner's lackadaisical attitude about the whole thing, could likely give me more details than I'd find in the file.

I glanced up at the clock. It was 3:25. Posner had told us quite a few teachers stayed until 3:30 on Thursdays, Adam Brant included.

"I'll be right back," I told Lance, who was starting a more in-depth look at Schroeder's file while we waited for Posner to produce the others. "I'm going to pay a visit to Brant before he leaves for the day."

Lance nodded. "You want me to stay behind and make sure Posner doesn't accidentally lose any files?"

"You know it, although as soon as I finish this visit, I think I'll get a search warrant to take all the files to make sure a few don't accidentally end up in the shredder after we're gone."

Although there was every chance I'd get Judge Neilson and he'd deny the warrant for reaching too far.

I left the office and headed for the main hallway in the school, looking for a student to ask for directions, but a sign on the wall labeled Science Hall pointed to the right, and soon I found the science wing. The classrooms were marked with the teachers' names, so it was easy for me to find Brant's room.

The only person inside was a teenage boy who was washing out a flask in a sink.

"Is Mr. Brant here?" I asked.

The kid glanced over at me. "He left."

I looked up at the clock. "Doesn't he usually stay until 3:30?"

"Yeah, but after that woman came to see him, he told me to finish the lab on my own."

I did a double take. "What woman?"

"She said her name." His mouth scrunched to the side. "I think it was Atty?" he said, sounding unsure. "She said she was someone's daughter, and he told her he wanted to talk in the hall."

"Andrea Baker?" I asked, but I already knew. Fuck. Why was Maddie here? More importantly, what had she found out to send her to him? "Did you hear what they said?"

He shook his head. "Nuh-uh. But he came back in, grabbed his keys out of his desk, and said he was leaving."

Goddammit.

I put my hands on my hips. "How long ago was that?"

"I don't know. About five minutes? Not very long."

"One more question," I said. "Where's the teacher's parking lot?" Then I added, "And do you know what he drives?"

"That's two questions," he said, setting the flask on a mat next to the sink.

Okay, smart-ass. I just gave him a dry look.

"They park behind the building." He pointed to the windows. "And I'm pretty sure he drives a Nissan truck. A red one."

I rushed over to the window to see if Brant was in the lot, but I didn't see him or a red pickup truck.

Damn it.

I pulled out my phone, about to call Maddie and ask her what she knew, but this seemed like it should be a face-to-face conversation.

Was Andrea Baker's death part of this? There was no denying that three people with ties to both cases were connected to the school—Maddie, Schroeder, and Ernie Foust. Then it occurred to me that I hadn't asked Posner about Ernie Foust.

I headed back down to the principal's office and discovered that he'd produced eight more files on teachers. "I'm going to need another file," I said. "The one on Ernie Foust."

He looked surprised. "We never had a complaint about Ernie. He was an excellent employee up until he retired about a decade ago."

"What was his connection to Andrea Baker?"

He blinked. "I don't understand."

"Did they know one another?"

"Ernie was the night janitor. He was the one who found Andrea in her classroom."

Shit.

"Did he see the murderer?"

"You would know better than me," Mr. Posner said in a smug tone. "Maybe you should check your *own* files."

He made a fine point. Too bad that file was lost. Now I really needed to find Ernie.

I filed a search warrant for all of the employment files and called for a uniformed officer to watch the office until I heard whether it had been approved.

We packed up the files we'd been given, took them to the station and locked them up, and headed to Darren Schroeder's house. He and his wife had just sat down to dinner.

"Darren," I said. "I hate to interrupt your meal, but I need to ask you a few questions."

Sherry asked us if we wanted to join them, and while the meat-loaf and mashed potatoes looked delicious and made my stomach growl, Lance and I declined.

Sherry ushered us into the living room, and we all took a seat.

"Do you have news about who murdered my father?" Darren asked.

"No," I said, turning on the recording app on my phone. "But we do have a few questions about when your father taught at the high school. I'm going to record our conversation so I don't have to take notes if that's okay with you."

"Yeah," he said, shooting a nervous glance to my phone on the coffee table. "Sure."

"Sherry, you had mentioned your father-in-law retired, but did you ever question that?"

"Yeah," Darren said with a dazed expression. "I thought he might have been fired, but that was years ago. What does that have to do with his murder?"

I ignored his question. "Why do you think he might have been fired?"

He glanced from me to Lance, then back to me. "He didn't get along with the other teachers. They pretty much hated him. Like I told you before, everyone did."

"But that's not why he was fired, is it?" I asked in an empathetic tone.

His face crumpled. "No. At least, I don't think so. He never told me anything, but my mother told me things right before she died."

"And what were those things?" I asked.

His chin dropped to his chest. "Mom said she thought he was having sex with his students. But I knew my dad. There was no way those girls were doing it willingly." Darren looked up. "I'm pretty sure I graduated before he started acting on his impulses. All of that came later. After my mother found his porn stash."

"His porn stash?" I asked.

His face reddened. "I never saw—never wanted to see it. But my mom found it. He had photos of teenage girls."

"From the school?" I asked.

He shook his head. "I don't think so. Mom found them in an envelope that had been mailed to him."

I shot a glance to Lance. We'd gone through his house, twice, and hadn't found a single piece of porn. Not even on his search engine's history. It seemed highly unlikely he'd gotten rid of it all, which meant he'd either stored it somewhere else or he'd hidden it so thoroughly we hadn't found it during our initial search.

Was that why his house had been broken into? Had the intruders been searching for his porn? If so, that meant someone else knew about it.

"When did you first become aware that he was molesting his students?" I asked.

"I don't know, maybe fifteen years ago?" he said, running a hand over his head. "But at that point, I didn't actually know anything. I suspected, but I had no proof. I even talked to a detective about it, and he told me not to worry. He promised he'd look into it."

"Detective Bergan?" Lance asked, and I was surprised he sounded so calm, when I knew he was furious.

"Yeah," Darren said. "That's him. I took him at his word, but nothing ever happened to my dad, so I figured it hadn't been true. And then, right before my dad retired, my mom called me, frantic. The father of one of the girls had shown up at their door with a gun. I told her to call the police, and I raced over to their house. The father was gone, but so was my dad. He came back a few hours later with a bunch of bruises on his face. He retired within a week or two. My mother died soon after that."

"Can you identify the father or the daughter? Did your mother know who they were?"

"No," he said, looking forlorn. "I was glad when he retired, because I knew the girls at that school would be safe from him."

I let his statement settle for a few moments before I continued.

"Darren, do you know if your father was tutoring or part of any kind of mentoring program where he might have been working with teenage girls?"

His eyes flew wide with alarm. "No! There's no way."

"Are you sure?"

"Even if the programs didn't know about his history—which, to be honest, the school didn't come out and share the news with people. In fact, the news media kept it shockingly quiet. But even if they had known, there's no way he would have been hired. He was *not* a nice man, and he didn't try to hide it. I can't imagine anyone would hire him to work with kids."

"Did he have a relationship with anyone that you knew of?" I asked. "A girlfriend?"

He laughed. "No. The older he got, the younger he wanted his women. He treated my mother like shit at the end. I moved her in with me so he could obsess over his porn and jack off in peace."

I resisted the urge to cringe. "Just the photos, or did he watch videos too?"

"Mom said he watched videos on his computer."

"We didn't find any evidence of porn on his desktop computer," I said.

He held my gaze. "He had a laptop, Detective. That's where he watched it."

Our search had turned up no sign of a laptop. Even if the laptop had died, where did he watch his porn? A tablet? A new laptop?

Of course, the obvious solution was the intruders took whatever device he used.

Shit, what if he'd watched it on his phone? Which we were currently locked out of.

"Thank you, Darren," I said, turning off the recording app and getting to my feet. "You've been very helpful. If you think of anything else, please let us know."

"Yeah," he said, looking confused as he stood too. "Why did you ask if he had a girlfriend?"

"We found evidence he might have been involved with someone," I said.

He snorted. "That man was incapable of being in a relationship. I'll bet he could only get it up for teenaged girls, and no girl in her right mind would willingly sleep with him. The minute he got fired, he lost his position of power."

So why did he have a fresh condom in his pocket? The implications were all too clear.

Chapter Thirty-Three

Maddie

I went home and started dinner. I was feeling out of sorts and confused about just about everything. I needed something, ached for it, but I had no idea what it was. I wanted to cry. I wanted to scream. I wanted to make men like Mr. Brant and Detective Bergan pay, but I didn't even know where to begin.

Aunt Deidre came downstairs for dinner, tired and withdrawn, and said she wanted to go to bed early. True to her word, she headed upstairs a little after seven. I wondered if I should make an appointment for her to see her doctor. Maybe alter her medication. Then again, she'd had her own ordeal this afternoon. Maybe her body was recuperating.

But her early night left me with nothing but time to myself, which was my worst enemy. I tried calling Mallory, but it went straight to voicemail. She sent me a text that she was on a date but would call me if I needed her to.

I'm fine. Just missing you. Can't wait to see you tomorrow night.

I put on pajamas and got ready for bed, even though it was only a little after eight, then went downstairs and turned on the TV. I was about to binge-watch *Bridgerton* for the fifth time when there was a knock on the front door. I froze, my paranoia getting the better of me. But I was being ridiculous. Based on the insistent pounding, it was probably Noah Langley, here to chew me out for talking to Mr. Brant. For all I knew, the man had filed harassment charges against me.

Crap. Why hadn't I considered that before? Then again, what I'd done could hardly be construed as harassment.

I grabbed a sweater from the coat tree, shoving my arms through the holes before I opened the door. I already had my mouth open, about to tell Noah off, but stopped short when I realized it was Peter McIntire.

Wrong night to show up on my front porch, asshole.

"Why are you pounding on my front door?" I demanded, one hand propped on my hip.

His mouth parted. He obviously hadn't expected my hostility, but he quickly recovered. "Why did you blow off your appointment with Burt?"

"Who?"

"Burt Pullman!" he practically shouted. "He said you had an appointment today, and then you blew him off without saying anything. I never took you as so inconsiderate, Maddie."

I gaped at him. Then my anger rushed in. "You don't even know me!" I said through gritted teeth. "How dare you presume to know the first thing about me!"

He took a step back, then drew in a breath, his shoulders stiffening. "You're right. I'm sorry. May I please come in so we can discuss this like rational adults?"

I filled the opening in the doorway and lifted my chin. "No. Did you run all over town telling everyone I was ghosting appointments?"

"What?" he asked in confusion. "No. Why would you say that?"

"When you didn't get your way back in high school, you sure

ran around calling me a cocktease." Apparently, this afternoon brought out a lot of unresolved anger issues.

"Jesus, Maddie," he said in disgust. "That was years ago. Why are you making such a big deal about it?"

"It was traumatic for me, Peter!"

"Look," he said in frustration. "You think I was in the wrong, and I've said I was sorry, so why can't you let this go? It really wasn't that big of a deal. We were just kids." He took a breath, his calm condescension returning. "Clearly, you're not thinking straight. Just let me in so we can discuss this."

"No," I snapped. "Maybe instead of chewing me out like I'm a child, you should be asking why I missed the appointment, but I'll save you the breath." I was so furious with him I wanted to roundhouse-kick him in the stomach so he would fall off the porch and land on his ass. Thankfully, I refrained. "Aunt Deidre wandered off today. I spent a good deal of the afternoon waiting for word on her and talking to the police. Thank goodness they found her and brought her home, so obviously I was here for that."

He blinked. "Maddie, I'm so sorry." His mouth twisted with regret. "I should have never made presumptions. I was just worried. Is Deidre okay?"

I ran a hand over my head. I just wanted to be done with this conversation. I wanted to be done with *him*. "Honestly, I don't know. She's upstairs sleeping and keeps slipping in and out of confusion."

His face softened. "I'm so sorry. I want to help."

I crossed my arms over my chest. Even without our previous history, I'd seen enough of Peter 2.0 to know he wasn't someone I wanted to associate with. "Thank you for everything you've done for us, but this is the end. I think you've done enough."

He glanced toward the side yard, then looked back at me. "I'm worried about you, Maddie. You're acting hysterical."

. . .

"Hysterical?" I asked with a laugh, dropping my arms to my sides. "Because I had the audacity to stand up to you and tell you no? You should leave, Peter."

"Maddie," he pleaded, moving closer. "If you'll let me in, we can figure out what to do next."

"There's nothing for *you* to figure out," I said, my voice rising. "You're not any part of this, Peter. In fact, in light of everything, I think it's best if I don't attend your cocktail party."

Anger flooded his eyes. "But I'm having it for *you*!" he shouted.

"So cancel it!"

"Maddie?" Margarete called out from behind Peter. "Is everything all right?"

He took a few steps back, and it wasn't until then that I realized how loud we'd been.

"Yes," I said, suddenly cold. I wrapped my sweater tighter around my body. "Peter dropped by to check on Aunt Deidre, but now he's leaving."

He shot me an unreadable glance before turning toward Margarete. "I'm so glad Deidre made it home safe and sound." Then he flashed her a smile. "How's your grandson enjoying that Japanese candy? Do you need me to order any more for you?"

Margarete looked to me, then shifted her gaze back to him. "He loved it. And I'll let you know if we need more."

Peter gave me a tight grin. "Maddie, I realize you've had quite a day, so perhaps a good night's sleep will help settle your nerves. I'll be in touch tomorrow."

I was about to tell him off, but then he blasted Margarete with the full force of his smile.

"Have a good night, ladies." He strutted down the walk to his car on the street, got inside, and pulled away.

Margarete stood there, watching him in confusion. For a second, I was too shocked by his audacity to speak—*hysterical?*—but then something struck me as odd.

"Margarete," I said. "Peter mentioned getting you candy. What was that all about?"

"Oh," she said, her hand on her chest as though trying to ground herself. "Peter is known for his special orders. If you need something and he doesn't have it, he finds it and gets it for you."

"Like Aunt Deidre's pickle juice."

"That's right." She frowned, staring down the street. "I've never seen him like that." She turned to face me with a look of concern. "Why was he so angry?"

"I don't know," I said honestly, because the more I thought about it, the odder it seemed that he would be so irate about me missing a consultation that had nothing to do with him. Was he that controlling?

"How's Deidre?" Margarete asked, her forehead creased with worry.

I leaned my shoulder into the doorjamb. "Honestly, I don't know. She slept until dinner, then went back to bed soon after. I wonder if I should take her to the doctor."

"That might not be a bad idea," she said. "She was out in the cold all afternoon. Maybe she's coming down with something."

Great. One more thing to worry about.

* * *

After Margarete went home, I poured myself a glass of wine and then had another, which made me tipsy and tired. My mind was whirling, and I needed something to help me calm down. I turned on *Bridgerton* while I finished the second glass and then drifted off to sleep on the sofa.

I woke to the sound of something in the kitchen. The Netflix screen prompt *Are you still watching?* was on the TV, making the room glow.

What time was it?

I listened to the silence of the house, the hum of the furnace, the wind blowing outside...the sound of breaking glass.

I sat upright. Someone was breaking into the house.

My phone was on the sofa, so I grabbed it and saw I had a missed call and a voicemail from Noah at 9:38, about an hour ago. I unlocked my screen and returned his call.

"Maddie, I told you it could wait until tomorrow," he grumped as he answered. He sounded exhausted. Had I woken him?

"Someone is breaking into the back of my house," I whispered, my heart racing.

"Get out. Now," he said, his voice tight and sounding panicked. "Go out the front door."

"I'm not leaving Aunt Deidre. She's sleeping upstairs."

"Then lock yourself in her room and wait for me," he said, sounding like he was running. "I'm on my way but I'm sending some units ahead of me."

"Noah," I said, terrified as I heard the back door squeak. "They're inside."

"There's probably more than one guy, Maddie. *Hide!* I've got to call the units, but I'm going to call you back. *Answer.*" Then he hung up.

How did he know there was probably more than one guy?

I realized whoever had broken in would be able to see me in the glow of the TV screen, so I frantically grabbed the remote control, trying to find the power button. However, I accidentally pressed play and the show resumed, the *Bridgerton* theme song blaring in the silence.

"Fuck!" I muttered under my breath and stabbed the off button.

But it was too late. They knew that *I knew* they were there.

Hide, Noah had told me, but I wasn't sure where to go. The front door was oh-so tempting, but I had to protect my aunt. I couldn't let them find her upstairs. So where could I hide? The hall closet? Run upstairs and risk them hearing the squeaky steps, drawing them up to her?

I had to stay down here.

I crouched in the corner between the sofa and the love seat, my back pressed to the wall. The shadows concealed me, but I realized that would be shot to hell if they flipped on a light. Then I saw a flashlight beam bouncing around the kitchen. Followed by a second. And a third. I could maybe fight off one intruder, but three?

How long would it take Noah to get here? Or a police car with lights and sirens?

The beams of light shone in the dining room, and a man whispered, "Spread out."

The basement door squeaked, the sound it made when it was being opened or closed. Two flashlight beams bobbed around the dining room, then moved into the edge of the living room. I could barely make out two dark figures.

Why were they here? What were they looking for?

Me?

The lights were moving across the room, and I knew that even if they didn't find me, they'd make their way upstairs. I had to draw them away from my aunt.

I made a snap decision.

Squatting next to the edge of the sofa, I shot straight for the entryway. I slammed into the staircase and then leapt for the front door, fumbling with the deadbolt as I heard cursing behind me.

I got the door open just as I felt a hand brush my back. Adrenaline and instinct kicked in. I flung my fist back as hard as I could, connecting with his thigh, then followed up with a roundhouse kick that landed in his face as he leaned over in pain.

I ran through the front door, screaming at the top of my lungs, but once I got into the middle of the yard, I turned to make sure the intruders were following.

A light drizzle was falling, and the yard was slick under my

Blind Bake

bare feet. This could make things tricky, especially since they were all wearing shoes.

The guy I'd kicked was stumbling out the door, clutching his nose, but his friend pushed past him, rushing down the steps. They were wearing jeans, dark long-sleeved shirts, and black ski masks. They also looked like they had on latex gloves.

They weren't playing.

The ski masks meant I wouldn't be able to scratch their faces. One less trick off the table.

Everything in me screamed *run*, but what if they went upstairs and hurt Aunt Deidre in retaliation?

Stay it was. I lifted my arms and took a fighting stance. When he saw I wasn't running, the second guy stopped and started taking slow, deliberate steps toward me. He was big, but I'd taken down big men before. I could stand up to him. Especially if he wasn't light on his feet and tried to use his brawn.

"What are you waiting for?" I shouted. The more noise the better. Maybe if there were plenty of witnesses, they'd leave.

A light flipped on in the house next to Margarete.

You can do this. You only have to wait for Noah to get here.

The guy tried to grab my arm, but I slid the foot on that side behind me, pivoting out of his reach.

He grunted his frustration and tried to go for my other arm. I did the same maneuver.

"You fucking bitch," he snarled, now reaching with both arms.

I ducked, shot a fist up to his groin, then shoved him to the ground when he crouched over in pain. Jumping to my feet, I saw the third guy come dashing out the front door as the guy on the porch finally stood upright.

"What do you assholes want?" I shouted at the top my lungs. "Three against one woman doesn't seem very fair!"

More lights flipped on. Sirens sounded in the distance. I only had to hold them off for a few more minutes.

The new guy made a run for me, and I told myself not to panic. I could do this, even though I was sorely out of practice.

I braced myself as he rushed toward me. Then, just before he reached me, I spun in a circle to the side, thrusting my fist into his solar plexus, hoping I'd been strong enough to knock the wind out of him.

He fell forward onto his knees, but the first guy was getting to his feet and the guy on the porch was now moving toward me.

Deep breath.

Should I run down the street?

No. I needed to stay put. Maybe I was being stupid, or stubborn, but I wanted Noah to catch these bastards.

With that thought in mind, my new goal was to hurt them enough to keep them from running away.

Both the first and second guys were advancing on me now. My heart was racing and so was my mind. Why were they after me? What did they want? Their objective wasn't to kill me, or they would have used some kind of weapon to do so by now.

I took several steps backward, continuing to move as my feet reached the asphalt. That might not work to my advantage if one of them managed to get me to the ground, but at least it wouldn't be as slick as the grass. Even if small rocks were digging into the bottom of my feet. I continued moving until I was in the middle of the road.

"Not so tough now, are you bitch?" the guy on the left growled.

"I've knocked all three of you on your asses, and I'm still standing, so you might rethink that statement," I sneered.

That enraged him, which was good. He'd be less likely to think things through. I just needed to figure out how to maim at least one of them.

The guy to my right lunged for me, and I spun out of the way, swinging my arm for his gut. But he was ready for me and grabbed my upper arm and hauled me to his side.

The second guy moved in closer, emboldened, and I gave him a hard roundhouse kick to his thigh, putting all my weight into it. He fell to the ground, screaming.

The guy holding me froze for a moment. "Fucking hell. I think you broke his leg!"

I spun with my back to him, scraping the inside of his calf and stomping the top of his foot with my heel, but it didn't have much impact since I wasn't wearing shoes and he had on boots.

"Ha!" he sneered, then grabbed my other arm and lifted me off the ground.

A dark sedan was coming down the street toward us, and I started screaming, "Help! Help me!"

The car stopped, but the driver didn't get out to help. He just waited, the car's windshield wipers swiping across the windshield. I could barely see the guy's bearded face.

Oh shit. He was their getaway driver.

My captor was carrying me toward the car, and I froze for a brief moment.

Move, Maddie! Think! This was *not* the time to panic.

How could I get out of this? My mind scrambled for an answer, and landed on…Noah. Which would have been more helpful if he were here. But then I remembered the demonstration we'd put on the other night, and instinct kicked in again.

I wrapped my foot around the man's calf, making it difficult for him to move as I started whacking his leg with the heel of my hand, aiming for his groin. My shirt was damp, and I started to slide down his body to the ground. His response was to squeeze tighter, making it difficult for me to breathe. I reached for his wrists, fumbling to find bare skin. If I could dig my nails in, he might release me on instinct, but when that didn't work, I reached behind me and grabbed the lump in his crotch and squeezed as hard as I could.

"Fucking bitch!" He dropped me, but in the process, he lashed out and punched me in the back.

I fell to the ground on my hands and knees as pain radiated throughout my body, stealing my breath.

A gunshot rang out.

"Leave her alone, or I'll blow you to kingdom come!" a woman shouted.

Margarete?

The guy tried to grab me again and another shot rang out. This one hit the car, based on the ping of metal.

My would-be captor got up and ran for the back of the car, but I could hear the driver shouting at him, "Get her, you fucking idiot!"

The driver opened the window and aimed a handgun at me. "Get in, or I'll shoot."

"No," I said, still squatting on the ground. "I'll take my chances right here."

The guy from the yard stumbled into the road, now moving toward me. But just as he reached me, I could hear sirens down at the end of the street.

He tried to grab my arm, and I whacked it away, then did the same with the other arm.

"I am never going anywhere with you," I grunted up at him.

The guy whose nuts I'd squeezed snuck up behind me and gave me a vicious kick to the back. I fell onto the ground on my side, gasping in pain, and he grabbed my feet and started to drag me toward the open car door, my stomach scraping against the pavement.

"Leave her alone, I said!" Margarete bellowed.

Another shotgun blast rang out. At least one of the car's windows shattered, but the guy continued to drag me, and his buddy had my arms now.

I kicked as hard as I could, getting one leg free. I continued to kick as I bent my elbows, forcing the guy who had my arms to lean forward to continue holding me. He fell forward, landing on my already aching back, but his weight pinned my body to the ground.

"Freeze!" Noah shouted. "Police."

Everything seemed to happen at once after that.

The driver fired a shot out of the window of his car, aiming toward Margarete and Noah's voice, and then several more shots rang out. The two guys abandoned me, scrambling into the back of the car, but the guy whose leg I'd kicked still lay in the street, wailing for them to get him—until another shot rang out and he silenced.

Their car shot into reverse, squealing at the end of the street as it whipped around and raced away.

I collapsed to the ground, trying to catch my breath, but then I remembered the driver had shot toward Noah and Margarete. I pushed myself up to look for them, terrified they'd been hurt, but Noah was already dropping onto his knees beside me.

"Don't get up," he said. "Tell me where you're hurt."

Relief washed through me, and I pushed myself to a sitting position, throwing my arms around his neck, and began to sob.

Chapter Thirty-Four

Noah

I struggled to catch my breath. Jesus. I'd nearly watched her get kidnapped. My heart was still racing. "Maddie? Are you hurt?"

She shook her head in the crook of my neck. "No."

I held her for a few seconds, my arms wrapped around the small of her back. What if I hadn't gotten here in time? What if they'd taken her?

A crowd had started to gather on both sides of the street. I really should get up and start handling crowd control until the patrol officers got here, but I couldn't walk away from her yet.

"Margarete," Maddie said between sobs. "Is she okay?"

I glanced over at the older woman. She was still holding her shotgun, looking like she was about to start running on foot after the speeding car.

"She's okay. Just pissed."

Maddie began to shake. She was wearing lightweight pajamas that were soaked through from the drizzle, and it was forty degrees outside. Or maybe the shock was setting in. In either case, I needed to get her out of the cold and rain. "Come on. Let's get you warmed up."

I wrapped my arm around her back, but she flinched and cried out.

A new wave of panic hit. Had she been shot? It wouldn't be the first time someone had been too overcome with adrenaline to realize it right away. I lifted the back of her shirt, looking for blood, but all I saw was a dark shadow that could be a blooming bruise. I needed to get a better look in the light.

"One of them kicked me in the back and the other one punched me," she said, pushing my arm away. She'd stopped crying. "I'm okay. Just help me up. I need to check on Aunt Deidre and make sure she didn't wander away in all the confusion."

More carefully this time, I wrapped my arm around her back and helped her stand. I had an overwhelming urge to pick her up and carry her into the house, but I suspected she'd fight me off like she'd fought off those men. Except I couldn't take her there. The house was now a crime scene. Thinking fast, I decided to put her in my car until I could figure it out.

Two police cars and Lance had pulled up after I'd run to Maddie, and Lance was now checking the pulse of the guy on the street. He stood upright and shook his head, not that I was surprised. The driver had shot to kill. Couldn't leave behind someone who might talk.

The patrol officers were holding people back, and one of them was taking Margarete's gun.

I led Maddie toward my car, but she resisted. "What are you doing?" she asked, her voice rising in panic.

"Maddie," I said gently. "You can't go in your house yet. It's a crime scene."

"But Aunt Deidre!"

"You can wait in my car, and I'll go get her, okay?"

She didn't look like she wanted to go along with my plan, but Lance had approached us and said, "Noah. Why don't you sit in your car with Maddie and start to take her statement while I check on Deidre." He winked at Maddie. "I know which room is hers now."

She reluctantly agreed. I put her in the front seat and turned on the car. We were silent for a few seconds. She was so tightly wound, I felt the need to loosen the tension a bit. "You didn't answer the phone when I called back."

She laughed, but it sounded manic. "I was a little busy."

I turned in my seat to face her, reliving the terror I'd felt as I drove up to the scene. I was still terrified. When I'd skidded to a stop, two men had been trying to drag her into their car, but she'd fought like hell. My heart swelled with pride. She was a fucking wildcat.

But they'd still almost gotten her. The thought stole my breath all over again.

"What happened?" I asked, then remembered I still had a job to do. I wasn't here because I was a person in her life. I was the detective on this case. I pulled my phone out of my pocket. "I'm going to record your interview, okay?"

She hesitated.

I reached over and took her hand. "Maddie, you were almost kidnapped. You're not in trouble. I just need to know what happened so we can track those sonsabitches down and put them behind bars. You can help me do that."

"Okay."

Lance emerged from the house with Deidre, but Margarete ran over and led them both over to her house. Maddie watched in silence, seeming to relax a little now that she knew her aunt was safe.

She gave me her statement, and I tried not to comment even though a range of emotions cycled through me—fear, anger, vengeance. If she hadn't been trained to defend herself, I had no doubt she wouldn't be in my car right now.

More police cars had arrived while we talked, including that of my sergeant. Before I talked to him, I took Maddie to Margarete's so she could check on her aunt, tucked safely into Margarete's guest room.

Once she was settled, I went out to give my sergeant my statement. He told me he was supposed to put me on administrative leave for firing my weapon—standard procedure, I knew the drill—but needed me to keep working on Schroeder's murder. So he settled for taking my service weapon as evidence and telling me I had to come in to discuss the situation in the morning.

Someone had taken Margarete's statement, and Lance told me she was none too pleased that one of the officers had taken her shotgun as evidence. Many of the neighbors had also given statements, and Lance told me their accounts were a lot more detailed than Maddie's *I fought them off until you could get here* statement.

I wasn't surprised.

"A few of them have Ring doorbells, so we're working on getting footage."

I nodded.

"You okay?" he asked.

I started to give him my standard "I'm fine" statement, but I really liked Lance. I wanted to be honest. "I'm not sure. She scared the hell out of me."

"Yeah," he said grimly. "Me too. You ran out of the station like your pants were on fire. I had no idea where you were going until I heard Maddie's name and you shouting for backup."

We'd stayed late, going over the employment files, furious that my search warrant for the rest of the files had been denied. "I should have told you. All I could think about was getting here."

"Sounds like it was the right move. They almost got her."

I felt nauseous. It had been too close.

"The coroner's team says it looks like the guy has a broken femur. You think Maddie did that?"

I gave him a grim smile. "She said she was determined to make sure there was someone for me to question when I got here."

"That didn't quite work," Lance said with a sigh. "Heard you got a good look at the car?"

"It's the same one as from outside Schroeder's house. Four guys. Guy with a bushy beard driving. They wanted her. Why?"

Lance shook his head. "I don't know. Ernie told Deidre she was in danger, and you said she talked to Brant. Did she make someone nervous?"

"What if *I* made someone nervous when I dropped by Cock on the Walk? I told them I was looking for Maddie. What if I tipped them off? Or maybe Bergan's accomplice thinks she knows something." I rubbed the back of my neck. "I don't know."

"She can't be left alone," Lance said. "They might come back."

"I'll stay with her." I wasn't sure she was going to like that, but too fucking bad. It was better than parking a patrol officer outside. It occurred to me that I'd just handed over my gun, but I wanted to stay anyway. I *needed* to stay. "Is the crime scene team done processing her house?"

"Almost. Not much to process. They broke the window on the back door and didn't do much more than walk through the house until they chased her out the front door."

I walked over to Margarete's to check on Maddie. She was sitting at the kitchen table, with a blanket wrapped around her shoulders as she drank a cup of tea. I was surprised at the relief on her face when she saw me, but then again, I was the person she'd called when she was in trouble. Not Lance. Not 911, although in hindsight, that's who she should have called. Something swelled in my chest at that realization.

I sat down in the chair next to her. "We're not sure why those men tried to take you, but they might come back. We need to have someone keep an eye on you tonight, so I'm going to do it."

Blind Bake

Her brow furrowed as though she was trying to determine how she felt about that.

"They're almost done processing your house. Do you want to stay there tonight or here at Margarete's?"

"You'll be there?" she asked.

"Yeah."

"My house." Then she added, "But Margarete said Aunt Deidre could stay here."

"Okay," I said. "I'll let you know when you can go home."

I went outside to find Lance. Even moving, I felt like a caged cat. "Any sign of the car?"

"Nope." He said with the ghost of a grin. "No men in the ER either."

I grinned too, but it quickly faded. "What the hell does Martin Schroeder's death have to do with Maddie? She just dropped him off. None of this makes sense."

"He dropped his phone. Maybe he misplaced the brown bag. Maybe that's what they were looking for at his house, and when they couldn't find it, they thought she might have it."

"Maybe. But why not tear her house apart too?"

"Good question," he said. "You gonna get any sleep tonight?"

For a split second, I thought he was insinuating I would try to sleep with her, but then I realized he'd meant I'd go without sleep because I was guarding her. "I don't know."

"We can go interview Brant at school tomorrow," he said. "And stop by and talk to Bergan's wife."

"And go to another autopsy," I said with a sigh. "Maybe the guy will have something on him that'll help us figure out who he worked for." But we both knew that was unlikely.

Half of the crime scene team finished with Maddie's house at around the same time the other half finished processing the street. When I went back to Margarete's to tell Maddie she could go home, she was still sitting at the kitchen table, looking almost exhausted enough to fall asleep there.

As we crossed from Margarete's house to the old Victorian, the last of the patrol cars were pulling out. Lance was leaving too, headed home to get some sleep. He'd gotten a patrol officer to cover the window of the back door with a piece of plywood they'd found in the garage, but I planned to make sure Maddie called someone to replace the glass in the morning.

I locked the door behind us, and she stood in the entryway as if trying to decide what to do next.

I stood behind her, resisting the urge to touch her. "Why don't you go up to bed? I'll stay down here and keep watch."

"I want to take a shower," she said, her voice breaking. "I can still feel their hands on me."

My gut clenched. I wanted to go out and find the bastards myself, but there were plenty of patrol cars already on it. What I was doing here, now, was more important.

"Okay," I said, the word getting stuck in my throat. "I'll be down here. You can go to bed afterward if you want." Then I added, "I'm definitely not a house guest, so don't treat me like one."

She hesitated, then started up the stairs, stopping on the third riser before she turned back to face me.

"Noah, at the risk of sounding like a helpless female..." Her cheeks flushed with embarrassment.

"You stop right there," I said. "I would never think of you as a helpless female. If you need me to do something, just ask."

"I don't want to be alone," she whispered, then hastily added, "I'm not asking you to take a shower with me. I'm not coming on to you."

I gave her a reassuring smile. "You want me to come upstairs while you shower?"

"Yeah, but if it's too weird, I—"

I started up the stairs, wrapping an arm carefully around her waist. "Come on."

When we reached the landing, she led me to her room, which faced the front of the house, and flipped on the overhead light. The room was more feminine than I would have expected. No, not just feminine—it looked like it was a time capsule from her preteen years. Soft pink walls. White bedspread. Frilly white curtains. A queen-sized bed was arranged between two windows on the wall to the left, and there was a small TV on the white dresser opposite it. On the third wall, there was a window seat flanked by white bookcases. There were two doors on either side of the dresser. I presumed one was to a closet and the other to a bathroom.

She grabbed a couple of things from her dresser, then started to go through one of the doors. "You can watch TV if you want. The remote's on the nightstand."

She didn't give me time to answer, just shut the door behind her.

Chapter Thirty-Five

Maddie

I nearly had to ask Noah to help me take off my shirt. I'd been sitting for too long, and my back was getting stiffer by the minute. I turned on the shower while I fought with the shirt, finally getting it off, thankful I hadn't had to deal with a bra. I was pretty sure I couldn't reach my arms around my back right now.

Before I got in the shower, I looked at my back in the mirror. I already had bright bruises spreading across both sides, but my right side had caught the brunt of it. I was lucky they hadn't broken any ribs.

I stepped under the spray and, without any warning, started to cry again. Why was I being such a crybaby? I was safe. I was lucky that my back and my slightly sore arm where one of them had grabbed me were the only injuries I'd incurred. I'd definitely given them more than I'd gotten. So why was I falling apart?

I couldn't help thinking about my mother. What had been going through her head when she'd faced her killer.

It was personal.

Had they drawn out her pain? Had they made her suffer? Had she been as terrified as I'd felt tonight?

I cried myself out, and the water turned cold before I got the conditioner out of my hair. I finally turned off the water and grabbed a towel. My back was starting to seize up, and I realized there was no way I could put on the oversize T-shirt I'd brought in with me.

Oh, Lord. I was going to have to ask Noah for help after all.

I pulled on my pajama shorts and wrapped the towel around my chest before I opened the door a crack. Noah had turned off the overhead light and flicked on the lamp on the left nightstand. He was sitting on the bed, his back against several of my pillows, his stockinged feet outstretched. The TV was on, but I was pretty sure he wasn't watching it. He swung his feet onto the floor when he saw me.

"Can you help me with my shirt?" I cringed. "I swear, I'm not coming on to you. I'm struggling to get my arms over my head. I barely got my hair washed."

He got off the bed and walked over, taking my shirt from me. "Turn your back to me, and I'll pull it over your head and help you get your arms through the armholes."

I was so embarrassed I couldn't do this myself. "Okay."

I turned my back to him, then let the towel drop off my back, holding it against my breasts.

We stood there for several seconds, Noah not doing anything, so I glanced over my shoulder to see him staring at my back in horror.

"It looks worse than it is," I said.

"Liar," he grumbled, gently placing his hand on my shoulder blade. "I think I should take you to the ER. You might have broken ribs or internal injuries."

His touch sent waves of heat through my body, but that wasn't why he was here, and I'd meant it when I told him I didn't want to be seen as a mistake.

"I don't have broken ribs. And I don't think I'd be walking

around if I had internal injuries. Help me get my shirt on so we can go to bed."

He tugged the shirt over my head, then gently helped me thread my arms through the sleeves, first the right and then the left. He took the towel and put it in the bathroom, then came back out with my hairbrush and a hand towel.

"Sit on the bed."

I sat cross-legged in the middle, and he sat sideways behind me. He wrapped my hair in the towel, squeezing out some of the water, then began to tenderly brush my hair.

Tears sprang to my eyes. After Mom's death, I'd never been with anyone who took care of me. I'd always been the caretaker. The doer. Now, as the brush stroked my hair, I felt vulnerable and exposed. Like I was giving Noah control, which was ridiculous. He was drying and brushing my hair. Shoot, I paid a hairdresser to do this very thing, but this was different, and my heart knew it. "You don't need to do that, Noah."

"I have a sister. It'll tangle if you don't brush it. Trust me. I heard my mother cursing her more times than I can count."

I closed my eyes, and I couldn't believe more tears leaked out, streaming down my face. "I think Martin Schroeder killed my mother."

He stopped brushing for a second, then resumed. "What makes you think that?"

"Did you know he molested some of the female students at the high school?" I asked. "I talked to my mom's best friend today. She told me that my mom thought he'd been molesting me, and she planned to confront him."

Noah stopped. "Did she?"

I twisted on the bed to face him. "I don't know. She went to meet *someone* that night. She didn't tell me who. I asked her not to go, but she went anyway."

He took my hand. "Maddie."

"Martin Schroeder didn't molest me, but my mother had heard rumors that he was inappropriate with a student, and I'd been acting moody and withdrawn. He was my chemistry teacher...so she put two and two together and got five." I pushed out a sigh. "She didn't ask me. Maybe she thought I wouldn't admit it. So she told Dawn she was going to confront him." I looked him in the eyes. "Noah, Dawn and a teacher named Eleanor and a few other teachers went to the police and told them they thought Mr. Schroeder might have done it. Do you know if Detective Bergan looked into it? Did Schroeder have an alibi?"

Pain filled his eyes, and he squeezed my hand. "Maddie, I don't know. We can't find her file."

I shook my head in denial. "What does that mean? Did it get deleted? Aren't there safeguards to keep that from happening?"

"It was never on the computer, and we can't find it anywhere."

I sat back, staring at him in shock. I wasn't sure how many more unwelcome surprises I could face today. "How is that even possible?"

He reached up and wiped my cheek with his thumb. "I have no idea, but Maddie, I swear to you, I'm doing everything in my power to find it." The intensity in his eyes convinced me he was telling the truth, and that he was just as outraged by the situation as I was.

"I think Adam Brant knows something."

His body stiffened. "Why do you say that?"

"I talked to him this afternoon. After I talked to Dawn, I stopped by his classroom and introduced myself by name, saying I was Andrea's daughter. He freaked out and made me go into the hall. I knew he wouldn't admit to anything, but he was acting guilty as hell, so I told him that I'd picked up Mr. Schroeder and he'd told me everything."

Noah froze, staring at me in disbelief. Then he pulled his phone out of his pocket and made a call.

"Lance. Send someone to pick up Adam Brant and hold him

until the morning so we can question him. Maddie told him this afternoon that Schroeder had told her everything." He paused, then grunted. "Of course he didn't. Make the call, then get some sleep so you can think straight tomorrow." With that, he hung up.

"You think Mr. Brant sent those men to come get me tonight."

"Honestly, Maddie," he said with a sigh, "I have no idea what to think anymore." He tugged me down onto the bed. "You need to get some sleep. I'll go downstairs."

"Don't go down there," I pleaded. "Stay in the guest room. Or..." God, I hated that I sounded so needy.

"I can sleep on the floor," he said softly.

"No. Please don't do that. You can sleep in the bed. We're adults, right? We can use self-control."

He looked uncertain, then said, "Yeah."

He got up and headed for the bathroom.

"There's a new toothbrush in the drawer if you want to brush your teeth," I called after him.

He closed the door. I turned off the TV and got under the covers. Then I waited.

I was nervous. What if he *did* think I wanted to have sex, not just sleep. *Did* I want sex? Part of me did. I felt like a teen with a crush around him, but I wasn't a kid anymore. Yet I wasn't stupid enough to think I'd be satisfied with just sex from Noah Langley.

He emerged from the bathroom, still fully clothed, then moved to the side of the bed and turned off the lamp. I could see him remove his pants and his dress shirt. The mattress dipped as he got into bed. I scooted closer to my side of the bed, but the pressure of the mattress on my back made me groan.

"I can sleep on the floor, Maddie," he said from beside me.

"No, it's just my back. I need to get comfortable."

"Roll onto your stomach." He placed his hand on my shoulder and carefully rolled me over and helped me get situated.

"I swear, I'm not usually this helpless."

"Maddie, you were viciously attacked and beaten. Stop. And trust me, if I get shot again, I'll have you help with my recovery as payback."

His comment stole my breath. "You were shot?"

He hesitated, then said, "About six months ago. The bullet narrowly missed my heart."

I reached over to touch his arm. "Noah. I'm so sorry." He'd just handed me another piece to the Noah jigsaw puzzle. One more clue as to why he thought he was messed up. I didn't take that gift for granted. "Did it happen on the job?"

"Sort of. I was off duty, but it was the result of a case."

Neither of us spoke, but I heard his rapid breathing. I wasn't the only one who was haunted by memories.

"You can google my name and find out what happened," he finally said, his voice rough.

I knew it had cost him to offer that, but that wasn't how I wanted to hear about what had likely been the worst day of his life.

"No," I said softly, stroking his arm with my finger, brushing the bottom of his T-shirt sleeve. "I'll wait to hear it from you. Just like I'll tell you more about my mother someday."

We lay in silence, and his breathing became more even. I thought he'd fallen asleep, and I was definitely dozing. I felt safe with him there. But I reminded myself that while that was good for tonight, it wasn't the basis of a functional relationship.

"Were you really moody enough that your mother thought Schroeder had hurt you?" Noah asked, surprising me.

"Yeah," I said. "But it was petty teenage drama. Stupid really."

"What happened?"

I released a soft, bitter laugh. "Oh you know, the age-old story of boy tries to get girl to sleep with him, and when she doesn't put out, he sets out to ruin her reputation."

"Who was it?" he asked in a low, threatening voice.

A shiver of desire ran through me. "You don't know him, Noah."

"Humor me," was his gruff response.

"Peter McIntire."

He paused a beat. "The guy who took your aunt home?"

"Trust me, I didn't like it any more than you did. But desperate times..."

"For what it's worth," he said, rolling onto his side so we were face-to-face. The room was dark, but enough light filtered in through the curtains to reveal his face to me, his eyes bright and intense. "I'm sorry."

"For what?" I asked in a whisper.

"For all of it, Maddie. Every last goddamned bad thing that's happened to you."

Oh, Noah. Why did he have to know the perfect thing to say?

His face moved closer, and for one equally terrifying and exhilarating moment, I thought he was going to kiss me.

I would have let him. He had shown me enough of himself for me to know we could have something beautiful together, only deep inside I knew neither of us were ready. Besides, he'd already broken up with a woman he loved because she wanted a family and he didn't. I'd be beyond stupid to start something with him knowing it would eventually end in heartache.

But his lips brushed my forehead instead. "Go to sleep, Maddie. I won't let anything happen to you. I promise."

I knew he couldn't promise any such thing, but for tonight, I let myself believe it.

Chapter Thirty-Six

Noah

It took me awhile to get to sleep, but once I did, I slept better than I had since before the accident. No nightmares. No restlessness. Which was weird since I'd had to discharge my weapon and fire at someone who was firing back at me.

I'd hoped to never have to draw my weapon on another person again, let alone this soon after Caleb. I'd worried that if it *did* happen again, I might hesitate and get myself killed. But I hadn't. I'd been so freaked out by the sight of them pulling Maddie toward their car that instinct had kicked in. The only thoughts I'd had were about saving her. My training had taken over after that.

Still, I'd expected nightmares. Anxiety. At the very least, some tossing and turning. I'd figured I wouldn't have any trouble guarding her because I would be awake anyway, my guilty conscience gnawing at me. But I'd slept like a rock.

Her hand was on my chest when I woke, the heat searing through my T-shirt and going straight to my dick. But it was also strangely soothing, like waking up next to her was the most natural thing in the world.

I studied her face, which was smooshed against her pillow. She looked so relaxed. So beautiful. I reached over and let my finger trace her jaw.

Last night could have ended very, very differently. Instead of sleeping with her, I could have been scouring the county looking for her. I could have found her bruised and battered body.

My throat tightened, and I wanted to grab some part of her and not let go.

Her eyes fluttered open, and she smiled up at me. "Good job not letting me get murdered in my sleep."

I laughed. Little did she know that I'd slept so well someone could have walked in and killed us both before we even knew what hit us.

Some guard I'd turned out to be.

"What time is it?" she asked. "I have to get ready for work at the coffee shop."

"Maddie, you just got your ass kicked last night. You can take the day off."

She shot me a glare so fierce it made me want to kiss her, which I was fairly sure would have gotten *my* ass kicked.

"First of all," she said, trying to push herself upright and groaning in the process. She made it to her elbows and stopped. "I did *not* get my ass kicked. I guarantee they look a hell of a lot worse than I do today."

Especially since one of them was dead.

I sat up, reaching over to help her up, but she swatted my hand away.

"Second, I have bills to pay, which means I need to work so my paycheck will be big enough to pay part of those bills."

I started to say something, and she pushed herself up the rest of the way, panting from pain as she pointed at me. "And please tell me my car's ready for me to pick up. If things settle down, I'd like to make some Uber runs this weekend."

I stared at her in disbelief. "You are *not* making any Uber runs this weekend."

"I need money, Noah."

"You need to stay *alive*, Maddie. If they tried to kidnap you once, they'll try it again." Now that I thought about it, though, the coffee shop might be the safest place for her today. Especially since I had to work. Surely they wouldn't be stupid enough to try to grab her from there. "I'll take you to Déjà Brew. What time do you need to be there?"

She started to say something, then stopped. "Do you really think they'll try it again?"

"Yes." When her face paled, I reached over and cupped her upper arm. "I'm going to make sure you're safe, okay?"

"How are you going to do that when you have to work too?"

"We'll worry about it one chunk at a time, okay?"

Shaking her head, she rolled out of bed, groaning. "I need coffee."

"You get ready. I'll start a pot," I said, getting out of bed. I grabbed my pants and shirt from the floor and carried them out to the hall.

I was in desperate need of a shower and clean clothes, but I put on my pants and headed down to the kitchen, tossing my dress shirt on the counter before I fumbled around for coffee grounds and filters.

A knock landed at the front door. I cast a glance upstairs, then decided I didn't really want Maddie answering the door, so I went and opened it, finding myself face-to-face with none other than Peter McIntire. He was wearing a blue and white checkered shirt, looking like he'd just stepped out of a fucking Vineyard Vines catalogue shoot. He seemed just as surprised to see me in my dress pants, white T-shirt, and bare feet as I was to see him.

"What in the hell do you think *you're* doing here?" I asked him in a growl.

Maybe it wasn't called for, but it was seven fifteen in the morning, and I didn't like that he was here. Besides, looking at him, I saw the innocent girl Maddie had been, called names and made to suffer because she hadn't given him what he wanted, what he thought he was owed.

The guy looked shocked by my hostility, but quickly recovered. "I could ask the same of you. Aren't you the detective investigating Martin Schroeder's murder?" He tried to look past me. *"Are you sleeping with Maddie?"*

"I don't see how that's any of your business, you asshole," I snarled. "Now leave her the fuck alone." I slammed the door in his face.

I suddenly wondered how Maddie would feel about that, but I was too worked up to really give a shit.

Was I jealous? Maybe, but most of my anger extended from what I knew Peter had done back in high school.

If Andrea Baker had confronted Schroeder, and Schroeder had killed her for it, part of me blamed him.

I started the coffee and headed upstairs to find Maddie sitting on her bed with a T-shirt in her hand and wearing a pair of jeans.

"Did I hear someone knocking on the door?"

"It was Peter McIntire," I said more shortly than I'd intended. "What the fuck was *he* doing at your front door this early?"

Her mouth dropped open. Then she shot daggers at me. "I don't think that's any of your business!"

"Maddie," I grunted.

She looked like she was about to tell me off, but the rage leaked out of her. "I don't want to fight with you, Noah. Plus, I need you to help me with my shirt." She cringed. "And my bra."

I stared at her like she'd just asked me to defuse a nuclear weapon. "Maybe you should go over and ask Margarete for help."

She gave me a patient look. "You were a perfect gentleman all night. You can help me with this."

She had a lot more faith in me than I did. Was she doing this to torment me? Maybe as payback for demanding an explanation for McIntire's presence? "I see the shirt. Do you have your bra?"

She pulled it out from underneath her shirt. It was black and looked fairly utilitarian. Thank fuck. Turning her back me, she set her bra down next to her. "Once you help me get my shirt off, I can put the bra on in front. I just need you to fasten it in back." She glanced over her shoulder with an ornery grin. "A good-looking guy like you probably has lots of experience with fastening bras."

More with unfastening them, but I was sure she knew that.

"Stand up."

She gingerly got to her feet, and I suddenly had major misgivings about our plan of action for the day. She could hardly lift her arms. How was she going to work? My misgivings doubled when I saw her back. It looked even worse after a few hours and in the light of day.

"Maddie, maybe you should stay home today. I'll get someone to come stay with you."

"You mean babysit me? I'd rather go to work and at least get paid. Trust me, Petra will baby the crap out of me."

Cursing under my breath, I pulled the T-shirt over her head and tossed it onto the unmade bed, then picked up the bra and handed it to her.

I was pretty sure I qualified for sainthood over this.

She lopped her arms through the straps and then held the bra to her chest. "You're going to have to pull the straps around."

I made myself think of Martin Schroeder and the autopsy I would be going to in a few hours as my hands brushed the silky-smooth skin next to her breasts.

The pathologist makes a Y incision, then uses a bone saw to cut the chest plate.

Her hair was to the side, exposing the curve of her neck, and it took everything in me not to lean forward and press a kiss there, which would lead to me tossing the bra to the floor, then turning her around and kissing her sassy mouth.

But she was vulnerable, and I couldn't take advantage of that, not to mention both of us had made it pretty clear we weren't ready for a relationship.

Which made me wonder once again why McIntire had thought it his right to show up on her front porch. Then again, I'd seen the way he'd looked at her in that parking lot. I knew why he was there.

"Has McIntire asked you out?" I asked as I carefully hooked her bra. The straps rested at the edge of her bruises.

"He's made it pretty clear he'd like to, and I made it *very* clear I'm not interested. However, he was never one to take no for an answer. Then Aunt Deidre wanted to have a dinner party. She invited him, but Peter insisted on throwing a cocktail party tonight instead. He invited 'all our friends from high school,' which I took to mean *his* friends."

I stood still, leaning around to look at her face. "Are you going?"

She hesitated. Which wasn't a no.

"Why the fuck would you do that, Maddie?" I asked in frustration. "After what he did to you?"

She turned around to face me, outrage flashing in her eyes. "Because some asshole detective had me as his number one person of interest, and I figured it would be up to me to clear my name. I was hoping to find out more about Martin Schroeder. And if I let Peter host it, I figured I could leave whenever I wanted."

I stared at her, trying like hell not to drop my gaze to her chest. "You're not going."

"*Excuse* me?"

My voice rose. "I said you're not going! Not with a kidnapping threat hanging over your head."

She moved closer until her chest was nearly touching mine. She glared up at me. "Let's make one thing perfectly clear, *Detective Langley*. You are not the boss of me. I will do what I want. If you

Blind Bake

want me to do something, ordering me is not the way to get it done." She leaned over to the bed and picked up her shirt. "Now help me with my shirt."

She didn't turn around this time, just stood in front of me, her eyes bright with anger.

Jesus, she was sexy as hell. Why was I torturing myself like this?

I took the shirt from her, silently telling myself to *simmer the fuck down*, and gently pulled it over her head and helped her thread her arms through the openings. This was more formfitting than the shirt she'd slept in, and the Déjà Brew logo was printed in white over her breast. It didn't help that I knew what she was wearing underneath.

She picked up her sleep shirt from the bed and tossed it into a hamper in her closet. "I need to go over and check on my aunt and Margarete," she said with less heat.

"I'll go with you. I'm not sure they should stay here today. Do you think Margarete would be okay with your aunt and her home health nurse spending the day over there?"

"Yeah."

I followed her downstairs, realizing she was right—I had gone all caveman on her, but I was terrified that something was going to happen to her. I needed to show her the party was a terrible idea. Because she was right—I couldn't order her not to go. "I'll go with you."

"To Margarete's?" she asked as she poured coffee into two travel mugs. "I thought that was a given."

"No. To McIntire's. If you really want to go, I'll go with you."

She stared up at me in disbelief. "You would do that?"

"Yes, if that's what you want to do."

Her face softened, and she put a lid on one and handed it to me. "I'm not going, Noah. I told him as much last night, and it pissed him off even more. He probably showed up earlier because he was hoping to change my mind. Especially since he spouted some mansplaining shit about giving me some time so I could think straight."

"Wait," I said, holding up a hand. "Why was he pissed off in the first place?"

"He was irrationally angry that I missed my attorney consultation yesterday."

"Why did you have an attorney consultation?"

She groaned. "I figured that's what a person of interest should do. Talk to an attorney. Peter and I went to school with Burt, so he helped arrange the whole thing. But it was supposed to be at two o'clock yesterday afternoon, and I was still dealing with the fallout from Aunt Deidre's disappearing act."

My irritation resurfaced. "You're not a person of interest. You don't need an attorney."

"I know, which was why I didn't care about missing it, but Peter was furious. He said I was being rude to Burt. He shouted so loudly Margarete actually came over to make sure everything was okay. That was when I told him I wasn't coming tonight."

"You're not going," I growled.

"I already *told you* I'd told him I wasn't," she said in exasperation.

"So we're on the same page."

She rolled her eyes and shook her head as she added cream to her mug. "So you're one of those kinds."

"What the hell is that supposed to mean?"

She gave me a pointed look. "You like to have the last word."

"I do not."

Her gaze sharpened, but she didn't say anything, proving her point.

Dammit.

Chapter Thirty-Seven

Noah

Margarete wholeheartedly approved of Deidre and Linda staying at her house for the day. I had no idea what I would ask them to do tonight. I planned to stay again, but I'd need to find someone to watch over them until I could come over, depending on how late I had to work.

I left Maddie with them and headed out to the front porch to make some calls. The autopsy was scheduled to start at ten, but the chief had just texted to tell me he was assigning someone else to watch it so I could have my nine o'clock meeting with him. I could drop Maddie off at work, run home to shower and change, and still make the meeting.

Then Lance and I could go question Brant.

I called Lance to check in with him.

"Any problems last night?" he asked.

"Nope. The chief assigned someone else to the autopsy, which frees up my morning. I have a meeting with him at nine, but then we can go question Brant. The sooner, the better."

"There's a problem with that, Noah."

My anxiety hitched up a notch. "And that is?"

"He wasn't home. We haven't located him."

My frustration mushroomed. "Send someone to pick him up at school."

"Wow," he said in a wry tone. "Why didn't *I* think of that?"

I scrunched my eyes shut and pinched the bridge of my nose. "Sorry. I just really want to corner this guy."

"And you think I don't?" he asked, his voice radiating frustration. "That's my school, Noah. I had Schroeder and Brant for teachers, and I had no fucking clue any of this was going on." He took a breath. Then his voice turned stone cold. "I want to nail those fuckers to the wall with railroad spikes. So don't presume you own the market on this."

"I'm sorry. You're right. We'll *both* get them."

"Damn straight."

"I'll call you when I get out of this meeting. Then we'll figure out where to go from there."

"Okay."

I started to hang up. "Hey, Lance," I said, at the last minute.

"Yeah?"

"You make a good partner. I'm going to see if we can make this permanent. That is, if you still want to deal with me."

He laughed. "Shut up and get in here so we can get to work."

* * *

Maddie came out a few minutes later, looking anxious. I pushed away from the porch railing I'd been leaning against to go to her.

"Everything okay? How's Deidre?"

"She's still tired, but she's not confused, thank goodness. However, she doesn't remember anything from last night."

"That's a good thing, isn't it?" I asked as I led her to my car. "That way she won't be traumatized."

"It would be if she'd been confused last night. But she wasn't…

and she woke up this morning wondering why she was at Margarete's."

"And that's a bad thing?"

"I think it's a *new* thing."

We kept walking, but I put a hand on her shoulder and squeezed. "I'm sorry. You don't need one more thing to worry about."

We stopped beside the passenger-side door, and she looked up at me. "Thanks for being here for me, Noah." She smiled. "And not just for making sure I don't get kidnapped and murdered."

I laughed. She had a way of lifting me from my dark places. "Yeah, well, that job isn't finished, so don't thank me yet."

She laughed too, then got into the car.

I headed downtown, and we drove in silence. My mind was whirling with the case and why those men had tried to kidnap Maddie. They obviously thought she had information they wanted. But what?

"Maddie," I said, my hand slung over the steering wheel. "Were you looking for Ernie to find out if he'd seen anything?"

"That and to make sure he was okay."

"What did he say to you in the parking lot?"

"Only that he thought I was in danger. He claimed they—whoever they are—had driven past my house. He was worried they'd think I knew something, particularly since he saw me at the crime scene the day we met."

"How did he know they'd driven by your house?" I asked, then added, "Maybe he was already staying in your garage."

"Maybe."

"Have you done anything else besides look for Ernie and talk to Brant that might have landed you on someone's radar and led them to try to kidnap you?"

"Not that I can think of." She hesitated. "Unless…"

"Go on."

"My old best friend from high school works at the hardware store. I found out at the women's meeting. All this thinking about the past inspired me to drop by and see how she was doing."

"How could that get you on someone's radar?"

"I found out she worked there because the person who told me also told me that she'd seen Martin Schroeder making some odd purchases there. So after our chat—" She made a pained look. "—I figured I was already there and curious, so I asked her if she remembered him coming in, and she did. She remembered all of it."

"What did he buy?" I asked, curious myself.

"A weird mix of things. Rat poison, rope, a hacksaw and some PVC pipe, and a blowtorch. He didn't know how to use it and got pissed when one of the workers asked what he intended to use it for. He said he only needed to know how to turn it off and on. Oh, and a padlock."

Jesus, that list sounded like it came out of the serial killer handbook. Was Martin Schroeder planning to kill someone but they got to him first? My second thought was that I hadn't seen any of those things in his house. Were they in his still-missing car?

"Anything else?"

"Well, then when I left, a homeless woman threatened me in the parking lot. She pounded on my window and told me to stop looking for Ernie. She said I was getting him into trouble."

I sat up. "Which insinuates she knows why he'd be in trouble. What did she look like?"

"I don't know," she said. "Older—medium height and build. Dark hair with lots of gray. Deep wrinkles on her face. She looks like she's led a hard life. She had a cart loaded with black trash bags. She wasn't with either of the groups. She was alone."

"I'll send a unit out to look for her. We'll see if she knows anything else. What's the name of the friend?"

"Colleen Nichols, but she's not involved. She's married and has three kids. No way."

I'd be the judge of that. "Who else might know about Schroeder's purchases?"

"The cashier, Ashley. The owner's daughter. She rang him up. Colleen saw it all because she was waiting to take over the register. But I doubt she was paying much attention to me. She was more worried that Colleen was talking to someone during her shift." She frowned and looked sad.

"Anyone else?"

She turned to look at me. "I've told you everything relevant to your case."

Which meant there was more she wasn't telling me. From the looks of it, it hadn't been pleasant.

"Any other snooping?" I asked with a grin.

She rolled her eyes. "It wasn't snooping, and no, I think that's it. Besides, why would showing up at the hardware store instigate someone to kidnap me? If anything, it proves I don't know anything."

I wasn't so sure about that. "What time do you get off?"

"Three."

"I'll come get you, or if I can't, I'll send someone else. But I'll let you know who."

I turned onto Main Street and gave Maddie a worried look. "If you get too tired and want to go home, call me."

She responded with a tired grin. "You're kind of going above and beyond, Detective."

"I have to take care of my former number one suspect," I teased. Then, because it had been eating at me since last night, I asked, "Why did you call me instead of Lance or 911?"

She was quiet as I pulled up to the curb in front of the coffee shop. "Because I knew you wouldn't let anything happen to me."

"How could you be sure?" I asked, unable to stop myself.

She gave me a sad smile. "I told you the other night. Like knows like, Noah." Then she got out and went inside.

Her words stayed with me. I wasn't so sure she was right about me, but I was determined as hell to find out who was responsible for her kidnapping attempt. I figured I was close enough to the hardware store to drop in on my way home. I should still have time to get home, shower, and make my meeting. Sure, I was a little rough, but I'd looked worse.

I pulled into the parking lot, and to my surprise, I saw the homeless woman Maddie had encountered yesterday. She was sitting at the corner, basking in the sun, her legs outstretched. Her eyes were closed, and I was pretty sure she was taking a nap.

I got out and walked over to her, wearing a jacket I found in my trunk instead of my rumpled suit coat. I tugged my wallet out of my pocket and pulled out a twenty-dollar bill along with a couple of fives. I stuck my wallet in my pants pocket, the fives in my jacket.

"Hi," I said, coming to a stop a few feet from her. "I'd like to ask you a few questions."

"Get lost," she said, her eyes still closed.

"I'm looking for Ernie Foust."

"Isn't everyone?" she snapped, eyes still closed, arms folded over her chest.

I squatted next to her. "Why do you suppose that is?"

One of her eyes squinted open. "You a cop?"

"Depends," I said with a sly grin. "Which answer will make you talk to me?"

"I ain't givin' no statements."

"I'm fine with that," I said, waving the twenty. "But I'm willing to pay for information. Off the books."

That caught her interest.

It was always tricky paying sources for information. Until you learned whether a source was trustworthy, you were basically throwing your money into the wind. Truthfully, I liked helping people, even if it didn't get me what I needed, but based on the smell of tequila emanating from her, I suspected my money would be buying her next bottle.

Her eyes widened. "What do you want to know?"

"Do you know where Ernie's hiding?"

She looked away. "He won't tell me, and he won't let me go with him."

"When did he start hiding?"

"Monday night. He didn't tell me any details, but he saw something bad happen. Said he'd be gone for a while."

"The murder?" When she nodded, I asked, "Who else is looking for Foust?"

Her gaze remained fixed on the bill in my hand. "I know there's a woman asking around about him. A cop too." She nodded to me with a wicked grin. "I suspect that's you."

I didn't respond.

She reached for the bill, but I lifted it over my head, out of her reach. "Those were the easy answers. I'm gonna need you to dig deeper. Who else is looking?"

She pulled her hand back. "What makes you think someone else is lookin' for him?"

I continued to stare at her with a bored expression.

"Tellin' you could get me killed," she said.

"I can offer you some protection," I said.

She snorted, then started to cough. "You're a funny man," she said when she settled down.

"So I've been told."

She eyed the bill again. "A rough-lookin' guy's been askin' after him. Mean."

"One of the Brawlers?"

She shook her head. "No. I know most of them. He's not one of 'em. He ain't from around here, neither."

"What makes you say that?"

"He asked how to get to the high school."

Shit. "How long ago was he asking?"

She grinned. "You're gonna need more than a twenty."

I pulled out a five, adding it to the twenty, and fanned them out. "Yesterday. After I told that woman to lay off."

"Did he want to know who else was asking about Foust?"

"He weren't no dummy."

I took that as a yes. "And what did you tell him?"

She made a come here motion, and I pulled out the other five.

She snatched all three bills and shoved them down her shirt into her cleavage.

"I told him she was Maddie Baker and she'd dropped Schroeder off to his death."

I scowled. Part of me was pissed at her for throwing Maddie under the bus like that, but at the same time, I also wasn't surprised. Was this guy associated with the guys from the Kia? Maybe that whole crew was from Chattanooga after all. But why were they interested in the high school? Had *they* taken Adam Brant?

None of this made sense.

"Anything else?" I asked.

She gave me a scrutinizing look. "You ain't like the other cops."

"How so?"

"They treat me like dirt."

"Yeah," I said with a sigh. "I'm sorry about that."

"You gonna pay me for information again?"

She was weighing her options. If I planned to use her again, she wouldn't feed me a lie for fear of losing her hookup.

"Yeah," I said. "I don't have a good outside source. I'm willing to come to you again if I need info."

She swallowed, looking nervous. "I think they're stayin' at the Bluebird Inn. A key chain from there with a room key dropped out of his pocket."

I stood and fished out my wallet, pulling out a ten as well as my business card. "Thank you,...?" I asked, prompting her to give me her name.

"Susan."

"I'm Noah. Noah Langley," I said, bending over to hand her the ten and my card. "I think we could work together again." Especially since she might have just helped me break this case.

I headed for the entrance of the hardware store, pausing outside to call Lance. "I just got a tip that a guy from out of town was looking for Ernie yesterday. The guy knew Maddie was asking around for him too. He needed directions to the high school. They're staying at the Bluebird Inn. Get some units out there."

"Will do. I'll head out there too," Lance said. "You're still going to your meeting, aren't you?"

It was the last thing I felt like doing, especially since I was itching to follow the lead, but the chief would possibly fire my ass if I missed it. Besides, it wouldn't be smart to go to the scene without a firearm. "Yeah, but keep me updated."

"Will do. Good luck."

I headed into the hardware store, walking up to the counter and showing the cashier my badge. "I'm Detective Langley, and I need to ask you a few questions about a purchase Martin Schroeder made last week."

Ashley, based on her name tag, swallowed hard. "Yeah, he was in last week." Then she gave me an account that was similar to Maddie's, with one exception. "His money stank to high heaven."

"Stank?"

"Yeah. Like buttholes and sweat. I washed my hands like five times after I touched it."

That was an interesting and gross observation. "I'd like to speak to another of your employees. Colleen Nichols."

She shook her head. "She's off today. Called in sick."

"You got any contact information for her?"

She opened up her cell phone and looked up Colleen's cell

number. I wrote it down, then headed out the back door to the parking lot. I still wasn't sure what to make of Schroeder's purchases. Where were they and who had he planned to use them on?

When I left, I noticed Susan wasn't on the corner anymore.

*　*　*

I got to the station a few minutes before nine, then headed straight for the chief's office. There would be an investigation into the shooting last night, of course, but the chief said there were over a dozen eyewitnesses who saw the driver discharge his weapon after I issued a warning. There was no misconduct that he could see. I'd been obligated to shoot to protect the bystanders and myself.

He waved his hand in dismissal. "Enough of that nonsense. What's going on with this investigation?"

When I filled him in on our recent progress, he seemed appeased. Especially when we got confirmation that four men driving a black Kia had checked into the Bluebird Inn on Tuesday and hadn't checked out. Lance and two uniformed officers had gained access to the room, and while no luggage or personal items had been left there, there was plenty of trash, along with blood in the bathroom we could use for DNA analysis.

We hadn't caught them yet, but we were closing in.

In the end, the chief told me to get back to work and said another weapon would be assigned to me. As I got up to leave, he motioned for me to sit back down.

I waited.

"How you handling this?"

"Excuse me, sir? You mean the case?"

"No." His face softened. "The shooting. You were placed in a situation where you were forced to fire your weapon. After your previous exchange of gunfire..." Mercifully, he didn't finish his statement.

I paused, unsure how to answer. "I wish to God I hadn't had to do it, but multiple bystanders were in danger, not to mention the victim was about to be dragged into the car. I did what needed to be done."

He nodded. "No hesitation?"

I wasn't sure if I should feel pride or shame. "None."

"Like you said, you did what had to be done. And if you hadn't, innocent bystanders, the victim, even you yourself could have been hurt or killed. If either of us had any questions about whether you are fit to be here, you answered them last night."

"Yes, sir," I said, looking down at my hands. I lifted my gaze to his. "I suppose I did."

"Good. Now go get the bastards who did this."

* * *

After I got my new weapon, I headed out to the motel to see the room for myself. The crime scene team was already there, photographing the space before they started collecting evidence. In addition to the large amount of blood, they had left trash from several fast-food restaurants—McDonalds, Popeyes, and Wendy's, along with a bag from the Piggly Wiggly that held empty chip bags and beer cans and discarded gas station coffee cups. The jackpot was the receipt for gas and snacks acquired at a Chattanooga gas station Tuesday night.

"I'll get started on pulling a warrant to get the information on the card from the gas station," I said, walking out of the room.

"There's a chance the card was stolen," Lance said.

"True enough, but we'll follow the breadcrumbs."

I had just finished filling out the warrant when I got a call from a patrol officer.

"Langley, we found your Kia. It's behind the Piggly Wiggly."

I told Lance, and we raced over to the grocery store in our separate cars, driving around to the back of the building. And there it was, complete with a shattered side window and a windshield and hood riddled with bullet holes.

"We found it back here after we responded to a stolen vehicle call," the officer said. "Some guy had too much to drink at the bar next door and left his truck in the lot overnight. Someone brought him by to pick it up this morning, but it was gone. When he figured out it hadn't been towed, he called 911."

"So they dumped the car here and took his," Lance said.

"Bought them enough time to get away," I said, then turned to the officer. "What time did the guy leave the bar?"

"About midnight."

"They left Maddie's street at about 11:05. If they'd stolen the car any sooner, the guy would have figured out it was missing last night. We could have had a BOLO out a whole hell of a lot sooner." That was frustrating as hell. And good luck on their part. "Do we have a BOLO out now?"

"Yep," Lance said. "The responding officer took care of it." He gave me a reassuring look. "Between the car and the motel room, we'll get prints," Lance said. "And DNA. There was blood in the back seat."

"How much?" I asked. I'd aimed at the gunman, but I could have hit the men trying to hustle Maddie into the car. Or Margarete could have.

"One of them could have had a bloody nose." He paused. "Or at least one of them could have been shot."

I wasn't sure how I felt about that, but I'd do it again in a heartbeat. "I'll call the ERs in the area."

If one of them were shot, they were going to need medical attention.

"The crime lab team should be here soon to get it processed. We'll see what they find," Lance said.

I nodded. "Yeah."

I slipped my phone out of my pocket and checked to see if I had any missed calls. Okay, so I was specifically checking to see if Maddie had called or texted. We were much closer to apprehending the men who'd attacked her, but we hadn't found them yet. I couldn't help worrying that they might get desperate and do something stupid like try to grab her from the coffee shop.

Lance leaned into me and whispered, "Call her."

I looked up at him in surprise.

"Look," he said. "You and I don't know each other very well, but it's obvious you like her and you're worried. So call her."

I gave him a dark look.

"Fine," he said nonchalantly as he pulled out his phone. "*I'll* call her."

He tapped on his phone, then held it up to his ear with a wicked smile. "Hey, Maddie. It's Lance. I was just calling to check on you. Any problems?" He was quiet, obviously listening to her answer. "Well, if you have any issues, you can call me too."

He hung up and grinned at me. "She's fine. Apparently business is booming because she made the news. But Maddie's boss knows she's not 100%, so she brought in another employee to help out."

"She probably hates that," I muttered.

"Guess you'd know if you hadn't been too chickenshit to call her."

I skewered him with a dark glare.

"Those looks don't scare me anymore," he said with a laugh. "I can see right through the Oscar the Grouch illusion to your soft, pudgy heart."

Rather than contradict him, I pushed out a grumpy sigh. "Yeah, well keep it to yourself."

He laughed but turned serious. "Look, I know you're a by-the-book kind of guy, and I appreciate that about you. I am too. But Maddie's not a person of interest anymore."

My glare was back and more intense.

"I know you came here to escape the bad shit that went down at the beginning of the year."

He was stepping into dangerous territory. "I'm not escaping shit."

"Fine, call it whatever you want. The thing is…I don't know everything that went down in your house or what led up to it, but I know you're a good person, Noah. You don't have to be alone. You can let some of us in."

A lump burned in my throat.

"Maddie's one of those people." He was quiet for a second, then grinned. "But if you're not interested, just say the word. She and I have a bit of history, you know."

"Fuck off," I practically growled.

He laughed. "That's what I thought. When this is over, let her know how you feel." Then he wandered over to meet the crime scene team that had just arrived.

He was right, but I wasn't ready. If I started something with her, I'd only fuck it up with my trust issues and moodiness. I needed to get my shit together first. Because I hadn't forgotten what she'd said at her front door the other night, and it was no less true now than it had been then. She *did* deserve better than what I had to offer.

But that didn't mean I didn't want her.

Now wasn't the time to deal with my fucked-up emotions. I needed to focus on the case, catch the bastards who'd hurt Maddie, figure out which of them—if any—had killed Martin Schroeder, and put some people behind bars.

We could only peek inside the car since we had to wait for the crime lab to tow it. I pulled Lance away to fill him in on what I'd discovered about Schroeder's purchases at the hardware store.

"Jesus," he muttered. "Was he planning to kill someone and dismember them?"

"I don't know." From what I'd learned about the bastard, I wouldn't put it past him.

"No one's been reported missing," Lance said. "So it looks like he didn't carry it out."

"Yeah." I glanced up at the grocery store, noticing several cameras. "We need to get copies of the surveillance footage from the Piggly Wiggly and outside the bar," I said.

I considered sending Lance since McIntire would be none too thrilled to see me, but then again, it might be fun to rile him up. And maybe I could find out what he wanted from Maddie. Maybe he was just trying to sleep with her. Hell, that was almost certainly what he was trying to do, but I didn't trust the guy. If he was the kind of man who'd slander a woman for not sleeping with him, he hadn't magically turned into a prince after high school. Life didn't work that way.

"I'll take the grocery store," I offered. "Why don't you see if anyone's at the bar yet?"

We split up and I went straight to the service desk at the Piggly Wiggly. After I introduced myself, I said, "I need to speak to your manager."

"I'll call Lucinda right up," the young woman at the desk said earnestly. Her name tag read Tracy. She called for Lucinda to come to customer service on the overhead intercom, then turned her attention to me. "I heard that car was involved in that shooting last night. Is that true?"

"That's what we're here to find out," I said. "You mentioned Lucinda. Is Peter McIntire here?"

Her face brightened at the mention of his name. "Sorry, Peter's not here."

"Is it his day off?"

"No," she said, shaking her head. "I don't know why he hasn't come in yet. Lucinda might know."

Maybe she would, but I had a feeling I could find out everything I wanted to know about McIntire from Tracy. Based on her reaction to his name, she was his biggest fan.

"How long has Peter managed the store?"

"Oh," she said, her face flushing. "He's the owner. His daddy signed it over to him when he retired a few years ago." She leaned closer and lowered her voice. "You know, the store wasn't doing so good when Peter took over, but he really turned things around."

"Really?" I asked, leaning my hand on the counter. "How'd he do that?"

She looked up at me, tilting her head and beaming. "He, like, really listened to the customers, you know? He calls us Cockamamie's friendly neighborhood store and insists on everyone being cheerful and friendly. He says we need to make people *want* to be here."

I grudgingly admitted it sounded like a good plan.

"He also started this program where we provide recipes for three different meals every week and run a sale on some of the items. Lucinda said it increased our profits by, like, twenty percent."

So Peter McIntire had a good business head on his shoulders, but I still didn't trust him.

"He has these events for seniors once a month, and he invites a guest speaker to come in and teach them things, like how to use their cell phones and computers and such. Oh! And he sponsors a lot of sports teams and even provides the drinks and snacks."

A woman with a toddler in the seat of her cart pulled up behind us. "Don't forget about the special orders," she said.

I turned to face her. "Special orders?"

"If you need something and we don't carry it, he finds it for you," Tracy said.

"Exactly," the mother said. "I wanted a specific kind of diaper rash cream for little Cooper and couldn't find it *anywhere*. Well, Peter had it for me a week later. He's a miracle worker."

I narrowed my eyes. "Does he charge more for that service?"

"He just charges what he charges," the mother said. "He's never given me an upcharge."

Which didn't mean he didn't jack up the price. I wasn't falling for the Saint Peter act.

"Hello, Detective," a woman said as she walked up to us. "I'm Lucinda. I hear you needed to speak to me."

I hadn't introduced myself, but then again, the lot behind the store was swarming with cops. It wasn't hard to figure out.

"That's right," I said. "I need to see surveillance footage from behind the store for last night and this morning."

"Is this about the car behind the building?" she asked, cringing. "Nasty business."

"Why didn't any of the employees notice it back there this morning?" I asked. "Weren't there deliveries or anything going on out there?"

She shrugged as she led me behind the counter. "Unfortunately, we see cars in all sorts of conditions around here. And sometimes they're parked behind the building. If it was still there tomorrow, we would have called y'all, but honestly, they're usually gone by then."

That seemed odd, so I filed it away for later.

Lucinda opened the door to what was presumably an office, and I thanked Tracy for her time before I followed her inside and shut the door.

I found Lucinda sitting at a desk with a computer monitor. A bank of screens on the wall showed the feeds from multiple cameras.

"This is a pretty high-tech setup," I said in surprise.

"Yeah," she said distractedly as she tapped on the computer screen. "Peter had it installed after his father gave the store to him."

"Gave it to him?"

She glanced over her shoulder. "Yeah. Stan was retiring, so he just signed it over to him." She shrugged. "Peter gives him money from the profits each month—I think they called it a buyout—but the two of them handle all that."

She turned back to the computer and continued pulling up the feeds as I stared at her, the wheels in my head spinning.

I pulled out my phone and texted Lance to get to the Piggly Wiggly office ASAP. Something about all of this felt off.

There was a knock on the door a few seconds later, and I reached over to open it. Lance appeared in the doorway.

"The bar wasn't open, so I was already on my way over," he said, his attention going to the bank of monitors on the wall. His eyes widened. "Wow. This is pretty state of the art."

"Nothing but the best," Lucinda said, but her tone lacked the enthusiasm of Tracy's gushing.

"You don't approve?" I asked lightly.

"It's overkill." She shook her head. "We've never had a single break-in. What do we need all this security for? My husband said Peter must have spent tens of thousands of dollars on it."

"Lucinda?" Tracy called through the still-open door. "We need a price override."

Lucinda heaved a sigh as she got out of her seat. "I've got to take care of this, but I've got the footage all cued up. If you'd like to take a look, it's pretty self-explanatory." Then she squeezed past us and walked out of the office.

"Ever seen anything like this setup in any other stores in Cockamamie?" I asked under my breath.

"No."

I sat down in the seat and saw that she'd backed the video up to 8 p.m. last night.

"There must be fifty feeds," I muttered, clicking the cameras that faced the back lot.

Lance pulled up a chair and sat down next to me. "And about half of them point outside."

I started playing all eight video feeds from the cameras pointed toward the back. We could see every inch behind the store, including the dumpsters and the wooden fence that ran along the back.

I fast-forwarded quickly until it hit the eleven o'clock mark and then slowed it down. At 12:10, the Kia pulled up perpendicular to a loading dock and idled.

"They're waiting for someone," I said under my breath.

"Who do you suppose they're waiting for?" Lance asked.

I slowly shook my head. I had my presumptions, but I was worried my bias was bleeding into my interpretation. I couldn't let that happen again.

The car stayed there for three minutes and forty seconds before the back door opened and a guy in jeans and a dark shirt got out of the car. He wasn't wearing a ski mask.

"That's definitely one of them," I said. "I recognize his outfit. But I guess they aren't as smart as they thought they were. Did they not realize they were on video?"

"Maybe they didn't feel threatened by the cameras," Lance said, his eyes glued to the screen. The guy walked up to the back door and pounded, waited a few seconds, then pounded again.

After about a minute he pulled out his phone and walked back down to the car and paced. He got into an animated conversation, then kicked the car tire and got back in the vehicle. The car pulled out of view. I stopped the tapes, then opened the video feeds on that side of the building. The car drove toward the street, and the front cameras gave us a clear view of it taking off down the main road.

"What the fuck?" I muttered, watching the car drive out of view.

"Obviously it comes back," Lance said. "Maybe they went back to the motel to get their things. We don't know when they left. All the guests we questioned claimed they didn't hear anything. Unfortunately, the type of clientele who frequent the Bluebird Inn aren't that enthusiastic about cooperating with police."

"Maybe," I said. "But they turned the opposite direction of the motel."

I fast-forwarded the feeds—now looking at the feeds from two cameras in the front, one on each side, and two from the back. The Kia reappeared on the street in front of the store at 3:12, coming from the direction of the motel. The side camera showed it stop next to a pickup truck. A guy emerged from the front passenger seat and went around to the driver's side of the truck and got in. The brake lights came on, and then the truck backed up and followed the Kia behind the store. The bearded guy parked the Kia in the spot where the patrol officer had found it this morning, then got into the truck's passenger side before it drove away.

"Where's the other guy?" Lance asked. "There was a driver and three other guys, right? They shot the one guy and left him in the street, and two other guys were trying to get Maddie into the car." He turned to me. "Where's the third guy?"

I sat back in my seat, the realization that there was a good chance I'd shot one of the guys hitting me center mass. "I think they dumped him."

"What?"

"They shot the guy they were leaving behind. What if I shot one of them and they knew they couldn't take him to the hospital so they disposed of him too?"

Lance didn't say anything, but he put his hand on my shoulder.

We sat in silence for a few moments. What did we do with all of this?

"Thoughts about Peter McIntire?" I finally asked.

"Oh, he's involved somehow. *How* is the question. Why does he need this much security? Is he dealing drugs?"

"One of the customers told me he offered special orders. He got her some rare diaper rash cream. It started after his father gave him the store. He put in the security a few months later."

He laughed. "He's got all this security for diaper rash cream?"

"What if he puts through other kinds of special orders?" I asked.

"Like what?"

"Illegal ones. Obviously those guys from Chattanooga aren't boy scouts. And it explains the security."

"Think we can get a search warrant to check out his storage in the back of the store?" Lance asked.

"Considering the judge denied our request to look at the school's employment files, I'm going with no. But to be fair, even I think it's a reach at this point. But..." I gave him a dark look. "That's not to say we can't ask to look around back there. Lucinda seems cooperative."

"Good idea."

I turned back to the screen. "But I want to take a look at something else first."

I set the program back to Monday morning and started fast-forwarding, concentrating on the area behind the store. Delivery trucks pulled in and out. Workers went out back to smoke. More delivery trucks. All moving quickly, in and out of frames. The lot began to darken as the sun lowered to the horizon, and at 5:40, a pickup truck pulled up behind the building. I slowed down the feed.

The truck idled for several minutes before a figure came out of the back of the store and stood next to the driver's door of the truck.

My heart started racing.

"That's McIntire," I said, pointing to the screen. I had no idea what he was up to, but Lance was right. This wasn't my imagination working overtime or the workings of a jealous mind—he *was* part of this. I just had to figure out how he fit.

The lights in the back of the building flicked on, giving us a better view of the driver, but his face was obscured.

They talked for less than thirty seconds. Then McIntire went back inside and the truck backed out and drove away, turning toward downtown.

I paused the tape. "It's headed toward the Bottoms."

Lance shot me a dark look and I could see he was wondering the same thing I was: had we just found Martin Schroeder's murderer?

I pressed play again. The truck had shown up at 5:40, which was before Schroeder's murder. Had the truck come back? I started fast-forwarding, keeping an eye on the feed.

"So did they plan to kill Schroeder?" I said, thinking out loud.

"Schroeder bought all that stuff last week," Lance said. "Maybe he planned on killing the guy at the butcher shop."

"Not likely. The only thing he had with him was that paper bag. Pretty much none of the stuff he bought would fit in there." Then I added, "Unless he'd already stashed it at the butcher shop."

"But none of it was there." He pushed out a sigh. "The murder scene was cleaned, so the murderer could have taken it with him."

"Maybe." I wasn't ready to paint myself into a corner with any theories yet, and something else was bothering me. Something more personal. "Why is McIntire focusing on Maddie?"

"What do you mean?"

I told him how Peter had shown up at Maddie's house both last night and this morning. "What does he really want?"

"Maybe he thinks she knows more than she's saying."

"I suppose that makes the most sense," I said, then slowed the video when the truck returned. Peter emerged from the back immediately, as though he'd been waiting for it. The time stamp was 6:45.

The driver got out of the truck and started shouting at Peter, pointing his finger at him. Peter ran a hand over his head and looked up at the camera. The expression on his face was one of pure terror.

I paused the tape. "What do you think he's so scared about?"

Then something else hit me. "That's Roscoe," I said, pointing to the screen again. "He was with the homeless guys. He's the one who told Maddie to go out to Cock on the Walk." I ran a hand over my head. "What the fuck is going on?"

On the screen Peter headed back into the store, then came out a few minutes later with a broom and a wad of something that looked like trash bags and shoved them at the man. Roscoe tossed the items in the back of the truck and drove away, heading back downtown. The truck returned two hours later. This time Roscoe didn't wait around for Peter. He just dumped two trash bags and the broom into a dumpster and drove away.

I practically jumped out of my seat. "We need to find out when that dumpster is emptied." Lance dashed out of the office while I pulled out my phone and called the patrol officer outside. "Lock down the dumpsters! And keep the crime scene crew. I think there's evidence in the trash."

Next, I called the station and told the sergeant to send out a unit to find Roscoe and bring him in for questioning.

Lance came back a few moments later. "Lucinda said the trash is picked up on Fridays, but apparently the trash truck broke down and hasn't shown up yet. We caught a lucky break."

"Hopefully, we've caught a few," I said. "But where is Peter McIntire?"

Chapter Thirty-Eight

Maddie

As I suspected, Petra babied the crap out of me, but word had gotten out that I was involved in the big shoot-out last night—the first in about five years, based on what plenty of customers said—and we were busier than ever. I couldn't keep up, and Petra had to call Cynthia in to help.

"I heard you kicked three guys' asses," Chrissy said in a wry tone. "I guess they hadn't seen the videos of you kicking that detective's ass."

"I guess not." Though if they had, they might have brought guns.

At noon, Petra told me to take a break and escorted me to a table with a cappuccino and a breakfast sandwich, telling me I had to stay until she came to get me in a half hour.

We usually took our breaks in the back, but Petra wanted me where they could see me. She was determined I wasn't going to be kidnapped on her watch.

Fair enough.

Lance had called to check on me earlier, and I'd be lying if I said I wasn't disappointed it hadn't been Noah.

I'd started to scroll my Instagram feed on my phone when a

shadow crossed over my table. I looked up to see Peter. He was wearing a blue-and-white checkered button-down shirt and a tan peacoat.

"Maddie?" He gestured to the chair in front of me.

I wanted to tell him no, but I needed to get through to him that I didn't want or need his help. This was the perfect place to make that happen.

Pressing my lips together, I gave him a curt nod.

Peter sat, clasping his hands on the table. He released a heavy sigh and gave me a pitying look. "I heard what happened last night. Are you okay?"

I shook my head, annoyed. I didn't want to discuss it with him.

"Maddie, I feel horrible. I treated you terribly last night. I'm *deeply* ashamed. You have no idea how sorry I am."

I wasn't sure what to say, so I said nothing. He obviously expected me to give him absolution, but I wasn't going to do it. Finding out my mother planned to confront Schroeder because of Peter's asshatery had unleashed my anger.

He shifted uncomfortably in his seat. "I had a horrible day yesterday, and I took it out on you. There's really no excuse, Maddie. I'm sorry."

I drew in a breath. "Look, Peter. We weren't friends in high school, and while I appreciate the effort you've put into helping me and Aunt Deidre, I think we should just let sleeping dogs lie."

He stared at me as though I'd just recited a poem in Chinese. "I don't understand," he finally said.

"What I'm saying is that I don't think our friendship is meant to be." Because of the manners that had been bred into me, I couldn't stop myself from adding, "I've got a lot going on in my life right now. I need to give all my extra energy to Aunt Deidre."

Relief filled his eyes, making me instantly regret what I'd just said.

"Well, surely you can spare time to come to my party tonight," he said as though I wouldn't be stupid enough to say no.

I gaped at him. This guy didn't understand the word no. Then again, I already knew that.

"Okay, good," he said. "Now that we've gotten *that* business out of the way, I can get to the real reason I'm here." His brow lifted and he looked serious. "I stopped by your house to talk to you this morning, and the detective who's investigating Martin Schroeder's murder answered your front door in a state of undress." He leaned forward. "I'm worried about you, Maddie. Do you really think it's a good idea for you to be sleeping with the man who seems intent on charging you with a murder you didn't commit?"

"I'm not sleeping with him, not that it's any of your business," I snapped.

"Well, thank God for that," he said, ignoring the last part of my statement. "You know he's trying to entrap you, Maddie. He's taking advantage of your vulnerable state. I hope to God you haven't told him anything."

"Thank you for your concern," I said, trying to hold my temper. "But I assure you, Peter, I'm a big girl. I can take care of myself."

"I know. Of course you are, but I can't help thinking about what your Uncle Albert would say. He'd want someone to watch out for you, and we both know Deidre can't do it."

I stood. "I need to get back to work now."

He reached out and grabbed my arm in a tight grip. Then, as though realizing what he'd done, he let go. "I'm sorry. I'm sure you didn't appreciate that, but I haven't gotten to what I came here to say."

I stood next to the table, crossing my arms. "You have thirty seconds."

"I really think you should talk to Burt," he said insistently. "I mean, what can it hurt?"

"I'm not a suspect, Peter. I'm not even a person of interest anymore. I have no reason to talk to Burt."

His eyes narrowed. "Is that what *Langley* told you? And you believe him?" He shook his head in disgust. "I thought you were smarter than that."

I shot him a harsh glare. "I think we're done here. Goodbye, Peter. Please don't come back."

I turned my back on him, and when I got behind the counter, he was gone.

I only hoped he didn't come back.

Chapter Thirty-Nine

Maddie

We spent the next hour going through trash bags, looking for the things Roscoe had tossed into the dumpster. Going through trash was my least favorite job in the world, but unfortunately for them, Officer Dunst and poor Officer Erickson got the task of going into the dumpster. We had located the broom and finally found two bags full of trash that looked consistent with the kind of detritus you'd find in a drug den —needles, syringes, basic trash, and a few pairs of latex gloves—and in one of the bags, a bloody X-Acto knife stuck to the side of the bag.

"Looks like we might have found our murder weapon," Lance said.

If that were true, we'd tied Roscoe to the murder weapon, and both him and McIntire to the crime, but it was all circumstantial. We needed hard proof.

We handed the bag and the broom over to the crime lab team, then headed back to the station to wash our hands a few times and grab some lunch.

"Still no sign of Roscoe?" I asked.

Blind Bake

"No," Lance said grimly. "And no sign of McIntire. Brant either."

We had a whole lot of missing persons in this case, and there were still too many unanswered questions.

Lance and I had just sat down to eat when he got a call from Officer Dan Sullivan, the high school resource officer. He put it on speaker.

"Lance, I'm not sure what to make of this, but I heard you and Detective Langley are working the Schroeder murder, so I thought I'd give you a call."

"We're listening," Lance said.

"A sophomore named Kendra Eggleston came to me this afternoon. She's sixteen. Good kid but her grades have been slipping. Never been in trouble, but her father's been arrested for a few DUIs. She's in my office now, and she's not doin' so well."

"What does that mean?" Lance asked, giving me a worried look.

"She just keeps crying and sayin' she knows something about Schroeder's murder and wants to talk."

"Try to keep her there," I said, grabbing my coat from the back of my chair. "We're headed there now."

Lance and I snatched up our food and hurried out to my car, finishing our lunch on the way to the school.

"What do you think she's going to tell us?" Lance asked, but based on his drawn face, he and I were suspecting the same thing.

"A teenage girl wants to talk about Schroeder?" I asked. "It can't be anything good." Yet it might be good for our case.

We were both keyed up by the time we pulled into the parking lot. As we walked up to the school, the resource officer met us at the door.

"The counselor took Kendra to her office," he said before we could ask. "Like I said on the phone, she's pretty much a mess." Then he added, "She wouldn't tell me or Mrs. Atterbury anything, though."

I nodded, then Lance and I followed him inside and down a hall. A bell rang and students poured out of the classrooms into the hall.

"Hey, Officer Dan!" several students called out, and he greeted many of them by name. It was obvious they liked him.

"How long have you been here?" I asked, knowing he wouldn't have built this kind of rapport with them within a few months.

"Three years," he said over his shoulder again.

"How's it hangin', Officer Dan? You still comin' to our practice?" a boy asked him.

"I said I'd be there," Officer Sullivan said with a laugh. "Why are you always doubtin' me, Trevor?"

Trevor gave him a complicated handshake and then moved on to class.

"Who was the resource officer before you?" I asked.

"There wasn't one," he said. "They didn't move me over until after the new chief started. He launched the program."

He led us into a room marked Counseling Office. It had a window that overlooked the hall, with a desk on the left side and a couple of chairs arranged under the window. On the opposite wall were two doors with nameplates—Mrs. Atterbury and Ms. Foster. The faint sound of crying came from the direction of Mrs. Atterbury's office. Officer Sullivan shut the door behind us.

He motioned to the door and said softly, "She's in there."

When we went in, Kendra was sitting in a chair next to an L-shaped desk. Her eyes were swollen and her nose was red from crying. Officer Sullivan had said she was sixteen, but she barely looked fourteen.

A woman in her thirties was sitting next to her, dabbing the girl's wet cheeks. She looked up at us with a grim expression. "You must be Detective Langley and Officer Forrester."

I nodded, then squatted in front of the girl so I was at eye level and not towering over her. "Hi, Kendra. I'm Detective Noah and this is Officer Lance. We hear you want to talk to us about Martin Schroeder."

She looked up at Dan. "Is my mom coming?"

He gave her a reassuring smile. "She's on her way."

Kendra nodded, then turned to face me. "She's going to be *so* angry with me."

"Honestly, Kendra," I said soothingly, "I think she's just going to be grateful you're okay."

She shook her head and wailed mournfully. "I was so stupid."

"Why don't you let us be the judge of that," I said, still squatting. "Do you want to wait for your mother before you talk to us?"

She shook her head. "I don't want to talk about it in front of her. It's too embarrassing. But I want her here waiting for me when I'm done."

"Okay," I said. "Would you like Mrs. Atterbury to stay with you?"

She nodded, and the counselor squeezed her hand reassuringly.

Officer Sullivan moved in two extra chairs for Lance and himself while I took a seat behind the guidance counselor's desk. I turned on the recording app on my phone and began.

"Kendra," I said softly. "Whatever you want to tell us is up to you. I'll probably ask some questions, but you're in charge of what you tell us, okay?"

Fresh tears streaked down her face. "I don't know where to start."

"Why don't you start from the beginning?" I said gently.

"From when Peter first offered me a job?" she asked, her eyes wide with fear.

Lance shot me a glance, but I kept my focus on Kendra. "Yeah," I said encouragingly. "That's a great place to start. Why don't you tell me who Peter is?"

"Peter McIntire. He owns the Piggly Wiggly," she said. "I met him when he sponsored my softball team. He brought us snacks and drinks, and he usually came to all the games. He even hosted a few parties at his house. He has a swimming pool, so we'd go swimming and he'd barbecue."

I nodded.

"I saw him talking to some of the girls, including my friend Amanda. Later Amanda told me that she did odd jobs for him. He paid in cash. They were supposed to keep it secret, only Amanda knew I needed money. I wasn't stupid. I knew it was probably illegal or he wouldn't be payin' cash. I mean, Jimmy Rector works as a sacker at the Piggly Wiggly after school, and I know he gets a paycheck because he complains that he has to pay someone named FICA." She made a face. "Anyway."

She looked up at me, defiance in her eyes. "My dad's a drunk. He pisses our money away on booze and his girlfriends. Mom tries the best she can, but half the time he takes her money too. She works so hard..." She started to cry again. "I thought maybe I could make some money to help."

"You're a good daughter," I said.

She glanced down at her lap, twisting a tissue in her hands. "So I told Peter that I'd heard about his special jobs, and that I really needed a job. I assured him I'd just heard rumors, so I didn't get Amanda in trouble. He told me they were supposed to be top secret. That if I ever talked about them, bad things could happen."

"He threatened you?" I asked.

"Not physically. At least not at first. He said it was all about helping people—the ones who needed the special favors, and also the people he hired. And if one person blabbed, it would hurt everyone. I'm good at keeping secrets. I've kept my dad's secrets for years, so I said I wanted in. At first, they were simple jobs. Taking a box to someone, that kind of thing. And then one day he asked if I wanted to work a party."

When she hesitated, I asked, "What did you do at the party?"

"It was a poker game at Peter's house. Six men. I didn't know any of them. Me and another girl were supposed to get them drinks. Peter had us wear short skirts and low-cut tops and high heels. The guys kept putting their hands up our skirts. Mostly they just touched my butt, so I let them, because I didn't want Peter to stop giving me jobs and they'd slip me a few dollars afterward. It was more than my daddy's friends ever did," she said in disgust. "Anyway, after that party, Peter told me that I'd done so well that he had a special job for me, but I'd have to be open to a man touching me all over." She stopped, then picked up a bottle of water next to her and took a drink.

"How long ago was this, Kendra?"

"At the beginning of the school year."

"Then what happened?"

"Peter said he'd send someone to the library to pick me up, and then he'd take me to the Bluebird Motel. I only had to spend an hour with the guy, and I'd get a hundred dollars, then they'd take me back."

"Who did you meet, Kendra?"

"Martin Schroeder." She glanced down at her lap. "It started out one time a week, but then it was two or three times a week." She looked up at me. "That was a lot of money, you know? All I had to do was let him touch me...and other things. But the last few weeks, Martin was acting anxious. He said he needed to see me—that he loved me—but he was out of money. He wanted me to run away with him. I was grossed out, but I told him I couldn't leave my mom. And then I told Peter."

"How did Peter react?"

"He told me that I'd done the right thing, but I wouldn't be meeting with Martin anymore and to remember that I couldn't tell anyone about meeting him."

"And when was that?"

"Last week. But then I heard Martin was dead and I started getting more and more scared. What if Peter thought I told someone?" She released a hiccup sob. "What if he killed me or my mother?" She looked over at Officer Sullivan. "That's why I wanted my mom to come here. Because then you could protect her, Office Dan."

He smiled. "I got word she's in my office. She's safe but worried about you."

Kendra's body sagged with relief. "Thank you."

Peter McIntire was a predator, and I wanted to personally slap the cuffs on his wrists. I only wished it wouldn't totally fuck up the DA's case against him if I punched him in the face first.

"Kendra," I said firmly, "I'm going to make sure they never come near you again."

Fresh tears streamed down her face. "Thank you, Detective Noah."

My heart ached for her, but I also felt motivated. This was a good reminder of why I became a cop. To help people who'd been victimized and abused and, as corny as it sounded, put the bad people behind bars so they couldn't hurt them again.

Officer Sullivan brought Kendra's mother to the counseling office waiting room, and I explained briefly what had happened. She seemed genuinely shocked, which was a relief. The only hint she'd had that something was off was that Kendra's grades had been slipping despite all the extra time she'd spent studying. I suggested that they stay with friends or relatives out of town, and she said they'd leave for her grandmother's up in Kentucky as soon as they left the high school. Then she rushed into the room, hugging her daughter and, through tears and relieved laughter, vowed to ground her for the rest of her life.

Lance and I thanked Officer Sullivan and told him we'd arrange for a more formal interview with Kendra in a day or two. Then we headed out to my car.

Lance called the station to see if there was any word on locating the guys from Chattanooga or Peter or Roscoe. They'd turned up nothing. I was ready to scour Cockamamie myself to find that bastard Peter McIntire. And then I was going to come up with so many charges, he'd never see the light of day.

Lance glanced at the time on his phone. "It's after three, Noah. What time does Maddie get off?"

I checked my phone. It was about ten after three. *Shit.* "Three."

I'd told her I'd pick her up or send someone. Had she left on her own?

I called her, needing to hear her voice and know she was safe, but it went straight to voicemail.

"She didn't answer," I said, feeling a sense of panic wash through me.

"Maybe she turns it off while she's at work," Lance said.

"She answered *your* call." Maybe she was pissed that Lance called earlier and not me. But then she would have screened my call. Not turned her phone off.

Worry filled Lance's eyes. "Why don't we call the coffee shop and find out what's going on?"

It was the obvious answer, and I mentally kicked myself for not having thought of it first, but something deep in my marrow told me there was trouble. I hadn't listened the night Caleb broke into my house. I was listening this time.

I looked up the number and called.

"Déjà Brew. This is Petra, how can I help you?" she answered cheerfully.

"Petra," I said, surprised by the tremor in my voice. "This is Detective Langley. Can I speak to Maddie?"

"She didn't do anything wrong," she protested. "Why do you keep harassing her?"

I took a deep breath. "She's not a person of interest, but she *is* in danger. Now can I talk to her? Please?"

She was silent for a long moment. "She's not here."

"What do you mean she's not there?" I roared, then took a deep breath and tried again. "When did she leave? Who did she leave with?"

"Uh," she said in a shaky voice, and I cursed myself for losing my cool. Now she was freaking out and struggling to think straight.

"I'm sorry, Petra. That was out of line, but I'm worried. When did she leave?"

"At three. When her shift was over. She went out to sit in the dining room and she said she was gonna call her bodyguard to come get her—although she refused to tell me who he was—but as she was getting ready to call, a man walked in and got her attention. He talked to her for about ten seconds and then they left together. She didn't even say goodbye, which is unusual for her."

My pulse pounded in my head, but I forced myself to stop freaking out and focus. The only way I could help Maddie was by thinking clearly. "What did he look like, Petra?"

"Really nice-looking guy. Blond hair. Tall. He had on a blue-and-white checkered shirt and tan pants. I figured *go Maddie* for getting such a handsome bodyguard."

Peter McIntire.

"*I'm* her bodyguard," I grunted, then hung up. Although some fucking bodyguard I'd turned out to be.

Fuck me.

I turned toward Lance, my mind whirring. "McIntire took her, and I have no idea where to look."

He checked his phone and looked up at me as he reached for the passenger door. "I think we found her. Someone just reported a disturbance on Main Street."

Chapter Forty

Maddie

When I got off at three, Petra sent me out to the dining room to wait for my ride. I sat there for a minute, trying to decide who to call: Noah or Lance. Lance was the one who'd checked on me earlier, which suggested that Noah had handed off that duty. Maybe he'd done that as a signal that he wanted to keep things professional.

Lance it was.

But as I was pulling up his number, I saw Peter making a beeline for me with a hard look in his eye. Good Lord. The guy really didn't understand the concept of the word no.

I groaned as he neared me. "Peter. I really don't want this to be ugly."

He gave me a cold stare. "I have an appointment for you to see Burt right now. He's holding the spot open for you. Last chance."

I stared at him in disbelief. The nerve of this man!

"No," I said, aggravated as hell. "I don't know how to make it any clearer."

He stared at me in disbelief, as though I was the first person to ever deny his whims. Then he recovered, his face shuttering. "You've left me no choice, Maddie."

He pulled back the flap of his jacket to reveal a handgun in the waist of his pants.

I gaped up at him. Was he serious? Had Burt promised him some massive referral bonus he didn't want to miss out on? I wanted to tell him to go to hell, but for all I knew he'd start shooting people to get his way. What a narcissist nutjob.

"Fine," I said. "But you really need therapy, Peter. This is not how you get your way."

"Turn off your phone and hand it to me."

Reluctantly, unsure I was doing the right thing, I turned it off and placed it in his outstretched hand. He slipped it into his pocket.

"Okay," he said, leaning into my ear. "Let's go out the front door. Don't make a fuss. We don't want anyone to get hurt."

"What the hell are you doing, Peter?" I whisper-hissed, but he gave me a soft shove toward the door.

I stumbled forward, and he grabbed my arm, leading me out to the sidewalk. He didn't let go, guiding me toward a car parked along the curb.

"You're in a no-parking zone," I said, pointing to the sign. "You're lucky you didn't get a ticket."

Seriously, where were the police when you really needed them?

He opened the back door of the black BMW and motioned for me to get in.

"Isn't his office just a block that way?" I asked, gesturing down the street. "Seems like it would be easier to walk."

"We're not going to see Burt. You missed that opportunity. If only you'd gone." He tsked, as if I were a stupid kindergartner who hadn't put away her scissors and was now getting them taken away.

"Well, if we're not going to see Burt, then there's no reason for me to get in your car, is there?"

He pulled back his jacket again. "I'm not sure you understand that you don't have a choice in the matter."

"Of course I have a choice," I snapped. "You're giving me *two* choices. One, I get in the car. Two, I stay right here and you…what? Shoot me? I'm going with option B, because I was taught to never get in the car with a man with a gun. I'll take my chances right here."

His face reddened. "Maddie, I am *not* having a good day. Do *not* push my buttons."

"Yet another reason for you to seek therapy, Peter," I said condescendingly. "They really have made great advances in anger management techniques."

He lifted his arm up to hit me, but I blocked it, my back screaming in protest, then twisted his arm behind his back, dropping him into a deep squat as he shrieked.

"Haven't you heard it's not very gentlemanly to hit a woman?" But the muscles in my back were already starting to cramp. I wasn't sure how long I could hold him like this. Or why I even needed to hold him.

What in the actual hell was going on here? Was he drunk? I hadn't smelled any alcohol on him. This couldn't be about the missed consultation, but I was really struggling to understand what he wanted from me.

People were watching us as they passed on the sidewalk, rubbernecking as they moseyed along. It was like they thought seeing a woman subdue a man was weird, but not weird enough for them to stop.

"You may have just signed Ernie's death certificate," Peter grunted.

My breath stuck in my chest, and I loosened my hold slightly. "What are you talking about?"

"Some very bad men are holding Ernie. If you want to save his life, you need to come with me."

I increased the pressure, twisting his arm. "Why do you have Ernie, and why are you threatening his life?"

A mom pushing a stroller with a toddler stopped next to us. "Do you need me to call the police?"

Did I?

"Yes," I said just as Peter said, "No." He glanced back at me, anger contorting his face. "Someone's life might depend on it, Maddie."

Crap. If he had Ernie, I had to protect him.

"Everything is fine," I said but kept up the pressure on his arm.

The woman's eyes narrowed. "Peter McIntire? *Is that you?*" Her mouth dropped open, and I could see she was just as confused as I was. "Thanks for getting that minted jelly for me. It went perfectly with the lamb."

"Yeah, no problem. That's what I do," he said through gritted teeth as he started to reach for his waistband with his free hand. The gun.

I kneed him behind his leg, and as soon as he fell to the ground, I dropped down and straddled his back, twisting his arm so that it bent at the elbow behind him. The drop sent a new wave of pain through my back, and his wild bucking to throw me off wasn't helping, but I maintained my hold.

"Peter's a little busy right now," I said, worried the idiot would do something stupid, like get out his gun and start randomly shooting bystanders. "He can chat later."

She hurried away, casting backward glances. I suspected if she called the police, it would be to report *me* for assault.

"Where's Ernie?" I asked.

"Those men have him at my house."

"What men?" Except the answer was obvious now that I thought about it. He was talking about the guys who had attacked me last night. "Why do they have Ernie?"

"They want the bag, Maddie. Just hand it over and everything goes back to normal."

"I am so confused," I said, shaking my head. "What bag?"

"The bag Schroeder had when you picked him up. Roscoe said he must have dropped it in the car."

Roscoe? As in the homeless guy? Then again, he'd seemed to know that Ernie was at the Bottoms on the night of the murder.

This meant Peter was connected to Martin Schroeder's murder, yet how?

It occurred to me that there was an easy way to find out.

Peter loved nothing better than to mansplain. Might as well play the Stupid Female role to the hilt and get as much information out of him as I could. "Why do you want a bag with a disgusting egg salad sandwich?" I asked. "That thing was rank."

"I don't want the sandwich!" he shouted, then tried to bolt upright. I put pressure on his twisted arm, and he cried out in pain. "You are such a fool!"

"Maybe so," I said, to provoke him, "but I'm not the one trying to find a sandwich that has to smell even worse now. Good Lord, if you're planning to eat that thing, I hope you have good health insurance. It has to be teeming with salmonella."

"I want what he had *in the bag*," he shouted. "My source said Schroeder put it in the bag!" He turned his head to look at me, pleading, "I need that USB drive, Maddie."

"What's on it?"

"Nothing you'd be interested in."

I barked a derisive laugh. "What? No recipes or makeup tips?" I put more pressure on his arm. "Try again."

"Proprietary pharmaceutical information."

What the hell? But shock made me loosen my hold, and he bucked up hard.

The movement caught me off guard and I flailed backward, my back landing on the concrete sidewalk. Sharp pain shot throughout my entire body and stole my breath for several seconds.

Long enough to give Peter the advantage.

"Here's what we're gonna do," Peter said through gritted teeth, not even trying to hide the gun he was pointing only a few inches from my face. "We're gonna get in my car, and you're gonna take me to that USB drive."

"Peter," I said carefully. "You're in trouble. Let me help you."

"You can help me by getting that USB drive!" he shouted at the top of his lungs.

Peter McIntire had officially lost his mind. Which made him extremely dangerous.

Several people were gathered on the sidewalk, watching us in horror. How did Peter plan to deal with all these witnesses?

"Get in the car, Maddie," he said through gritted teeth. When I hesitated, he swung the gun to point it at a woman in the crowd.

A chorus of shrieks rose up, and people toward the back began to scatter.

I scooted backward, trying to get up. "Okay. Don't hurt anyone. I'll come."

"I knew you'd see it my way. In the back."

I gingerly got into the back seat, my back screaming in pain. How was I going to get out of this?

One step at a time, Maddie.

He slammed the door behind me and got into the driver's seat and took off like a bat out of hell, tires squealing.

Jeez, where are the police? Where is Noah?

Peter rounded a corner, and I flew across the seat. Could I open a door when he came to a stop sign? Would he actually *stop* at a stop sign?

That answer was a big fat no. He drove through them like he was playing *Grand Theft Auto*.

"Where did Martin Schroeder get proprietary pharmaceutical information?" I asked. "I mean, he was a crap chemistry teacher."

"It wasn't his, Maddie! Keep up!"

"You're making it kind of hard when I'm worried about dying in a fiery crash."

"You should be more worried about getting strangled by the buyer's goons."

Shit. "The guys who tried to kidnap me last night."

I didn't need to ask why they planned to strangle me. It hadn't gone well for them last night, and they obviously blamed me for that. Strangling someone was much more personal than shooting them.

My mother had been strangled.

Think, Maddie. Focus.

"So, obviously you screwed up," I said. "You didn't give the buyer the USB with the information, and now they're pissed."

He gripped the steering wheel and leaned forward, shouting at the top of his lungs, "I didn't screw up!" He took a deep breath, then said more calmly, "I didn't screw up."

"Well, Martin Schroeder got your information *somehow*," I said in a know-it-all tone, "so I beg to differ."

He released a loud growl, then took another deep breath. "Fine. It was probably my fault. The supplier called to discuss the handoff of the USB drive, and then I called the buyer to confirm I'd be bringing it to him Monday night. I didn't realize that Martin had let himself in my house until after I'd made all the arrangements. I went to the bathroom, leaving my phone on my desk in my study, and Marty got both contact numbers from my recent calls. He was still there when I came back."

"Why would Martin Schroeder come to your house?" I asked in confusion.

"Because I'm a very important man, Maddie. You would have been lucky to have me." He swerved around a car in our lane and almost ran into an oncoming truck that blared its horn. Peter ignored it and maneuvered back into our lane, narrowly missing a head-on collision.

"So your interest in me wasn't entirely for the USB drive," I said dryly, trying to hide my fear that he was going to kill us both before we got to his house. "I'm flattered."

"As you should be," he said smugly, obviously missing my sarcasm. "Marty and I had an arrangement. He had a certain peculiarity, and I helped provide what he needed."

I recoiled in disgust as the meaning of his words sank in. "You mean he was a pedophile, and you gave him children to molest."

He made a face. "It's not that seedy. The girls were compensated for their time."

"So Mr. Schroeder came for a scheduled molestation *at your house?*"

"Don't be stupid, Maddie. Nothing like that ever happened at my house. It was either at the store or some other location. Marty met them at the Bluebird Inn."

"So why was he at your house?"

He pushed out a sigh. "He was there to kill me. He was upset that I kept raising his rates, but it was becoming harder and harder to find girls willing to accommodate him, and he was *such* a pain in the ass. The final straw was finding out he'd tried to circumvent me and work out a deal with one of my girls. So I cut him off. High and dry. I should have realized he was an addict, and cut-off addicts lash out. When I came out of the powder room, I found him in my kitchen with a butcher knife in his hand. It was a Rachael Ray knife, so I knew right away he'd brought it with him. Rachael Ray. Can you *imagine?*" He snorted. "I only use Miyabi blades."

"Oh my God," I said before I could stop myself. "You are *such* a snob."

He shot me a superior look in the rearview mirror. "And that snobbery saved my life. I threw my crock of organic Celtic sea salt in his face. He dropped the knife, and I pushed him out the back door. After he left, I found two Cockamamie Hardware bags with rope and a hacksaw and a blowtorch. That was when I knew he was a problem."

"*That* was when you knew he was a problem?" I asked in disbelief.

But Peter ignored me. I had a feeling he needed to talk this out, and since he seemed to balk at therapy, a hostage who was about to be murdered was the next best thing.

How was I going to get out of this?

He hadn't tied me up. I could jump him from behind, and sure we might crash, but I'd probably survive. My chances at his house were much slimmer. But I believed he *did* have Ernie, and what if they killed him if I didn't show up quickly enough? Ernie had tried to protect me. I had to try to return the favor.

"Late Monday I got word from my buyer that he was nervous about the change of plans. But *I* hadn't changed the plans, so I called the supplier, who said he was about to hand the USB drive off to my courier at the new location. That's when I figured out what Marty had done. He was trying to steal the drive out from under me. Only the joke was on him. He'd stolen the three-digit code for the buyer to access the encryption key, but it had changed since last week. He had the wrong one."

"I bet he laughed at that," I said dryly.

"He never lived long enough to find out," Peter said. "I had Roscoe send him a text from his phone, pretending to be one of the buyer's goons. He changed the location of the handoff to the butcher shop and told him there'd be a ten-thousand-dollar bonus for his trouble. Of course he leapt at the opportunity. I told Roscoe to kill Marty at the butcher shop. But I insisted he needed to do it with something other than a gun. I didn't trust that any guns I or he owned couldn't be tied to previous crimes through ballistics. So he slit his throat."

I gasped in horror. While I knew Schroeder had been killed, I realized I'd assumed he was shot. But shooting someone was one thing, cutting their throat...that felt personal too. And evil.

Peter shrugged, then took a corner, fishtailing through the intersection. "It worked. They don't even know what the weapon was. My source in the department keeps me informed of such things."

He had a source in the police department? It skeeved me out to think one of Noah and Lance's colleagues was feeding him information, but it made sense. It explained why he'd gotten away with so much shit. "Do you know why my mother's murder case file is missing?"

His eyes widened. "It's missing? I know Bergan worked with Brian Summit and made Marty's previous molestation cases disappear, but I don't know why *her* file would disappear."

Officer Summit? The guy who'd shown up at our house to take Aunt Deidre's missing person report?

Peter's face softened. "For what it's worth, I'm sorry for how I treated you back in school. Especially after your mother died."

That pissed me off. "Fuck off, Peter."

He burst out laughing. "You wish. Sadly, there's no time. Those men want that drive, and I suggest you tell them what you know as quickly as possible to avoid any more suffering than necessary."

He skidded into the driveway of an antebellum home that looked like it belonged in a magazine. When he caught me gawking, he said, "Do you have any idea how much it costs to keep a house this old and size in good repair?" Then he got out of the car.

I needed to save Ernie, and I knew in my gut that if I went in that house, not only would I not save him, but I'd wind up dead too. My best chance to save him was to find a way to call 911 and pray Ernie wasn't killed before they showed up. I tried to open the back door to bolt out of the car and make a run for it, but Peter had planned ahead and engaged the child locks.

Like *seriously*, how had he not gotten pulled over during his suicide run? The police in this town were worthless.

He opened the back door, but I was ready for him. Lying sideways on the seat, I kicked him hard in the chest, sending him sprawling backward onto his butt.

I scampered out of the car, my back making me move slower. I'd just gotten out of the car when he tackled me to the ground and I landed on my back. The pain made me see stars.

Dammit.

It took everything in me to ignore the pain and try to get to my feet, but he got up first and started to haul me with him.

He wrapped his arms around my chest, and I bent forward, flipping him over my back but not without a high cost. My body felt like it was on fire.

He got up and stood upright, his face red, then leaned forward over his legs, panting. "Just give up, Maddie."

I noticed his gun in the grass. It must have fallen out in our scuffle.

Could I reach it?

"Never."

He tried to grab me again, but just then a streak came flying from the street, toppling Peter onto the grass. A fist slammed into his face, and it took me a second to realize it was Noah, and he looked *furious*.

Noah rolled Peter over onto his stomach, then wrenched Peter's arms behind his back and slapped on handcuffs. "Peter McIntire. You're under arrest for reckless driving."

I stared at Noah in shock. "Are you *kidding* me?" I shouted. "What about *kidnapping*?"

Noah shot me an aggravated look. "It's enough for now."

Gunshots rang out from inside the house, and I remembered that Peter had said the bad guys were inside.

Noah dove for me and pain shot though my body as he flattened me to the ground, covering my body with his.

More gunshots came from behind us, piercing the windows of the house. About thirty seconds later, the gunshots stopped, and the front door burst open. Noah jumped to a squat and tugged me behind Peter's car, but not before I saw Ernie walking out with his hands in the air.

"Don't shoot," he shouted. "They're both dead!"

Police rushed the house, and Lance went over to Peter and pulled him to his feet.

I was sitting on the driveway with my legs outstretched, with Noah squatted beside me.

"Are you okay?" he asked, his voice shaking as his gaze searched me up and down.

"Well, I'm going to need a deluxe massage to work out these muscle spasms in my back, but other than that..."

Relief filled his eyes, quickly followed by anger. "Why didn't you call me when you got off work? Why in the hell would you go with McIntire?"

"Oh, I don't know," I grumbled. "Maybe because he had a *gun*."

He remained silent.

Yeah, I thought that was a pretty good comeback too.

"Did no one call the police after that Main Street debacle? *Seriously*," I grumped, getting to my feet, or trying to. I grabbed the bumper to pull myself up. Noah tried to reach for me, but I batted his hand away. "I've got this."

He watched me with a mixture of amusement and irritation as I finally stood upright—well, almost upright. I was still slightly hunched.

"Peter is behind Martin Schroeder's murder," I said. "He had Roscoe kill him for a USB drive with some proprietary pharmaceutical shit on it." I waved my hand, irritated at Noah and grumpy from pain. "But he was going to kill him anyway because Schroeder went to Peter's house to kill him last week. He left behind some Cockamamie Hardware bags with his purchases, blowtorch and all."

Noah stared at me in disbelief.

"What?" I snapped. "I'm a good listener. Anyway, those guys

who tried to take me were hired by the buyer. I have no idea who *he* or *she* is." Then I shot him a glare. "I can't do *all* the work for you."

He looked like he wanted to kick me in the ass, so I was surprised when he wrapped his arms around me. We stood there for several seconds before I let myself relax and sink into him, my ear pressed against his chest. I could hear his still-erratic heartbeat. Finally, several seconds later, he said softly, "Has anyone ever told you that you're a massive pain the ass?"

"No," I said truthfully. "After I left Cockamamie, I think I've spent my life trying to not rock the boat." Was that another reason I'd put up with Steve's crap for so long? "I guess you're the exception to the rule. You bring out the worst in me."

He pulled away slightly, looking slightly wary. "Do I?"

I caught sight of Ernie in my peripheral vision, and I called out to him. "Ernie!"

Noah dropped his hold on me and took a step back.

Ernie had a blanket wrapped around his shoulders. There were bruises on his face. "Miss Maddie, I was so worried about you!"

"Me?" I protested. "You're the one who was kidnapped and beaten."

Noah snorted. "Like you weren't," he said under his breath.

I turned to him. "Officer Summit. He worked with the detective on my mother's case to make other cases disappear. He also fed Peter inside information. You might want to look into that."

His face went blank. Then he took off running for Lance. There was even more commotion as Noah found Officer Summit in the crowd of officers and slapped handcuffs on him.

I turned back to Ernie, who'd been watching the drama unfold with plenty of interest. "Ernie, are you really okay?"

"Yeah, I tried to protect you, Miss Maddie. I told them you didn't have the USB thingy they wanted. I tried to get them to leave you alone."

"Thanks, Ernie. And no more of that Miss Maddie nonsense. I think this makes us friends now."

He smiled, but it quickly faded. "I lied, Miss...I mean Maddie. I lied to the police because I knew there was someone crooked on the force, and I didn't know who to trust."

"Well, Peter blabbed about the crooked one, so I think it's safe now. What did you lie about?"

"I told them I had no idea what they were talkin' about when they asked me if I knew what Martin Schroeder had in his bag. I do know." He hesitated. "I took it."

"What?"

"I was sitting outside because some drug shit had been going down out there, and I was determined to help clean this town up. Get names and force the police to bust the dealers. The last person I was expecting was Martin Schroeder. He was lowlife scum, but I never took him for a druggie. Then you left, and I heard screaming a few minutes later. Well, someone had propped the front door open, and I went in and seen that Roscoe and Schroeder. Only Schroeder was dead." He shook his head. "God-awful sight. Schroeder was lying on the floor and there was so much blood." He sounded haunted by the sight. "His neck..."

I reached for his hand and held on. He was going to have nightmares from that for the rest of his life.

"I had brought a board with me and I knew that Roscoe would kill me next, so I smashed the flashlight and everything went dark. I ran for the door. I could hear him fumbling around behind me, but when I opened the front door, I saw the bag Schroeder had carried in. It had been tossed to the side. Figured he either hid it or dropped it. I thought there might be drugs inside, so I picked it up and ran." He paused. "I found a USB drive inside a rotten egg salad sandwich. I thought about turning it into the police, but like I said, I knew someone on the police force was bad, and I figured it had something to do with Peter McIntire. He's been doin' some shady shit for a few years now." His eyes widened. "Pardon my language."

I shook my head. "Don't worry about that. So you hid?"

"I did. I stayed by the river that first night, then watched the crime scene. I saw you come by, and I was worried those goons would see you, especially after you and that detective got into a yelling match. See, they were watching too. That's when I decided to go stay in your garage so I could watch over you. Sorry if I scared your aunt."

I put a hand on his arm. "It's okay, Ernie. She knows you were protecting me."

"I followed you to the women's meeting on account of I didn't want you figuring out that I was staying in your backyard."

"You walked all that way?"

He waved me off. "It's not that far, and I'm used to walking."

"But those guys caught you."

"Not until this morning. I went by your house to check on you, and they snatched me up." He gave me an apologetic look. "I'm sorry I wasn't there to protect you last night. But after y'all figured out I'd been staying in the garage..."

"Ernie, you might have gotten yourself killed." I paused, studying him, then said, "I guess the million-dollar question is where's the USB drive?"

"I hid it," Ernie said. "No one's gotten it yet."

"Where did you hide it?" I asked.

"Inside a gallon of paint in your garage."

Chapter Forty-One

Maddie

Lance was rushing past us, so I stopped him and told him about the USB drive. He grabbed Noah, and soon all four of us were headed to my house, bringing Ernie so he could show them the location of the paint can before they took him in for questioning.

Noah was tense the entire drive, not saying a word, and Lance kept shooting worried glances in my direction.

"Are you sure you're okay, Maddie?" Lance asked. "We got so many calls that a crazy man had shoved a gun in your face on Main Street, tossed you into the back of his car, and took off like a maniac."

"Why didn't you tell me any of that?" Noah grunted. "All you told me was she was in McIntire's car and headed to his house based on the 911 calls about the erratic driver in the BMW."

Lance shrugged. "I was worried you'd lose your shit."

Noah's jaw tightened so much I was afraid he was about to break a molar.

Ernie led us straight to the paint can. He'd put the whole bag—sandwich and all—in the paint, making sure the paint covered it.

Lance found a garbage bag and put the whole can inside, then

Blind Bake

brought the whole mess out to the backyard and opened the paint can lid. Wearing a pair of gloves, Lance reached in and pulled out the sandwich bag dripping with pink paint, then opened the bag. A powerful, pungent odor blast out of the bag, making us all stumble back, gagging. Poor Lance was left holding the bag and looking like he was about to lose his lunch as he pulled the sandwich out and opened it.

Noah, Ernie and I were covering our noses—me with both hands, Noah in the crook of his arm. Poor Lance had tears streaming down his face, looking like he was about to vomit as he picked a USB drive out of the rotten egg salad mixture.

Noah held out an evidence bag for Lance to drop the drive into, then backed far away as quickly as possible.

Lance slapped the two slices of bread back together, a few pieces of egg mixture dropping onto the ground, then shoved the sandwich back into the paint and slammed the lid on top. He tossed his gloves into the garbage bag, and tied it all shut, not that it did much good. The backyard was permeated with the smell.

"Good hiding place," I said to Ernie from behind my hands.

He made a face and shrugged.

Lance announced that they needed to take the drive and bag to the station. They also needed Ernie to come with them to give his statement.

"I have information too," I protested. "I need to give a statement."

Noah pierced me with a stormy look. "You stay here. We'll take your statement later. I know enough to question the other people wrapped up in this. I want you to stay here." Then his voice broke. "*Please.*"

I stared up at him, and somehow I knew that what we'd had last night and this morning was gone. Noah had gotten what he'd needed from me and now he was done.

But that was a big fat lie. I saw the fear in his eyes when he showed up to Peter McIntire's and last night. I saw the affection in his eyes this morning. I saw the longing and the sorrow now.

Noah wanted me as much as I wanted him, but he was terrified.

"Okay," I whispered, tears filling my eyes.

He stared down at me, looking like he was about to break, then turned and left.

* * *

Lance had told Margarete it was safe to come home, and she told him they'd be over as soon as she, Aunt Deidre, and Linda finished a game of canasta.

Mallory turned up around six, asking why my neighborhood smelled like rotten eggs. She was pissed that she'd missed all the excitement, then babied me once she got a look at my back.

After we got Aunt Deidre tucked in bed for the night, we stayed up late drinking wine in my room, lying on the bed. I told her about Noah and how I was already so messed up over him.

"I think that was goodbye, Mal. He's obviously scared. Plus, he says he's messed up." I glanced at her. "And you know, if I've learned one thing in my thirty-four rotations around the sun, it's that when a guy tells you he's messed up, you believe him."

"Hmm..." she said thoughtfully as she picked a fuzzy nub from my comforter.

"Hmm, what?"

She propped herself up on her elbow and looked me in the eye. "That's a very mature observation, Madelyn Baker."

I threw a pillow at her and made her wine slosh onto her hand, which she promptly licked off.

"Seriously, Maddie," she said, settling the pillow I'd thrown at her next to mine, then lying on her side so we were face-to-face. "I know it's hard to let him go, but you deserve a guy who's all in, and Detective Hot-Stuff sounds like he's not ready for that."

"Yeah," I said, bitter disappointment washing through me.

"And frankly," she said, "I think you need to spend some time figuring out who *you* are and what you want. It sounds like Noah Langley's not going anywhere. Maybe he'll get things figured out at around the same time you do."

"Maybe." But I wasn't holding my breath. "He gave up a woman he loved because he was so opposed to marriage and kids, and we both know I want that. It doesn't seem smart for him to make that mistake twice."

Plus, when I was honest with myself, I was pissed and hurt that he'd found out that Peter was involved earlier in the day but never called to warn me. I knew things were classified and all, but why hadn't he at least let me know Peter was dangerous? It felt like a massive betrayal.

* * *

I didn't sleep well, so I was sure I looked pretty rough when Lance showed up at the front door around ten the next morning.

"Hey," he said with an apologetic look. "I'm here to take your statement." Then he added, "Noah's tied up."

He was lying, and he *knew* I knew it, but it wasn't his fault that Noah Langley was a chickenshit.

He was silent for a moment. "Sorry, Maddie."

I forced a smile. "There's nothing to be sorry about. Come on in. Let me get you a cup of coffee."

We settled at my kitchen table, with Mallory hanging back making faces about how hot he was—*mostly* out of his view. Thankfully, he seemed amused.

I told him everything that had happened yesterday, including Peter's bizarre confession.

"I'm surprised you didn't want my statement yesterday," I said.

"Well, in an interesting development, Peter sang like a Sharpay wannabe auditioning for *High School Musical: The Musical*—enthusiastically."

I laughed. "I'm not sure whether to be impressed or frightened by the fact you could make that analogy."

He laughed too. "A casualty of living with a younger sister." He leaned closer and said, "For what it's worth, I can sing a pretty good rendition of 'Bet on It.'"

"If you don't snatch that man up, I will!" Mallory called out from the living room.

I rolled my eyes. "Why would Peter confess to it all?"

"Because the Feds showed up and offered him a plea deal before he even opened his mouth."

Figured. Assholes like Peter McIntire always seemed to get off easy. He always had in high school.

"The Feds were interested in Peter's supplier, who'd come across some proprietary information from a pharmaceutical company, as well as the buyer. Peter told them everything they wanted to know in exchange for a greatly reduced sentence in a federal prison."

They'd found Roscoe and charged him with first-degree murder since his fingerprints were on the X-Acto knife.

Two of the goons were found shot dead at Peter's house after the police gun fight, one had been killed in the street in front of my house, and the fourth was found dumped on the side of the road on a country road outside of town. He'd been shot twice—once in the stomach, which had made him lose a lot of blood, and once in the head, which had likely come hours later. Thanks to Peter, they knew who had fired the headshot.

When Peter had originally suggested I call Burt Pullman, he had done it "for the right reason"—to help me. But then he'd realized I was the Uber driver who'd dropped Schroeder off at the butcher shop, and he'd blackmailed Burt, for whom he'd acquired some exotic fish for his saltwater tank, to listen to my story and encourage me to spill my guts about the USB drive.

In a weird way, Peter had tried to protect me.

"I also thought you might want to know how you got dragged into all of this," Lance said. "Why Schroeder called an Uber."

I gaped at him. Weirdly enough, I hadn't questioned it. At least not since yesterday.

"He drove his car out to the industrial park, but it broke down. Roscoe had called with the location and time change, and he panicked. So he called an Uber."

I got dragged into hell all because a pervert's car broke down.

"Roscoe dumped it in the Briny River, but it's being dragged out even as we speak.

"Thanks for telling me that," I said. "It's a lot more than I ever got during my mother's investigation."

"Speaking of which." He shifted uncomfortably in his seat. "There's one more thing I need to talk to you about, Maddie." Lance glanced over his shoulder and caught Mallory's gaze. "You might want your friend with you for this."

My breath caught. "You're scaring me, Lance."

He didn't respond.

Mallory hurried in and sat next to me, taking my hand. "Go on," she said. "We're ready."

He drew a breath. "We think Martin Schroeder murdered your mother."

I expected to feel shock. Anger. Relief.

I felt nothing.

"Noah said your mother planned to confront Schroeder. We corroborated that with Dawn Heaton. Also, we've interrogated Adam Brant."

"What?"

"He confessed to knowing about Schroeder's previous molestations and helping them to cover it up. He also knew about Schroeder's irrational grudge against your mother. In fact, before her death, Brant had been worried that Schroeder was about to hurt her. He said Schroeder kept making vague threats. We think she confronted him about molesting you, and he lost it. Between his already existent rage and the fear that his molestations would be made public, well, we think he lost it and killed her." He was silent for a moment. "I'm sorry, Maddie."

I didn't say anything. I didn't know what to say.

"For what it's worth, Brant brought his concerns to Detective Bergan, who swept them under the rug. We've gone to Bergan's house and found a bunch of missing files that Bergan had made disappear." He hesitated. "But we can't find your mother's. I assure you that we're still looking." Empathy filled his eyes. "We can't release any of this information to the public, and there will never be a trial, Maddie, so we'll have to settle for knowing what happened. Justice has been served."

"Not as far as I'm concerned," I said, my voice breaking. "Justice would have been if Schroeder had suffered. He didn't."

Mallory pulled me into a sideways hug, resting her head on my shoulder. "Mads, I'm *so* sorry."

We were silent for several seconds as the shock and the pain sank in.

"Which brings me back to Ernie," Lance said. "Maddie, he was there the night your mother was murdered, and he feels responsible. He's always wondered whether he might have been able to stop it if he'd cleaned the English hall sooner."

I realized what he wasn't saying. "Ernie found my mother."

He nodded. "That's why he felt so protective of you. He feels responsible for your mother's death. He was determined to make sure the same thing didn't happen to you."

I blinked back tears as Mallory squeezed my hand.

"That was very sweet of him," she said. "It's nice to know

someone was watching over her. Speaking of which"—her gaze hardened—"where is your partner, Officer Forrester? Really?"

He looked her in the eye. "He thinks it's best if he makes a clean break."

I hated that they were talking about me like I wasn't even here. I hated that so many people knew Noah had discarded me so easily. Without even a goodbye.

Noah Langley could go fuck himself.

***

Lance left and Mallory encouraged me to take a nap, saying she'd stay with Aunt Deidre. In fact, they were planning on frying chicken later.

I woke to the sound of the doorbell and voices downstairs. I heard Mallory say, "She's upstairs resting, if you want to go see her."

My heart leapt, and I let myself dare to hope that Noah had changed his mind. That he would at least tell me goodbye. But when the door opened, it was Colleen standing in the doorway, holding a bouquet of grocery store flowers.

"Still your favorite?" she asked with a hesitant smile.

"Of course," I said, sitting up and wincing in the process.

"I heard you got your ass kicked," she said with a laugh.

"You should see the other guys." But then I realized it was pretty morbid since all four of them were dead.

"I owe you an apology," she said, still standing in the doorway. "I was pretty horrible to you."

"I'm sure it was nothing less than I deserved," I said.

She walked over and carefully sat on the edge of the bed, setting the flowers next to me. "Your momma's death did a number on you. I should have been more understanding."

I shook my head. "It's no excuse. I should have been more

supportive of your decisions." I gave her a bright smile that felt so fake I let it fall. "But there was some good news in all this mess. Lance says they think they've figured out who killed Momma."

"What?" she shrieked, then looked relieved. "After all this time? Who was it?"

"We have to keep it quiet." But Colleen had always been good at keeping secrets, so good I'd nicknamed her the Vault.

"Of course," she said eagerly. "Who?"

I took a deep breath. "Martin Schroeder."

Her face paled. "What?"

"It's a long story, and honestly I can't tell you all of it, but what it boils down to is that they think Schroeder killed her."

Colleen stared at me in confusion. Then she sat back and gave me an apologetic look. "Maddie, Mr. Schroeder didn't kill her."

"Lance told me they were pretty certain."

She looked like she was going to be sick. "They were wrong."

"How can you know that?"

Horror filled her eyes. "Because I was with him, Maddie."

I shook my head. "What do you mean you were with him? It happened on a Thursday night, Colleen."

She glanced down at her lap. "We weren't at school, Maddie. We were at the Bluebird Inn. From six until long after ten."

The significance of her words sunk in, and I felt like *I* was going to throw up. "*Colleen.*" I couldn't believe what she was saying. "How? I never...*Oh. God.*"

Her gaze lifted as she shook her head. "It's all water under the bridge, and it only happened a few times. I know there were a few rumors, but most of them weren't true."

"But he still molested you," I said, fighting the urge to cry. "Did he..."

"Rape me?" She was quiet for a few minutes. "It wasn't violent if that's what you're asking. But he did use his power to get what he wanted, so yeah. He raped me."

"Colleen. I never knew," I said in a rush. "I never even suspected. I'm a terrible friend." How had I not seen it?

"You stop that," she said firmly. "It started right before your momma was killed. You were going through your own hell."

"Still. I'm *so* sorry."

She squeezed my hand. "I've been thinking about it since you came by the store." She paused. "I think that's why I stayed home to marry John. He made me feel safe."

"Does he still make you feel safe?" I asked hopefully.

She smiled. "Safe enough. I have a hard life, but I *do* love him."

I wasn't sure what that meant, but I'd let it go for now.

The shock of Colleen's statement was starting to settle in, and I realized she was right. If Martin Schroeder had been with her from six until ten that night, that gave him an alibi. There was no way he'd killed my mother.

Which meant her killer was still free.

* * *

I hope you enjoyed *Blind Bake*! I have a special bonus scene with Noah that takes place after the book ends!
Get access through my newsletter.
http://bit.ly/DGSnewsletter

There's more coming from Maddie and Noah!

Bake Off
Maddie Baker Mystery #2

About the Author

Denise Grover Swank was born in Kansas City, Missouri and lived in the area until she was nineteen. Then she became a nomad, living in five cities, four states and ten houses over the course of ten years before she moved back to her roots. She speaks English and smattering of Spanish and Chinese which she learned through an intensive Nick Jr. immersion period. Her hobbies include witty Facebook comments (in own her mind) and dancing in her kitchen with her children. (Quite badly if you believe her offspring.) Hidden talents include the gift of justification and the ability to drink massive amounts of caffeine and still fall asleep within two minutes. Her lack of the sense of smell allows her to perform many unspeakable tasks. She has six children and hasn't lost her sanity. Or so she leads you to believe.

denisegroverswank.com